# Mark Me
IMMORTAL VICES AND VIRTUES: HER MONSTROUS MATES

MILA YOUNG

Mark Me Copyright © 2023 by Mila Young

Cover art created by Trif Book Cover Design

Editing by Personal Touch Editing and Virtual Author Services

Visit our books at
www.milayoungbooks.com
www.milayoungshop.com

All rights reserved.

No portion of this book may be reproduced in any form or by any electronic or mechanical means, including information storage and retrieval systems, without written permission from the author, except for the use of brief quotations in a book review, and except as permitted by U.S. copyright law.

For permissions contact:

**mila@milayoungbooks.com**

This book is a work of fiction. Names, characters, businesses, places, events, locales, and incidents are either the products of the author's imagination or used in a fictitious manner. Any resemblance to actual persons, living or dead, or actual events is purely coincidental.

# CONTENTS

| | |
|---|---|
| Immortal Vices and Virtues | vi |
| Mark Me | ix |
| | |
| Prologue | 1 |
| Chapter 1 | 11 |
| Chapter 2 | 24 |
| Chapter 3 | 34 |
| Chapter 4 | 45 |
| Chapter 5 | 56 |
| Chapter 6 | 67 |
| Chapter 7 | 80 |
| Chapter 8 | 91 |
| Chapter 9 | 100 |
| Chapter 10 | 115 |
| Chapter 11 | 129 |
| Chapter 12 | 140 |
| Chapter 13 | 151 |
| Chapter 14 | 161 |
| Chapter 15 | 174 |
| Chapter 16 | 184 |
| Chapter 17 | 202 |
| Chapter 18 | 211 |
| Chapter 19 | 222 |
| Chapter 20 | 233 |
| Chapter 21 | 242 |
| Chapter 22 | 259 |
| Chapter 23 | 273 |
| Chapter 24 | 283 |
| Chapter 25 | 302 |
| Chapter 26 | 312 |

| | |
|---|---|
| Chapter 27 | 332 |
| Chapter 28 | 342 |
| Chapter 29 | 358 |
| Chapter 30 | 370 |
| Chapter 31 | 385 |
| Chapter 32 | 400 |
| Epilogue | 417 |
| Demon's Chocolate Cake | 421 |
| About Mila Young | 425 |

# DEDICATION

*For Sam, who I can't thank enough for your unwavering support, dedication, and passion.*
**Love, Mila**

# Immortal Vices and Virtues

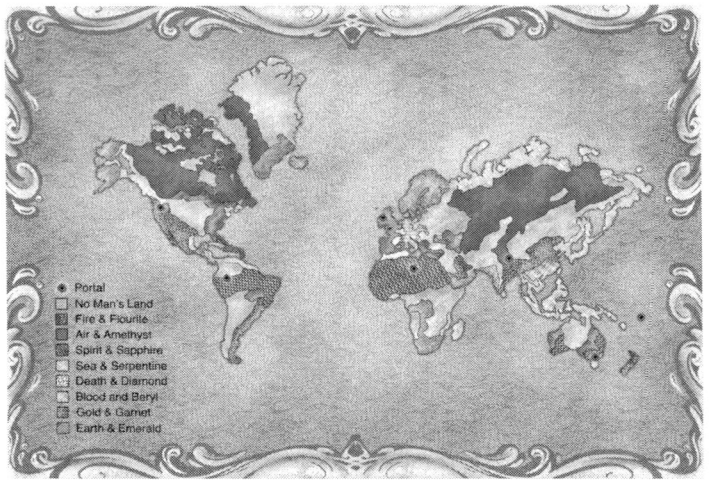

**The Houses**

House of Gold and Garnet

House of Blood and Beryl

House of Air and Amethyst

House of Earth and Emerald

House of Spirit and Sapphire

House of Death and Diamond

House of Fire and Fluorite

House of Sea and Serpentine

**No Man's Land**

No Man's Circus - Portland, Oregon

**Supernatural Syndicates**

*New York City*

Manhatten - The Wards - Shifters

Brooklyn - The Roses - Fae

Staten Island - The Outcast Coven - Witches

Queens - The Divine - Angels & Demons

Bronx - Clan Tepes - Vampires

# MARK ME

**I'm marked...but I won't be tamed.**

Loss has scarred my life. I've trained relentlessly, endured unimaginable pain for one goal—to face the beast who watched me, who came for me. But took my family instead.

There's nothing I won't do for vengeance.

Until three sinful and unhinged monsters find me, emerging from the shadows with sharp teeth, and with claws that could pull apart my life as easily as they do the buttons on my dress.

They think they can break me... Absurd.

Yet I'm caught in their twisted war in a world in ruins and fraying at the edges. They won't leave me alone, insisting I belong to them. That they'll make me irrevocably theirs.

Resisting the fantasies they promise grows harder with every passing day, and it scares me how easily I've started thinking of them as my own monsters.

But I remind myself I obey no one. Especially when I'm starting to suspect that they had a hand to play in my family's death.

They aren't the first monsters I've faced. They'll most certainly be the last...

# PROLOGUE
## BILLIE

They say your life flashes before your eyes just before you die... Well, mine came on broken dreams, with a nightmare slipping into reality.

You see, someone entered my room in the middle of the night.

The creak of the floorboard has me shrinking back against my pillow, the thumping of my heart growing louder. I scratch my arm where the marks etched my skin, the feeling like biting ants, like they always do when I'm afraid.

The sky gives a thunderous crack, and I flinch beneath the blanket, the drumming of the rain against the window insistent. My thoughts fly to my parents coming to check on me, that I might be imagining things.

Then another small creak sounds in the room, and I know I'm mistaken.

My eyes snap open, searching the darkness.

There...

A shadow lingers in my room, darker than the moonless night. It's not my mom or dad; it can't be by the size of the shadow. Shivers rake down my spine as it moves closer.

I scream, but the intruder is at my side in seconds, a large, rough hand pressing down on my throat, cold and merciless.

The darkness, the strength, his *shush* sounds more like a growl.

I thrash, my hands flailing for anything to grab hold of, connecting with my diary laying on my bed. It has never been more useful than now, as I frantically whack it against my attacker's face.

Surprised, he releases me for a split second, long enough to scramble off my bed in the opposite direction.

Dad taught me to fight because that was the only way to survive.

*Run, Billie girl. Run and hide until I come find you.*

But the shadow's hand grabs my foot.

No, please, no.

Screaming, I kick him in the stomach and grab for the lamp on the bedside table just as he tackles me on the bed with such force we're thrown forward. My world morphs into an explosion of sparks and shards as the lamp crashes to the floor.

I fall out of bed, the shadow coming with me, both of us hitting the floor with a thud. I ache all over, crying, thrashing against the monstrous form that looms over me.

"Stay still." There's the growl again. "I promise to make this quick, Billie."

He knows my name.

The shadow knows my name.

This isn't random. Not a break-in. The stranger's here for me.

I tremble beneath him because I know dangerous monsters live in my world. I've heard the stories and seen the death on the streets, even when my parents think I don't.

Now, one of them has come for me...

Panic swallows me.

I fight against him, punching, biting, but he might as well be a boulder and completely immovable.

The room spins as I claw at his arm, my screams shrill. Then Mom's voice calls from somewhere in the house, distorted and far away.

"Billie!"

In my moment of horror, hope trickles through me.

The shadow's grip tightens around my throat, darkness blurring my vision at the edges of my eyes, stealing my breath. Madly, I gouge at his arms with my fingernails, trying to loosen his hold. With my other hand, I reach up, wrenching at the mask hiding his face, and just as I do, the door to my room crashes open.

He pulls back abruptly.

Dad roars into the room like a demon, lunging at the man killing me.

Mom is a shadow behind him, her eyes wide, my name on her lips.

"Get off her, you bastard!" Dad commands like the dominant wolf shifter he is, crashing into my attacker, both of them slamming into the wall.

Hysteria.

Madness.

Shaking uncontrollably, I drag myself to the corner of the room, curling up and hugging my knees as tears fall. I flinch at every punch, every grunt. I scratch my tingling arms, fingernails digging into skin as the sticky slick of my blood covers my fingers.

My mom comes for me, and I reach for her, sobbing.

It's also when the darkness gives birth to another shadow, a taller, grunting figure. With an unearthly snarl, he flings his arm out, and it tosses my mother into the wall with such brutality, I cry out. Then the second figure lunges for my father, who's still fighting.

Mom's whimpering but on her feet, her body's fuzzy as she shifts into her wolf form. Her golden fur glimmers in the moonlight streaming through the window, her elongated teeth gleaming as she charges at the newcomer.

Then chaos explodes.

The room is savage violence, blurring in front of me, and I'm not sure where to look, unsure of what I'm seeing.

Fierce growls.

My parents are flung like puppets, but they never stop fighting, never stay down.

The battle is a mess, and somehow, I find my voice.

"Stop! Just stop!"

My dad's back slams against the far wall with a sickening thud, the moonlight glistening off the blade in the shadow's hand who has him pinned.

I jolt to my feet, my legs weak and heavy, and I rush closer, shouting, "Don't hurt him!"

Dad's gaze swings to mine.

Heartbreak and sorrow swim in his eyes. He knows this is the end. I see it written on his fallen face, and I want to die there along with him.

With a guttural snarl, the shadow thrusts the knife into the soft flesh of my dad's chest. Blood spills, his eyes huge, a whine on his lips.

A scream explodes out of me as his body drops to the floor.

I frantically scan the room for Mom and find her lying by the door across the room, gasping for air. She's clutching her bloody stomach as the first shadow rises to his feet by her side. Then he comes toward me with a mission.

My muffled whines choke in my throat as tears escape. I tremble ferociously, a piercing burst of shrieks on my lips.

I... I'm standing there in my bedroom with my dead parents. With two enemies who'd come for me but took them.

Anguish. Fury. Heartbreak. They wrap around me like barbed wire. My marks flare up once more, worse than before, and searing pain streaks down my arms. The pain is a welcome distraction, a reminder I'm still here, still breathing.

Bile rises in my throat, and I can't think straight, can't speak.

Suddenly, the script of ancient words etched on my arms bites into my flesh. Their blue glow lights up as the shadows freeze, their attention on me.

A manic, burning fury thumps in my veins, and I feel nothing but utter rage from what's been taken from me.

"Billie," the shadow calls me once more in that raspy, deep voice, as if it has a right to say my name.

"Shut up," I snap. The script on my arms lifts off my skin with ease, lighting up the room, revealing the men in heavy, black cloaks, with hoods, with black masks.

The ancient words swirl in the air between us, stretching, taking the shape of two thin swords. My mouth drops open. I've never seen this before... Their hilts slip into my hands, fitting like a glove as I curl my fingers around them, liking how they feel. Something hums up my arms, filling me with bravery I never knew I had. At fifteen, I had used my dad's throwing knives, but never a sword... never like this.

A primitive cry rips from my mouth, and before I have time to process it, I let the anger inside me take control.

"Interesting," the bigger intruder presses, as though I'm a fascination to be admired.

Well, fuck him.

Something strange happens, as if the swords have a mind of their own, guiding my hands and directing my arms in swift, powerful strikes. With each swing across the space between us, the blades whoosh through the air, and I'm rushing toward the first shadow who doesn't react in time.

My blades cut right across his torso like he's made of liquid.

Blood splatters across the walls.

He falls like a sack.

I should be scared, should stop, but when I raise my gaze to the second shadow, still concealed behind his mask, hysteria comes over me.

"You killed my parents," I shout.

"I knew you could be special." The monster spins the blade in his hand nonchalantly. "Not that it matters."

Ice forms in my veins, then comes the twisting anger burning in my heart.

"Who are you?" My voice holds power, even if standing close to him I realize how much smaller I am in comparison.

His laugh, a deep, cruel sound, ripples across the room.

I tighten my grip on the swords, lifting my chin. If there's one thing I've learned from Dad, it's that to survive, you must use what you have, even teeth and claws—even magical swords I'd never seen before. Sometimes, the only thing you can do is fight.

The floorboards creak under the weight of his monstrous presence as he steps forward.

"Stay back." My heart squeezes tighter. "You saw what I did to your friend."

"I have no friends," he snaps, his knife raised, something blue glinting from its sharp edge, just like my swords.

Magic.

Suddenly, a loud crash booms in the house like a bomb exploded. Like something has smashed the front door open.

"Draven!" A male's voice rings out for my dad, echoing from downstairs. It's our neighbor, a family friend. Then there are several other thundering footsteps rushing about.

"Upstairs!" I shout for them to hear me.

With my swords pointed at the monster in front of me, the shadow pauses, his gaze sliding to the hallway and back.

I seize the opportunity, channeling every ounce of anger, of desperation, into one swift motion. My sword's motion matches my intention, cutting forward, biting right into his raised defensive arm.

Blood bubbles on his hand, and he quickly covers it with his sleeve, hissing.

Thunderous footsteps rush upstairs, and the shadow recoils with the speed of the wind.

I leap at the killer once more, an angry groan rolling in his chest.

Before I can strike again, he swoops to the side, and I miss him.

He yanks the body of his fallen friend off the floor. Then with a speed that takes me by surprise, he launches himself out of the window, smashing the glass and disappearing into the darkness.

For a moment, I stand there, my heart pounding in my chest, the swords melting into strings of script that float in front of me, then slip onto my arms. The adrenaline that has been coursing through my veins ebbs away, leaving behind bone-deep exhaustion.

My father's empty eyes stare into the night, and the image weakens my knees.

Our neighbors burst into the room, finding the chaos, the death, the end. I don't hear their shouting, their terrified words. I stumble in slow motion and throw myself at my mother's side, desperately snatching her arm where she still breathes.

Tears roll down my face.

Her inhales are shallow, her eyes fading, and she's already back in her human form.

"Mom, please get up." My fingers lace with hers in an aching grip.

Someone behind me touches my shoulder. "Billie." But I shrug them off.

Mom's eyes find mine. She's all I see in a world of terror swirling in the depths of her gaze, touching me deep in my soul. She draws a shaky breath.

"My little cub," she croaks. Her fingers shift, moving weakly toward her neck where she's wearing her gold pendant just like mine, and a low whimper comes from her chest.

"Promise me." She coughs, blood spilling from her mouth, and everything inside me hurts. She points at the necklace and pendant around my neck that matches hers, her arm too weak to reach for it. "Never take yours off, no matter what. It keeps you protected. Or he'll find you again."

"You know him, don't you? Who is—"

Her eyes glaze over, the life slipping away from her even as I watch.

"Billie," she gasps. "Leave this house, change your name, don't go to anyone else in the family, or he'll find you."

"Who is he?" I plead.

But with one last quivering breath, her hand falls limp in mine.

"Mom, no!" The room tilts as I clutch her lifeless hand, my dad's unmoving form mere feet away. I sob.

My neighbors lift me up to stand, but I can't balance on my own legs. Someone else in the room is calling for the authorities.

For me, my world burns around me. I'm in the wreckage of my past, alone with the whisper of my mom's warning in my mind and the memory of my parents' final breaths forever seared into my heart.

# CHAPTER
# ONE
### BILLIE

**6 Years Later**

"You won't believe it. I've made my first kill," Sasha gushes in a whisper across the table from me. We're on the oversized balcony at my workplace, and I glance around to make sure no one hears my best friend's excitement.

Don't get me wrong. I'm over the moon for her, but at the same time, I'm shocked to hear it coming from her. Yep, I'm full of contradictions like that.

"You didn't!" I blink at her in disbelief, unsure if I've heard right. Sasha's a damn good bounty hunter, but she doesn't kill. She once spent an hour meticulously rescuing a spider from our home, so she could release it back into the wild. Staring at her, I ask, "Or is that meant to be a metaphor for something?"

"Oh, you're hilarious." She giggles, genuinely finding my question laughable. "Look, I've brought us cake to celebrate." She nonchalantly sets down two small, white boxes that seem far too ordinary for the gravity of her announcement.

A rush of wind flutters through her aquamarine-colored hair that's neatly styled off her face in soft waves and accentuates the bright blue vibrancy of her eyes. Her lips are full and heart-shaped, and she's absolutely stunning. She might appear like a pushover at her five-foot-three height, but she's the complete opposite when it comes to her job, especially coupled with her luring power to capture fugitive targets.

Being a mermaid definitely has its perks.

"Wait... I'm still confused. So, you actually killed someone?" Anyone else making such a claim wouldn't surprise me. Mercenaries for hire, spies, smugglers, assassins, guards, and so many others call this city home. Death is part of our lives.

South Africa, where I've lived my whole life, falls under the reign of King Kaspian. He rules over the House of Gold and Garnet, which spans several countries around the world under his control. He's located in the headquarters in Reykjavik, Iceland. Our house represents wealth and prestige, and we have the largest concentration of mercenaries.

Individuals from other houses across the world often hire our specialists for their unique skills.

The world, of course, wasn't always like this. Once, when humans ruled, a series of portals opened up across Earth, bringing magic into the world. Chaos broke out, destroying so much, including many humans, before a semblance of order took place. That was how the houses were created, how different supernaturals were assigned to them. Now, everyone must join a house.

The benefit of living in the House of Gold and Garnet is the sheer wealth it possesses. While other places around the world may have lost a lot of technologies that once existed, such as planes and other travel vehicles, the use of expensive magic gives our residents that luxury. Though there are still plenty of things that no longer exist, like something I've read about called Google.

"Fine, I see how this might be unbelievable," Sasha elaborates, whisking me out of my thoughts. Her hand reaches out to squeeze mine. "But the horned asshole I was hunting would have killed me, so in a way, it was self-defense, but after doing it, I feel more... alive. Why did I wait so long to make my first kill?"

"Are you okay?" I lean closer, studying her face for any signs that she's pretending she's fine. It wouldn't be the first time.

"Yeah, for sure." Pushing the hair out of her face, she pulls out glittery sunglasses from her bag and sets them on her face. They only add to the spectacular vibe she carries. "Can't say the same for the poor sucker."

"So, you're fine then to start showing signs of becoming a siren?" I worry about her because my friend is fickle with emotions. Tonight, she might end up crying that she took a life and doesn't want to end up a siren like her abusive family. Thing is, mermaids can become sirens by drowning someone while kissing them, essentially stealing their voice. And the more people they kill in such a manner, the more connected they become to the ocean and even a body of water. If they continue to kill, mermaids will become sirens and could reach a point where they can no longer grow legs to leave the water.

With a shrug, she simply murmurs, "Maybe, but the taste of his voice is… addictive, still buzzing through me. Plus, it might help me with my bounties as my lure strengthens. Who knows, it might even be fun to draw in more bad guys to their doom."

I eye her, smirking. "Does that include Pacific, your new squeeze, and has he shown you his kraken side yet?" Pacific's a powerful man who had a huge bounty on his head, and my girl caught and bagged him. Then dated him, of course.

"You leave him out of this. Besides, he still hasn't confirmed he's a kraken shifter." She lifts her chin high, her lips pinching in a cute, excited way. "We're still in the beginning stages of dating."

I laugh because I can already tell she's smitten with the guy.

"You know I'll support you, no matter what, as long as you're safe."

"I know, babe. I'm there for you, too." She leans forward, her elbows placed on the wood table between us. "But I have more news, and I think you're going to like this part. I found something for you." Her smile beams.

The last time I saw her this elated, she'd gained a promotion at work.

"Don't keep me hanging then," I tease.

"While I was down by the dock, wrestling with that brute, he dropped his bag. The contents spilled out, knives and all sorts of torture weapons, though I suspect they might have been sex toys. He also had folders upon folders of documents. They ended up blowing on the breeze, and I snatched a few handfuls."

"What were they?" I press forward against the table as if being closer might make her speak quicker.

She blinks at me. "Names of mercenaries' targets."

My shoulders pull back as my mind swims, but trepidation surges that somehow my name has found its way onto those papers.

"There were dozens upon dozens, then I spotted your parents' names."

A cold, gnawing sensation grips my heart. "Are you sure?" My voice is barely above a whisper as I try to make sense of her finding.

She nods, and gone is her earlier smile, replaced by a furrowing brow.

"Lorelei Tempest and Draven Tempest are quite unique names, but I didn't see your name on there. The papers looked old and used, like these lists were made years ago. But all the names were crossed out, you know..." She pauses, refraining from saying the word *killed*. "The bastard claimed they were mementos from successful hits, records kept by mercenaries, and he was going to sell them to make a fortune with collectors."

"D-Do you have the list?" I grapple with keeping my voice steady, needing to see if my name is on one of the documents.

Her lips flatten, and she sighs heavily. "Sorry babe, but that was when he lunged at me and we both tumbled into the ocean with all the papers, which were destroyed."

My breath catches in my throat as a sudden flare flashes across my mind—the monstrous shadow towering over me while I lay in bed all those years ago, the fatal blow, my parents' lifeless bodies. My fingers curl into fists in my lap, and inhales get trapped in my lungs. I hate how even after all this time, I'm close to crying at the mere mention of my parents.

"Was there anything else in the documents?" I asked in a strained voice.

Her soft gaze meets mine. "At the top of the papers were different names scribbled, which I assume were the mercenaries responsible for those hits. I memorized the one with your parents listed. *Bryant Ursaring.* Almost sounds like a bear shifter's name, doesn't it?"

The unfamiliar name echoes in my ears. The darkness of my past thumps in my veins as I hold back the tears in my eyes, the images of my dead parents flashing in my head.

I spent the past six years trying to discover the truth about that savage night. It's also why I recently started working at FaeEcho, a magic communications company based in South Africa. I'd failed to find the killers myself, so I figured I'd use their extensive database to discover any possible leads about the hit. But without a name, it had been harder than finding a pin in a haystack.

*Bryant Ursaring.*

I finally have a name... a lead.

I roll the name over my mind, already hating the sound of it.

*I'll find out who the hell you are.*

Before I remember moving my hand, my fingers twirl on the golden family pendant around my neck. I slide the tip of my thumb over the detailed wolf's head, which is surrounded by intricate patterns and symbols etched into the gold. Mom once told me the image represented strength, loyalty, and unity, though I haven't felt that way for a long time. Following my mom's instructions, I'd never taken it off, but every time I look or touch it, my heart squeezes until it hurts. I miss my parents devastatingly.

"Sorry, babe." Sasha shuffles closer to my seat, around the table, and throws an arm around my shoulders, drawing me nearer.

I breathe easier in her company.

Sasha smells like the fresh ocean breeze with a floral tinge, a scent that always settles my nerves. She's the only one who knows the full story of my past, the only one I've shared my grief with. When I left my family home, Sasha was the first person I'd met on the streets, and she offered me a place to stay in exchange for doing work for her. Mostly, stealing things from stores, which she'd then sell to make money. She's just a year older than me at twenty-two. We've been inseparable ever since.

Now, she's given me a chance to hunt down and destroy the ghosts from my past.

"I love you, you know that." I hug her tighter.

"Okay, okay, don't get all sentimental on me. Now, I want to celebrate with you my first kill and eat cake because these won't last long in the sun." Sasha hugs me tighter, and I adore her. She's always been there for me, and I'll do anything for her.

"Agreed. Let's see what you've got for us."

Bouncing back into her seat, she pushes one box in front of me, and I raise the lid as she does hers. Here I expected a layered sponge cake with extra cream to drown in, but instead it's a dome-shaped gelatinous dessert... I think. The sunlight reflects through me, and it's exquisite, but edible?

"Hmm... is this a trick cake?" I furrow my brow at my friend, who's watching me with a grin. "You know cake is my weakness, but this is challenging, even for me."

"I went for something a bit healthier since I'm watching my diet," she explains in all seriousness.

My eyebrows shoot up my forehead sarcastically at the mention of cutting back on *cake*.

"Try it before you freak out. It's a Japanese raindrop cake made with natural spring water and agar powder, molded to resemble a raindrop. You need to pour the contents from the small container over it. Isn't it gorgeous?"

"I'm not sure if I should eat it or mount it at home on the wall." I burst out laughing before pouring the deep brown syrup that smells like honey. Then I scoop out a spoonful and slid it into my mouth. It gives a slight resistance when I chew it, then it suddenly melts on my tongue in a sweet explosion of water and sugar. "Wow. I think it just rained over my tongue."

"Told ya."

"Surprisingly, I love it. We need more treats but also some with cream," I say. "We'll celebrate properly tonight, and I'll pick up more treats." Then I dove back in for more because something about the cake is addictive.

Half an hour later, Sasha had taken off, and I made my way back to my desk, my thoughts consumed.

*Bryant Ursaring.*

The name sails across my thoughts, and before long, I'm not hearing the soft keyboards clicking around me or the hushed conversations around me from the other cubicles. Instead, I'm frantically searching through the database for Bryant. I open several case files on various companies who are late with their payments to appear like I'm investigating.

At FaeEcho, we offer a means of delivering messages and packages, which comes at a high cost, but considering many in the House of Gold and Garnet may have used the service at one stage in their lives, a lot of information is stored in the database about their orders.

I glance over to the photo of my parents on my cubicle wall, a longing whistling through me. "I'm going to find those bastards and make them pay," I whisper, reaching over to touch their faces.

The sleeve of my shirt pulls up my arm, revealing the edge of the script etched in my skin, giving a faint glow in the shadowy light. I've been taking fighting training, along with meditation and Tai Chi classes, since I'm told it helps center my energy to harness my magic. So far, I've had some luck in drawing out the magic on my skin. Sasha insists it's connected to the shock of my parents' death, but there had to be a way to fully engage the power again. A few times, I felt the tingling on my skin, but that's where it ended.

Wolf shifters like me shouldn't have such power, but I'd been born with the markings. My parents called me their special miracle as I was a premature baby, implying the magic was a result. I doubt they knew the truth, seeing they were never able to explain it.

Pulse racing, I return my attention to the screen where I watch the list of Bryant Ursaring names pop up on the screen from my search.

Three potential matches.

"Right, I got this." I steel myself for the task of sifting through each profile, finding their files and reading them all until something jumps out at me.

An hour later and still nothing. The office falls quiet. It's taking longer than I anticipated. The first Bryant uses our service weekly from various countries in the Gold and Garnet House, and his files are enormous. The database doesn't exactly state what their profession is as non-mercenaries live in our house as well, so I can't simply search by mercenary and narrow it down.

Stretching my back, I keep going. My boss isn't in today, so there's no question about not getting my project work done.

But by the time I reach the third name, I'm starting to think this is a waste of time when something on the profile catches my eye.

Or more specifically an address—13 Dark Spire Street.

My gaze strains, bulging as I stare at my parents' home address where I grew up, where I haven't been back to since the night I lost them.

Are you kidding me? Bryant had sent us a letter!

Frantically, I tap on the keys as my heart races faster. With a flare of anticipation flooding me with anger, I scan the delivery details.

He sent it two days before the attack.

Contents... it only states *invitation*.

There's a chill in the air, and it's worming its way into my bones. Leaning back in my chair, staring at the screen's glaring light, I think back to my parents canceling an event that night at the very last minute due to my mother not feeling well. They were meant to go out, but they never told me where.

The truth plays out in my mind.

Bryant had tried to get my parents out of the house so they could attack me. My parents pulled out at the last minute, so the two monsters coming for me had no clue that we weren't alone.

My parents died because of me... I've lived with that for six years. The only way I survived the guilt that threw me into depression for years was the incongruous thrill that one day I'd get my revenge.

I push toward the monitor once more, my fingers flying over the keyboard.

Information is bare on Bryant, with the exception of where he sent the invitation from.

Lapland, Finland.

Icy determination pours through my veins as my fingers curl into a fist. I'd tracked him down to a location, a place that should reveal more on Bryant and who he worked with, who the two attackers were, and why I mean anything to them to kill.

Wringing my fingers now, things are feeling real. Of

course, it's not inconceivable that I might be barking up the wrong tree, and Bryant is not one of the killers. But a clue is a clue, and damn if I don't dig up all of Lapland until I dish out all the dirt on him.

I am the wolf shifter who got her parents murdered.

I am the wolf shifter who's been hiding, changing my name from Billie to Mina to everyone but Sasha, dyeing my hair to a deep brown, never removing my protective pendant—whatever it takes to remain undetected. It's why I work in the office of FaeEcho and not down in the stores with clients.

Those thoughts make me shiver from how I'd been living my life. I remind myself I'm also the wolf shifter born with a powerful magic that saved me that night. And I will find a way to wield it.

But I can't think because of the nausea building in me.

I will redeem my parents, no matter the cost.

Taking a deep breath, I glance at the word *Lapland*, well aware Finland is also ruled over by King Kaspian. Three powerful mercenary dukes manage the region, along with their grandfather.

The Dukes of Lapland—treachery, wealth, and indomitable power. Everyone's heard of them. I've never met them, but there's enough information spreading about them to know who I'm dealing with.

Khaos, the eldest, part wolf shifter, had once hunted down thirty shifters for stealing from him. He tracked down each one, then killed them without remorse.

His brother, Eryx, carries gryffin blood in his veins.

He's so sly, he moves with the shadows, and if he catches your eyes, consider yourself dead.

Then the youngest, Tallis, comes with demon heritage and is said to command control over anyone he crosses paths with his incubus power.

Not too much is said about their parents, except that their father had three wives and that their grandfather is the God of Forests in Finland. So, they're a powerhouse family and feared by many.

The trio hold the lives of countless mercenaries, trackers, hunters, and a number of others in their grips, and they lord their powers and position over anyone who dares to threaten them.

However, those in power *have* fallen before. So, if these Dukes had a hand to play in the attack that night, they're going down. The Dukes approve every hit that leaves their borders, so they know enough for me to start with them.

My gaze shifts to my parents' picture.

"I think I've found the monsters." I'm already making plans in my head on booking my flight to Finland, what I'm going to take with me, and the best way to get into their estate without drawing attention to myself.

Of course, I'll have to tread carefully, covering my tracks meticulously, but if I do this right, I could have the Dukes eating out of my hand. Then I'll find out who came for me six years ago.

The Dukes are powerful, feared, and dangerous, but they haven't met me yet. They have no idea what's coming their way.

## CHAPTER TWO

KHAOS

"Our operation has been compromised," Clark begins in a steady breath as he clears his throat nervously, standing in the doorway of my executive office.

Bitterness fills my mouth. It's not what I want to hear now or ever, not when it pertains to the meticulous structure we have in place for all the mercenaries, trackers, and every last one of the hunters who operate under my territory, under my rules.

"Explain," I demand of my advisor, the room tightening around me.

Clark sucks in a sharp breath, shoving a hand over his already well-gelled hair. He's not a large man, but what he lacks in size, he makes up for in shrewd intelligence, and that's why I hired him. Today, there's a sheen of sweat on his forehead, so I expect bad news, especially after he barged into my office unannounced.

"Several hired hits haven't been recorded, or... paid for."

The beast inside me stirs, clawing at my flesh to escape and rip into Clark.

"How many are we talking about?" I'm on my feet, crossing the room in several long strides.

Stiffening, he says, "Hard to tell, especially when we're still manually discovering the discrepancies."

I blink at him, narrowing my eyes. He needs to understand how ridiculous he sounds, coming to me with a problem before establishing the scale of the issue.

He squares his shoulders, and I do like *that* about Clark. He doesn't back down from me, even if he should be fucking afraid.

"I received a complaint from a client with an incomplete job who said she paid in blood to the mercenary and wants a refund. Except, there's no record of the hit in our system. I chased up said mercenary, and here's the thing. I remember the guy since I recorded his job myself and matched him up with the customer. I entered it into our books in the registry room, but when I went to check, the assignment wasn't there." He's pacing now across my room.

"Okay, so we slipped up on a few clients' dealings." It's not the first time a job hasn't been recorded properly. It's happened before, so it isn't a huge deal, as long as it's caught and corrected.

"If it was just a few, I wouldn't be bothering you with it, Khaos." His words tumble out quickly as he pauses and turns to meet my gaze, lips in a taut line.

He only refers to me by name when his patience is stretched thin, but I'll let it slide this time. After all, he's served loyally by my side for years as the Head of Mercenary Transactions, and directly reports to me. Now, I intend to hear every damn detail of what has rattled him.

"I reviewed other assignments I recall coordinating, and I urged some of our team to do the same. Roughly, ten to fifteen percent of those tasks vanished from our records."

At a quick calculation, that's close to sixty jobs a month, lost. Fuck!

"How the hell could they simply vanish if they were duly noted in our record books?" I mentally dissect the process we built, pairing our team with clients globally, extracting half payment up front and the rest after the job's completion. The fundamental rule when dealing with backstabbing bastards is you doggedly pursue them for payment, or you won't see a dime. I have a team who manages that, yet these payments have been unwittingly sliding through our grasp.

"How has no one noticed this until now?" My voice climbs.

Clark's shaking his head. "I'm working on finding out." As a raven shifter, he's cunning and has a knack for uncovering secrets, so I have no doubt he'll get to the bottom of it, yet it doesn't calm the fires flaring in my veins.

"I want to know how long this has been going on." My words spit out. "Tear the damn system apart. Find the issue and fix it. I want a full report first thing in the morning."

Clark flinches but holds my stare. "Yes, Your Grace." His voice darkens, and he excuses himself from the room.

What I hate more than being lied to is someone stealing from me, right under my fucking nose.

I march to the window and pull back the heavy curtain to look at the landscape. The city of Rovaniemi, at the heart of Lapland, stretches out as far as the eye can see. The edges of Finland, the boundary of our home, have been my life for as long as I can remember. From a young age, my grandfather, the God of Forests, raised my two brothers and me as rulers of this land. With my parents not around, his stern words still echo in my head from childhood.

*You're a Talino, part god, and my grandson, and that means a powerful Duke who's in control. You command respect and never demand it. You lead and never follow.*

My beast growls inside me, furious at the news from Clark. The primal urge to release my wolf lurks beneath my skin. He's always humming inside me like a time bomb, starved for escape, commanding we take action immediately.

I shut my eyes, my hand resting against the cool glass of the window, and take a deep inhale, driving him down. The revelation of the broken infrastructure is an obvious indicator that things have slipped through the cracks and from my grip.

Drawing away from the window, I stride out of the room with determination to get this fixed before anyone outside the estate gets a wind of it.

My boots muffle against the thick, plush rug. Rich, dark wood covers the walls, gleaming under the warm light of the wrought-iron chandeliers. My grandfather built the estate near the city of Rovaniemi as a central place to control the country. With his wife, my grandmother, he insisted he wanted a home steeped in history with portraits hung on the walls, my parents and us as children. Every time I pass them, the moments captured in the pictures feel too distant to be real.

Yet he doesn't even live with us. In his position as Sovereign to King Kaspian, he moved our headquarters south of Finland to Helsinki.

Now, my brothers and I report to him from our home in Lapland, feeding him updates and a portion of our earnings to share with our king of the House of Gold and Garnet. My grandfather's been preparing me to one day take over his position, and I welcome continuing to serve our king. That means getting on top of the current fuck-up.

Reaching Tallis' room, I find it empty and the bed a complete mess. Sheets are strewn on the floor, pillows across the room, a towel draped over the table, his wardrobe hanging open to a fallen coat. Shoving out of there, I make my way upstairs, knowing where to find him. I reach his game room, aka Tallis' torture chamber, up in the west wing that faces the mountains in the distance, with large, arched windows for plenty of natural light.

He's there. Of course, he is. He's predictable.

Tallis is leaning over a scruffy-looking man chained to the wall, and I know instantly he's a fox shifter by the earthy and skunky sting in the room and by the way my wolf's hackles rise.

Agonizing pain and terror twist the man's expression, staring at me with desperation in his eyes, as if I, of all people, would be his savior. Tallis chops off another finger with pliers, sending the man into a hollering scream. Blood spurts over Tallis' apron and the tarp covering the floor.

Trick is to take our enemies to the edge of death, then they'll tell you anything, do anything for you. Though I'm stumbling in the dark here about what he's done wrong. But if Tallis is involved, it was something against the reigning house.

"Brother," I call out to distract him from his fun.

Tallis twists toward me, wearing a wicked grin, his ink-black hair falling to his shoulders in disarray, and eyes black. He looks every bit the demon he is—untamed, ruthless, and carrying unspeakable abilities.

"You finally decided to join me. About fucking time, Khaos. I told ya, too much of that bureaucratic crap will shrivel your dick and make you go cross-eyed. You need to spill blood, release your wolf."

I snort a laugh at his theatrics. "I came here for something else."

He raises an eyebrow. "And that would be?"

"Looks like we have a breach in our network." I don't worry that the fox shifter hears it all. I know Tallis well enough to understand the man will never see the light of day outside this room again.

So, I explain everything Clark told me, along with my theory I'd just come up with that it's an internal job and someone else is collecting our payments. His brow furrows because my half-brother rarely overreacts unless it somehow impacts him directly.

"Then you came to the right person. I'll fuck them up real bad." He breaks into his fake maniacal laughter.

"Calm the hell down. First, we need to find out who's doing it, but for now, I need you to monitor Clark, make sure he's not part of this… oversight." It's not that I don't trust Clark, but I don't trust most people. If there's one thing I can rely on in this business, it's that those closest to you will stab you in the back. My grandfather always taught me that in such situations, first ensure those around you aren't involved, as they are most likely responsible. My immediate family are the only ones I trust implicitly, so I know Tallis will dig up the truth.

"Spying on the spy." He nods, his hands dripping in blood, the guy behind him whimpering. "That's exciting."

"This is serious, Tallis."

"I know, I know." He raises his bloody hands, one still gripping the pliers. "Consider it done."

My brother's blasé response is infuriating, testing my patience on more days than I prefer to admit. But over the years, I've learned it's as much a part of him as is his intense eyes that never miss a beat.

I turn to leave, needing to track down Eryx next, when an explosion of glass detonates behind me. Instantly followed by a violent burst of wind that screams into the room.

Ducking out of pure instinct and covering my head, my wolf is in my throat, ready to fight whatever's coming for us. I whip around, a growl on my throat just as a gargantuan form hurtles in through the smashed window like a tornado, claws first, a horrendous gust following in its wake.

"Fuck, Eryx, not again!" I snarl, not in the mood for his manic hunts, letting himself lose control. The difference between him and me is that I work hellishly hard to train my wolf from taking me over, while Eryx lets his animal side rule him.

His massive gryffin form—body of a lion, head of an eagle—decimates the entire section of the wall around the window, tossing broken stones and dust into the air. I throw myself aside to avoid being struck. Enormous wings spread wide, each beat raising the dirt farther, the tarp on the floor flapping at the edges as my other half-brother slides into the room.

He clutches a colossal reindeer in his talons. The animal's eyes are wild and terrified in its final moments.

Eryx crash lands, shoving me up farther against the wall with a wing, Tallis in the same position across from me. All the while, he slides forward, and the reindeer's antlers spear right into the man bound to the wall, silencing him forever.

It's in the dust storm that I'm trying to comprehend the madness around me. A primal response consumes me at the dead animal, at my brother's stupidity. Annoyance flares in my veins at the hulking figure of the gryffin.

Before I can react, a fiery explosion comes from Tallis' direction, lighting up the space. A ball of fire slams into the gryffin's side, doing nothing more than making him flinch.

"Eryx, you fucking idiot. This guy was my kill, and he

was about to spill, but you stole *my* moment." Angry flames flicker across Tallis' hands. He's staring incredulously at his victim impaled by the antler, shaking his head.

A grin tugs on my lips because the whole situation is too ridiculous not to be funny. I school my smile just as Eryx's body shimmers, and he's in human form within seconds, standing in front of us in his birthday suit. Blond hair cascades down to his chest, matching his golden eyes.

"Didn't see him there," he grunted. "My feathers must've been in the way."

"You've got feathers for brains, asshole. Crash landing into my game room… I ought to pluck you bald and hang you on my wall as a trophy." Tallis is snorting flames. "Told you before not to hunt near the city and the mansion 'cause you know how you get. You're no better than some fucking dragon, hoarding shit, but for you, it's your kills."

"He has a point," I added, meeting Eryx's sly grin. We once encountered a horrendous smell in the mansion, only to discover a small mountain of half-eaten carcasses in the basement. His gryffin has a ferocious appetite of the gods and is never sated, which also makes him terrifying to everyone else and extremely useful when we're taking on big jobs.

"Well, I brought us meat for the feast." Eryx flicks dust off his head, looking rather proud of himself, then glances over his shoulder at his destruction.

"Congrats, Eryx. You've successfully created the world's first man-deer kabob. And now, you owe me a new suspect," Tallis snaps, turning back to his perished victim.

I step over the dead deer's legs and the rubble.

"We have bigger problems to worry about than Eryx's catastrophic entrances." My gaze flickers to the mess the room's become, announcing loud enough for both my brothers to hear.

"I think there might be a traitor among us."

## CHAPTER
# THREE
### BILLIE

No one just waltzes into the Duke's estate without a personal invite.

But I have a few options. Posing as a prospective client, a newly minted mercenary seeking a job, or even a security specialist offering to evaluate their mansion defenses. All things to potentially grant me the access I need and, more importantly, to the brothers themselves. The looming problem is I don't have credentials for those lies, and I suspect the Dukes are the kind of men who will carry out a background check on a random person turning up in their estate. The situation might end in a one-way ticket to my death.

The brothers are mercenaries at the top of the food chain and are not known for compassion.

Nope, those options won't work, so Plan B comes into play. Enter the mansion inconspicuously as a menial worker, which means I won't get the brother's direct attention, giving me time to spy and discover who the hell is Bryant Ursaring.

With Plan B zipping through my mind and all the scenarios I need to be prepared for, I flew to Finland, and now I'm sitting on the back of a magic-fueled motorbike, my arms tight around the transport guy, Ivan. We're cutting through the dense thicket of pine trees in the forest, the terrain bumpy as hell, my insides shaken to smithereens. We're way past the Dukes' estate because who I need to see lives out in the middle of nowhere, and I haven't seen him for over six years. I'm nervous as hell and hope he'll help me get into the estate.

I'm thankful it's not winter, or I would have frozen like a popsicle by now. Instead, it's June, the onset of what they call summer here. But for someone who grew up in South Africa, this temperature feels a lot more like our winter season.

Ivan's driving like a lunatic, swerving left and right, my backpack proving a hindrance from the weight. I try to maintain my balance each time he takes a corner too sharply, which distracts me from the fact that I'm actually in Finland doing this. I might have had a small freakout moment in the airport's bathroom this morning, but I'm all right now, I'm a powerful wolf shifter armed with blades.

I got this.

With my fingers digging into Ivan's sides, gripping his leather jacket, I grit my teeth because *I* asked to be taken into the forsaken woodland outside the expansive city of Rovaniemi. And I'm ready.

An hour later, my butt's turned numb, and we finally come to a stop in front of a small log cabin in the woods. Moss covers the walls, looking like it's part of the woods.

An old worn porch surrounds the home with a few wooden chairs for lazing about. The place is secluded, the perfect hideout for a recluse... or a murderer.

"Awstin's waiting," Ivan grunts over his shoulder at me, parking the bike to the side of the home. "I'll wait out here for your return ride into the city."

Ivan must work for Awstin, since he arranged to have me picked up from the airport, which I appreciated for keeping a low profile.

"Thanks," I grumble, climbing off the bike and adjusting the straps of my bag. Then I stretch my cramped up back and take in the crisp, mountain air. The porch creaks under my weight as I approach the door, losing my chance to knock as it swings open.

Awstin greets me with a crooked smile, and instantly I'm taken to my childhood to the one time I recalled him visiting us in South Africa, just weeks before my parents died, and he brought me Salmiakki, aka salty licorice. My parents hated it, but I loved the candy. His light hair is wiry, as is his beard, but whiter than I remember, his eyes a dark-blue sky color, just like my dad's.

I don't know him much aside from what my parents told me, but I was told he was too busy to visit us.

"Uncle," I say, throwing myself into his arms.

*"Leave this house, change your name, don't go to anyone else in the family, or he'll find you."* Mom's voice plays loudly in my head.

Now, I'm breaking my promise. But as I stand in my uncle's embrace, inhaling that woodsy, earthy scent of his wolf, it reminds me so much of my dad that I have to blink away tears. The hole in my heart is made worse because I know it will never heal, no matter what.

"Oh, Billie, I thought I'd lost you, too." He pats my shoulder, and something chokes up in my throat. "I'm terribly sorry about your parents."

My pulse thunders overtime, more tears rising to my eyes, and when he pulls away, I try to school my emotions. I fail miserably and I sniffle, wiping my wet cheeks.

"Come, come inside." He loops an arm around mine and drags me indoors as he quickly shuts the door behind us. Then I drop my backpack down.

"You know, I tried to find you for so long. So, when you contacted me out of the blue, I jumped with excitement. Which is a big thing for an old man like me."

He has me laughing as we move into an open-plan room to a table with stools, and I'm instantly hit by the scent of freshly brewed coffee. Stacks of paper and books, along with a shortwave radio, are cluttered on the wooden coffee table by the hazelnut-colored couch. There's something comforting about the cabin. The extra coats and boots by the door tell me he may not live here alone, and I notice him staring out at Ivan, who's leaning against a tree in the yard smoking.

"I wanted to come to you earlier, but I couldn't," I murmur, not wanting to say too much and draw him into my troubles. Even being here is a risk, yet I'm so close to finally finding who attacked us that night, I can't let this chance pass me by.

My uncle studies me from the kitchen, where he's

pouring two cups of coffee. He brings them to the table before handing one to me.

"Never thought I'd see the day when your hair's as dark as the woods at night," he comments, amusement lifting the corners of his lips.

Grinning, I reach up and curl a lock of my dyed hair around my finger. "I thought I'd mix things up," I quip playfully, remembering the moment I decided to color my hair. It had been Sasha's idea to help me not stand out so much. As I stared in the mirror, watching my blonde strands darken, I cried as another part of my old life slipped away.

"It suits you," he adds, bringing me out of my thoughts. "Now, when you contacted me, your message sounded urgent. I'm guessing you're not here to catch up about the past or tell me where you've been for the past six years." He studies me, taking all of me in, and I meet his stare evenly.

Do I trust my uncle?

I'm honestly not sure yet, but out of all the extended families, he's the only one who visited us, the only one my parents ever spoke of fondly. So, I'm willing to believe he couldn't have had a hand in the attack.

"I wish I could lay it all out for you," I say. "But the House of Gold and Garnet is no stranger to secrets and danger. I don't want you caught up in my mess, but I could really use your help."

"I understand," he responds, his keen gaze softening. "Your dad was a good man and an even better brother. He saved my bacon more times than I could count, and the world is much darker without him." He pauses for a moment, then clears his throat. "He confided many things to me, and rest assured, I'm in your corner. So, tell me what I can do?"

A rush of emotions floods me, and my hand instinctively tightens around the coffee cup as I lift it to my lips and sip the nutty-flavored coffee before lowering the mug.

"I'm looking for someone, and I think he might work for the Dukes of Lapland or perhaps used their mercenary services. So, I need help to get into the Dukes' estate without suspicion. Perhaps I can go undercover as a maid or something." I lick my lips, trying to calm my nerves, noting how silent my uncle had fallen, how his face reveals no reaction. My knees are bouncing under the table as I continue.

"I remember Dad saying you were a Safe House Operator, and you managed some of the safes in the Dukes' estate where they stored the rarest of bloods. That you're familiar with the place. That you have connections."

My thoughts are ticking over, and I'm watching his every movement, trying to see if his facial expression reveals anything. Perhaps I can say something to show that I'm looking for my parents' killer, but my mind and emotions are snowballing and rushing away from me at a million miles an hour.

My uncle places his steaming coffee cup down on the table.

"Do you have a name?"

"Bryant Ursaring." Sitting still, I ignore the tightness around my throat.

His lips pinch as his gaze lifts to the ceiling, his brow furrowing.

"The name doesn't ring a bell from any of my circles." Then he's looking right through me. "Tell me you're not trying to find your parents' killer?"

A blink is my only response. Lying isn't an option, as he'd see the truth on my face. I'm not great at hiding emotions, so I remain silent. His deep sigh echoes in the quiet room, and I can tell he already knows the answer.

There's something about him that nudges my caution aside, insisting I trust him. Soft light from the window and shadows from indoors give him a striking resemblance to my dad. My chest clenches with a desperate wish to rewind time and bring back my parents.

"There might be other ways I can help you find Bryant without you involving the Dukes. They're dangerous and unpredictable."

I lean forward, taking a shaky breath. "You can?" Coming here might have been the smarter decision after all.

"Trust me, you don't want to bring the Dukes' attention to you." He smiles softly again. "You can stay with Ivan and me. I have a spare room. I will start putting out feelers for Bryant."

The perfect moment shatters into an explosion as the front door to the cabin rips right off its hinges. I flinch hard, my heart attempting to break out of my chest as a tide of midnight black-uniformed guards sweep into the home.

Adrenaline shoots me out of my chair, my uncle

doing the same, icy shivers racing down my spine. The quick flash of their gold emblem on their chests isn't enough to let me know where they're from, but my mind isn't exactly thinking straight.

"What's going on?" I ask, swiftly curling my fingers around the hilt of the blade that rests at my hip. Every survival instinct in my body roars to life, hitting my veins like electricity, and I'm recoiling from them.

Everything changes in an instant.

My uncle's hand locks on mine, and we're both running through the kitchen to the corridor for the rear door.

"Run. Don't stop, whatever you do," he commands in a hoarse whisper, his gaze darting between me and the guards behind us. The floorboards thump with their boots, the corridor echoing with their shouts.

"Halt." That's the only word I hear as the roaring ocean of my panic blocks my ears.

"Who are they?" What in the world is going on?

The backdoor is mere steps away, and my uncle reaches it first, throwing it open.

But before I can take another step forward to escape, a vice-like grip latches onto the back of my neck, wrenching me backward.

I cry out, my feet tangling as I'm ripped out of my uncle's hold. The sharpness of the pain across my neck leaves me momentarily breathless as I teeter for balance.

My uncle's swinging around to get me, our gazes clash in a fleeting moment, his filled with torment. He unsheathes blades that rush out from under his sleeves, and slashes at the first guard coming for him, but when three others shove past us to reach him, he throws himself out of the door, vanishing from my line of sight.

I wheeze, thrashing against the guard holding onto me. I slam my heel into his foot and in a hot surge of fear, I twist to face the two of them. With the blade tip gripped tight in my hand, I hurl it at one of the guards. It spins through the space between us. He darts out of the way, the knife smacking him in the shoulder. All while I'm grabbing another one from my boot.

Spinning to the brute reaching for me, I swing the knife in my fist. It arcs out in front of me, tearing a line across his chest. The uniform splits from the cut, along with a thin line of blood from where I only grazed him. That's also when I catch a better glimpse of the emblem on his uniform of a golden tree.

The unmistakable symbol of the Dukes.

*Fuck!*

"You little bitch!" he snarls.

I recoil, fear spiking through me in a manic flurry. Why are the Dukes' men after me? Are they connected to the killers hunting me down after all?

In my alarm, I snatch another blade tucked at the back of my belt, brandishing both weapons while squaring up to two guards. They tower over me, but they don't scare me. It's who they work for that worries me.

One of them barks in laughter.

Wait, he thinks this is funny? Fine, I can give him something to really laugh about.

With a deep, guttural growl from my inner wolf, I hurl myself toward him. My knee slams up against his crown jewels as I climb him like a thick tree, the sharp edge of my knife kissing his jugular, driving him backward. He hits the wall, howling like a wounded animal as his knees buckle under him. In the process, he shoves me off him, his fist knocking into my arm. One of my knives slips from my grip and is accidentally tossed across the hallway.

I throw myself at him once more, pressing the tip of my blade to his face. I'm glaring into his eyes as his laughter's cut off in a strangled gasp.

"Now that I've got your attention. What the fuck are you doing here?"

Just like that, a thick arm is thrown around my neck, and I'm pulled off the second guard while he snatches my hand with the blade.

"Son of a bitch!" the wounded guard grumbles, groping his groin, getting to his feet, and coming at me. He snatches me by my hair, and I whimper at the burning pain.

"The Dukes just want to ask you some questions. So, will you come easily or do it the hard way?"

"Questions? About what?" I tense all over, my heart thundering against my ribcage. "Get the hell off me." I kick my heel into the guard's kneecap hard enough to know I've knocked it out of place. He snarls in my ear, and I rip free of him.

"Fuck, fuck!" he's howling, clutching his knee.

A sudden shadow falls over me, but before I can face who it is, a blinding pain ripples across my head, a powerful force that has stars erupting at the edges of my vision.

The world spins as a sense of weightlessness takes

me over. My legs crumble under me, and I hit the floor, darkness encroaching. I fight it with everything I have, then I hear someone say, "The other two got away."

With a weak half-smile on my lips, everything goes black.

## CHAPTER
# FOUR
### BILLIE

An icy splash of water crashes across my face. I flinch awake, ripped out of the black depth of my unconsciousness, spluttering and gasping.

I squint up from my chair at the gleaming overhead light, and a grinning guard casts a shadow over me. It's the same guy I kicked in the jewels earlier, and now he seems rather pleased with himself.

"Where am I?" I groan, shaking the water from my hair while droplets run down the sides of my neck.

He grunts in response, his square face not quite finished smirking at my expense. When I tear my sight from him and find we're in a terribly white, barren room, I can't help but shudder that this is when he's going to start torturing me. Save for a few metal chairs scattered along the walls, there's nothing else.

Why hasn't he tied me up, then?

Grabbing my arm, his grasp like iron, he hauls me to stand.

"It's your turn," he says.

Before I can form a single word about what he's talking about, he's hauling me into a corridor that's bustling with other people. That takes me off guard, my attention swinging left and right, trying to piece together the jigsaw puzzle I'm in. Shifters and supernaturals, dressed in casual or uniform attire, are scattered around as if they are waiting for their turn to audition or something. I don't see a pattern of how they are all connected.

Except that they're all watching me, their chatter dying down, and that feeling of confusion steadily tightens my chest harder and harder.

"My turn for what?" I mutter, struggling against the guard's grip, slightly nauseated at my situation as I speed to keep up with his long strides.

He turns toward a door at the end of the corridor and pushes it open, then shoves me inside. His large hand against my back rams me forward.

"Have fun with her," he growls at the man waiting for me inside, then leaves us with a hasty slam of the door.

I stumble before a figure sitting across a round table from me who doesn't appear intimidating. He's on the smaller side, yet his presence seems to fill the white room. Black hair is slick with gel and shiny beneath the lights, combed out of his eyes. Dressed in black trousers and a fitted shirt, he's in his chair, one leg crossed over the other, leaning back, while he stares at me intensely. The room is overbearingly hot, as if someone's cranked up the heat.

"What's going on?" I ask. "Where am I?"

"My name is Clark Ashenfeather, and I give you my

word you're safe." He gestures at the chair across the table for him with a hand, yet the invite feels like a sparrow being invited by a hawk to share its nest.

I slide into the seat, figuring there's only one way to find out where I am, and that's listening to the man with a narrow, beak-like nose. As I settle into the seat, my hand subtly brushes against my boots, and a sinking sensation fills me. My two additional knives are gone. That asshole took them. Though I sense the reassuring hardness of the neck knife concealed in a small sheath I've stitched into the front of my bra, making it close to undetectable.

"Nice pendant," he comments, his attention falling to the gold emblem swinging from the chain around my neck. It's customary to show it to anyone upon entering their country or even sometimes their home to show that you are a citizen of the House of Gold and Garnet. Sometimes, they ask for your blood to be spilled over it for true patronage to the district. Locals aren't always trusting of newcomers from other houses. "Can't say I recognize that design."

Swallowing my nerves that he might recognize my family crest if he looks too closely at it, I say, "There are lots of different ones out there." Then I tuck the pendant back under my shirt, hating how much my hands shake. "Must be tough to keep track of them all. Anyway, you were saying who you were…"

"I work for the Dukes of Lapland." His gaze drills through me as though he's reading my thoughts, sending a shiver down my spine. "You're here because we're trying to uncover some gaps in our information."

Could he be any more vague? Yet there I am, my insides quivering at how closely Clark studies me as if he knows something about me I don't want him to. I blink, panic warring within me as it burns my insides out, yet I sit still, faking how jacked up I am in fear.

"A-And that's why your guards tore into the cabin and attacked us like criminals?"

"Unfortunate things." Not a flicker of a reaction on his face, no remorse either. "So, let's begin, miss...?"

"Mina Carter," I provide, throwing him the fake name I've been using. When he researches me, he'll find my ordinary life and job at FaeEcho, and that I'm a wolf shifter from a simple family. I've been pretending for so long, I now feel more comfortable hiding behind this persona than revealing the real me.

"Hmm, Mina," he repeats, letting the name roll on his tongue as he scribbles something on a notepad. "Tell me, how long have you known Awstin?"

"A couple of years," I reply, my stomach clenching at the mention of my uncle's name.

Clark hums in acknowledgment, scribbling more in his notepad and holding it in a way that makes it impossible for me to read it.

"And when was the last time you visited our estate on a job?"

My heart drops. Work? What the heck is he talking about? I push out a nonchalant shrug, thinking fast. "Can't really say I remember. You know how it is, with so many jobs, and right now, I'm still rattled from being attacked by your guards."

A faint smirk pulls at his mouth. There's a certain

pleasure gleaming in his eyes, as though he relishes knowing just how roughly the guards handled us.

"Where did you gain your training, Ms. Carter," he asks in a nonchalant voice that might as well belong to a machine.

As I consider his question, I realize the heat that has my clothes clinging to me. My answer sticks to my dry tongue, and I feel parched in my throat.

"South Africa," I answer truthfully, even if I'm unsure what work he's specifically referring to.

"Is that where you were born?"

I nod, squirming under the growing heat of the lights and his intense stare. His calm demeanor isn't helping me keep my cool, nor does the glass of water untouched in front of him. The perspiration running down the side of the glass makes me swallow the dryness in my mouth. I'd kill for a sip right now.

"How about you tell me why you're grilling me when I did nothing wrong?" I ask, my voice cracking, my gaze instinctively falling to his water. It's so close, and I can practically feel its coolness on my lips.

His dark stare flickers to me, a sly grin slowly etching on his mouth when he reaches for the glass, and my breath hitches as he brings it up to his lips, pausing just for a moment as if savoring it. Then, ever so slowly, he tips the glass, and the water flows right into his mouth.

I want to hurt him as I stay hypnotized, watching him swallow it. A droplet trickles down his chin. My heart pulses in my throat, but I know the game he's playing, so I school my thirst.

He sets the half-empty glass on the table, his gaze sharpening.

"And in what capacity are you working with Awstin? Installing safes or... breaking into them?"

Wait! What?

The room spins, my insides tightening as I put two and two together.

He's not after me, but my uncle. They think I'm working for him, and it's obvious they have no idea I'm his niece. As alarming as my situation is, this discovery is my lifeline.

"Look, there's been a mistake here," I begin, noticing the brief flare of surprise in Clark's eyes, but I keep my voice steady, needing him to believe me. "I'm just in town visiting Awstin as he's an old friend. Nothing more."

His cold eyes narrow on me, and I shift in my seat uncomfortably, hoping they don't think I'm lying and finish me, then bury my body somewhere no one can find. I haven't come all this way not to find out who killed my parents.

"Your friend is of interest to us. If you are merely visiting him, then you are of no use to us. We *will* conduct a background search on you, so I suggest you don't leave the country for now. I am to assume we will find you at Awstin's home?"

My breathing grows ragged, my pulse thumping in my temples as I lean forward. "Is my friend in *real* trouble?"

Clark arches a thick eyebrow. "Has he done something we should be worried about?"

What has my uncle gotten himself into? And how is it related to the people out in the corridor? It scares me to think he'll have mercenaries coming for him if it betrays the Dukes.

"He's always been a trustworthy man who keeps his word, so I doubt he's done anything wrong." I plead his case, desperate for him not to end up dead.

That's when an idea slides into my thoughts. Clark reports to the Dukes. This might be my chance to take up the matter with them. What's the worst that can happen? They kill me... I almost choke on my breath.

Straightening, I force a smile to appear cooperative. "I want to speak to the Dukes, please."

Clark's features contort to where I worry he's about to have a seizure, except he breaks into a laugh, shaking his head as though I'm an amusing child.

"Do you have an appointment?" he mocks.

"And if I manage to get one, will you take me to them?" I press, my muscles tensing at him laughing at me.

"Highly doubtful it'll happen this year or the next. But everything comes with a price. Everyone who is brought to their attention must provide a sample of their blood as payment," he murmurs. "And if you want a chance, I need your payment upfront, now."

I really hate this guy. Sure, in the House of Gold and Garnet, many payments are made with blood, which is normal, except I don't trust him one inch. There's a reason I've hidden my real identity, and I sure as hell won't give a drop of my blood to a worm like him. Especially if he tests it and discovers there's magic in my blood and I'm not who I said I was. One false move can mess this up for me, and I've never been this close to finding out about my parents' murderers.

"Hmph, I thought as much," Clark huffs dismissively, pushing up from his seat. He saunters over to the door, opens it, and raises his voice, calling for the guards.

My heart beats faster as my chance slips away.

With desperation settling over me, I spring to my feet as the heavy footsteps of the guards grow louder, approaching the room.

"Wait!" my voice strains because I'm not ready to leave.

He pauses but doesn't turn around, waiting for me to continue.

"I'll make the payment, double, after I speak with Dukes. You have my word," I counter, hands sweaty and pressed to my stomach as if I'm going to be sick.

"No deal." He steps back as the idiot guard barges into the room with a sneer, his rough hand clutching my arm, pulling me out of the room.

*No. Please no.*

Panic curls under my ribs, and tears burn my eyes. Pain erupts in my arm. He's gripping so hard, stopping blood circulation in my arm. I resist the urge to draw my blade because I'm so close to the Dukes, and I can't blow this.

I'm fighting against the guard's grip when Clark's gaze fixes on my arm, right where the sleeve has pushed up to my elbow, the faint hint of the cryptic words etched on my forearm visible. His dark eyes bore into my arm, and I hastily push my sleeve back down.

A chill of apprehension climbs through me as the room seems to shrink around me. It's alarmingly clear Clark is not a man whose curiosity I want to provoke. I swallow hard, tasting the bitter tang of worry.

"What's that on your arm?" he hisses, pointing at my arm with his chin.

"Just a tattoo, something I got done as a teen."

His scowl deepens, staring at my covered arm for too long, then looks at me with cold eyes. "Throw her out," he finally caws.

I plead, "Wait, please. I'm open to negotiating so I can meet with the Dukes."

The guard hauls me down the corridor away, and Clark doesn't glance my way but slips back into the room.

The fucker! On the bright side, he didn't demand to inspect my arm, but devastatingly, I might have just lost my chance to confront the Dukes.

Led through the dimly lit corridors, the guard's constant hauling hurts my arm, but nothing aches as much as the devastating sensation that I failed.

"Please," I implore. "There's a misunderstanding. Just let me speak with Clark again."

A snort ricochets back at me from the guard, and my heart beats frantically the farther we travel through the building. Before I know it, I'm being rushed outside the building into the blinding sunlight. I squint as my eyes adjust at a sight that absolutely blows me away.

Manicured lawns stretch out in front of me like an ocean of green. Gold statutes pepper the landscape, shimmering beneath the daylight, and the lofty golden gates in the distance add to the whole opulent appearance. I've never seen anything so indulgent. Many in the House of Gold and Garnet are rich, but the Dukes are on a whole different level of affluence.

There's no doubt I'm in the Dukes' estate, the one place I came to Finland to enter. Except, that dreadful ache curls in my gut that I'd fucked up my chance.

I tug against the guard's hold while taking in the sights, gaining myself a stern jerk from him that has me tripping over my own feet across the stone pathway that glints with flecks of gold.

At that moment, I catch a whiff of midnight jasmine, tangled with a potent masculine scent of mahogany on the breeze, followed by the smell of wolf.

The rest of the world immediately dims as I take another deep inhale, desperately wanting more. It curls around me, intoxicating, searing into my mind, pulling at something deep within me that scares me.

My stomach lurches so hard I'm going to be sick.

I know what it is immediately...

It's the undeniable feeling of finding my fated mate.

They say when you meet your soulmate, you instantly know. And this is it... a punch right to my chest.

With a shuddering breath and my heart thrashing wildly in my chest, I nervously twist around. My line of sight clashes with the most striking man I've ever seen. Pale blue eyes narrowed on me are all I see, filled with a startled intensity and recognition that I'm his fated mate. That he's mine.

His gaze widens, his shock thick in the air between us. He feels it, too. That's how these things worked.

My pulse thumps erratically at the sight of him because this can't be happening. Not now.

Even before I can process the reality of my world spinning out of control, the guard's grip slackens from around my arm. He falls to one knee, his voice booming out.

"Your Grace."

My heart seizes in my chest. Is the universe laughing at me?

I've found my mate, and he's not just any man, but a Duke!

## CHAPTER
# FIVE
### BILLIE

Every instinct in my body goes alert.

The Duke's irresistible scent lingers in my head, twisting me inside out, that midnight jasmine and mahogany smell so powerful, it fogs my thoughts. The fierce reaction of my body to him confirms in that moment of terror that he *is* my fated mate.

It's real... Fuck, it's real.

Every wolf shifter dreams of one day finding their mate, but not me. I don't have time for that when I have killers to hunt down. So, this can't be right, especially not with a Duke from the same regime who most likely sanctioned my parents' death.

Once you've found your partner, it's for life, and your body will crave him. The thought makes me quake ferociously, but with each inhale, the tightness in my chest confirms we're bound together.

Suddenly, I can't breathe, my pulse roaring in my ears, my knees trembling. I'm recoiling from him and from the guard, who doesn't seem to notice. He's still kneeling and bowing his head in front of his Grace.

My world cinches around me until it's too much, moving too fast. I need air. I need space. Before I know it, I'm running in the other direction.

I pray that what I feel is an illusion and that my body is stressed or something because I'm not sure I can do this.

The wind rushes past my face as I sprint across the lush lawn, doing the complete opposite of what I came here to do. I don't even know where I'm heading, but I need a quiet corner to find my breath and collect my thoughts.

When a huge shadow falls over me, fear pummels through me that the guard's on my heels. He'll hurt me, and right now, I'm not exactly thinking straight, so I might do something I'll regret later. Still, my fingers close around the hilt of the neck knife tucked into my bra.

A strong hand grasps my arm, sending a jolt of electricity through my body. In a swift motion, he swings me around and pushes me against a tree. The large figure presses against me, trapping me. Struggling against the hold with my fingers around the hilt, I quickly blink up, already holding the blade at his throat. God, he's huge.

Then, my breath catches as my eyes meet his.

It's the Duke... my fated mate.

How can things have become so complicated?

His scent swirls through my senses, intoxicating and captivating, the musk weakening my legs. As if I have zero control, I take another deep breath, filling my lungs with him. My knees wobble, but something else is happening to me.

This close to me, those primal instincts flare wilder within my chest. A ripple of desire turns in my stomach while my skin heats up, a fire burning between my thighs.

Up close, he's more beautiful than I could have imagined. His face is all strong angles, a shadow of growth across his square jawline, and full lips that should soften the dangerous air he carries… but it doesn't.

"Tell me, *mate*, do you have a name?" He's not pulling back but pushing against the blade biting into his flesh like nothing in the world frightens him.

Maybe I'm foolish or scared, perhaps both as the words pour from my lips.

"It's a mistake. I can't be your mate." My voice trembles, and I hate how little authority I hold over myself. "Now, get off me."

Rich, dark-brown hair, short and windblown, falls into a wild mess, a few strands tumbling over an eye. Irises so pale, it's like I'm staring into the winter's sky. They're also cold, but something wild is roaming behind them.

I glance around me but we're alone.

His hand slides down to my chin, his knuckles tucked underneath, tipping my head back to stare up at him.

My cheeks flush.

I lift my gaze all the way up to the Duke. Layered with muscles, he stands close to six foot five, compared to me at five foot eight. I'm tiny next to him, and something about him towering over me turns me into jelly.

He's a mountain in front of me, those blue eyes focus on me once more.

"Let's try again. Or shall I just call you, wild girl?" I can almost feel the heat underneath his skin and hear the rumbling of his wolf deep inside.

Part of me debates running as fast from him as possible, but the other part, a section of myself I barely recognize, is drawn to him so severely, it leaves me winded.

"M-Mina," I manage. "You can call me Mina."

"That wasn't so hard. Now, Mina, either cut my throat or lower your blade." There's a sense of controlled power around him, like a wolf holding back from pouncing on his prey, yet his muscles are corded and ready for action.

As much as I prefer to keep him at a knife's length, I also don't want to have the Duke on my bad side. If I put aside the thought of him being my fated mate, the opportunity to finally ask him about his mercenaries plays on my thoughts. I will deal with the whole bonding thing later on.

After all, a true bonding between mates doesn't truly take hold until we have sex. As much as the Duke is sinfully gorgeous, I like to think I have some semblance of power to resist that from happening. Even if that overwhelming sensation from deep in my chest surges through me once more, the one where I'm fighting for breath, where I'm feverish, where my heart drops.

He doesn't look like a patient kind of person, but looks are deceiving. He hasn't threatened me yet, but his lips are curling into the most dangerous smile.

"Who would have guessed that today I would meet

my fated mate," he says in a rugged voice that's deep and too sexy to be legal. "You can call me Khaos."

I finally lower the blade from his throat and tuck it back into my bra, noting the red line against his flesh from the pressure I applied. I watch a single drop of blood roll down his Adam's apple from where I actually broke skin.

*Oh, shit!* My stomach coils into a fiery pit that I've made the Duke bleed.

*Way to go, Billie. The moment you meet your fated mate, who just happens to be a dangerous Duke of Lapland, you cut him with your blade.*

"Come with me," he commands. "We have much to talk about." His hand slips down and takes mine in his, swallowing it with the sheer size of his grip. The touch is like fire, flushing over my skin.

I'm still drowning in the sheer shock of the situation to resist as he starts walking me across the lawn. I follow him for the reason that, yeah, I need to talk to him, too. And privacy would be better.

His pale blue, wolf-like eyes hold mine, and I might as well be floating from how quickly things escalated. His skin is a rich sun-kissed color, hair a deep brown, with short wild locks blowing in the breeze. He wipes the blood from his neck with the palm of his hand, never saying a word about it, and I inhale a sigh of relief he doesn't promise to punish me. Which I expect, considering everything I've heard about the Dukes.

My heart thunders in my chest. I study his features while my body floods with heat at the sight of him.

Is that normal? It has to be part of the fated mate connection, that sharp edge of attraction causing my body to flip with arousal and my nipples harden. I'm getting high just from standing next to him, which I know is wrong. No way should a fated mate connection be this dramatic.

Nerves lift the hairs on my nape, and butterflies burst to life in my stomach. My body is ruling me while my head hasn't had time to process everything.

"Let's go," he says with a grin on his lips. His grasp tightens around my hand.

What the hell is wrong with me that I'm letting him take control over me as we start walking?

These Dukes have god blood in their veins, so who says Khaos doesn't have some kind of captivating ability to lure me? The more I think about it, the more I tense up. I slide my hand out of his.

He pauses and turns to me, his gaze tracing down my body, lingering a bit too long on my breasts before lifting to my face.

"Is everything alright?"

"Maybe we should talk out here," I suggest, fighting the fog in my head. "I don't make a habit of taking off with strangers into their homes."

He laughs. The deep, rich sound ignites my nerve endings and slides all the way to the apex between my thighs. I stare at his mouth, curious to know how it'd feel on my body, especially down where I'm aching to be touched.

"It's safer inside," he insists, his voice demanding. "Are you ready?"

I shudder at the strength of desire that crashes into me like I've never felt before.

"I-I just need some fresh air," I say, stumbling from him. "I'm not feeling myself."

His inhales deepen, nostrils flaring as a primal growl rolls from his throat. My chest immediately sticks out toward him in response as a pressure builds deep in my gut.

Hell, what's wrong with me?

Khaos studies me carefully, another snarl purring from him. I tremble all over, the sound like a vibration rippling over me and consuming me.

"Please stop making those sounds," I gasp breathlessly.

His full lips pinch. "Interesting."

"Maybe I'm coming down with something," I suggest as my pulse throbs through me. I'm burning up at this stage.

Khaos steps into my personal space, his hand tracing my jawline. Moisture drenches my panties with such intensity, the world spins. I push his hand away from me.

"What are you doing to me?" I snap.

"Wild girl, what you're feeling is natural."

I back away, shaking my head, hating what he's saying. My insides quiver as sweat trickles down my spine, and my mind rages with rationalizing what's going on.

I've caught a bug, the change in temperature has impacted me, or the Duke has a power of captivation and is toying with me. The latter seems like the most reasonable explanation. Every time I stare at this beautiful man, I clench my thighs together.

"This isn't natural. I was perfectly fine before I met you." I came here to find my parents' killers, not my fated mate and to completely lose control of myself.

"On the contrary." Khaos closes the distance between us once more, not understanding that I need space from him. "You're not only my fated mate, but I can smell the heady slick of your heat pouring off you."

My cheeks turn to fire at his words. I blink at him, pushing against him, but he grabs my arm, not letting me go.

"No, you're wrong... that can't be right." Heat only comes two weeks after a full moon once you've met your fated mate, and definitely not this quickly. Besides, we're only a few days out from a full moon, and wolf shifters like me shouldn't react this severely around our mate after meeting them for only a few minutes.

His nostrils flare once more, taking in my scent, and his lips curl into a grin.

"You smell so fucking delicious." His eyes glint, seeming to almost change color into their wolf form as if he's losing control.

Fear squeezes my insides. A sharp stabbing pain comes from my stomach, and I whimper, wrapping my arms around my middle.

"We need to go inside." He reaches for me. "I can help with your pain."

"Don't touch me." I recoil, seriously scared of how I'll react to his touch, how I'll become putty for him, and I don't even know this man. "Just give me a moment to calm down."

His features darken, a feral expression, his true face instead of the fake one he's been showing me. His breaths quicken, his chest pumping for breath, and the noticeable bulge in his pants tells me he's struggling as much as I am. The difference is that he seems to be better at mastering his body's reaction.

"Then follow me indoors, and I'll find you a place to rest. On the way, you can tell me what business brings you to my estate?" There's hunger in his eyes but a hardened edge to his voice. "And you don't need to be afraid of what your body is going through. It's normal."

My heart hammers, and I'm not even sure if I'm walking straight, but I take one step after another alongside him.

"This isn't normal. We just met, and it shouldn't happen this fast."

He smirks, somehow taking my words as a compliment that he's so irresistible, and I can't help myself. I roll my eyes, making sure he notices.

"Okay, talk then," he states.

Swimming in confusion, I decide to tell him the semi-truth.

"I was being questioned by a rude man called Clark and shoved around by the guard after they broke into my friend's cabin while I visited him. I was brought in for questioning." Sweeping my gaze to the Duke, he just nods, his forehead now a furrow of lines, and darkness dances under his eyes.

"And you're from Lapland?" he asks as if he's skeptical I'd be a local.

Another sharpness comes across my stomach, and I moan, the heavy feeling inside me not helping me move faster.

"South Africa," I push out, holding back from showing him how tight I feel all over.

Without another word, he guides me past the building the guard had brought me out of, and we travel along a stone path that delivers us to a set of lofty metal gates at the rear of the property. Beyond the gates lays an extravagant mansion, a great expanse of dark obsidian stone with lofty windows on all four levels. The sun's reflection gives it a mirage effect of sparkling crystals. It comes complete with a dark, pointy roof. A winding path cuts through a sparse forest of pine trees that leads up to the grand arched doorway. The entrance steps are flanked by imposing gold wolf statues.

With a flick of Khaos' hand, the guards swing open the gates. Stepping through, I immediately feel as though I've crossed the threshold into another realm.

Pushing down the heated desire consuming me, I focus on what's around me to distract myself. As we stroll along the path, silence envelopes us as though the metal bar fence surrounding the estate is able to shut out all external sounds. All I hear is the distant whisper of the breeze swishing through the pine trees and the crunch of our boots on the pebbled path.

Pines line the passage, needle-like-leaves flutter in the freeze, and shadows flitter deeper in the woods. It has to be a trick of the light.

My gut twists, and it's not just from arousal, but that I've found my fated mate and I'm simultaneously going into heat. He's taking me into his mansion, but for all I know, he signed off on my death years ago. I've gained exactly what I wanted in Finland. An audience with one of the Dukes, which I'll take.

I just have to find a way to control myself. And under no circumstance am I to throw myself at the Duke of Lapland.

# CHAPTER SIX

ERYX

Surveying the wreckage of Tallis' game room, I grimace at the destruction I'd caused. Furniture overturned, scratches on the polished floor and walls, the bloodstains where my deer had stabbed his victim.

It had been accidental on my part. Sometimes in my animal form, I become so engrossed, so enthralled in the hunt, the rest of the world simply fades away.

Still, Tallis cherished his game room, and as the youngest of us three, he's always trying to prove himself. That's why I've arranged for a crew to clean up the mess and rebuild the wall with the hole in it. Otherwise, I'll have to listen to his constant whining.

He's short-fucking-fused when things don't go his way. Like the time he set the office building at the front of our estate on fire. To be fair, I thought it was warranted, considering my grandfather forced him to take a mercenary job targeting a girl he'd crushed on hard. To the point he'd refused to use his incubus lure on her. So, when he had to hand her over for delivery to the king, after discovering she was a spy against us, he lost his shit.

Shaking off the memory, I give one last glance to the room being renovated, then head downstairs. Murmuring voices catch my attention... a female voice I don't recognize has me intrigued. Curiosity leads me around the corner, and there in the main hall is Khaos with a dark-haired girl, their backs to me. Her head is level with his shoulders, but my gaze traces her trim legs in tight leather pants, the nice curves of her ass, and the long-sleeve top that hugs that hourglass figure. Deep-chestnut hair is pulled up roughly into a bun, loose strands tumbling past her shoulders.

Who the fuck is she?

Is Khaos hiring a new mercenary?

They continue walking to the end of the entry hallway, and I'm tracking them on silent steps, left in the wake of her perfume—the candy-sweet scent of her slick, the dewy fragrance of roses, caramel apples, and crisp mountain air... all belonging to her.

The smells slam right into me at my core, shattering me, squeezing my heart, and gripping my balls as if the scent has taken hold of me and now owns me.

I stumble on my feet, not expecting any of it... and especially not the combination of finding my fated mate and that she's starting to go into heat.

A low growl grumbles in my chest, and instinctively, I mouth, "Mate" under my breath, as if she controls me now. I'm urged forward, anxiety and anticipation billowing through me to know that she's mine.

As a half-god, half-gryffin, our grandfather insisted that anything could happen when it came to our love life. There was no guarantee of being matched with a fated mate.

Yet here I am.

She's a beautiful surprise. I haven't seen her face, but I'm already smitten, already planning on stealing her away to be mine, mine, mine.

For so long, I accepted I might not find my soulmate, and I didn't have to like it, but I'd learned to be comfortable with it. Mates don't have to be fated to fall in love, but when it happens, it's like having the stars and the constellations in the sky align with destiny.

The pair stop several feet in front of me when they encounter Rez, our messenger in the estate, a young rabbit shifter who zips through our estate with urgent messages. Our grandfather hired him, and we all suspect it's his way to keep tabs on us.

I halt, leaning a shoulder into the wall. Playing with the ring on my finger, I twist it soothingly over and over, my attention locked on the pretty girl.

I've never experienced such an intense need toward anyone, nor the overwhelming urge to sweep her into my arms and discover everything about her. Every muscle in my body tenses as I trace her body from head to toe, noting the way she keeps her distance from my brother, yet she keeps stealing glances at him, thinking he's not noticing. But Khaos sees everything.

Whether or not she knows it, she's smitten with my brother, and it makes me curious if she's as special to him as she is to me? Our father had three wives after all, each a fated mate, so maybe it's in our lineage that she's all of ours.

Do I like that idea?

Perhaps. I'm not sure yet. It all depends on if my brothers intend to keep her all to themselves or share?

I may not understand the full extent of the obsession ruling through me, but I want to discover who she is. I inhale deeply, needing more of her scent.

She whips her head around and spots me, no doubt having heard me. She gasps. Shattering ice-blue eyes clash with mine, and a painful ache bleeds into my chest at how absolutely spectacular she is. The hairs on my arms rise, and my cock thickens as my heart thunders. Lust unfurls through my body at her beauty.

It isn't just the depth of her gaze or the wild fray of the loose hair feathered around her face that captivates me. It's something raw, an invisible connection drawing us together. The longer I stare at her, the more I notice there's something odd about her dark hair against her light skin that doesn't fit, as though she isn't exactly herself. I can't explain it, but what I do understand is the unspoken recognition billowing between us.

She's inhaling the air deeper, and I grin as she realizes who I am to her.

Her breathing hitches, her eyes wide, and I watch the transfix of curiosity to fright cross her face. Amusing. Skin flushed moments earlier now pales.

I step forward, expecting her to pass out, but instead she recoils from me, bumping right into my brother.

Khaos pulls away from Rez and turns toward me with relief in his exhaled breath.

"Eryx, meet Mina, my fated mate," he gloats with a grin. "I'll answer your questions later, but for now, you need to take extra good care of her and deliver her to my office until I return. I have an urgent issue to attend to."

My emotions ignite into a flame that I'd been right. "It seems she has a lot more in common with us. She's my fated mate, as well."

Khaos straightens, looking disappointed at first, then schools his features, his gaze drifting to Mina.

I picture myself growling as I fuck her hard, my fist curled in her hair, and I make her scream—how else am I going to secure my lifelong bond with her?

"Do you feel the same connection with him?" Khaos asks as if my word isn't enough, which tells me just how deeply invested he is in the girl already. It's rather amusing, considering my brother is reserved with his emotions, so this will be interesting.

She stares between the two of us. "I don't really understand how it's possible," she begins.

I smile, hypnotized by her sexy, melodic voice.

Khaos glares my way. "Fine, we'll sort this out later. Take her to my office and grab Tallis to join us. I suspect he's involved as well."

He turns to Mina, as though he's struggling to leave her side but has second thoughts. He clears his throat and marches down the hallway with Rez on his heels.

"Are you ready to have fun?" I murmur, stepping toward her. "Are you excited to find yourself as our fated mate? I do love to play with my toys."

She tenses, her lips thinning, chin high, and I'm smitten with this rebellious side to her.

"I'm not one of your fangirls," she snaps, her words clipped. "I've heard about the sea of females fawning over you three, who you sleep with, dump, hurt. That's not me, so don't waste your time."

Stepping closer, a rumble breaks over my throat at the intensity of her scent. She can fight it all she wants, but I see the way she trembles, how she can barely keep herself up on her feet in my presence.

"Nature seems to have other ideas," I say, grinning, and she lowers her attention to me twisting my ring around my finger. "It's a family emblem." The gold signet ring is engraved with the family tree. She just blinks. Any other female would be swooning by now... evidently not her.

Every instinct inside me calls me to her, demands I secure our bond at this moment, but I have patience. Her resistance doesn't fool me, but I'll let her believe it does. In truth, I like her feistiness. I want her to fight me, to run from me. Adrenaline pours through me at the thought of chasing her.

Except, I'm not dealing with one of our 'fans' as she called them. She's my fated mate, and that means she needs to come willingly.

"Okay, let me give you a tour of the place you'll be calling home."

Her mouth drops open. "Home?"

"What did you expect? That we would let our fated mate just slip away?" I add, starting a casual stroll. She falls in step beside me.

With a huff, she says, "You know, I have a life. My home, a job, friends. I can't just desert them all."

"Yet, that's exactly what's going to happen." A spark of awareness flicks through my mind. She's seething on the inside, cursing me, perhaps. I see it in her fisted hands and stiff posture. But she must understand the cardinal rule of our kind—once you find your fated mate, you hold on to them fiercely until the bond is sealed. Then she's with us forever... an idea that excites me.

I didn't expect to have my world turned upside down by meeting my fated mate and settling down, but I'm not one to fight fate.

"Besides," I add nonchalantly, sliding my hands into the pockets of my pants, attempting to adjust my growing cock caused by her tantalizing scent. "How far do you think you'll get once your heat really kicks in?"

"I-I don't think it's a heat. It's a... reaction to stress. Or whatever this is between us," she stammers.

Her denials irk me. The truth is staring her in the face, but I let her hold on to her illusions. We've just met. What I find fascinating, though, is her resistance. Why is she fighting her nature? Anyone else would be on their knees, ecstatic to be our fated mate. Yet she looks ready to plunge a dagger into my heart.

We travel in silence, and I decide to take the scenic route and spend the time getting to know a bit more about her. I guide her to two double doors and push them open to our grand library.

"If you like to read, you will find every kind of book you desire."

She peers inside, not saying much. As she steps past me to get a better look, her scent wafts over me, distracting my focus. I'm not great at concentrating at the best of times, and now it's a hundred times harder.

When she steps out without a word, I steer her down the hallway to the other end, and we enter the pool room, which gains a gasp from her sweet lips. Not surprising since this room was crafted from magic made to resemble the interior of a mountain. Cavernous walls littered with quartz crystals reflect the dim lights and cast a glow on the water. Steam wafts from its surface. At one end of the long pool, a waterfall cascades from the crest of a rock formation, the sound of the rushing water filling the silent space.

"The pool is carved right out of the stone," I explain, admiring the way her eyes take in the surroundings, the way she blinks as if she's uncertain the place is real.

"It's beautiful."

"The water's warm." Stepping into the room, I crouch and dip my hand in. Her blue stare tracks my every movement, her pink lips parting slightly in wonder. "The water has healing properties, and it might help soothe the ache from your oncoming heat."

She's flushing, her cheeks so red, it does things to me, makes me picture her slipping into the pool, naked and soaking wet. I'm not doing myself any favors, so I head to the doorway.

"It's not too deep if you're worried about being unable to swim."

"I can swim. I grew up in South Africa by the water," she offers, which I take as progress.

Halting near her, I say, "I sense resistance between

us. Do you have a boyfriend back home? Dump his sorry ass."

She cuts me a stare, narrowing her attention. "The stories are true about your arrogance."

"So, I take that as a no to having a boyfriend?"

She shrugs. "You made it clear it doesn't matter. And why the kindness? Rumor has it I should have been flayed and paraded around town by now."

I bark a loud laugh at her bravery. "I've heard the gossip, and some of it is true. When I'm not in a hunter mode, I'm easy to get along with, laid-back. Unless you want me to treat you like the whispers suggest?" Watching her carefully, I hold her stare, and she doesn't glance away. I admire her for her tenacity.

"You do you. I was just noting that you're not as terrifying as they make you out to be."

Another laugh rumbles through me.

"Trust me, you never want to see that side of me." Even as I say the words, I offer her a devilish smile, and there's no missing the slight tremble that courses over her. It's a strange thing, my primal satisfaction bringing her fear, knowing how easily I can affect her.

Returning to our tour, we head up to the next floor, and she pauses in front of a family portrait—my father surrounded by his three wives, standing in front of our mansion.

"My father," I explain, a tightness in my gut at the mention of him. "With his three fated mates. The one in the middle is my mom." I refer to the blonde with curls down to her waist, clinging to my dad's arm, a wildness in her eyes, looking unimaginably content. It's been too long since I've seen that smile...

"Your father had multiple fated mates, too? Must run in the family." She distracts me. My muscles tense, my heart slams against my ribcage, and the desire to drag her up against me intensifies.

Clearing my throat, I answer, "Apparently. Trust me, I'm as shocked as you are about finding my fated mate today."

She pinches her lips to the corner of her mouth, then glances at the painting and back at me. "They live on the estate, too?"

"No," I respond, not elaborating, not needing to talk to her about my parents.

I move down the corridor, and her soft footsteps follow.

When my father had gone missing, his wives, including my mother, went into hiding and remained isolated ever since. Being ripped apart from your fated mate is devastating, and that was the only way they coped with their loss to avoid going completely insane. When a fated mate dies, their partner doesn't last much longer.

He was last seen over twenty years ago in Portland, thrown into a dangerous portal to Arcadia, a world of shifters ruled by Pan, the King of Arcadia.

Those who went in years ago never returned, and the few who had stumbled out by some miracle, have zero memory of their time in Arcadia. Today, the portal has been fixed, and it's open, but there's still no sign of my father. Deep in my soul, I know he's lost somewhere from where he'll never return. Part of me has made peace with that... other parts haven't. My grandfather once said, *carry the memory, not the weight of our loss*. I deal with that by not thinking about my parents when I can avoid it.

The tickle of Mina's scent draws me to her, its sweet scent engulfing me and tugging me out from my past.

"Where are we?" she asks, glancing around at the lavish corridors, the tone of her curiosity bringing me pleasure.

"Somewhere you'll be spending a lot of time," I answer with a lion's grin.

Her brows bunch up, looking ready to pepper me with questions, but before she gets the chance, I thrust open the door to Tallis' bedroom.

Tallis is sprawled across the couch, his nose buried in a book, more engrossed in reading than the company he keeps. A thin, naked brunette is straddling his hips, riding his cock, her tiny tits bouncing crazily. Her moans go unnoticed by him.

Classic Tallis, never focusing on his meal.

An incubus doesn't have to feed as frequently as my brother does, and part of me thinks it's his version of eating out of boredom.

A gasp slips past Mina's lips, coaxing Tallis to finally take notice of us. He lowers the book from his face and pauses.

"So, you're still trying to make it up to me for wrecking my game room by bringing me an offering? Excellent taste, brother." Yet the moment his nostrils flare, taking in a deep breath, his gaze lands on Mina, his eyes going wide, just like hers.

I smirk, watching the realization crash over him. He'd once told me he doubted he had a fated mate, which was fine with him. I'm eager for him to feel the same thrill I did at discovering how wrong we've both been.

With an awkward movement, he lifts the girl off his lap, and gets up clumsily, book still in hand, marching toward us with a raging hard-on.

"Fuck man, put it away," I snarl, squinting not to see it.

Mina retreats from the room and waits a few steps down the hall, murmuring to herself.

"Wait." Tallis strains out, making a sound on the brink of cracking.

Something potent and animalistic flares in his black eyes. Yet beneath the wildness lies fear, which is the opposite of his usually composed appearance.

"Is that..." He can't even complete his sentence, his attention darting between Mina and me.

"Yep," I admit, unable to hide the smile on my lips. "Mina's our fated mate... all of ours."

His features twist in disbelief. "Why the hell did you bring her in like this?" he growls.

"How was I supposed to know you were fucking? Besides, who cares? We found our fated mate."

Tallis' mouth opens, about to argue further, but then he straightens his shoulders and takes a sharp inhale.

"Get dressed and meet us in the office." I turn my back to him, leaving him to his turmoil. I search the hallway until I find Mina standing at the end of the hall, staring out a window, the sunlight bright on her face.

I can't help but grin.

"You better buckle up, princess," I murmur, excitement storming through my veins. "You have no idea what you're getting into."

## CHAPTER
# SEVEN
### BILLIE

Three fated mates?

Goosebumps flare over my skin, and I'm close to fainting.

This has to be a joke.

It's got to be impossible, a mistake, utter madness.

Yet the force that whispers in my soul that they're mine runs wild and untamed through my veins, demanding I stop fighting nature.

Nothing has prepared me for these three Dukes, and I've only just met them. Especially the dark-haired brother with black irises. I can't stop thinking of that girl riding him. I'm not jealous, of course not. I force my mind to remember that the fire-spitting sparks in my chest at seeing her straddling him are my hormones and animalistic reactions to my fated mate attraction.

Me? I don't care what he does or what any of them do.

Priority is to find my parents' killers, then later, work out how to deal with my fated mates. But for now, I have no intention of pushing them away until I get what I need out of them.

Eryx shoves open the door to an office, and as I pass him to enter, his hand presses against my lower back to guide me. My breath catches, and my nipples knot from that single touch.

Pushing forward to put distance between us, I take in the refined office—a dark mahogany desk with shelves filled with books and bottles of spirits and a leather lounge at the opposite end of the room. I can't help but notice the floor-to-ceiling windows that offer an awe-inspiring view of the woodlands.

I stroll toward them, drawn to the beauty. Sunlight filters through the dense pines, varying in shades of lush green on the sloping landscape. In the few areas where there are open patches of land, they're covered by wild purple and butter-yellow flowers. Absolutely beautiful.

Eryx shifts next to me, and I feel his gaze burning into my side. It's almost as if he's memorizing every detail, every inhale, every inch of my body. I'm not used to this kind of scrutiny, not to mention his proximity has him radiating a raw, compelling energy that tugs at me.

My toes curl in my shoes, and I struggle to hold back my reaction. It's hard to fight the desires, especially when I'm wrapped up in his captivating scent of cedar wood and crushed pine leaves. Beneath it is a strong hint of his manly scent, something warm and heady.

This is Eryx, a Duke of Lapland, a fierce mercenary I should fear, yet a deep hunger licks through me for him.

I twist my head toward him. He's standing a couple of feet away, one shoulder pressed against the window, his hands in front of him, and he's fiddling with the gold ring on his finger. His golden hair tumbles to his shoulder, and his skin is tanned just like Khaos', except his face is more angular, with high cheekbones and a firm jawline. His eyes are ridiculously striking and mesmerizing, as if I'm not just looking at Eryx but standing face to face with his gryffin. It's slightly intimidating.

He grins at me, complete with teeth, and when he looks at me that way, it's like a thunderbolt has struck me. The promises of what he'll do to me in his smile send a shiver down my spine. Warmth stirs deep in my gut, igniting the longing I never knew existed inside me.

"Not everyone enjoys being stared at so intensely," I say, hoping he gets the message.

"Lucky that's not us," he replies, a broad smirk tugging his lips wider. Despite his casual clothing—low-hanging jeans clinging to his powerful thighs and a Henley top following the curves of his muscular torso—his presence screams brash arrogance and regal authority, as if the air around him bends to his will.

He's too much, yet it's enthralling... and a bit terrifying, leaving me covered in goosebumps.

Pushing himself off the window, he squares his wide shoulders, exuding raw power that's impossible to ignore.

"Tell me, what's it like in South Africa?"

I exhale to speak about a topic I'm comfortable with.

"Absolutely gorgeous. Beaches, mountains, vineyards. Everything is under the same sky and in close reach to where I live in Cape Town. I mean, it's stunning but also a dangerous mess, yet the busy city still crawls under your skin, you know?"

His eyes never leave me, and there's something addictive in the way he hangs onto every word.

"I'm sure it's not just about the scenic views," he states, his attention sliding over my face and dipping down into my throat. "I've heard the place is a melting pot of cultures, so it must be incredible to meet so many people."

"It sure is. I mean, the streets aren't always safe, true, but something about the place is real and infectious. It stays with you once you live there."

"You'll find Finland just as captivating," Eryx adds, as if reconfirming I'm not going anywhere.

Then he gives me a wink, which sends a flutter through my chest—a reaction I instantly squish down like I'm stomping on a roach—and I turn away from him.

"I'm sure, but just so you know, I haven't yet agreed to stick around here."

Just as I move away from Eryx, the dark-haired brother strolls into the room, and my legs instinctively stop moving, my feet frozen in place. I tell myself to move, step away from him, but all I can do is stare, taking in how incredibly irresistible he appears.

Thankfully, he has clothes on now because the image of him naked and his huge cock is etched into my mind for eternity. I almost wish I hadn't remembered that part, seeing how anticipation and arousal now tighten my stomach.

The play of emotions on his face is difficult to read, even so, my body flushes at his presence.

He runs a hand through his hair, the color of midnight, falling loosely around the hard planes and angles of his face. I'm drawn to those deep eyes that seem to see right through to my soul. I'm also intrigued by his clothes and just how spectacular they look on him, made to fit him precisely—fitted black pin-striped pants, a dark button-up shirt rolled up at the elbows. As though he's come in fresh from a mercenary hunt. Leather bands wrap around his wrist, one featuring the same golden tree symbol as Eryx's ring.

As tall as Khaos, he steps deeper into the room, his presence commanding attention, but when he walks in, it feels as if I'm about to face down the devil. A pulse ripples over my skin at the sight.

"Who's not planning on sticking around?" he asks, his voice dark and smooth.

My pulse thunders in my ears, and once again, I have to remind myself that these Dukes are spellbinding but lethal. They are also my fated mates, and that's a far more complicated discussion I haven't had with myself yet.

"Finland is enchanting," Eryx answers before I can, studying me. "Tallis here can attest to all the excitement we have." He's smiling at me as if there's an inner joke between them, yet I don't know the punchline.

Turning back to Tallis, I roll his name over in my mind, liking how precise it sounds, much like his attention focused on me.

"Why would our fated mate ever think of leaving her home?" Tallis asks, circling me like a hunter does his prey.

Eryx doesn't miss a beat. "Maybe she's getting cold feet."

"Really now?" Tallis' laugh echoes in the room, his eyes sparking with mirth. "Isn't the whole fated thing supposed to be, you know, absolute?"

"I suppose." My cheeks burn up. "But I see nothing here that feels like fate to me."

Eryx bursts out laughing. "She's just burned you, brother. We're keeping her."

Tallis pauses in front of me, glaring down at me, a challenge glinting in his black eyes.

"You're our fated mate, and by the perfume in the air, your body is already preparing for us. That makes you ours. You do know that, don't you?"

"Lucky me," I murmur sarcastically, shifting my gaze between them. "And you do realize that if you want to be my fated mates, you'll have to earn it, right?"

Silence swallows the space between us as a grin curls on my lips while the two of them exchange glances as if I'd surprised them.

*One point for me. Zero points to the Dukes.*

"What, you think this was a free ride?" I quip.

Eryx laughs. "Hear that? We have to earn our keep. This is going to be fun."

Tallis just studies me with those eyes that look like sex, as though he's mentally preparing himself to accept my challenge.

I won't admit it, but part of me thinks maybe they're right. This could be fun, or it could be a disaster. Either way, we're fated mates, and while I'm stuck here, I need to work on discovering who the hell my parents' killers are. That means spying on the Dukes' business and discovering where they keep the records of the mercenary jobs they assign.

"Where's Khaos?" Tallis asks, strolling across to the office couch at the end of the room and dragging a chair to place it in front of the sofa.

"He shouldn't be long," Eryx mutters, lingering close to me.

"Well, how about we start," Tallis insists, then taps the chair, glancing my way. "For you, my firecracker."

Peeling myself away from where my shoes had glued themselves to the floor, I cautiously approach the chair. Their presence in the same room is like I'm suffocating on their masculine scents, twisting my arousal into overdrive.

My skin tingles, breathing grows shallower, but I got this.

The brothers watch me lowering myself into the seat, crossing my legs, and leaning back into the plush fabric, their gazes drilling into me.

"Is this an interrogation?" My voice sounds steadier than I feel on the inside, especially with the heat between my thighs feeling like an inferno.

"Just getting to know one another." Eryx takes a seat on the couch with his brother, smiling like everything is rainbows and unicorns. I appreciate the attempt he makes to put me at ease. While Tallis... there's something antagonistic in the way he's acting toward me, and I swear I see flames behind his black, demon eyes.

It's been years of planning, training, and honing my fighting skills, of investigating... These are the only things that kept me from losing my mind. So, I'm not giving up.

"Feels very much like a blind date," I murmur, my words slipping out before I can clip them.

"You've been on many dates?" Eryx's question cuts through the air. The intensity behind his words is explosive, as if he's about to ask for their addresses so he can pay them a visit. Or maybe I'm just being paranoid?

I shrug. "Not really."

"Blind dates, huh, *Mina*?" Tallis chuckles from his side of the leather couch, a dark amusement etching over his facial features. "They're like unwrapping a package where the gift inside could either be a gem or a ticking time bomb, seeing as most folks love playing hide and seek with their real selves."

Eryx glances at him. "What the fuck are you talking about? You really need to work on your jokes."

Tallis' piercing eyes remain locked with mine, and a wave of dread washes over me as I second-guess myself. Is he intentionally calling me out, seeing through my lies? The weight of his scrutiny makes me sweat bullets while my heart pounds faster at being exposed.

Part of me wonders if this is the time to come clean about who I am, as it's easier to explain it now, except what if they know about the hit on my family? Would they try to hide the truth to not appear as the bad guys? Not to mention, they'll never leave me out of their sight after discovering I already lied to them. But if they had a hand to play in my parents' murder, I'm not sure I can ever look at them again.

I'll stick with the same plan. I only need a few days,

tops, to find out information... once I get a lay of the land in the estate, that is. Then, if they are involved, I'll tell them the truth, standing over them with a blade to their throats.

"Okay, let's start. Name, address, age," Tallis grumbles, distracting me from my thoughts.

"Mina Carter, 13 Acacia Street, Cape Town, and I'm twenty-one." I pause, keeping my breathing steady. "And what about you two... age?" I command, my gaze never leaving Tallis. My lies roll off my tongue with ease, but if I'm answering questions, so will they. I hold my composure and don't shift in my seat, but in truth, I've never felt more exposed than at this moment.

"Twenty-Seven," Tallis answers.

Eryx leans back on the couch. "Twenty-Eight."

It hits me that despite their ruthless reputation, they're on the younger side of a normal wolf shifter lifespan, which is normally three to four-hundred years old.

"Now, what do you do for a job?" Eryx continues.

"A menial data entry job. Nothing exciting." Not that I need to ask them what they do, when it's publicly known they run an enormous mercenary business out of Finland.

"I noticed the family crest on your pendant," Eryx asks. "Are they back in South Africa? Are they in the data entry business, too?"

His questions hang in the air as I try to keep facts straight, growing heavier with the mention of my parents.

Images flash in my mind like shots slamming into me, over and over, so suddenly, it takes me off guard.

Blood.

Lifeless bodies.

Empty eyes.

Tears... heartbreak shattering me to pieces. I haven't recovered; I know that. The room thickens around me, making breathing difficult, and the prick at the corners of my eyes comes too fast. I'd give anything to have my parents in my life again. Give up my happiness, my future, even my fated mates...

The past crowds into my head, stuffing it with the darkness that is slowly suffocating me.

Silence.

I try to find my voice, but it's lost somewhere with my sanity.

The thoughts stay with me as I force a response.

"They're... they're gone," I finally get out, my voice barely a whisper. "I lost them years ago."

The oppressive silence leaves me trembling in my seat, and I nervously tuck my hands under my thighs to stop them from shaking. I don't know how I'm ever supposed to move on from their loss when I drown every time I think of them.

Eryx is suddenly at my side, crouching in front of me, his warm hand resting gently on my knee. "It's okay. Everything's going to be okay."

Those simple words hold more impact than he'll ever know. I lift my gaze to his amber eyes, feeling as though, in those few seconds, he somehow understands the storm I'm facing, the bomb ticking beneath my rib cage, threatening to explode at any moment.

I offer him a grateful smile. "Thanks, I appreciate it,

but I'm okay."

"Have you ever been to Finland before?" Tallis asks, leaning forward, forearms resting on his thighs. He suspects something. I can see it in his intense stare.

Eryx stands, taking my arm and lifting me out of my seat. "She's had enough," he tells Tallis over his shoulder, then back at me. "I'll have one of the maids show you to your room. I'm sure everything is overwhelming today."

Tallis' gaze lingers on me, and I'm left wondering what he's thinking. With the fog in my head, the desire in my body, and the lure of my fated mates, Eryx is right. Being interrogated is the last thing I need.

"I'd appreciate that." My voice still carries a trace of vulnerability I hadn't planned on.

Eryx escorts me out into the hallway, where he calls to a girl maybe a few years older than me, wearing black pants and a button-up matching shirt, looking more like a bodyguard than a maid.

"Helmi, can you see Mina to her room?" Eryx asks, to which the girl nods in response.

She promptly threads her arm through mine, and we're walking away before I can even process what happened. As I steal a glance over my shoulder, I catch sight of Eryx slipping back into the office, shutting the door behind them.

The whirlwind of emotions and revelations leave me reeling, my gut hurting at how quickly things spiraled. But something about Tallis threw me off balance.

What exactly have I got myself into?

I can't shake the feeling that something far more dangerous lurks in the shadows, waiting for me.

## CHAPTER
# EIGHT
### TALLIS

"She's lying to us. She's not who she says she is," I spit out as I barge into Clark's office in Vanguard Manor, located just outside the gates of our estate. It's where we run our business from, but right now, it's my brother, Khaos, I need to speak with, and he's staring at me from behind the desk with a puzzled expression.

"Is that why you dragged us here?" Eryx shuts the door behind us, strutting into the room, his upper lips curling up into a sneer. "To spout your suspicions?"

"Perhaps, Eryx,"—I snarl back at him, noting from the corner of my eye, Khaos is sighing heavily—"you've lost your head already to her tantalizing scent that you can't see danger in front of you. Has her heat clouded your judgment?"

"I'd like to remind you, little brother, that not everyone possesses your paranoia," Eryx mutters, stuffing his hands into his pocket. "Not everyone is out to get us."

The urge to hurl a chair at his smug face rises through me. He loves to dig up the past, knowing how to push my buttons. Clenching my jaw, I can't stop the damn unwanted memories spinning on my mind, or the feeling of fucking vengeance for the first girl I fell in love with. A sting of betrayal and my own stupidity reminds me why I shouldn't so easily trust Mina, my fated mate.

I know I have fucking trust issues. I'm broken at the core, and now I'm expected to accept a soulmate who has my paranoia flaring up like a bonfire. I'm still drowning in the ashes of my past, trying hard to see the truth clearly, but my instincts are off the charts with Mina.

It's a memory I don't need, and I shake my head to dislodge those images of Sereia, of her demolishing my heart and trust into dust. She proved she was a web of lies, and I let her walk all over me. Fuck. Never again.

Eryx studies me, and today, he pisses me off more than usual.

"What are you going to do when you find out your little firecracker is nothing but a mirage? What then?"

He grunts without even trying to conceal his disbelief.

"Did you come here to bicker, or do you actually want something?" Khaos' loud bark slices through my staring match with Eryx. Turning to my oldest brother as he hands off a stack of papers to Clark, he gets up to face me. "Now, what's the issue?"

Clark lifts his chin, more intrigued than he should be, but I also know how much he enjoys drama.

"Mina's not her real name, so what else is she lying

about?" I announce, part of me wondering if I'm wasting my time. My brothers do their own thing, anyway.

"Explain," Khaos demands, tilting his head to the side, his attention completely on me.

Eryx huffs, standing several steps behind me by the door. I can tell he's already so smitten with her, she could threaten him with a blade, ready to strike, and he'd urge her to make him bleed.

I grit my teeth.

"It's because of the slight change in her voice, a fraction of a tone that just... shifted. The small uptick of her heartbeat at the same time, like she's speaking rehearsed lines and trying to keep the lies in check."

My brothers remain silent, Khaos' face unreadable, but I know him. He keeps his emotions close to his chest. Doesn't mean his mind isn't churning with suspicion, too.

"Then there were her eyes," I continue. "Her pupils dilated like she was prey facing her predator, not her potential mates, when she stared at us."

Eryx released a hollow laugh. "You just contradicted yourself," he quips. "Of course, the girl's afraid. She discovered her fate is tied to us. Plus, your delightful charm would unsettle anyone."

Stiffening, I hate admitting that my brother is even partially correct.

"Fine," I concede, annoyance pricking at me. "She's nervous, scared even, I get it. But she's still lying about who she is." I've tortured and questioned enough people in my life to smell a lie a hundred feet away.

"I have to agree with Tallis on this." Clark's voice cuts

through the silence. He's the last person I expect to take my side. He and I have never seen eye to eye after I burned down half of his building. Then again, anything with him leaves an uneasy feeling in my gut.

Khaos rounds the desk to join us, his lips pressed into a thin line.

"There *was* something peculiar about the ease with which she drew her blade with me," he muses.

Clark gasps. The guy's always been so overprotective of my brother, he'd do anything for him. Like the time he made a pact with a vengeful spirit, binding it to Khaos' service, to watch him day and night. It was hilarious at first, until the spirit started turning on us, so we had to exorcise it.

"She concealed the blade down her top, and drew it with an aptness that seemed far from ordinary for a data entry clerk."

"See, I'm not the only one who suspects something strange," I state, thankful it's not only me with my head screwed on straight.

"Remember, every member of the House of Gold and Garnet knows how to handle a blade. They might as well be born with one in their hands," Eryx says, his voice calm.

"Perhaps," Khaos adds. "But there was a precision in the way she held the knife to my throat. She was faster than I could react, and it takes a considerable feat to surprise me like that."

"Your grace, the sheer act of threatening you with her weapon to your throat is a direct offense," Clark declares.

Khaos ignores him. I know my brother well enough to understand that he doesn't always play by the rules, especially if it involves something or someone he's interested in. Which Mina is to him.

Don't get me wrong, I harbor no hatred toward the girl. She's fucking strikingly beautiful, a captivating vision. The thought of stripping her, bending her over the desk, and fucking her sweet cunt has crossed my mind... more times than I'll admit. But before I give in to anyone again, I need to know exactly who I'm surrendering to. I won't be duped again.

"She's lying and hiding something," I insist.

Eryx, who's been unusually quiet, is radiating irritation from his stiff shoulders to his heavy breathing. But whether he likes it or not, he has to face the truth.

Clark, from his position behind the table, turns completely toward us.

"Could you remind me how Mina ended up in your estate to begin with? The last time I saw her, I'd completed the interview and had my guard escort her off the property." His voice comes out controlled, but there's a rigidness in his expression, as if he's wrestling to keep his anger in check. "And I'm not sure if you are all aware, but she was brought here by the guards on suspicion of being involved in the missing mercenary jobs and payments."

At his insinuation, I tense, but before I can reply, Eryx beats me to it.

"Hold on. You're implying she's guilty, yet you're the one who let her go? Maybe you should reconsider your tone and refrain from judgment. Regardless of what anyone in this room thinks, remember, she's our fated mate."

Clark pales at my brother's words, his mouth falling open in dramatic shock. "Your fated mate? Each of you? Are you certain?"

I find Clark's overreaction toward her odd. Just what happened between them during the interview?

Khaos rolls his eyes at the exchange, but answers firmly, "Yes, she is."

Heaviness sinks through the room, and I feel it in the pit of my stomach. I understand why Eryx is so annoyed at us. He wants us to embrace the situation and move on. Except what about Mina?

She didn't exactly appear over the moon joyous at the news, even with the first signs of her heat calling us to her.

"If you barrage her with these questions, you're going to scare her away." Eryx's voice echoes in the room. "She's already said she hasn't decided if she's going to stay with us."

"She can't leave," Khaos snaps.

"That's what we said," Eryx continues.

"Then we need a different approach," I suggest.

"I got it," Clark cuts me short. "Get a sample of her blood and we test it. She's bound to be in our database. And if not, we have connections."

"I don't see her agreeing," Eryx states, his voice growing bitter. "But Tallis can ask her, seeing he started this whole fiasco."

"We should try the Reflection Ritual," I suggest, not in the mood to keep arguing with Eryx over this. I'll get the evidence to show him. "The ritual's a sure way to confirm her truth without cornering her or making her jump through hoops."

I meet Khaos' eyes, the uncertainty etched in the lines on his forehead. The ritual sends a rush of anticipation through me. It gives us the chance to uncover the truth about her, and if I'm wrong about my suspicions, I'll gladly swallow my pride and admit it.

"Maybe the ritual isn't such an outrageous idea," Khaos admits, which has me grinning. "Tallis, make the arrangements. Clark, bring me up to speed on Mina and the circumstances of her arrival."

Clark seizes the opportunity, launching into a torrent of explanations. Eryx, less accepting, shakes his head, and storms out of the room. That's my cue to exit as well.

As I step into the cold corridor, a bold resolve uncoils inside me at the thought of her undertaking the ritual. At that moment, I imagine her defiant eyes, and I'm eager to face her head-on. I'm certain of one thing—Mina's truth will be an encounter worth every scar.

I march back into the grand mansion, my boots thumping against the marble floors with purpose. The corridors are quiet, the flutter of servers only rushing about during meal time, celebrations, and when visitors arrive. Especially my grandfather. I prefer it quiet.

Approaching her room on the third floor, not too far from ours, I'm ready to confront her. I'd give anything to get rid of the mistrust wrapping around my insides like barbed wire. I raise my hand to knock on her door, and just as my knuckles make contact, the door swings open, revealing an empty room.

Frowning, I step inside, my gaze darting around the spacious place that looks unoccupied. The four-poster bed sits untouched, the dresser and wardrobe remain closed, and the lush fur blankets on the chest at the foot of the bed lay undisturbed.

Moving across the plush rugs, I approach the bathroom, half expecting to find her there, but I'm met with silence and a rising sense of suspicion.

Where the hell is she?

Pivoting on my heels, I stride out of there when a petite figure appears, and I jerk to a stop. It's the maid who took Mina to her room.

"Helmi," I begin. "Mina's not in there."

She blinks up at me, the wheels spinning beneath her dark gaze. "I-I left her here, Your Grace," she stammers. "She told me she was tired and would get some rest."

"And you saw her enter the room?"

"Yes, sire." She nods, her curls bouncing with the movement. "She strolled in and shut the door behind her."

"And you haven't seen or heard anything unusual after that?"

"Nothing. I've been walking past the room regularly in case she needs anything."

My little fated mate snuck out of her room and past Helmi, making her even more suspicious.

I dismiss the maid with a curt wave of my hand, and as she scampers away, I decide to track Mina down. She can't have gone far. Entry in and out of the mansion is heavily guarded, and unless they receive word from my brothers and me, no one is to leave or enter the premises.

As I take off and start my search, a thirst to uncover her and what she's up to feels more potent than ever.

## CHAPTER NINE

BILLIE

It's funny how life works. One minute, I'm working for a communications company, unsure if I'll ever find the truth. The next, I'm sneaking around a grandiose estate belonging to three dangerous Dukes, searching for evidence that they arranged my parents' murder.

I rush across the long rug of the uppermost floor on silent steps, the urgency for answers pressing against my chest, especially after Tallis all but called me a liar earlier. How long before he gets his brothers on my case, and they uncover why I'm here?

Will my status as their fated mate save me from what they have in store for me?

I came here for a mission, and nothing will stop me. That means doing things fast before I'm kicked out... or worse. The thought of losing my fated mates tightens around my ribs. Listen to me, freaking out over men I've sworn to fight if they came between me and the killers.

The agony that comes from being apart from them will be nearly unbearable. That's the nature of the bond between soulmates. But I cling to the hope that if I avoid sealing the bond, the pain might be more manageable. That is, as long as I refrain from sleeping with them... I sigh as a wave of my heat ripples through me at the mere mention of them.

I can't even let myself think about how we'll deal with the consequences or how we're supposed to make this work.

Already, I feel a headache brewing from overthinking.

Glancing around, most of the doors are locked, their secrets hidden away. While I fumble with the pin in my pocket which will grant me access into those rooms, I scope out what's up here and if I'm alone.

A distant murmur has my pulse speeding and me glancing over my shoulder, convinced someone's on my tail. There's nothing there, so I hurry my walk.

I turn the corner of the corridor that leads to a dead end, but in front of me stands an oversized arched window with a golden frame but no blinds. Beyond it lies Rovaniemi in the distance. It's spectacular. I stumble forward where the city spreads out like a fairy tale, its winding river, the Kemijoki, shimmering beneath the sun like a blue ribbon. Bridges criss cross it, the banks peppered with homes. Beyond the city is the dense carpet of forests. The place is mesmerizing. I've always been bewitched by Cape Town back home, but this place holds something special.

As much as I'd enjoy exploring it, I don't have the luxury right now. Retracing my steps, a door sitting ajar catches my attention. On impulse, I rush over and push it open softly.

There's no one inside, but the sight has me stopping dead in my tracks, my eyes close to bulging. It feels like I've stepped into a planetarium because of the thousand tiny points of light glinting from the ceiling.

Pulling the door closed behind me, I step inside, a gasp on my lips.

The first thing I notice is the wall-to-wall collection of celestial charts, marked with dozens of dots in red. The maps are everywhere. Then my attention falls on the feathers scattered here and there, as if someone's been keeping chickens in here. Except, these belong to dinosaur-sized chickens.

I pick up a gold feather that's the length of my arm, the spine rock hard, the feathers silk soft. Some are nestled in a glass vase, others across tables or bookshelves, their colors ranging from bright gold to pitch black. They are gorgeous. I drop the one in my grasp.

The reality of who these belong to isn't lost on me. I'm in Eryx's room, and these must be his gryffin's feathers. I should feel scared, but I'm too excited to explore the place to worry about him right now. Besides, I won't stay long. Who would have thought that a mercenary like him was into astronomy?

Desks and chairs, shelves and storage cupboards are all pushed away from the middle of the room for the main attraction. The massive telescope points toward the window where its designs curve upward into the ceiling across one wall. The day's light glances off its polished surface as I stroll close. My hand hesitates over the eyepiece before I finally lower my eye to the lens.

"Wow. I need one of these," I murmur to myself.

Through the telescope, the world sharpens, then in the blue backdrop, I notice the moon. Even in the light of day, it's visible like a ghost in the sky.

The creak of the floor sounds behind me, and I snap back, swinging around, but the moon remains etched into my retinas. Someone's across the room from me. Blinking to clear my vision, I stumble back and bump the telescope, pushing the optical tube to face the room instead of the window.

My heart freezes in my chest, and an expelled sound of air rushes from my throat.

Tallis stands in the doorway, filling the space, a menacing figure. His arms hang casually by his sides, yet every muscle in his body bulges against his clothes, screaming power. Raven-black hair falls around his strong face, windblown as though he's been running.

"Eryx's going to be livid," he says with his deep, gravelly voice, lifting his chin toward the telescope I'd accidentally bumped from its original position.

"Well, you shouldn't have startled me then," I counter. Straightening my spine, I embrace my courage despite trembling at being busted. I still remember the conversation back in the office with him and Eryx, where his suspicious gaze made me question my plans.

Now, he's staring at me exactly the same way.

"You left your room," he murmurs, taking a step closer.

Instinctively, I move back, a twinge of wariness prickling across my nape. I've never been face to face with a demon before, and there's something almost unsettling about him. It might be because he also has godlike blood in his veins, making him unpredictable and formidable. What exactly is he capable of?

"And why are you following me?" I challenge as my heel taps the edge of the desk at my back. His proximity awakens the storm inside me, my heat rising in a crescendo, boiling me from the inside out. My stomach flutters, heat flushing right between my thighs.

The Duke is built like a god, and he's so sure of himself, so damn arrogant. It should make me sick. Instead, goosebumps ripple down my spine at the intense attraction I feel toward this stranger... my fated mate.

The corner of his lips quirks upward, his nostrils flaring at my scent. I really hate how easily my body gives me away, or how he stands so close to me that I inhale a hint of smoky, charred wood in the surrounding air, reminiscent of camping fires lined with an aroma of wild cherries. It invades every inch of me, making concentrating close to impossible, especially when the first thing that pops into my mind is an image of my thighs wrapped around his face as he lowers himself between my legs.

Fighting my body, which screams for him, my panties grow wetter. Biting my lower lip until it hurts, I regain some normal brain activity.

"Do you always answer with a question?"

His words wash over my face, and I feel the rush of

adrenaline through me. I might as well be touching a lightning rod with the aggressive way my body responds to him. He doesn't move away, but towers over me, the muscles in his throat flexing when he swallows. Looking up, I catch his furrowed brow, the frown that looks more confused on his face than angry.

My mind barely grapples with the emotions and desire flooding me before a new thought pushes its way forward.

"Wait!" I state, shoving my palm to his chest as he attempts to step closer when we're already a breath's wisp apart. Heat sears into my hand, the sensation reverberating up my arm. Not a good idea to touch him. "Are… are you using your incubus allure on me?" My voice trembles more than I want it to.

A rich, deep laugh bursts past his lips, curling around me.

"Trust me, little firecracker. If I were, you'd be stripped bare already, on your knees, and begging for me."

I clench my jaw, unable to form a coherent thought, let alone the anger I'm feeling. Sparks of desire he's giving off tighten in my stomach, threatening to overshadow everything else I feel.

"Believe it or not, I'm not your plaything," I grit out. I refuse to be the submissive damsel in distress, but the simmering heat within me has a mind of its own, undermining me at every chance it gets.

"Good to hear," he states. "Then how about we talk?"

My breaths come in shallow gasps as his words settle in my mind.

"Sure, we can talk." I shrug, but the mountain of a man isn't moving away from being in my personal space. I'll take talking over him torturing me if he knew why I asked the questions.

"We haven't exactly gotten off on the right foot. Maybe I can correct that."

I can't help but smirk. "Yeah, I guess it would be shocking to be caught with your lover when you discover you have a fated mate," I say a bit too quickly, that earlier ridiculous jealousy still clinging to my ribs.

His strong jaw clenches. "She was a... one-time thing," he explains, his tone surprisingly honest.

"Oh, so you've had a few of those, I'm guessing? Being an incubus and all," I say, fighting to keep my tone light. I know that I have no right to take out my jealousy on him when fate mushed us all together completely out of the blue.

A wicked grin unfurls across those delicious, full lips, and I really dislike how my body reacts to the dangerous allure of his smile.

His hand lifts, fingers gingerly tracing a path across my cheek, his touch leaving a trail of fire in its wake. The sensation sweeps through me like a tornado, shuddering me to the core. My legs wobble beneath me, lust fluttering through my stomach while my thoughts fog over, consumed by a singular desire—pleasing him.

Fire pulses between my legs, and I clench them in the shadow of the massive demon who blocks out the rest of the room.

"Tallis," I purr, then suck in a sharp breath, well

aware I'm staking my claim on him with that single word.

He's here, impossibly close, hunching nearer, and those gold sparks in his dark eyes glint. The sight of his gorgeous face so close to mine leaves me quivering in anticipation.

*My firecracker*, he whispers in my mind, his lips not moving, but one side of his mouth pulls up. The sound of his husky voice calling to me is like a siren's song, billowing in my mind.

*You don't need to flinch from me. Not when I can't stop thinking about lifting you into my arms and licking you all over, inhaling your scent so deeply, I lose my mind. I'll fulfill your every fantasy. Fuck you again and again. I'll show you what it really means to have me as your fated mate.*

Arousal spears through my body, and my mind empties as a groan grazes my throat. The pleasure pouring through me is so intense, I can't stop myself from moaning louder.

As quickly as the feeling came over me, the fog in my head sweeps aside, leaving me swaying on my feet. I stumble and catch myself from falling straight into his arms.

I pull away from him, and his pupils dilate, a hunger on his face that wasn't there before.

"Wh-What did you do to me?" I gasp, my heart pounding in my chest.

That damn smirk lifts higher, amusement dancing in his black eyes.

"A small taste of my power. Now, you'll know what it feels like next time you doubt me. Though, as my fated mate, I shouldn't need to use my power... except to feed." There's something unsteady in his voice, as if his touch backfired and affected him as much as it did me. Wait... feed? I shiver.

His whispers are still whirling in my mind, and my skin feels too tight, my nipples too hard. With it comes the dread slowly creeping in at the true depth of the danger I'm in. His power, the ease with which he used it and controlled me, hits like a sledgehammer. It's a terrifying thought, but with him holding my gaze, my nerve endings tingle.

My shoulders cinch up. "Don't ever do that again without my consent," I say, my voice shaky, knowing that without boundaries, he'll render me completely powerless.

He licks his lips, tilting his head to the side, studying me.

"Well, you wanted to talk, so go ahead," I say, working hard to keep any bitterness out of my voice and not show him he's got the upper hand. But I'm shaken, and I have a nagging suspicion he's the kind of man who picks up on the smallest nuances in others.

"I have no desire to harm you," he begins as though he can read my mind, yet believing him is another thing. "But we've recently experienced some problems with potential breaches at the estate, so we've implemented extra security for those coming into our mansion."

Swallowing the confusion of where he's going with this, I nod for him to continue.

"All new visitors must take a small test to ensure they are who they say they are."

My thoughts scramble. We've circled back to this initial problem, haven't we? All my attention focuses on him strolling across the room, kicking aside one of Eryx's feathers.

"What sort of test are we talking about?" I force out through gritted teeth.

"Just a simple reflection test to confirm your identity." He walks over to the telescope to point it back at the window from where I'd shoved it aside.

"You're not one to trust easily, are you?" I can't help the defensive edge to my words.

"I once trusted someone who said they loved me," he says, on a sigh. "It turned out to be a lie. So, yes, I struggle to trust easily."

The fact he admitted something so intimate has my shoulders pulling back. Someone had hurt him, betrayed him? Guilt lances through me, seeing I'm walking a similar line.

With a deep breath, my response pours out of me.

"I know how that feels. My parents were murdered, and I have no clue who took them. They took the only people I truly trusted from me." I hadn't intended on sharing those details, but maybe it's for the best. I want him to understand that while I may have my own agenda, it isn't about betraying him. It's about uncovering my own truth.

He bows his head slightly. "Sorry to hear that."

"Anyway, I... I'll think about it. Just give me some time," I finally respond, deciding that buying myself a couple of days to investigate is all I need. I'm not naïve. I understand the irony of my situation. It doesn't escape me and neither do the risks.

Tallis doesn't respond right away, and his stare is difficult to read. I hate that guilt claws at me, tugging at the edges of my sanity, but I remind myself this is about my parents, about justice.

It's not like I chose to be their fated mate, even if my heart beats faster in their presence, and my heat erupts because of them, so I can't deny that they distract me.

"Two days." Then he steps across the room.

"I accept. Thanks." I can't be completely uncooperative because in the next two days, I might have all the answers I want. Then I'll plan my next steps.

"So, what exactly do you do here?" I ask, deciding that's my cue to change the conversation. "There are so many rumors about how you and your brothers run a mercenary business."

Tallis takes a long pause to answer, his intense gaze narrowing as he's clearly reading deeply into my question.

"It's not that complicated. We have a range of skilled individuals who report to us. We hire them, then match them to various jobs we receive from around the world, but the really important jobs, we take care of ourselves."

I can't help but shiver at hearing the satisfaction in his voice at mentioning the latter.

"And all your hired help lives in Finland?"

"No, but the majority are local." He lingers by the telescope, shadows dancing across his features.

"Then what happens? You confirm these matches down in that business building outside the mansion gates?" Holding myself still, I fight the urge to fidget at the precise questions I'm throwing at him.

His mouth tightens. "Something like that."

I try to keep my attention focused on a map sprawled out on a table, but my mind races, connecting the dots— the Dukes would have had to approve the hit on my parents. Or are they just blindly accepting all jobs to get paid?

"I'm curious... how do you decide if someone deserves to be on a hit list?" I ask casually, trying to sound interested, not that I'm spying.

"We take our jobs seriously, and every single job is carefully researched. Believe it or not, there are some jobs we don't take on. For example, we axe any hits put out on children. But this is all information available from any of our staff if you'd rather grill them."

I pause for a moment. Is that why the list of names Sasha had found listed only my parents and not me? "I see. So, then—"

"Why all the questions?" he asks, his voice dangerously soft, his footsteps closing in behind me.

"It just occurred to me, how does one decide who deserves to die or live?"

"You realize you live in the House of Gold and Garnet, where so many work in mercenary jobs?"

I twist around, resting against the table to face him standing several feet away.

"Do you blame me for being curious? Everyone knows about the Duke brothers, and the rumors are savage. So, I'm trying to work out how far-fetched and what I've gotten myself into."

"I don't care what anyone says," he growls, strolling closer, feeding the flames of arousal lingering just below the surface. "I've heard what they said, but if I gave a fuck about what nobodies outside our business thought of me, then I'm in the wrong job and family." He grins to himself.

Stiffening at his words, I clench my hand. Does this mean the rumors are true that the brothers sign off on anyone being killed without a second thought? Except, earlier, he admitted they vetted all jobs.

My mouth opens with other questions when he steps alongside me. His gaze sweeps over to the constellation map behind me, and I turn to where he's pointing to a star sign, Scorpio.

"Did you know this constellation is often associated with bravery and focus, but it also can symbolize mistrust and secrecy?"

"Are you saying you're born under Scorpio?" I tuck a loose strand of hair behind my ear, waiting for him to respond.

Stuffing his hands into the pockets of his trousers, he nods, then leans forward over the map, murmuring, "According to Eryx and the endless discussion on constellations, those like me are passionate, stubborn, and possessive." He pauses and twists his head to glance at me. "Basically, we don't take betrayal lightly."

My heart shudders in my chest while my libido tightens with the desperation to climb him. I mentally shake myself to rein in the arousal.

Straightening, he looks me up and down. "Guessing

you're either Gemini or Aquarius, both known to clash with Scorpios."

I chuckle because that's a first—a demon using astrology to explain our complicated relationship.

"I've never really been into the signs," I explain, strolling away from him. "My preference is to believe that I can lay out my own fate and not have it predestined."

He pushes off the table and crosses the room, where he opens the door and stands there.

"When your grandfather is the God of Forests, you start to believe that fate has us all by the balls. Now, let me walk you back to your room, and I'll arrange for clothes and food to be brought to you."

He isn't asking and speaks to me like I'm a prisoner. To him, I'm a stranger in his home, and if it wasn't for our soulmate connection, I'd be dead or kicked out of the estate by now. But while I'm here, I won't let him get under my skin. I need to stop shaking and letting him see the impact he has on me.

Once I arrive at my room, I head inside and close the door immediately as Tallis turns to call the maid. I press my back against the cool surface, trying to slow my racing heart.

Somehow, I managed to spend time alone in the company of a demon and lived for another day. Not to mention, I miraculously am still wearing my panties. As much as I hate to admit it, Tallis is nothing like I expected. There's depth to him, and here I assumed he was just a monstrous brute.

He's not to be messed with, I can tell, and betrayal is huge for him, so he's going to most likely turn on me once he discovers my truth. Except... I didn't come here for him. I might end up being with him and his brothers, something I'm still torn on, but I have a mission to complete.

All I can do is pray I survive.

# CHAPTER TEN

## ERYX

I've never been one to suffer from insomnia, but then again, I've never had a fated mate before.

Deep inside me, my gryffin, Echo, stirs, flexing his wings at every thought of Mina. He's damn excited to meet her firsthand, but when he comes out, controlling him has never been my strength, so his wish will have to wait.

But it's Tallis' fucking paranoia getting into my head. That's the issue. Of course, I want to give Mina the benefit of the doubt, but maybe the Reflection Ritual wouldn't be such a bad idea.

So, here I am, pacing in the semi-darkness of the corridor outside her room, contemplating trust, the truth, and the gorgeous woman asleep in the room, just feet away from me. A single light hangs from the ceiling, barely piercing the thick night. Not that I need it. I have exceptional sight and can spy a rat from a hundred feet in the air. So, a poorly lit corridor is a piece of cake if anyone stirs.

Who knew fated mates came with sleep deprivation? I snort a sarcastic laugh to myself.

Suddenly, a muffled cry slices through the night like a dagger.

I stiffen at the sound coming from Mina's room, and panic grips my heart, fierce and desperate. Lunging, I snatch the door handle, only to find it's locked. With a powerful shove of my shoulder into the wood, I snap the lock, a splintering crack reverberating in the otherwise quiet night.

I barge into a room swallowed by darkness, frantically scanning the area and expecting to find someone hurting her. She's in the middle of the large poster bed, painted in the blue glow from the moon, still asleep. She's thrashing around, tangled in the sheets, caught in a nightmare by the look of it.

Knots form in my gut, and my first instinct is to drag her from her distress and into my arms, but I don't want to frighten her on her first night with us. So, I stand there, desperately holding myself back. Her sugary, caramel-apple scent pours over me, laced with the heady scent of her slick, which I'm already addicted to. My cock pulses to life, my heart thrumming faster with that urgency to climb into bed alongside her, to make her mine.

One bite.

That's all it takes to bind us, and she's not going anywhere.

Khaos and Tallis will string my balls up for all to see if I so much as make her bleed. They don't have to admit their obsession with our little fated mate, but it's there, roaring behind their gazes.

And me? Never felt such compulsion over a girl before.

Dark hair fans out across the pillow, some strands sticking to her sweaty forehead, stirring something new inside me.

Primal. Protective. Possessive.

She's fucking beautiful, and my cock's throbbing.

The blanket has slipped to her waist, revealing a white tank top that's twisted from her thrashing. I trace my gaze from her tousled hair to her bare shoulders and down to the curve of her waist, partially exposed. A sudden whimper slips from her lips, and like a spark of magic, an instinct buried in my gryffin's soul shoves me forward, my knees bumping the edge of the bed.

"Shhh. It's okay, I'm here," I whisper.

It's just a dream, but I want to know what monsters fill her nightmares. I want to rip the fuckers out of her dreams, but for now, I draw back and pull up a chair from the dressing table and set it beside the bed. Flopping into it, I watch her, my fingers aching to trace her body.

Fuck, my pulse is roaring in my ears, and arousal punches through me.

Giving in would be so easy, but I'm not weak, and I won't push her... not tonight.

My gaze traces over every inch of her gorgeous body. I know how easy it would be to crawl between her legs, my head deep between her thighs, take in sharp inhales of her sexy scent, then wake her with my mouth.

Breathing slowly, I calm my shit down before I strangle myself in my pants.

Her eyes move rapidly behind her shut eyelids, and the longer I stare at her, the more I can't bring myself to wake her up. She'd end up startled, maybe screaming with fright, maybe hurling whatever she could grab at me. Except, perhaps that might be what I need. A huge argument to get all the emotions out of me, then head out and kill something. That would make me feel like my old self again.

Time ticks by, and her nightmare never relents. She tosses and turns, and sounds like cries on her throat tear at my insides. Watching, helpless to do anything, chokes me.

Nightmares I know well, and a pain gnaws at my gut from my past.

Cold.

That's what I remember the most. How quickly it sinks into your bones and takes up residence. Shivering at the memory, already feeling the icy grip slithering up my spine, I stiffen.

Darkness.

That's what consumed me. I'm not talking about ordinary darkness but the hellish abyss where you lose your mind, and even when you escape, a part of you remains there.

I shake myself to shove those memories aside, but Echo shifts within me, agitated, and unleashes a bone-chilling shriek in my mind. My skin tightens, my insides turning like they do every time he forces himself out, deciding it's his turn to take the wheel and deal with the darkness instead of me.

My fingers curl into knots, knuckles white as I shudder in my seat, a growl on my lips.

Straining against the force, I murmur, "Easy."

Staring at my fated mate, calmness ripples over me… long enough for me to shove him back into his box and calm the hell down. A flare of amusement surfaces at how fast her beauty distracts Echo. The moment I met her, I felt his compulsion for her.

"Hey, buddy," I whisper, speaking to my gryffin. "What are you gonna do if you take over? Snuggle with her? You'll scare her half to death."

No response. I make a mental note to release him tomorrow for a long flight, which settles him.

Her lashes flutter against her cheeks, her breathing deepening, and she's completely oblivious to my presence. Moonlight kisses her skin, and it's impossible to look away. She rolls onto her side, her back to me, making a small, breathy sound in the process.

I consider leaving her to sleep, but my protective instinct constricts around my chest, and I settle back in my seat.

"Sleep, Mina…I've got you." I notice a silvery glint sticking out from beneath her pillow. It's the sharp tip of a blade—her blade. A girl after my own heart. There's a blaze of admiration in my thoughts. She's quite the warrior, this one.

Night stretches, only broken by the rustle of sheets as she moves around.

In the peaceful silence of the night, it feels like she has always meant to be here.

## Billie

*THE AIR THICKENS with the scent of decay... death.*

*Glancing around, I have no idea where I am.*

*I'm standing in a vast ruin, an ancient and crumbling stone structure with no ceiling. The heavily pregnant moon hangs low, casting the world in its eerie glow.*

*Around me, shadows stretch out in every direction.*

*My gaze pauses on a small pile of skulls and bones that glistens under the moonlight, sending a shudder through me. Already, I hate this place.*

*"Hello," I call out. When I turn away from the remains, I sense movement in shadows, the change in the air, and my skin ripples with coldness.*

*Heart thumping, I pull back from a figure lurking in the periphery of my vision.*

*Glowing white eyes.*

*My instinct to run doesn't pan out when my feet freeze in panic.*

*"Sh-Show yourself," I stammer, my throat parching.*

*Hands emerge from the dark, reaching out for me with elongated, claw-like fingers.*

*I shove myself backward, but more hands come for me from every direction. Chilling and ruthless, they tug at my clothes, my hair, my body. Fingernails dig into my skin, scratching me.*

*I shove them away, wincing at the pain.*

*The moment any of them touch the line of script etched down the length of my arms in a thin line, the shadowy hands flinch back, their hisses filling the night. Good, let them all burn for all I care.*

*Frantically, I push them off me, terror twisting my insides. But with it comes a flicker of anger that they're ganging up on me.*

*The wind whistles past, carrying the echo of laughter, chilling me to my core.*

*On bare feet, I lash out at the hands clutching me, my movements jerky and desperate. But more join in, rougher this time, shoving, scratching, and pinching.*

*I whimper.*

*"Enough!" I finally yell out, thrashing against them.*

*One of them shoves me in the chest, and my legs buckle out from under me. Darkness closes in around me, towering, menacing.*

*Then a single shadowy figure steps forward, taller than the rest, staring down at me.*

*Goosebumps sweep over my skin, except for my tattoos, which itch. They glow brighter the closer he gets, and with it, a savage force rises through me.*

*Scrambling to get up, the others hold me down just as the figure crouches in front of me, its features obscured, all except two glowing white eyes. I can't stop shivering.*

*Its sharp claws stretch out, reaching for me.*

*"Get away from me," I growl, my wolf baring her threat in my chest.*

*But the figure ignores my warning, snatching my arm. The hiss of steam and painful sizzle of its skin has the figure wrenching back.*

*I don't feel a thing, but I use the moment to wrench myself free and scramble out of the darkness and into the moonlight.*

*Everything stills.*

*The shadows stir and press themselves against the invisible barrier of darkness that contains them. They make clicking sounds, which echo around me, making me sick.*

*I recoil as far as I can without stepping into the utter dark.*

*The figure abruptly leaps into the air, its shadowy form expanding and blotting out the moonlight.*

*In the thick of the dark, the monsters move. Twitching and squirming, they shove forward like manic creatures.*

*They erupt toward me in a war cry made up of clicks. Chills sink into my skin, and I scream, backing away, but they crash into me, ripping my balance away, and I fall to the ground, yelling.*

*They rush at me, suffocating me, stealing everything from me...*

WITH A STARTLED GASP, I wake up, my eyes snapping open to a white ceiling. Cool sheets are soaked with sweat, clinging to my skin, the remains of the nightmare still holding onto me. Heart hammering in my chest, I push myself to sit up in bed, the ancient ruins and dark shadows replaced by the soft glow of the morning sunlight spilling through the window.

My stomach hurts at the thought of the freaky dream that's haunted me since I lost my parents.

"Goddamn shadows."

Pushing my legs out from the tangled sheets and

swinging them over the side of the bed, I stumble across the cold wooden flooring to the en suite bathroom to wash away the grime of the nightmare.

Next thing I know, I'm clean and standing in front of the wardrobe, filled with clothes hanging off the racks. Tallis had ordered the maids to bring them to me. I'm slightly in shock at the sheer number of outfits. Each is more extravagant than the next, using only the finest silks and fabrics. I have no idea if they'll fit. There's also a drawer with brand-new underwear and bras that look about my size, so I pick a black set and slip them on.

I skim my fingers over the expensive clothes, mostly gowns, until they land on a pair of thick, tight-fitting pants that look like leather but feel more lush. These are more my style, even if they are an expensive design. Stepping into them, I enjoy the way they hug me, as if they're made for me. Next, I select a long-sleeve, white t-shirt with a deep V-neckline. Pulling it on, the fabric feels velvet soft.

I don't give any thought to how the maid knew my size, appreciating having clean clothes to wear. Last, I reach for my boots—familiar and comfortable with their worn-in-feel—and step into them. A glance in the mirror, and my reflection isn't hideous. I look half-decent, as if I might belong in this mansion. Quickly, I brush my dark, wet hair out of my face and head out of the room.

The door swings open easily, though I swore I locked it last night. Inspecting the locks, I notice a chunk of the doorframe is ripped away.

A shiver ripples up my spine that perhaps someone

broke into my room as I slept. Or had I been sleepwalking... again? I really hope it isn't the latter. I've seen a shrink to deal with my past and managed to stop sleepwalking. The kind that made me run into things and break doors in my dream-state attempt to escape the shadows.

Running a finger over the splintered wood, I sigh, hoping I didn't do this.

Out of my room, my boots echo through the hallway as I contemplate where to start finding information on the mercenary, Bryant Ursaring. Before I make it several steps from my room, a figure comes bustling around the corner. It's Helmi, the maid from yesterday, hands full of a pile of clean sheets.

"Morning, miss," she greets me with a warm smile, coming in my direction in her black pants and a button-up matching shirt uniform. "Are you ready for breakfast?"

"Now that you mention it, my stomach is growling." I laugh softly as she pushes into my room and leaves the clean bedsheets on the table, then joins me in the hallway.

"Then let's not keep you waiting."

Strolling alongside her, I enjoy her easy-going personality, which makes me feel more welcome than the Dukes did.

"Do you enjoy working here?" I ask, considering the rumors I've heard of the Dukes painting them as brutes. I follow her onto a grand staircase, red carpet running down the middle of them.

"I do. You see, the Dukes' grandfather, his grace,

Talino, saved my great-grandparents from a rogue bear attack in the woods, and to show our gratitude, someone from our family is to serve the Dukes in every generation."

"Doesn't that bother you?" The idea sounds ridiculous. I can't imagine living tied down to a centuries-old debt.

She giggles, her dark blond curls bouncing on her shoulders. "You make it sound like it's punishment, but it's not. I choose to work here, to pledge my service to them. I'm quite proud of my position. The Dukes have always treated me with respect. Besides, it's a small price to pay. If my great-grandparents had perished that day, I wouldn't be alive today."

"Of course," I answer, guilt burrowing through my gut that I'd said the wrong thing.

With a flighty wave of her hand, she has me following her once we reach the end of the steps. She leads me down a winding corridor, the walls draped in tapestries, columns topped with flames. The place carries a dark medieval vibe, as though I've stepped back in time.

Suddenly, Helmi pauses and turns to face me, and I halt before walking right into her. She's a foot shorter than me, so I would hate to bowl her over in my rush for food.

"Miss, I hope you don't find me too bold, but..." She licks her lips and glances down the corridor to where a door sits open, and bright light spills into the hall.

"What is it?" A slight panic bunches up in my chest that she's about to reveal some danger I'm in.

"It's just that yesterday, I saw the agony you were in with your oncoming heat." She studies my face, trying to see what my reaction is.

My insides stiffen at the mention, but it's not like I can keep hiding from it.

"Yeah, it's confusing me. It shouldn't be happening at this time of the moon cycle, or so fast."

Her lips pinch together, her features serious as she leans in, a faint scent of soap and honey wafting around me.

"I've heard it said," she begins in a low voice, "that the quicker the heat appears, the stronger the bond between fated mates becomes. They say it becomes harder to break, even if you reject them."

I blink at her, not loving the sound of experiencing an intense heat. A sense of confusion flares over me. Is this what she wanted to tell me?

"Alright," I respond.

"But miss," she continues, fiddling with something hidden in her pocket, her gaze darting from mine to behind her and back to me again. "Sometimes, the heat can take weeks to fully pass, especially seeing as you've only just met your fated mates. But I have something that can help suppress your heat for a short period, so it doesn't happen so quickly."

Her offer catches me off guard. Suppress the heat? I'll be honest, I've never heard of such a thing, but I hadn't exactly been reading up falling into heat.

Part of me wants to grab the opportunity with both hands while another part rings alarm bells. Sounds a bit too good to be true, and the last thing I need is to make a bad situation worse. Swallowing hard, I glance down at her pocket, then back up at her worried expression.

"It's fine if you don't." She blinks a lot, seeming to shrink in on herself.

"No, I appreciate it, but I need time to think it over, that's all." Her offer is tempting, but I won't jump into the unknown, especially when, so far, I've managed to tame my heat and not do anything crazy. I'm sure that's a sign I have this under control, and if it gets worse in a couple of weeks or so, then I'll consider the opportunity.

"Of course." She gives me a slight nod, with a hint of a smile curving on her lips. "I just want you to know you have options before it gets more serious and you fall pregnant. I saw my older sister experience heat when I was young, and she suffered horribly after her fated mate rejected her."

I almost choke on my own breath. This is going too fast. No one said anything about pregnancy.

Helmi is watching me, waiting for a response about her sister. I'm still reeling from her bombshell, but still I manage to push out a question.

"Is she okay now?"

"Oh, yes. She ran away with a lynx shifter, and she already has five little ones."

"Sounds like she found her happiness after all." I keep thinking about what she said earlier, and I'm not ready to have children... When the room spins, I lean against the wall in the corridor to stop myself from falling over.

"She certainly did." There's no bitterness in her voice. Then she straightens. "Come, I've kept you long enough from breakfast." She grabs my wrist and tugs me from the security of the wall.

Maybe food will help the nausea.

I decide I like Helmi, even if she says more than she should. She reminds me of Sasha, who I miss terribly. I could use her right now, but my friend knows I'll be gone for a while. I do hope to catch her up on the crazy soon enough.

My life has been mostly about survival, and now I'm on the verge of being swallowed up by an ocean of unknowns. It's overwhelming. Up to this point, I hadn't given thought to fated mates or going into heat, let alone having babies.

# CHAPTER
# ELEVEN

KHAOS

Tonight marks the Midnight Sun Gala, the one event that sees all the high flyers and big shots in Finland gather together. But it's not about celebrations. This is a well-oiled machine of networking and appreciation, a chance for us to tip our hats to our allies and remind them why they stand by our sides.

In truth, I can't stand the damn thing. The empty conversations, superficiality... it all gets under my skin, but the responsibility instilled in me by my grandfather is something I can't shrug off. He drilled into me the importance of rewarding those who've got our backs, a commitment I've taken to heart.

However, I can't stop my mind from returning to Mina. I've ensured she won't step foot outside the mansion and into the gala tonight. I figure it would be too much for her. The whispering voices, the curious stares, and the bombarding questions would overwhelm her.

For now, we keep her from prying eyes, keeping her

as our secret, shielded from the wolves prowling around, at least until we know her well enough ourselves. So, I've purposefully left her in the dark about tonight's event and instructed the guards at the mansion entrances to ensure she stays inside.

The way she pushes against her attraction to us plays on my thoughts. What gives her the audacity to turn away from us? Something tells me she'd bolt if she had the chance, yet she remains. There's something else she's after...

I stiffen at the last thought. The future I'd envisaged with a fated mate isn't exactly unfolding as planned, but whether she likes it or not, she's ours. I refuse to lose my mind over a woman we had just met, a woman who might be spinning lies.

The problem rests in the constant battle between my head and body, and right now, they're anything but in agreement.

I bunch up my shoulders at the grim reality. If not for our connection, Mina would likely be dead right now. There wouldn't be any room for hesitation because that's who I am—a cold-hearted bastard who relishes his job a little too much.

My brothers and I have our own reasons for thriving in this business, for taking satisfaction in eliminating those who dare stand in our way.

There's a darkness that lives in Tallis, one that reveals itself when he's on the job. Eryx loves the thrill of the chase, the high-stakes game, much like the primal instincts of any predator.

But me?

I carry the weight of my inherited responsibility to never disappoint my grandfather. Ever since our father disappeared and our mothers went into hiding, it was me, as the eldest, who had to pick up the pieces. The running of the business, looking after my brothers, and the new life we were forced to embrace with our grandfather. And I'll be damned if I'm not spectacular at what I do.

Pushing open the door of the Vanguard Manor, I stride inside. The usually bustling halls are noticeably quiet. Most of the staff are helping with last-minute preparation for the gala or tending to their own affairs… except for Clark. If I don't insist, he'll work through the damn event.

I march through the grand building, heading toward the far end where Clark's office is. As I pass a room, a glimpse of pitch-black hair catches my eye. Along with it, there's the familiar, smoky scent of Tallis, mingling with the faint smell of dust.

Pausing in the doorway, I glance back into the room. Tallis is hunched over a pile of files, his usual impeccable clothes covered in dust. The glow from the database computer screen illuminates his concentration, lines of information running across the monitor as it downloads data. Curiosity peaks, and I lean against the doorway.

"What the hell are you up to?"

Tallis glances up at me, his hair messy, surprise in his dark eyes.

"Looking into our fated mate," he admits with a raspy voice, as if he hasn't taken a sip of water in hours.

My eyebrows arch upward. "Clark could have done

this for you." At the mention of this, I realize he still hasn't come to me with an update on investigating our missing data. Something I'll remind him of when I speak to him shortly.

Tallis snorts, tossing a sidelong glance my way. "I'd rather juggle live grenades than ask him for anything."

His reaction isn't new. The pair have always been at war, more so since Tallis burned down part of the Vanguard Manor, including the main office that almost got Clark as well.

As entertaining as their banter can be, I'm curious about what he's discovered.

"So, what did you dig up?" I cross my arms over my chest.

As Tallis rubs his temples, I step inside, then prop myself against the edge of the cluttered desk.

"Not much concrete to go on yet," he admits. "I found some skimpy details on her parents, and they don't appear to be in the mercenary trade. Otherwise, we'd have an entire file on them. There's a daughter, Mina, which checks out. The address matches what she gave us, but this... this is spotless. People's records are never this clean and slim on details. Something's missing."

"Any updates on finding her friend in Lapland? The one she supposedly came to visit?"

Tallis huffs, shaking his head. "Checked out the owner of the house, and he passed away a couple of years ago, and there's no record of who the place has been left to since. Even his name, which we have on record for work he's done for us, is a first name only.

Someone fucked up royally in collecting information for our records."

Sure, when living with many mercenaries who are hiding secrets, tracking them down isn't always easy. They use fake information for their places of residence, but anyone working through us is researched. So, what the hell?

"That's why I'm narrowing down a short list of parents who were killed together in South Africa over the past decade." Tallis glances at me, offering me a wry grin. "Considering how high the death rate is in South Africa, it's a broad search, but it's a start."

"I appreciate you taking the lead on this."

He shrugs nonchalantly, never one to soak up praise. "It's as though Mina and everyone she knows are ghosts," he murmurs, a hint of frustration in his tight shoulders, in the way his breath comes slightly faster. "Either she's fiction, or she's done a spectacularly good job of covering her tracks of who she really is. Good thing I convinced her to take the Reflective Ritual tomorrow. Then we'll know if she's lying."

"I see..." I lick my teeth as I push off the desk and take a few steps toward the door, curious more than ever to have her take the test and uncover the truth. "Keep digging, but don't be late for the festivities." Ignoring his grumbling, I step out of the room, and the hallway stretches out before me, dimly lit and deserted.

Too many pieces about Mina don't fit together—her parents' death, her friend in Lapland and how they're connected, her arrival here, and hiding her real identity.

I have enough to distract me, but after tonight, we'll get to the truth—one way or another.

## Billie

THE DAY WAS a blur of me wandering aimlessly through the colossal mansion, my search and digging through the Duke's mercenary business coming up empty. The mansion is just a home and nothing more. The brothers themselves were nowhere to be found. Instead, the place was a chaotic jumble of staff members scurrying around in a frantic frenzy, doing who the hell knows what. It wasn't until I pinned down Helmi that I discovered the Dukes are hosting a party on their property tonight, and the preparations are in full swing.

Of course, I'll attend, even if I haven't been invited. The mansion, unfortunately, didn't offer me any leads on the mercenary, Bryant, and I suspect the answer lies in the building next door where Clark grilled me on my arrival.

And a party?

The perfect cover for me to sneak off the estate and break into that building.

So, with the clock already nudging past nine in the evening, I ransack the closet, hunting for an outfit that's comfortable, dressy enough as a cover if I'm questioned, and allows me to sneak around.

Given the deal I had reluctantly made with Tallis—waiting two days for his truth detection test—my time is running out fast. Once they uncover the truth, I'll be under constant scrutiny, maybe even chained in their dungeon.

The thought rushes me in my urgency to make tonight count and find an answer to my parents' killers.

Finally settling on a dress in a midnight hue decorated with tiny sparkles in the fabric, I can't help but be reminded of the Finnish landscape. The gown follows every curve as I slide it down my body and leaves little to the imagination from the low-cut neckline. Its long sleeves conceal the glowing ink on my arms, which is the very reason I chose this outfit. A daring slit runs down the middle, stopping at the upper reaches of my thigh, and has me turning on the spot to see how much is being revealed.

"As long as I avoid running or any brisk movements, I should be fine." I laugh to myself since that is the opposite of sneaking around, but from my options, it's the least awkward dress to rush around in that still has long sleeves.

Quickly I collect my thigh strap from the pocket of the pants I wore yesterday—never leave home without it—and thread my foot through it. I pull it up my leg to where I can wear it comfortably on my thigh, then I slide my small blade into its concealed pocket. I twist the strap so the blade sits at the front of my thigh and when I release the fabric of the dress to fall over it, I find it loose enough that the slight bulge and strap aren't noticeable.

In the heels, I'm higher than I'm used to, but I can walk in them comfortably. Besides, I can easily discard them when it's time to slip out of the mansion grounds and into the Dukes' business manor just past the gates.

Quickly attending to my hair, opting for a loose updo that frames my face, I apply minimal make-up, using what Helmi kindly brought to my room, along with the clothes.

Staring at the tightness of the fabric once more, I'm unsure if I can do this. I don't need any of the Dukes' attention, and this dress is attention grabbing. I should change outfits... yeah, perhaps pants and a shirt will be acceptable.

Today, I've been lucky enough to have my heat remain at bay, so I'm praying it stays that way. Perhaps what I experienced was a once-off, a shock to the system of meeting my three fated mates.

Just as I move toward the closet, the door with the mysterious, broken lock swings open to Helmi. She pauses in the doorway, her eyes bulging.

"Miss, you are simply stunning!" Her gaze trails up and down my dress, leaving me slightly uncomfortable. Walking around me, she makes strange sounds, smiling. "The Dukes will lose their hearts and minds when they see you tonight."

"Maybe it's best I change then?"

"No. Sorry Miss for my directness, but that dress is made for you. Don't you dare change. Own how beautiful you look. Let them see you are their queen."

I burst out laughing because that's the last thing I'm thinking about.

"I came to find out if you wanted dinner, as you hadn't eaten earlier," she says, blushing. "There's plenty of food outside at the gala. Come, let me guide you."

Her persistence is clear. She's determined to place me

front and center with the Dukes, isn't she? I had planned to keep a low profile, avoiding drawing attention while studying the guards at the estate's entrance gates. Yet the thought occurs that it might be less conspicuous if I was seen associating with the Dukes. Should I face any difficulties at the gates, they might even serve as a handy excuse.

"Alright then, let's do this," I finally give in.

We're heading along the hallway in no time, my fingers dancing along the edge of my dress' split. Noticing my fidgeting, Helmi keeps glancing over, giggling to herself.

"Oh, Miss, don't worry. I've been to so many of these galas, and I have never seen anyone so spectacular."

"Well, I have to give you credit as you brought me the dress. Thank you."

Her smile is contagious as we move downstairs. I hold on to the banister with my life to not trip on my heels.

"I work closely with our tailor on new outfits she creates. She says I have a good eye."

"Have you thought of creating designs yourself?" I ask as we finally leave the stairs behind and follow a lengthy corridor that leads us straight to the backyard doors of the mansion. My nerves already twist in my gut.

"Indeed, I have." But before she can expand, a female's urgent cry echoes from another room up ahead.

Helmi suddenly bolts away from me and into the room. With a blaze of worry, I dart after her.

I come to a stop in a partial kitchen where there are tables layered with food to be taken outside to the guests. There's a woman, only a few years older than me, teetering and losing the balance of a massive tray of hors d'oeuvres. Helmi rushes to her rescue, and I throw myself into action, snatching several of the gourmet nibbles into my hands before they plunge to the floor. With Helmi, the woman steadies the platter, and I set the morsels in my hands on a table nearby.

The maid's face goes paper-white, her breaths coming in short gasps. "Thank you so much." She refuses to meet my gaze. "You shouldn't have gotten your hands dirty."

Helmi quickly gives me a paper towel, even though my hands are practically spotless. The maid shuffles off, her tray clutched in her grasp, making her exit through a side door, and disappears outside.

The perfect route to join the gala but not make a grand entrance.

"Well, that's my cue," I admit and start striding toward the same exit.

"But Miss Mina, that's not the proper entrance for guests."

"It's fine, Helmi." I shake my head and reassure her, "This is exactly what I prefer."

Stepping outside, the sky is breathtaking, a splash of vibrant oranges and serene blues. Despite it being late in the evening, the sun that never goes fully down this time of the year drenches the landscape in a surreal dim light.

I lower my gaze to focus on not falling over and walk on my toes to avoid my heels from sinking into the soft soil. At the rear of the mansion, there are bright lights strung across the yard, soft music, and the ring of chattering voices.

Drawing in a cool inhale of fresh air, I steel myself, mumbling under my breath, "I can do this."

Pivoting on the balls of my feet, I move in the opposite direction toward the entrance gates in the distance. At that same moment, Tallis and half a dozen men in suits round the corner, howling with laughter.

My heart scales up to my throat, threatening to spill out at the sight.

*Shit. Shit. Shit.*

I whip back around and hurry toward the paved area behind the mansion where the party is. With my face flushing, I realize there is no time, hoping Tallis didn't spy me heading in the wrong direction.

I ease myself out of the shadows to join the party. But, as soon as I take my first step into the lights, a palpable shift in the air becomes noticeable. It's as if every conversation has been muted, and every single eye is fixed on me. The weight of their stares is intense, especially in these heels, which are already wobbling beneath me.

With a slow twist of my head, I lift my gaze across the sprawling yard. All the faces glancing my way fade into a blur, except for one—Khaos. His piercing gaze locks with mine, a storm of irritation swirling in his icy eyes.

His jaw tightens.

I haven't just entered the gala—I've walked right into a storm.

## CHAPTER
# TWELVE
### BILLIE

S tepping into the battlefield, I'm completely out of my comfort zone and in the thick of it. Uninvited to a party held by the feared mercenaries of Finland, I have every eye at the outdoor gala studying me.

I had one simple goal—keep low-key and figure a way to slip past the entrance gate and into the business manor to check their records. Yet here I am, about to challenge Khaos across the yard with his friends, and he looks ready to burst with rage at seeing me at his precious party.

So, what's a girl to do when surrounded by mercenaries?

Smile, play it cool, and mingle, even if my teeth are grinding. And try my best not to overthink that my parents' killers could be here. Not that I'd recognize them since I never saw their faces.

Breathing deeply, I concentrate on fitting in. If I act confident, that's what they'll see. If anyone talks to me, I can discuss the art of knife throwing, ask them if they collect weapons, and heck, if all else fails, even throw in a couple of bad assassination jokes to get them to leave me alone.

All the bravery in the world vanishes the moment I glance over at Khaos, who's ignoring who's talking to him. His icy eyes are locked on me. The man's pissed, and obviously, he doesn't want me here. Well, so sad for him. I'm here now.

Still, his gaze bores into me, his silent accusation that I've overstepped his bounds hanging in the air between us.

Damn him, and damn him twice for looking dangerously handsome. His suit is so black, it gleams under the dancing firelight from the torches, his shirt and tie matching. The blood-red fitted vest adds color against the dark. Deep brown hair, short and neatly parted, brings out his intense blue eyes. He stands taller than those near him, looking every inch the god that runs through his veins. Broad-shouldered, the man is large, and everything about him screams predatory sharpness.

I hate that I notice all this about him and that my heart beats faster at the sight of him. This isn't the time to forget my mission and get caught up in his attraction. With someone else joining the conversation near him, he's distracted enough to drag his attention off me.

Inhaling deeply, I listen to Tallis' deep laughter from somewhere behind me, a sound that covers me in goosebumps and wobbles my knees.

Standing around is an invitation for one of the

brothers to approach me. All that's missing is Eryx, but I know he's around here somewhere, watching me, too.

With determination not to fail tonight, I set my sights on the buffet table. If I'm going to weather this storm, I need to blend in and get everyone's focus off me. Especially the *storm* named Khaos, who will find me soon enough. I'm banking on him not making a scene at his party when he finally confronts me.

Weaving through the crowd, I take in the decorations in the open yard. My sight skims the surrounding tall, majestic trees, covered in strings of lights that are draped like stars falling. More of them loop around the outer perimeter of the paved area, stealing the shadows creeping in from the woods that stare at us from the woodland backdrop. An eclectic band is set up in one corner of the yard, playing a soft tune that complements the hum of conversation.

Nearby, there's a couch covered in blood-red cushions. I spot several more around the enormous yard. In front of me are three long tables covered in black linen with white rose bouquets bursting from glass vases while curling thorns stretch out across the tables of food. My mouth waters for the rich cheeses and fruit, and I'm not one to shy away from eating.

I fill my plate with canapes topped with caviar and crème fresh, smoked salmon, petite bruschetta, and cured meats. With my plate full, I'm ready to move away before I lose control at the table devoted entirely to desserts. The third table, with plates of sliced, dark meat, decorated with an extraordinary set of reindeer antlers, screams, *warriors eat here.*

That's also when a shadow falls over me.

"Excuse me, Miss," comes a male's voice.

My hand freezes mid-air, the tips of my fingers inches from the petite, gold-rimmed fork. I half expected it to be Khaos, but this voice lacks his rich timbre and the undertone of a threat. I remind myself if I mingle, I'll draw less attention to myself. Before I can stop myself, words are pouring out of my mouth.

"Tell me, why don't assassins ever play hide and seek?"

When he doesn't respond but clears his throat, panic settles in.

*Great job. Tell a stupid joke to a man who could kill me ninety-nine ways with my fork.*

I daintily grab the utensil.

"Because good luck hiding when they always have you in their sights."

I lift my attention to the man with a half-smile, hoping he gets my joke. Blinking back at me isn't a guest, but a young waiter. His expression is brimming with confusion as he stands in front of me, a silver tray with filled wine glasses balanced in his hand.

"Um, I meant, would you like red or white wine, Miss?" he says with a light curl on his lips.

My cheeks flush, blood pounding in my ears with humiliation. With a tight smile, I shake my head and dart away from him with food.

*Great job, Billie.*

I wonder if anyone noticed my embarrassing moment, but I've done worse. I keep repeating in my mind, *I can do this.*

Then Khaos steps into my path farther ahead. He stands like an ominous adversary ready for a showdown, his piercing stare unfazed by the onlookers, his jaw rigid, and his brow furrowed.

Drawing in a deep breath, I decide I'll get this over with now.

Just as I steel my nerves and take my first step forward to confront him, an explosive group of men emerges from the side of the house where all the guests are arriving, howling Khaos' name like a battle cry. Their laughter streams over the music and boisterous chatter around us.

Suddenly, the energy in the yard shifts, cheers rising and glasses clinking.

I have no idea who the newcomers are—four men, all in pressed suits, with wild looks in their eyes. By the looks of it, they are a party favorite.

With one lengthy stare at me, Khaos exhales loudly, then pivots in the men's direction, that earlier scowl morphing into something jovial. Of course, it's fake, it's so obvious, yet no one seems to care. He approaches his friends, taking long strides, his voice streaming louder, welcoming them.

As relief washes over me, I use the moment to glide past the crowd.

Suddenly, a man with a stock-barrel torso slides in at my side. Graying at the temples, he's built like a tank, the fabric of his black penguin suit pulling taut across his arms and chest. Agile, he swings around to stand in front of me, effectively blocking my view with his body. He grins at me with that look that screams, 'It's your lucky day.'

I roll my eyes, which he either doesn't see or ignores.

"I can't believe no one has introduced us yet," he says with a gravelly, oily voice.

His lecherous stare lowers down my front, lingering too long on my chest. My skin crawls, and I'm close to kneeing him in the balls, but that's not exactly conducive to keeping low key.

"You belong to Khaos, right? Everyone's talking about his newest toy," he states with an arrogant lift of his head.

I glare at him, my fingers twitching to grab my blade and carve a big dick symbol on his forehead, so everyone sees him for what he is. How the hell does everyone know I'm with the Dukes? And why the hell is everyone talking about me?

Another thought pops into my head. If I belong to Khaos, then jerks like him would leave me alone. Of course, I hate the idea, but the more I think about it, the more sense it makes.

"Yes, I do," I confirm through hissed teeth.

The man grunts, rubbing a hand across his square jaw. His muddy green eyes flick to Khaos at the other end of the yard with his back to us, then back to me.

Taking in a sharp breath, I take in his musky odor that reminds me of an animal barn with a powdery smell. He's a shifter, but honestly, I couldn't care less.

He leans closer. "Khaos wouldn't notice if you vanished into the woods, now would he?" A filthy smirk tugs his lips wider. "I've heard he shares his toys, and you're a lovely doll."

My hackles rise, and I almost gag, but part of me thinks he'll enjoy seeing my reaction, so I square my shoulders.

"Oh, I don't doubt it. But you know very well that when Khaos finds out, and he will, you'll be lucky if he just feeds you to the pigs. The man has a penchant for making minced meat out of anyone who crosses him. Haven't you heard?"

The color drains from his face, and while he lifts his head, standing tall, I catch the subtle tightening of his jaw and the unease in his expression.

His hand shoots out, and an iron grip snatches my arm. My breath hitches in surprise, the plate of food I'd been holding onto getting wrenched from my grasp. He thrusts it into the hands of a passerby, who appears just as surprised, but they don't question it and shove it at a waiter.

I tug on my arm to free myself.

"You don't need food," the older man growls, his face flashing with irritation.

"There you are," Eryx calls out from my right, stealing my furious response. He strides in, strong, the guests seeming to part for him as he nears us.

As I yank my arm free, Eryx shoves himself between the man and me, facing him toe to toe. Tension ripples through the air and slams into me, traveling up my arms as my hairs stand on end. I rub my arm where his fingers left red bands on my wrist.

I shift aside, panic grabbing hold of me at the war about to break out.

"Do we have a problem here?" Eryx asks, the silkiness of his voice not hiding the heavy darkness of his threat.

The man sneers at Eryx. "Remember your place, boy." An arrogant smirk tugs at the corners of his mouth.

A few bystanders turn to watch the situation unfolding.

Eryx bursts into crazed laughter, a low rumbling sound that sends chills through me. If I was the man, I wouldn't be challenging a gryffin shifter, but it's his life.

"Let's make this simple for you. She is ours. That means she's off-limits to your filth. Don't so much as look at her, or I'll tear your face off. Don't push me, Darcon, or you won't see me coming, and I'll fucking destroy your whole family."

"For her?" he snorts. "Maybe you should keep her locked up then, letting her come out here, perfuming. What the fuck do you think's gonna happen?"

My heart thunders at him blaming me for his reaction. Anger blazes over me, and with it comes a taste of bitter embarrassment that others can sense my heated scent even on a day when I feel no symptoms. My skin prickles while rage bubbles through me, hot and sharp.

"Kill him," I murmur out of the biting anger swallowing me.

"You heard her. She wants you dead. Think I should listen?"

There's a moment of silence. The smell of Darcon's fear is sour. He blows out a loud exhale, making his lips tremble and steps back in retreat, a harsh expression forming on his face.

Another figure emerges from the crowd, a younger version of Darcon, with a confidence that makes him noticeable. He places a hand on Darcon's shoulder, and their gazes meet, but the older man shakes his head.

"Stand down. We're all good." Restrained frustration lines his voice.

The younger man, with light brown hair and a square face, hesitates, his gaze drifting to Eryx and me, but then gives a nod. Both men turn away and disappear into the thickening crowd of guests.

Eryx turns toward me, his hand taking mine, enveloping it. The warmth of his touch races up my arm and through me. Leading me away at a brisk pace, he navigates us out of the crowd.

"You shouldn't have come," he murmurs, guiding me toward an unoccupied couch.

I glance at him. His strikingly impeccable suit screams authority. The high-collared jacket is tailored to fit his broad shoulders and tapers down to his waist, making it look as if it was crafted on his body. Gold frames the edges of his jacket and the sleeves, and the buttons glint in the flames. His golden hair is drawn off his face, emphasizing his chiseled features.

It's getting hotter out here the longer I steal glances at the Duke, who looks like a man who's stepped off the battlefield, not someone attending a gala. Despite his clothing, the wildness still burns behind his stare.

"I didn't realize the party was exclusive," I say, trying to keep my voice steady.

"Mina." He leans in closer, the fire from him leaping over to me, his scent of cedarwood and crushed pine leaves smothering me. "These men are animals. To them, you're a young deer... irresistible and delicious."

I swallow as a chill grates at the back of my neck.

Eryx's breathing is heavy as he keeps glancing over his shoulder at Darcon.

"Is everything okay?" I ask.

"I'm going to kill the fucker for touching you."

Looking back and scanning the crowd, I can't see the man, so I push forward, and Eryx joins me.

"I just want to forget about him."

Once we reach the couch, I sit, thankful to be off my heels. Eryx is still on his feet, studying me, but his brows are pulled together.

"What?"

"Don't go anywhere. I'll be right back." Then he vanishes into the crowd.

He's going to kill Darcon, isn't he? I shift uncomfortably on the couch, not feeling guilty because that old asshole made his bed. Except now, I really notice the way the other vultures are leering at me.

There's a hollow feeling in my stomach that has little to do with hunger. Torches flicker, casting shadows across the lavish party, and everywhere I look, I now see predators. The truth of Eryx's words sinks in. It's no surprise because of where I grew up, yet being surrounded by so many dangerous men with dark, hungry looks is unnerving.

Heat rises to my cheeks when my gaze lands on Tallis.

He's on the far side of the yard, closer to the mansion, and in deep conversation with a woman who's every bit as stunning as the vibrant night sky. Her glittering white bodysuit leaves nothing to the imagination. She laughs at something he says, and jealousy slides through me like venom.

Of course, I shouldn't care who he talks to or laughs with, but seeing him engrossed in conversation with her makes my heart slam against my ribs. It's almost as if my body knows something my mind refuses to admit.

Clenching my hands in my lap, I remind myself I can't afford to feel this way or lose control. I would sneak off now if I thought Eryx wouldn't track me down fast, so I'll wait a little longer, then make a break for it.

Until then... I keep staring at Tallis with the blonde beauty and can't deny the bitter jealousy strangling me.

The longer I stare at them, the more I fear I'm about to do something really, really stupid.

## CHAPTER THIRTEEN
### BILLIE

I step forward, my attention narrowing on Tallis and the jump-suit woman. Her white outfit catches the twinkle of the flames in the yard, making her mesmerizing, and despite my distance from them, I catch the full strength of her lips into an enchanting smile as she chats with Tallis.

He's chuckling at her words, a relaxed tilt of his body toward her. That earlier knot of jealousy hardens, and I hate my reaction. It's ridiculous. Tallis' an incubus, and it's his nature to draw people in, especially women, yet the sight of them together has my blood boiling.

Dressed in all black, there's no suit and tie for him, just raw masculinity. His pants are fitted tight, leather that molds his powerful thighs, and a shirt clings to his sculpted chest. A thick belt cinches at his waist, its silver buckle glinting, providing the only break in color from his black outfit. Even his hair, pitch-black and disheveled, frames his face as if he worked hard to achieve that style.

It's not just how irresistible he looks, but the smoldering expression in his eyes, the way his lips twitch at the corners in a smirk. Everything about him screams sin. The only thing missing is a long leather coat to complete his image as the lord of darkness.

Another step forward, I mull over the idea of introducing myself, even if I'll come across like a jealous girlfriend. Except, why should I care? Does it matter when I have no idea what's going to happen between us long term?

A blond man saunters up to them, his gaze locked on the woman. In one fluid movement, he wraps his arms around her waist, drawing her against him. She giggles and leans in as he presses a kiss to her neck.

Relief splashes through me. She's with someone else. I just learned something about myself tonight. I told myself I wouldn't be the jealous kind. When I found the right man, I'd never get all psycho if he talked to another girl.

Now, look at me. Geez, what happened to me?

I quickly retreat and sink back onto the couch, tugging on my dress across my thighs in order to not flash the crowd. My heart is still slamming in my chest at my crazed reaction.

"Get a grip," I murmur under my breath, blaming the whole fated mate thing. How else can I explain my irrational jealousy? All these emotions are messing with my mind.

Lifting my head, I find the woman and her partner are gone, and Tallis is talking to someone else, an impossibly handsome man. Roughly the same height as Tallis, this man demands attention. He's built and muscular, wearing a well-tailored suit that hugs his form. He runs his fingers through rich brown hair, just long enough to sweep it back from his face. Those dark eyes glint with a spark of red whenever the light strikes them. He's irresistibly handsome, and something about him is hard to ignore. His beauty is the dangerous kind, carrying with it mystery and darkness.

The man reaches for the pocket in his jacket and pulls out a handkerchief, pristine white material fluttering in the breeze. His fingers slide over it in a rhythmic pattern. There's something almost sensual in the way he touches it that captivates me to find out more.

The pair are chatting, leaning in close, laughing like they've known each other for eternity.

Movement from the crowd up ahead takes my attention to Eryx, pushing free from the guests and strolling my way with a huge grin. He's balancing a plate loaded with delicacies and a glass of something bubbly in his other hand.

"For you," he says, handing me the plate, and my eyebrows raise at the mountain of food. "I don't want you to go hungry, and I noticed that asshole, Darcon, took your plate away."

I smile at his kindness, slightly taken aback at his gesture. It's not what I expected.

"I sure hope we're sharing this."

"Of course," he replies, sitting next to me on the couch. The cushions dip slightly under his weight, then he sets the drink on a small table next to the couch.

My attention falls to the plate in my lap, unsure

where to begin because it all looks delicious. I start with the small cheese balls, noticing Eryx watching me.

He breaks the silence between us. "I saw you watching him."

Confusion sets in, and I narrow my gaze at him.

"Who? I've been people-watching since I arrived."

His gaze flicks over to where Tallis and his friend stand.

"You were checking out that vamp talking to Tallis. You know, Jas is super dead? Is that what you're into?"

I blink at Eryx slowly and deliberately in response to his latter comment, then a lopsided grin spreads over my lips.

"How can someone be *super dead*?"

Thinking about the mysterious vampire makes sense now—the deadly allure, his hypnotic attraction, and his unusually pale skin. So, a demon has a vampire as a friend... They'd have a lot in common to talk about—death, killing, draining someone, that sort of thing.

"He's a vampire with a dark necromancer influence," Eryx explains, studying me the whole time for a reaction.

I guess I'm not the only one living with a green-eyed monster tonight, seeing his brother has a bromance going on with his buddy.

"Interesting. I bet they often create havoc." I munch on some of the food with one of a dozen toothpicks, piercing the items on the plate. Eryx shrugs and reaches over for a slice of the dark meat. He wraps it into a tight roll with his fingers and pops it all into his mouth.

"They got real close a few years ago when Tallis lost his crap and burned down part of the Vanguard Manor next door. His girlfriend dumped him, and he went crazy. There were others trapped inside, including Jas, who we rescued. Jas got a severe burn on his back, a scar that refuses to heal. I suspect it's because Tallis' fire is a hellish blend of demon and god blood. But instead of going ape shit on us, Jas ended up getting Tallis to calm down and talked him off the proverbial ledge." He digs into the food like all that talking has made him hungry.

I just stare at Eryx, half of me unable to believe how incredibly handsome he is this close up, and the other half shocked by what I've just learned.

"Oh, wow. Tallis must have really loved this girl."

He watches me for a long pause. "Interesting. Your first question is about Tallis' ex."

"You don't have to scrutinize everything I say and do. I'm just curious. I mean, an incubus having a girlfriend when he can have anyone he wants... that's intriguing."

"If you say so."

A strange awkwardness fills the void between us, so I go back to eating.

Eryx finally twists toward me in the seat, a mischievous glint in his eyes, then looks over to the two men in conversation across the yard.

"So, how many people have you killed today?" he says, donning a dramatic, Dracula-esque accent, catching me off guard with confusion. In an instant, he clears his throat. "Only ten today," he answers his own question in a deep, gravelly tone, meant to imitate Tallis, I assume. "I've spent the day getting this suit sewn directly onto me to look irresistible."

I stifle a laugh, realizing he's dubbing their voices to his own interpretation.

Without missing a beat, Eryx keeps going with his Dracula impersonation.

"Ah, it suits you well, my friend. I barely had the chance to partake in the blood of five virgins today."

Laughter spills past my lips as Eryx mimics their hand movements, too. When Jas runs his hand through his hair, Eryx says, impersonating Tallis, "I like what you did with your hair."

In the spirit of his entertainment, I jump in, answering for the vampire, "Ah, and your hair is also slicked back in perfection."

Eryx straightens, holding onto Tallis' tone. "It's so hard being this hot, but I'm trying to impress this new girl. I really hope she likes my tight pants."

I giggle, glancing over to Tallis, turning on the spot to answer a waiter at his back, and I continue as Jas. "Do give me another twirl. Let me see your ass again."

Eryx chuckles. "As much as I know you'd like that, my eyes are on the new prize now."

"Intriguing," I say. "What's so great about her compared to me?"

"Well, for one, I don't cross swords, and two, I'm hoping to get myself a taste of her sweet p–"

"Pardon me, Eryx," a male says, cutting us off.

We glance up at a man in a waiter's suit who looks apologetic.

"Sorry, but your attention is being called over to his grace." He turns and points to Khaos, who has his back to us, deep in conversation with a small audience of people. "Your brother insists you join him right away."

"What does he want?" Eryx asks, close to growling.

The man shrugs and swallows nervously. "It's something about negotiations."

Irritation flares over Eryx's face, then he turns to me. "Sorry. Duty calls, but don't go anywhere, okay?"

"Of course. I'm good. I've got my food and drink."

He gets up, hesitates for a moment, then with a grunt, he strides away with the waiter.

Left to myself, my gaze involuntarily drifts to Tallis. His conversation with Jas has turned serious, and I decide this is the break I need.

Setting the plate on the table, I stand and silently slip away from the crowd and down the opposite side of the house where guests are arriving. Shadows engulf me as I move on silent steps between lofty trees on my left and the stone mansion to my right.

I barely reach the far corner when a twig snaps behind me. Heart racing, fear drowning me, I swing around.

Standing behind me is Khaos, his expression cloaked in shadows.

*Fuck.*

He prowls forward, those pale blue eyes eerily wolf-like.

"Why are you following me?" I manage to ask.

"Who told you it was okay to attend the party?" he counters, a growl lingering in his throat. His breaths speed up, and I can tell he's restraining himself around me.

"I didn't realize it was an invitation-only party." I bite off each word sharply.

His guttural snarl rumbles in his chest, and my pulse picks up.

"Mina, it's not that I wouldn't invite you, but it's dangerous. You think I didn't see the situation with Darcon? Eryx coming to save you?"

"I can look after myself," I huff.

"You don't get it, do you?" Khaos steps closer, towering over me. His scent, mahogany and midnight jasmine, wraps around me, warming my insides. I've never had anyone make me feel this way from their scent and voice alone.

"Two of his sons were watching you from the sidelines, ready to collect you and steal you away into the woods. Any way they could sneak you away from us. Those bastards trade in females, but first, they break them, each of them taking turns."

A gasp cuts across my throat as a shiver trails up my spine.

"I-I didn't know. Why would you associate with them?"

He gives me a deadpan stare at my stupid question. Of course, he's in the business of killing. And really, how much can I trust Khaos and his brothers?

"I need you to trust our decisions."

How can I when I barely know them when they could have played a role in killing my parents?

"I'll return to my room," I state abruptly, starting to move past him when he grabs my hand. An earth-shattering spark of electricity dances up my arm and flutters down to between my thighs. Khaos may be huge and intimidating, but his touch still floats across my skin, and I am unable to deny how much I like the way he feels.

"Mina." His voice is rugged and deep, with a hint of impatience. "Where were you going just now?"

I twist back around to face him. The air shifts, his thumb stroking the inside of my wrist, and a shudder flares down my body.

"Just a walk. Too many people at the party."

Under his piercing attention, my stomach clenches and my nipples tighten. His earlier scent thickens, and it's potent, igniting arousal from deep within me.

If I stay here a second longer, he'll keep getting under my skin, then the next thing I know, I'll be spreading my legs for him. Then where will that get me? Bound to a mercenary for life. And the scary part is I'm not even mortified by the idea. Goes to show how much this fated mate thing is wrecking me.

Nope. I don't have time for that, so I shake my hand to release myself from his grip.

"Why do you fight me?" he demands.

"I don't even know you," I say the first half-truth that comes to mind, but each time I inhale his masculine scent, I sway on my feet. Swallowing, I try to slow my breaths and how hard my heart hammers. So far tonight, I've managed to keep my arousal under control. Now, with him standing in my space, with all those muscles and his biceps flexed, moisture collects between my thighs.

His stare lowers to my lips, and his fingers wrap

around my hand once more, and with it comes a warmth that strokes me. Everything about him hypnotizes me, seduces me, and I'm not even sure if he knows how hard I'm fighting to resist him.

One thought at a time—like removing my hand from his and stop touching him would be a start.

"You're my fated mate. That already secures you to us and tells you that you're safe with us."

My insides twist because suddenly he's closing the distance between us, a hazy glaze spreading over his eyes, and his hold squeezes slightly.

I'm drawn into those blue eyes. They call me to let myself fall into them. Before I can make sense of my thoughts, his arms loop around my middle, and I'm pinned up against the mansion. His body presses into mine, the thickness in his pants nestling against my stomach.

Another deep inhale of his scent, and my toes curl, every inch of me insisting we belong together. Unbearable heat sweeps through my body, every inch of me desperate to feel his touch.

Some tiny part of my mind screams for me to pull away, and I want to—gods, I need to—yet my body isn't responding. I'm too absorbed with the Duke's body pressed flush against mine.

A keening sound grazes my throat.

*Move away from him.*

But I can't.

It feels like the only solution is to strip and feel him naked up against me, to have him take me. Right now.

## CHAPTER
# FOURTEEN
KHAOS

She trembles in the shadows, her back against the wall at the side of the mansion and away from the party.

My body tenses, every primal instinct demanding I claim what's right in front of me, what's been driving me insane from the moment I crossed paths with her.

She stares up at me. This tiny thing, large cerulean eyes filled with desire and fear. Her chest rises and falls quickly, her nipples pressing against my chest, and that heady, addictive scent wraps around me like barbed wire. Thick locks of hair tumble over one side of her face, the rest blowing in the breeze. Her rosy lips part for breath like she can't get enough air. Despite the hunger in her expression and her heavy scent, I sense the tension in her muscles, as if she's going to fight me.

I brace myself, but in truth, I fucking love her feistiness. She has no idea how stunning she is, fighting me while her body sings for me. She's so ready for the plucking, her heat escalating so fast, I know she's close to hitting her crescendo.

Then she'll cry for us to fuck her, but it's always easier if she doesn't fight her primal nature.

She exhales out a purr, her cheeks blushing.

"You're giving me mixed messages, mate," I tease, as my pelvis grinds against her. My hand slides down her side, caressing the edge of her full breast.

She gasps, and I fucking adore how easily her body reacts to me.

"It's pretty clear to me what I want."

"Yeah?" Her palms are flat against my chest, but there's no pressure behind them. "And what's that?"

Her mouth parts, but only a tiny purr escapes, and she scowls at her lack of control. It impacts me, too.

A flare of arousal ripples through me, down to my cock.

"Don't even think you're getting lucky," she finally manages. Her fists strain as they grasp my shirt, as if she can't decide if she's going to rip it off me or push me away.

"There are some things you can't fight." I twirl a finger across her hip, lowering my touch.

"That's not helping the situation." Her voice is barely audible.

"I think it is. You seem to have a problem with listening to what your body wants, so I'm going to help you."

"Perhaps you're the one who's lacking control," she huffs, lifting her chin.

"You think so?" I tilt my head to the side. "Then tell me you don't want this." The words fall from my mouth easily, the challenge thrilling.

Quivering against me, her breaths grow uneven, speeding up, matching my thumping heart. My touch slips down the front of her thigh, tracing lower over the fabric of her dress until I find the high split. My knuckles graze the smooth skin of her thigh. She shivers at my touch, the sharp intake of her breath a confirmation of the electricity between us.

"That's what I thought," I whisper close to her, resting one palm on the wall of the mansion behind her. My touch glides higher as my gaze holds hers. When I touch something cold, something metallic strapped to her thigh, I pause. A blade.

A grin plays on her lips, vanishing just as quickly as I push the fabric aside and take hold of the hilt, holding it in place.

"Smart girl to bring a weapon to a dangerous party. But weapons are forbidden on my estate." Her cheeks flush red, and that frightened, vulnerable look has my balls tightening. "Fucking beautiful."

"Maybe you should be more worried about yourself right now."

I break out laughing at her adorable threat. Her body vibrates in response, as though she's attuned to my reaction, and I can't get enough.

Who the hell is this girl? She walked into my life a day ago and now stirs up emotions I didn't know I was capable of.

Still holding onto her blade in her leg strap, my thumb runs small circles across her bikini line, her skin smooth and delicately soft. An inferno pours off her, her body slack against me as if she's given up trying to fight me and barely holding on, yet her stare screams the opposite.

Our lips are inches apart, and I wait for her, but she never makes a move. Her stubbornness is outstanding. Everything about her is going to haunt me every second I'm away from her.

"Be a good girl and admit you want me," I encourage. Not waiting a second longer, I let go of her blade and pull aside the elastic of her soaked panties.

She gasps, her inhales racing, but she doesn't stop me. I'm starving to feel her, to show her what I can do for her.

Craving this moment with her has been fucking brutal.

With the back of my fingers, I run them across the slick line of her bare pussy.

She makes a tiny moan but doesn't push me away. She's compliant, needy for me.

My cock hurts for her.

"Is this what you need?" I groan.

She sways against me, her grasp on my shirt tightening, but she tears her gaze from mine. Gone is the fiery girl fighting her urges. She's not frantic. I let the fantasy play in my mind of fucking her hard against the wall. I want her more than I realized—to see her squirm, to scream, to stare into her eyes afterward when she can't escape what she wants...me.

The burst of laughter and voices stream down to us from the party. How long before someone finds us? Because when I fuck, I take my time. And the first time I claim my firecracker, it won't be quick.

Our gazes crash, and she mouths, "Khaos." A sound of complete surrender, her body shuddering.

My damn heart is pounding in my head, blood diving south and leaving me dizzy.

"You're killing me," she purrs, and I love hearing those words.

"You want me, don't you, gorgeous?"

Leaning forward, our foreheads touching, I don't kiss her, not yet. Watching her as my fingers spread her lower lips, I press against the slick heat of her drenched pussy, my hand engulfed in her burning inferno. Circling her clit, her hips rock at my touch.

I've never wanted to fuck someone so badly in my life.

Tiny pulses dance off her body, rippling over me, twisting around my cock. He's craving release to the point of feeling strangled.

Her hypnotic groans escalate as she loops her arms around the back of my neck.

I slide two fingers into her center, and they come out completely wet. Pushing them in and out, I have her clinging to me, her mouth so close to mine, I inhale her breath.

"So goddamn gorgeous," I whisper, caught up in the moment of plunging into her.

She bucks against me, whimpering for more, pushing her legs wider.

Darkness frays at the edges of my sight from my ache, but I don't reach for my cock. Not tonight.

"Let me hear you scream." I finger that sweet pink hole, my thumb teasing her swollen clit.

Expecting her snarl, I instead sense the trembling of her pussy around my fingers.

I barely register the rest of the party as Mina comes undone over my hand. A cry rises from her throat, and I press my mouth to hers, stealing the scream. She tastes of honey, so sweet, so decadent that my cock hardens like he's about to burst.

We kiss ravenously, our lips sliding over one another, tongues dancing in an unspoken battle. She's everything...

Her body thrashes and writhes, her pussy squeezing my fingers as more slick slips out.

Then I feel it—a sting, sharp, sudden, and painful.

Her teeth sink into my lower lip. I curse, pulling my head from her, the metallic taste of blood on my tongue.

"Bloody hell!" I purposefully leave my fingers fully plunged inside her, holding onto her as I lick the blood from my lips. I'm a bastard on the best days, and anyone else who draws blood from me would be dead by now, but with Mina, I want more...

Gasping for air, a smirk plays on her face. Something else crosses her face, something other than lust... excitement. My gut flutters with anticipation that she enjoyed hurting me beyond getting her revenge.

"You can't just take what you want," she answers, still catching her breath, then pushes my fingers out of her.

The strong perfume of her scent doesn't help the situation in my pants. Especially when I place my sticky fingers into my mouth. She tastes as sweet as I expect.

She watches me, looking ready to snatch my fingers away from my mouth. That makes me suck on them harder, then I lick the last bits off. Her clenching her thighs and enjoying the show don't go unnoticed by me.

"You feel better after that, don't you?" I whisper. When she doesn't respond but fixes her dress, her lips pinched tightly, I continue, "You're welcome, and now you owe me a favor."

She scoffs a laugh, even if her cheeks are blazing red.

"You're lucky I didn't stab you."

My nostrils flare, and I bark a laugh.

"And you're lucky I'm letting you keep your blade." I leave out the part where the last person to bring a weapon into my home ended up chopped into a dozen pieces and fed to the wild creatures living in the woods.

She's still panting, her face flushed, showing me she loved it as much as I enjoyed giving it to her, even if she won't admit the truth.

"Well, I hope you got your kicks, because that won't happen again."

My cock throbs at her feistiness. She actually thinks what I did was for my pleasure only? If that's the case, why does it feel like my cock's in a vice? She has no idea that without my help, she'll be in pain most of the night.

She turns on her heels to walk back toward the party, and I grab her wrist. She spins around, staring at me with surprise.

"Let go of me," she pleads firmly, as if the walls she has up between us are about to come crashing down.

"Not going to happen. As long as there are guests in my home, you won't be in their company without me or my brothers."

Her eyes widen, yet her gaze hardens. She tugs her wrist against my grip, but I hold on to her.

"So far, I've been nothing but hospitable with you, but if you keep pushing me, I can't be held responsible for what I do next."

She stares at me intensely, then groans.

"You can walk me back to the mansion door."

As we turn to stroll back, a grin pulls on my lips. Even if she's furious, she's captivating. And if she's shocked by tonight, she's going to be in for a rude awakening when her heat comes into full effect.

### Billie

My heart is in my throat, my head is spinning, and arousal is still pulsing deep in the pit of my stomach. With burning cheeks, embarrassment swallows me at how easily I gave myself to Khaos with barely a fight.

The worst part is that he knows he won, and I hate him for it.

I hate his cockiness.

I hate the way he grins when he keeps glancing over at me, his grip tight around my wrist.

I hate even more that he's escorting me like a child.

I have to find another way to get past the guards at

the doors, then the main gates to reach the Vanguard Manor, as Eryx had called it.

Sighing, we emerge from the shadows into the party crowd, which has doubled since I left it. Khaos guides me on fast steps, slipping through the chatting masses, though most are distracted by something at the other end of the yard.

An oversized birdcage on a platform that wasn't there earlier now has a crowd surrounding it. Two women are inside, scantily dressed in strips of silk, but what grabs my attention is their long, sharp claws for hands. They're hissing at one another, baring their sharp teeth. Suddenly, one launches at the other, a feral growl ripping from her throat. The explosive collision has them both slamming into the metal bars of the cage, rattling it.

The crowd goes wild, cheering and yelling for more.

I roll my eyes at their barbaric behavior, but before I can say anything, Khaos' name is being called over the crowds. Immediately, I spot his boisterous friends from earlier coming toward us. Tension ripples off Khaos, his grip on my wrist tensing. He maneuvers to stand in front of me, shielding me from them. I'm starting to learn that all of his work colleagues are predators.

Glancing around, I spot Tallis not too far ahead of us, near the mansion door, his back turned our way... which gives me an idea.

"Hey, Khaos, you go to your buddies. I'll get Tallis to take me to my room. I'll be fine." I tear my arm out of his grasp and start walking away, but he snatches my arm once more. He glances over my shoulder at his friends, then at me like he's about to argue.

Then he hauls me closer to him in a heartbeat, and I'm swallowed by his masculine scent. Before I can push him off me, he growls in my ear.

"Go straight to Tallis. Don't push your luck with me."

He lets me go, and I scowl at him, then step toward Tallis. Bossy asshole.

His friends arrive, slapping him on the shoulders and back, grilling him about where he'd gotten off to. A couple of the men sniff him, then howl like coyotes. Goosebumps run down my arms at how quickly they pick up my scent on him, which makes me want to leave the party even more. Before long, he's engulfed by the men and the crowd.

With him out of sight and Tallis still not glancing my way, I slip away unnoticed, retracing my steps the way we'd come. Only near the corner of the mansion stands a huddle of men in suits, and a few of them are already leering my way.

A shudder slides down my spine. If I've learned anything tonight, it's that once I head down the side of the house in the shadows, they'll trail after me.

Pausing for a split second, weighing my options, a flash of red at the edge of my vision catches my attention. I glance over to the woods that stretch out beyond the yard and find it strange someone's rushing in there. Then I remember Awstin, my uncle, wore a red top when I last saw him.

"Awstin?" I mutter, squinting into the dark after him. Could it be him? Had he come to find me... rescue me? Except... he can't be here. It's too dangerous.

Before I know it, I dart away from the party, my eyes

glued to the spot where the figure vanished just at the edge of the woods. Sneaking a glance behind me, I find no one's noticed my disappearance, but when I turn back around, there in the distance stands the man I spotted. He's too far away to see clearly, but I swear it's Awstin.

He's got his back to me and turns to glance at me over his shoulder. Shadows hide his face.

Then he waves for me to join him.

"Awstin," I mutter, fear collecting in my chest that he'd risk his life to come for me. My feet are already pushing forward.

My skin shivers that someone will see him.

He moves deeper into the woods, vanishing from my sight. The hairs on my arms shift and I pull out the blade on my thigh strap, just in case I'm being tricked. I desperately want to believe it's Awstin. He's the last living relative I have, and I'm not ready to lose him, too. But if it is him, I'm going to chew his ear off at risking his life like this.

Taking slower steps, I lose sight of him and I pause.

I'm not a fool and just can't risk the danger out here. But I'll wait near the edge of the woods to see if he returns.

With the party farther behind me, I stare deeply at the shadows, not seeing a flash of red again. That ominous sensation bites into my skin, so I turn away from the forest.

I retreat to the party when something snatches my dress and yanks me backward, wrenching me deeper into the woods. It happens so fast, the earth beneath me seeming to fly with how fast I'm being flung. I lose my footing and end up tumbling to the ground. Rolling a few times, I finally come to a stop. A muffled shriek escapes me as my heels fly off my feet, but I'm still gripping my blade.

My dress catches on something and rips loudly as I drive myself to my feet, leaving my legs exposed to the cool night air. The world tilts around me for a few seconds as I find my bearings, discovering I'm in a small clearing surrounded by a dense forest. And that a broken log tore my dress.

Up on my feet, wincing from the scrapes and bruises, I turn on the spot only to discover I'm not alone.

I shudder at the beast standing at least twenty feet from me.

Eyes glint in the nightless night. The creature has gnarled fur and a long snout that's snorting out hot breaths. Its front hooves beat against the earth, sending a chill racing down to my bones.

I'm face to face with a huge, black bull with sharp, curled horns that have my name on them. What the hell is a bull doing out here?

Panic claws at my chest as the beast grunts.

The world around me slows, the sounds falling into the background. I can practically feel its hot breath, the ground trembling each time it smacks another hoof into it.

Those few moments where I'm frozen in fear stretch into an eternity, and I'm suffocating on how in the world I'll get out of this.

As if the universe has decided to make my life hell,

the beast's roar fills the night and charges, nostrils flaring.

My life suddenly flashes before my eyes, but instead of my parents, the first thing to pop into my mind are the three Dukes.

What the hell?!

## CHAPTER
# FIFTEEN
### BILLIE

Madness burns in the beast's red eyes.

It charges at me, the ground trembling. All the while, my heart's furiously pounding against my ribcage, and my mind's frantically trying to tap into my magic—the same one I've struggled all these years to summon, to control—and I come up short.

Instinct kicks in, and I desperately run away through the woods, the bull's hot breath practically on the back of my neck.

A scream rips from my throat, but the party's music and explosive chatter drowns it out. No one's going to hear me. No one will come to help me, but later, they'll find me dead, trampled by a goddamn bull.

Fuck this. I sure as hell didn't come this far to be taken out by wildlife.

I snatch a dead branch from the ground and whip around, already swinging. My short knife poised in my other grip, I'm ready to stab this beefster to death. Then they can add it to the menu at the party.

But it's so close, it exhales all over my face with the breath of death, coming to a screeching halt. The sight chills me to the bone.

My branch breaks against his horn, crumbling in my hand. Fear smashes into me that this is my end, and I lock up, my mind blank, my body shaking.

I swing my knife at its face, but in that same split second, the bull makes a strange swing of its head, missing my attack. In a flash, the side of its massive skull whacks into my side, knocking the wind out of me. I'm hurled across the woodland, pain echoing deep in my body.

The world blurs as I scream because of the pain. I slam to the ground, rolling a few times, groaning with aches. I'm going to have bruises for days if I survive. Already, I feel the tingling of my body healing—being a wolf shifter is a lifesaver.

The world tilts, and a thought hits me—if the bull wanted me dead, it would've done it already. Why didn't it?

I barely push myself up when a monstrous shadow engulfs me, freezing my insides and leaving me no time to react.

The animal's on top of me, shoving me down onto my back with his long nose. A putrid, hot exhale scorches across my face. Its eyes are filled with insatiable hunger, and I shudder. Snorting, it digs at the earth beside me, its horns glinting in the dim light.

I pause for a second, recognizing the musky odor flooding me—a barnyard stink with a powdery smell. Hell, no! This isn't a wild bull gone mad. It's that major ass, Darcon, who'd hit on me back at the party. He's a bull shifter!

Trapped beneath the asshole, I simmer with fury. With it comes that familiar buzz that pulses down my arms, the kind that belongs to my power.

About damn time.

I hadn't planned on killing the animal, because I don't dance that way, but knowing I'm dealing with a first-class asshole, all bets are off.

Something slimy nudges my thigh.

Quickly, I glance down my body and see his fifth leg dangling there, all red and throbbing.

Ewww.

My mind goes empty with terror and rage. The fucker hasn't killed me because he's going to rape me...

I vomit a bit into my mouth.

He lingers there, grunting and staring at me. I slam my knife into his face, but he jerks out of the way at the last second. The blade slips and plunges into the thick muscle between his shoulder and neck.

Blood spurts out, warm against my face, and he unleashes a deep guttural snort, piercing my ears. He shakes his head furiously, and I quickly drag myself out from under him.

I scramble backward, then rush to my feet. It's also when I catch a glint of something red through the woods around us. Hell, if that's Awstin and he doesn't help me, I no longer have an uncle.

My body shudders while my arms are itching to the point of biting pain. Rapidly, I shove my sleeves up past my elbows, and the ancient script inked on flesh glows brightly. It's already peeling off my skin, like it did the night my parents died. The thought alone floods me with a savage anger about what was taken from me.

With my legs wobbling beneath me, I recoil from the monstrous thing who's grunting, blood rolling from the knife sticking out of him. Flaming eyes are on me in a flash. The bull lowers his head and his broad, muscular shoulders flex.

Between us, my ink floats, morphing into two thin swords at least twenty-four inches in length, with a pale blue glow. They're a part of me, and I have never seen anything more beautiful and perfect at the time I need them most.

With the hilts slipping into my hands, fitting like a glove into my grasp, I catapult myself forward. Bravery fills me as adrenaline thumps in my veins, and I let it control me...

Anger.

Retribution.

Survival.

Like the first time I used my weapons, they guide me like a puppet.

"Come get me!"

The bull charges, head down, its curved horns aimed right at me. I throw myself to the side at the last possible moment and slash at his flank with the magical swords. One blade's edge bites into his thick flesh, blood bubbling to the surface. He growls ferociously, twisting fast for a stocky beast.

Shoving aside the fear gnawing at my insides, my body moves almost of its own accord. I spring toward him, as he does me. Next thing I know, I've hurled myself ahead into an arc and flip over the beast, my blades rushing down the sides of its back. Deep cuts mark him.

Look at me! That move's spectacular. No idea how I did that, though.

Landing behind him in a perfect gymnast post, I whip around. I turn away from him just as his hind leg delivers a brutal kick to my left arm and steals my grin. Stars dance in my vision as I'm thrown to the ground, then the searing pain hits. I cry out, my arm on fire, pain shooting up into my shoulder.

The sword in my injured grip disintegrates into magical particles that float in the air, which slide back into place along my arm as though it knows it's useless right now.

Tucking my arm close to my side, I retreat as the bull pivots in my direction. Gasping for air, I steel myself, needing to stay focused, or this time, the dick will kill me. He's bleeding all over the grass, but he's not stumbling. Hot gusts of breath rush from his flaring nostrils, fury blazing in his black eyes.

To hell with letting myself collapse or giving in to the searing pain that hurts so much my eyes are watering. Sweat drips down my spine, and I shake away the shivers that engulf me.

The bull rushes me, faster this time.

Gritting my teeth, I shoot forward, the sword feeling weightless in my hand. In a swift motion, I throw myself into a slide on my hip, right between the bull's front legs, between those deadly hooves. With my good hand, I stab the blade up into its soft underbelly, using all my strength and the force of momentum to drive it deep and slice him open.

I'm out from under him in seconds as blood and other stuff pours out. Up on my feet in a flash, I snap around, sword pointed at him.

"Told you not to fuck with me," I gasp,

The bull gives one final shudder, a painful bellow, then stumbles forward before crashing to the ground. His exhales are ragged before he goes still. His body starts quivering, then in seconds, he's shrinking, fur replaced by skin and before me lies a dead Darcon in human form.

Khaos will be absolutely thrilled when he discovers I killed one of his guests. Let's add guest murderer to my growing list of achievements in this damned place. Just brilliant, Billie.

Exhaling loudly, I collapse onto my knees, my body shaking with adrenaline, with agony. I'm still grasping my sword while my other arm is killing me.

The crunch of twigs has me snapping my attention up.

Two more enormous bulls burst into the scene, eyes glowing with a feral intensity. Somehow, they're bigger than Darcon. I took him down on my own, but what chance do I stand against two?

Their gazes funnel on Darcon... lifeless as a log.

My heart thunders in my ears, and despite the pain, I'm on my feet, tightening my hold on the sword. Panic drums in my chest, not sure I'll survive this battle.

They grunt furiously. I won't outrun them. A tree... I

could get out of their reach, but the nearest tree is a pine and too thin. Crap. I need a different one.

The bulls leap forward.

A desperate cry falls from my lips. I'm down to one sword and an injured arm, so I'm not going to win this fight. I'm not stupid to believe otherwise.

It's not a weakness to run, so I sprint in the opposite direction.

Darkness crashes over me as if someone switched the lights off, quickly followed by a half-roar, half-screech, terrifying me down to my soul.

I shudder, almost losing my footing as I twist my head back around.

Something gigantic, with an expansive wingspan, shrouds us in darkness.

This time I scream.

I just know with a horrifying truth, I'm going to die today.

If the bulls don't trample me to death, then whatever the fuck that is will finish the job.

The creature swoops down, and the beating of those massive wings sends a shockwave of wind through the air, colliding into me and taking the bulls off guard. They come to a screeching halt, and their heads snap up at the newcomer.

With the bird's movement, it lets the dim light back over us, and I catch those magnificent feathery wings as it descends with a grace that astonishes me.

I finally see it clearly.

A large eagle head with piercing golden eyes and a fierce black beak. Wings just as dark, enormous with the underside covered in gold feathers. Talons sharp as razors on the front legs are ready to grasp and tear while its lion's body ripples with muscles, covered in a golden-brown fur, and a long tail curls at the end with a tuft ball.

He releases a keening cry.

I'm rooted on the spot, my breaths wedged in my lungs, shocked at Eryx in gryffin form. Of course, it's him... gryffin are rare, and I've never been happier to see him.

His eyes meet mine. My heart's racing, and all I can think is that I'm not going to die today after all.

He lets out a deafening roar, a sound that seems to shake the earth, yet the party in the distance still continues, louder than before, if that's even possible.

The two bulls grunt up at him.

Wings beat heavily, creating gusts of wind that whip through the trees, sending the branches into a wild thrashing. Leaves and twigs lift off the soil, twirling in mini cyclones.

I shove myself up against a tree, as one bull, disinterested in the gryffin, swings my way, snorting with fury.

Pulse pounding in my ears, I raise my sword, ready to do whatever it takes.

Eryx maneuvers toward us in the air, coming for the poor sucker barreling my way. Wings tucked close to his body, he dives, talons outstretched.

I see the train wreck coming for the bull, yet I can't look away.

The clash is fast and brutal. Talons sink into the bull's sides, and the gryffin's beak snaps shut around the animal's neck. The snap of bones is loud, and its final breath comes out as a gasped exhale.

He tosses the bull to the ground, only feet from me, and it transforms into its human form—the young man who'd placed his hand on Darcon's shoulder at the party.

A shiver wrecks through me, and my gut twists with bile at the sight. My adrenaline's off the charts, and I recoil from the body.

The second bull takes its chance, twisting away from us and darting into the woods, its movements frantic. Eryx doesn't waste a second. Wings beating in the air, he gives chase.

I watch them both disappear from view into the forest. An explosive screech streams out from where the trees sway violently. The piercing whines and cries of the bull escalate, the savagery leaving me clenching my gut.

The sword in my grasp begins to dissolve, transforming into a line of ancient words that glide through the air and slide back onto my arm, melding seamlessly with my flesh. How I wish I could summon this power on command, rather than having it awaken only in the face of death.

A deafening squawk has me flinching and glancing up as the gryffin bursts out from the treetops, a lifeless body in its claws, torn in half.

Oh, shit!

Eryx dumps him near his friend with a sickening thud.

I gag at the sight, shaking. I still have a dead man's blood on me, and I choke out a cry. I try to wipe it off. My arm is biting with pain. Shaking, I'm not sure what to think or feel, only that I'm hurting.

The sweep of air collides into me once more, and the gryffin is coming for me, eyes narrowing on me.

My blood turns to ice.

"Eryx, no! Don't do it." I back away, terrified that he sees me as something to eat.

Powerful wings stretch wide, the golden tips of golden feathers standing out against the dark ones. Then he lunges at me with terrifying speed.

Fear chokes me.

I stagger backward, my mind screaming that he's going to hurt me, or worse...

He's there in a thundering rush, the wind slamming into me, knocking me off balance. My legs buckle, and I fall over when strong talons curl around my waist. They're gentler than I expected, and I'm off my feet. The ground falls beneath me as we move too fast, the world becoming a blur.

"Eryx, stop!" I cry out, but my words are lost in the wind.

There's no response or any sign that he heard me. My vision tunnels, and terror claws at my chest at how fast and high we're moving.

With a desperate cry, the world fades away beneath me. The gryffin's grip tightens around me, then everything goes black.

# CHAPTER
# SIXTEEN
## TALLIS

The insistent pounding at my door wrenches me from sleep, and I'm still dazed as I stumble out of bed, groaning.

Knocking comes again, louder this time.

"Still your soul, I'm coming. This better be important." I grunt to make sure they hear me as I drag my feet over the cold floorboards. Morning sunlight might be drenching my room, but it feels far too early for whatever this is. I barely slept a couple of hours after last night's party. An event I normally used to feed, yet last night, I couldn't get Mina out of my thoughts. It's ridiculous how I still don't trust her, yet I can't bear to even touch another woman now.

I yank open the door to Helmi standing there in her maid's uniform, her eyes round as disks, brimming with panic.

"Your Grace, something bad has happened! You need to come right away," she cries in a strained voice.

"What?" I blink at her, confused and yawning. "Guests still passed out in the cage or something?"

"No, Your Grace! Please hurry. He's got Mina. Eryx has her!" she pleads, and I'm surprised I can make sense of what she's saying at the speed she's speaking, her words tumbling over one another.

I yawn, rubbing the sleep out of my eyes.

"What do you mean, he has her?" I run a hand through my hair, frowning.

"His gryffin–"

I stiffen at the word.

"Fuck! Where?" I demand, my heart scaling up to the back of my throat as I rush out of my room.

"The basement." Her lips pinch, holding my gaze. "Your Grace, you may want to put some clothes on first."

Right. I glance down at my naked self, then dart into my room to throw on the first clothes I find, last night's party pants and a shirt. I'm back in the corridor, doing up my buttons while on the move.

"Go get Khaos," I call out over my shoulder at Helmi. "Tell him to meet me in the basement."

Rushing through the mansion and down the stairs, I hurtle myself over the banister, leaping from the third floor down to the first. Landing with a thud, I dart toward the basement.

If Eryx hurts her, if that damn gryffin's done anything to her, I'll tear them both apart. My blood's like angry lava bubbling in my veins. All other thoughts vanish, and I'm left with terror gripping my insides.

I charge down the basement steps, instantly tasting the faint blood in the air in the back of my throat. Is it hers? Everything the gryffin brings down, he maims and toys with until they die.

Downstairs, I lunge at the oversized door sitting ajar, my breaths heavy as I draw it open. Sunlight spills into the room from a tall window at the top of the wall, illuminating the sight before me.

A chill wraps around my heart.

Mina's lying unconscious on a mattress, still wearing her dress from last night, except it's torn and bloodied. I clench my fists, glaring at Eryx in his gryffin form, holding her, embracing her from behind with a possessive intensity. Long talons are tucked around her middle, a lion's leg thrown over hers. I realize she's not wearing any shoes, and her feet are filthy, covered in dirt like she's been running through the woods.

Those beady bird eyes lock onto mine, his tail whipping against the mattress, clearly agitated. His sharp talons curl tighter around her protectively. I still can't tell if he's keeping her as his plaything before he eats her or if he's keeping her safe from harm.

Massive wings are half spread, one under her, the other behind him, muscles taut. A shrill erupts from his beak, a warning for me to back the fuck off, or he'll attack anyone who gets between him and Mina.

The hairs on my arms rise, and fire burns through me. If he's killed her, I'll destroy him. I've seen this look on him before, usually when he drags a kill down here, and we try to take it away from him.

Except... Mina's still breathing, her chest rising and falling.

Thank fuck.

So, how the hell do we get her away from him?

"If I learn that's her blood all over her dress and you were responsible, I'm going to burn you to a crisp, asshole," I snap, my body tense, fists tighter.

He hisses at me, the feathers around his neck fluffing out.

Thundering steps rushing down the stairs have me turning to find Khaos marching toward me, his face pale. He steps in alongside me in the doorway.

"Sweet fucking gods! How the hell did this happen?"

"Party, I'm guessing," I mutter, my gaze locked on the pair. "She's breathing, so she's not a meal... yet." Relief eases the anxiety tightening in my chest to know she's still alive.

Khaos curses under his breath, his shoulders stiff, and for a long pause, we just stare at them.

Khaos exchanges a knowing look with me—we've been here before. Not exactly like this, but we regularly deal with Echo's mayhem. Like the time he dragged an enormous moose into the mansion, then released it because he wasn't hungry anymore.

"When she wakes up, she's going to scream and panic. That'll set off Echo, and who the fuck knows how he'll react," Khaos murmurs.

I clench my teeth as the image plays out in my mind.

"I suspect she's already met Echo, which could be how she ended up passed out, so she may not panic. The girl's a fighter."

Khaos clenches his jaw. His gaze blazes with fury and frustration as he shakes his head.

"I truly believed she'd heed my words. I warned her

at the gala. Told her explicitly to go straight to you, so you'd walk her to her room. When I didn't see her, I assumed she was safe. But I fucked up by trusting her word to remain in her room."

Every muscle in my body tenses.

"Wait, she never spoke to me last night. She was with Eryx the last time I saw her. And assuming his obsession with her and hatred of socializing, I figured she'd be safest with him."

"Fuck, now I need to know. How did she end up like that, and why does she have blood all over her?" he growls, his knuckles turning white as he tightens his grip on the door frame.

"Not sure, but I'll find out." I run my fingers through my messy hair, exhaling deeply.

Khaos isn't listening, completely captivated by Echo holding onto Mina. The gryffin stares down at Mina's unconscious body, making a strange, deep chirping sound.

"Look at him," Khaos murmurs, keeping his voice low. "He's gushing over her. He's not going to eat her. There's something different. That damn gryffin has never shown this kind of... attachment."

"Then we tempt Echo away from her, maybe with food, and hope he doesn't go mental on us when we take Mina from him." I glance at Khaos, and his brows are drawn together. He knows as well as I do that with our powers, we'd be able to stop him, but it means hurting him. My brother's gone through enough torment in his life that I won't bring him more agony.

"We can try to see if food works, but we won't force

him," Khaos suggests. "We wait and watch, and once she regains consciousness, I'll explain to her to remain calm. If she tries to leave on her own, he might release her."

A chill of dread settles over me. "If he gets aggressive, the last option is to tranquilize him."

"Fine," Khaos grunts.

"We take turns watching them," I state. "While you take the first shift, I'm going to find out what the fuck happened to her."

Khaos nods, and I charge upstairs, the image of Mina in Echo's arms etched on my brain. I'm trembling, fisting my hands, hating that we have to wait to get her away from the gryffin.

Out in the backyard, the morning sun stretches its golden fingers across the landscape, highlighting the remnants of last night's party. Empty glasses and plates are strewn about, and several guests are draped over the outdoor furniture, fast asleep.

Our team is already at work cleaning up the mess.

But all that fades into insignificance.

Staring at the woods behind our home, I dash forward, urgency in my mind. Trees are denser, shadows stretching across the land.

Did she come out here alone last night? Why?

Following my nose, I take in deep inhales, gliding between the trees when I pick up the metallic tang of blood. The dampness of mud is heavy, but there's no missing the acrid scent.

Running forward, I move with speed, letting the breeze that carries the smell guide me. Then I spot it several trees away—bodies heaped together near a tree while flies buzz around the corpses.

My gut twists.

A chill ices my insides as I move closer to understand what we're dealing with.

Darcon. That's the first face I see, his dead eyes, and like his two sons by his side, they're all naked. Had they shifted into their bull forms at the party? Why the fuck would they do that?

One of the son's bodies is gruesomely torn in half. Clearly Echo's handiwork. The weight of the discovery pushes down on my shoulders.

A family line has just been eradicated on our premises. I don't give a fuck about them, but the repercussions could bite us in the ass hard. But if these men dared to harm Mina, Echo's actions might be justified. If he hadn't finished them off, I would have done the deed myself.

I'm taken slightly off guard by how quickly my protection over her rises in me.

Fated mates come once in a lifetime, and I'm not going to sit back and allow anyone to harm her. The shit between us and the truth she's keeping will come out. I'll make sure of it because the truth always does. Then we'll deal with that, but this fucking bullshit is gonna come back to us.

Our grandfather, Talino, is traveling right now, but he's always placed importance on politics and keeping face with others, including our enemies. So, to have a close ally murdered on our territory is going to send ripples out into the community.

Personally, I think it sends a strong message.

Fuck with us, and you'll pay.

Our grandfather, the God of Forests, won't agree. He's going to be fucking pissed.

## Billie

Blinking awake to the yellow hues of a light bulb overhead, I'm buzzing with confusion. When my gaze settles on the gryffin behind me, fast asleep, cradling me in his firm grasp, my memories catch up.

Me in the woods.

Darcon attacking me.

Eryx bursting onto the scene and taking out the other two bulls.

Now, he's breathing heavily behind me, and I can't stop the tremors that sink through me at being so close to his gryffin. When I'm in my wolf form, it's still me, and I'm aware of what's going on, so this is just Eryx. He wouldn't hurt me, right?

Then why is he still in his gryffin form?

The stiffness in my limbs and the lack of pain in my injured arm tell me I've been in the strange room, lying on a mattress, longer than I should have been. Not to mention a pressing bladder issue that's demanding my attention.

I attempt to wriggle free, but the moment I stir, his grip tightens, drawing me closer to his enormous body. He radiates heat that swallows me, but it's also intimidating to be in the arms of such a beast.

Twisting onto my back, I glance up, gaping at how tiny I am against him.

"Eryx?" I whisper. "It's you in there, right?"

The huge eagle tilts his head forward, eyes opening and on me, but I can't see his facial expression to understand what he's thinking, which is slightly terrifying. Right now, I feel like I'm in an eagle's nest as his next feed.

A low rumbling purr resonates in the lion's chest. It doesn't sound like a threat, but more of a primal claim.

"Thanks for helping me in the woods," my voice trembles out. "But think you can loosen your grip a bit?"

He doesn't move, and fear skids over my skin that I'm dealing with a wild animal. Perhaps Eryx doesn't have control over his gryffin. A shiver coats my skin... except he hasn't hurt me yet.

Gathering my courage, I reach over with a tentative hand and trail my fingers over his feathers around his neck. Despite the dread smothering me, the gryffin is breathtaking. His reaction to my touch has him ruffling his dark feathers. I flinch back initially, a surprised giggle escaping from my lips when he does nothing more.

He leans in, and the side of his head nudges mine gently, as animals do in bonding moments. Warmth fills my veins, and I'm ninety-nine percent convinced he's not going to kill me on purpose. But with his possessive hold, I doubt I'll get far from him if I try to run.

"You're really big, you know that?" I tell him. "And you can be intimidating. But I need to visit the bathroom. Maybe you can let me go?"

Does he even understand what I'm saying?

His talons constrict a bit more around me in response, and I sigh. I also take that as him knowing what I said.

"Okay, this is how it's going to be then," I murmur under my breath.

His gaze never leaves me, his silence thickening the air as confirmation that I'm not going anywhere, but that growing pain in my lower stomach sharpens.

Glancing up at the gryffin, I hold his stare.

"Look, I-I really need to pee. You can take me to the bathroom and wait, and I promise I'll return to your room. I mean, where do I have to go? But..." I gnaw on my lower lip, discomfort growing with every passing second. "Otherwise, I'm about to soak your mattress, and we both don't want that."

I stare at him, pleading with him with my eyes. A biting ache causes my body to shudder involuntarily. I squirm against him, a whine in my throat. I have no idea if gryffins understand English, but he's about to find out very soon what I'm saying.

Instantly, his talons retract from around my middle, and he hastily rises with a swiftness that surprises me, considering his size. Except, his sudden movement nudges me and shifts the weight of the mattress, which shoves me off and sends me tumbling onto the cold floor.

I don't waste a second and scramble to my feet, reminded of the impressive size of the gryffin whose head scrapes the tall ceiling, his wings tight against his side.

The door to his room in the basement suddenly creaks open, and I whip around to find Tallis standing there. His hands are glowing orange like they're going to burst into flames.

"Back off," I warn him. "He's not going to hurt me, but I'm about to wet myself, and I won't hesitate to push you aside."

"Charming as ever," Tallis states, stepping aside and opening the door wider.

I shoot out of the room and into the main basement area, then head for the stairs. But before I can take a single step, a large taloned arm loops around my waist, steering me back and pushing me to another door in the basement.

"Bathroom's that way," Tallis calls out in a smug voice. "Looks like Echo doesn't plan on letting you stray too far."

"Yeah, I noticed." So, the gryffin has a name? Interesting, I don't know of anyone who names their animal side. "And what's your plan then to help me get away from him? Surely, you've encountered this behavior before?"

"Absolutely. With prey, he brings it into the house before he eats it."

I swallow hard, not wanting to hear that. Instead, I sprint into the small bathroom and slam it shut behind me, then bolt to the toilet.

Just as I relieve myself, the door swings open.

I let out a squeal, finding the gryffin shoving his fat bird head inside, along with his front legs, his gaze on me.

"Hey, get out!"

From somewhere beyond the doorway, Tallis is

laughing. Thankfully, he's not joining us in the bathroom as well.

The gryffin doesn't move.

"Fine," I huff, accepting my lack of privacy. "For prestigious Dukes, I didn't think you were into watching someone pee."

"I'd take it as a compliment. Echo's smitten with you. He's never acted like this before, so I'm guessing after he saved your ass last night in the woods, he's claimed you as his little doll to protect."

Tallis's words spear through me. He already knows what happened?

"Truthfully, I was already in charge of the situation last night before he arrived."

Echo unleashes a shrill sound, his front paw scratching the tiled floor between us, eyes piercing into me.

"Geez, fine, you helped. And I already said thank you." I lower my head, unsure I want to have this conversation while I'm on the toilet.

"So, do tell?" Tallis asks. "How did three members of the same family, a close ally to us, end up dead in our woods?"

"Can't this wait until I'm finished? It's hard enough to go to the toilet with giant eagle eyes watching me."

"I found your discarded shoes in the woods," Tallis continues on, regardless. "What I'm curious about is why you went into the woods in the first place. Were you searching for a way to escape from us?"

Frustration bubbles in my chest, and I finish up quickly. I push my dress down to cover myself while sliding my panties up. Shooting Echo a glare, I murmur, "Are you satisfied now?" I quickly wash my hands at the sink and dry them.

He merely retreats, giving me room to step out.

Tallis is leaning against the wall when I emerge, looking entirely too relaxed and entertained by the situation. The faint light in the basement casts shadows across his striking features. Eyes that are a temptation, despite being dark as the night. There's a ruggedness about him, a wildness that draws me to him, even when he has me agitated.

Refusing to give into my arousal, I tear my attention from him.

"So, that's a yes to you attempting to run from us?" Tallis insists.

I pause, my breathing quickening.

"For your information, that creep, Darcon, tried to force himself onto me in the woods. I killed him, then his sons came. Echo took them out. Otherwise, they would have killed me. If you want to call that escaping, go for it."

Tallis's face pales as he pushes off the wall, dread etched across his face.

"Did he hurt you?" he asks with a shaky voice.

Before I can respond, Echo nudges Tallis aside with a forceful flap of his wing, sending him into the wall. With a soft motion, he then ushers me back into his room in the basement. He follows me in, squeezes himself through the doorway, and swiftly shuts the door in Tallis's stunned face.

"Well, I guess I'll be out here, making sure you're okay," he says through the door.

"Yeah, great help you are," I answer.

Echo returns to the oversized mattress, flopping down on it, then his front paw pats it for my return. All I can look at are those huge, curled talons.

Despite the unsettling situation, the last thing I want is to anger a gryffin. So, I take a seat on the edge of the mattress, tucking my legs beneath me, and glance at him.

"You know, I've never been this close to a gryffin before. In fact, you're the first I've seen. Back in South Africa, there are so many different creatures, but your kind is not one of them."

He studies me, holding me in his eyes. They are pools of gold that captivate me. There's intelligence behind them, but also his humanity, a hint of recognition that makes my heart squeeze.

"Can you understand me?" I ask, my voice trembling. "Are you in there, Eryx? I mean, I know you are, but can you hear me? And why aren't you coming out to talk to me?"

Echo's head tilts to the side, an almost child-like gesture of curiosity.

"I just want to understand and make sure you're okay, too," I say softly as his tail flicks around my waist, the fluff tip landing in my lap. I gingerly touch the unexpectedly soft tuft.

Silence stretches out between us, and his tail, still curled around me, drags me closer to him with ease. I don't fight it and lay down beside him, which is what he wants. I figure if I keep talking to him, he might eventually change into Eryx. I rest on my head on my bent arm, my back to him, his warmth radiating over me.

"I'm curious. Why do you want to keep me here and watch over me?"

There's no response, not that I expected it, but it would be nice. A few more seconds pass when a spark of electricity zips over my skin. The mattress behind me rises as if he's getting up.

I twist my head over my shoulder to see what he's doing, and my breath catches in my lungs.

Eryx is there, the gryffin gone, his piercing amber eyes meet mine, and a wide smile spreads across his lips.

"Hello, gorgeous," he purrs.

I melt on the insides at the sound of his warm, honeyed voice.

Blinking a few times, I'm slightly shocked at how quickly he changed back.

"I can't believe it's finally you again. Here I thought you were going to stay in gryffin form and keep me captive in this room."

I roll around to face him, my gaze traveling across the face of this gorgeous man, who also just happens to be completely naked.

He chuckles with a lopsided grin, the conflict in his amber eyes darkening. Reaching out behind him, he drags the blanket over his hip to cover himself. A gesture I can't thank him enough for because I can't stop staring.

"I'm doing this for your benefit," he teases, glancing down at the blanket. "Or else you'll lose control."

Flushing with fire, I can't even laugh. Instead, I give

him a small giggle, which sounds forced even to me. Who am I kidding? With us being fated mates, resisting him is becoming harder by the day.

He guides a stray strand of hair behind my ear while I'm fighting the urges inside me that have my fingers tingling to run them across his chest. Muscles on muscles. The man is built, and I hate how much I'm drawn to him.

I glance up to look into his eyes, my breathing picking up, and I'm starting to think that staying here with him like this is a terrible idea.

"My relationship with Echo is complicated," he says after a few moments of silence. "What he wants and what I want doesn't always marry up, but we make it work."

"You don't have full control of him?" I ask softly.

"Depends on the day of the week." He chuckles as though he's accepted this and now laughs it off.

I want to better understand it, but I won't push him, not until he's ready to open up to me.

"Thing is, when he takes over, I'm not always aware of what he's doing. Sometimes, he'll let me in; other times, he shuts me out."

I gasp, and he runs the back of his fingers tenderly across my cheek.

"It's okay," he reassures me. "He's not taking me over. We complement each other. Besides, he completely adores you... almost as much as I do."

Blushing, his words leave me giddy. Yet my thoughts are still stuck on the pain in his eyes, as though he's trying to brush the whole situation with him and Echo under the rug. Shifters don't lose control of their animal side or let them take control. Well, at least not the ones I've known. But this is something else with Eryx, something darker.

"So, last night, do you remember what happened?" I ask, curiosity filling me.

"Who do you think instructed Echo to eliminate those bastards coming for you?" He shifts closer. "I'll always keep you safe, Mina. You can trust me."

Can I? I don't know, especially if he can't always control his gryffin, right? Besides, I feel horrible knowing I'm keeping secrets from him and his brothers. My chance to investigate the Vanguard Manor went out the window during the party, and just thinking about it has me tensing.

"Anyway." Eryx's voice is soft, drawing my attention back to him as he continues, "Earlier, you asked me why my gryffin and I kept you in the room, watching over you."

"Yeah?" I ask, leaning in closer with curiosity. "Why's that?"

His hand is on my arm, stroking over the sleeve of my dress, sending delicious shivers down to the pit of my stomach.

"I want you to know that I won't rush things with you. I don't want to scare you," he says, his expression full of sincerity. "My intention is to take my time, draw out our time together, and make you feel comfortable. That way, you'll never leave us."

My heart shatters. It also makes me slightly swoon

that this powerful, terrifying, and unpredictable man is showing me a side to him that is tender and genuine.

"That's beautiful," I whisper, unable to voice that I still haven't decided what I'm going to do once I find out the truth about my parents. I'm trying really hard to keep a distance between us, even as fated mates, even with my heat flaring, but they're making it harder.

"I mean it, Mina."

For a heartbeat, I almost correct him about my name, but I remain still, my breaths racing at how easily he's making me lose my head. I pull my gaze from him and start turning away before I say something I'll regret. There's an ache in my chest, hating myself at that moment, scared to death of how he'll respond when he finds out I lied. I remind myself I shouldn't care, yet the ache burrows through me.

"It's okay." His hand settles on my arm when I have my back to him, his breath on my cheek as he leans in. "I don't expect you to feel the same way about me yet. That's why I'll take my time. But I also think we need to start being honest with each other as fated mates."

I freeze, my chest heaving for oxygen.

"Wh-What do you mean?"

"Want to tell me exactly what you are?" he whispers in my ear. "Wolf shifters rarely have magic that slides onto their skin like yours did."

## CHAPTER
# SEVENTEEN
### ERYX

Silence.

My little wolf girl has fallen quiet, so I clear my throat and ask her again.

"How is it a wolf shifter like you possesses magic?"

She's still lying in front of me on the mattress when she finally twists around to face me. There's concern etched into her brow, and I can tell she's wrestling with her answer. Lips pinched tight, she exhales as if she's come to a solution. I'm completely entranced by her, knowing I can stare at her all day and never be bored. She's spectacular and has me intrigued to discover all her secrets.

"In all honesty, I don't know," she answers softly. "I was born with the marks on my arms, which seems to be the source of my ability. My parents were both wolf shifters, and they said that there could be magic in our family bloodline, which might explain it."

Drawing in her scent deeply, searching for a sign of deceit. I find none. No perspiration, no shakiness in her voice. She's not lying and genuinely believes what her parents said.

Yet something doesn't add up, and I suddenly sound like Tallis, who should have been a private detective with how much he loves to dig up background on everyone he meets. The guy's got trust issues, but now, I'm wondering if he's onto something with Mina not telling us the entire story.

Flashes of last night play on my mind as I remember watching her fight, the blue of her sword glowing, alive with energy. There was a strength that pulsated through the air I doubted she even knew existed, but it had thumped under my skin like it was a living, breathing thing. Just as quickly, the sword she'd been using disintegrated and vanished onto her arm as if it were part of her.

Damn, I've never seen that kind of magic. I can't shake the feeling that this is so much more than a bloodline ability passed on through generations.

"Can I see it? The way the magic manifested into a sword, then slid back onto your skin, was astonishing."

Nibbling on the corner of her mouth, she hesitates. "No one knows about these. Only my best friend, and well... I guess you since you saw me."

"You're safe with me." The temptation to reach over and draw her closer heightens by the second, but first, I need to see her magic. "We're fated mates, and that means no secrets between us."

She swallows hard and takes her time, then pushes the sleeves of her dress as high up her arm as she can.

My gaze sweeps on the strange markings. It looks like

an ancient script I don't recognize, running down the length of her arms in a straight line. They have no color but are etched into her skin.

"Can I?" I ask, reaching for them.

"Go for it."

Under my fingertips, I can't feel them. Her skin is smooth, as if it's been painted on her skin, which isn't how they look. Yet a buzz of energy jolts up my arm at our connection. It curls inside Echo and me. Whatever the magic is, it's part of her and alive.

"Fascinating."

"They also glow in the dark." She says with a grin, almost excited as she rolls closer to tuck one arm between us, so it's shrouded in shadows.

True to her word, the marking gives a faint blue glow, and I'm completely hypnotized. If I thought she was fascinating before, I'm completely blown away now.

"Can you show me the sword?" I ask eagerly. I've seen all sorts of magic, but this is unlike anything out there.

Laughing nervously, she rolls onto her back and glances away from me.

"You're going to laugh at me when I tell you I don't know how. Don't get me wrong, I've been trying to master it, but I fail miserably each time I do. It comes out when I'm in grave danger. It's not like they came with instructions, and my parents were no help." She pauses for a moment, staring up at the ceiling, a change in her demeanor I've noticed each time she speaks about her parents.

Their loss has really impacted her.

"I'd never laugh at you. We'll figure it out together, but you need to share everything you know, okay?"

She swallows once more, which is enough to tell me she's hiding so much more. We've only just scratched the surface.

When she doesn't respond, I say, "You're not alone with this. I'll help you every step of the way."

Tilting her head toward me, she meets my gaze, a strong female staring at me with determination on her face.

"What if I don't want to find out more? What if I'm happy with things the way they are?"

"Everything happens for a reason, Mina. And from what I've heard, for all you know, you could be cursed." Tallis answers from the doorway.

We both twist to glance over to my brother, who strolls into the room, hands deep in the pockets of his pants.

Mina stills at his arrival, her breathing speeding up, those deep eyes tracing over his body. As aloof as she behaves, her body isn't hiding her attraction to my brothers... or to me.

"I doubt it's a curse," I answer. "The magic was protecting her, giving her the ability to defend herself."

"Maybe now's not a good time to talk about this," she suggests, pushing herself to sit up, her voice shaky. Her gaze darts between Tallis and me, her shoulders curling.

My brother, always with his detective mind, seems not to notice her discomfort, or he ignores it. He moves to sit down on the mattress next to her, his brow pinched from his concentrated expression.

Silence fills the room, but I have no intention of pushing her. I can see there's also pain in her past she's not telling us about.

"I'm not going to torture you," Tallis says, studying Mina. "But I'm curious. It's not every day you discover a new type of magic."

"You make it sound like I'm a lab experiment," she says with a half-smile, her gaze darting between us once more in that nervous way. "This is actually the reason I never showed anyone. They'll have a thousand questions, then they'll prod further. But how can I explain something I don't know?"

"Let's leave it for now," I say firmly, my gaze lifting to Tallis, who doesn't notice my subtle hint. He's too busy gawking at Mina, and I can't tell if he's going to lean in and steal a kiss or start interrogating her.

He reaches over, placing a hand on her bent knee, and something inside me growls—an inferno of jealousy sweeps over me—something that comes right from Echo. She's not pushing him away, and it's hard not to let Echo's jealousy tear through my chest.

Calm the fuck down.

"It's okay," Tallis murmurs. "There's no rush. We have all the time in the world to discover what you're experiencing." He gives her that spectacular smile that makes girls fall to their knees for him, and I don't hate him for it—far from it—but if he oversteps his boundaries and hurts her, we'll have a problem.

"Thanks," she says, then glances at me with a smile.

She fidgets on the mattress, a sheen of sweat on her brow. Is she that nervous? "Trust me, it's no fun having something weird about you stand out."

I can't help but laugh out loud. "You're talking to us," I point out. "We're the strange ones here. Look at me with a gryffin who doesn't listen to me, and then there's Tallis with his hellish fire that goes rampant when he gets angry and his over-the-top trust issues."

My brother gives me a deadpan glare. "That's not really that strange."

"It could be," Mina chimes in, her eyes sparkling. "Depending on how obsessed you are with it."

Snorting, I laugh and swivel on my ass to better face my brother on the other side of Mina, tugging the blanket over my lap to keep myself covered. "Tell her about the last time Khaos had a friend staying over. You flew halfway across the world to interrogate the poor girl's grandmother under a spotlight for hours to find out if she was who she said she was."

"Wow," Mina says with sarcasm in her voice. "That's intense. I'm definitely in good company then."

She laughs, and I love hearing the sounds she makes. I study the curve of her full lips, the way she occasionally nips on her lower lip. No girl has gained my interest as intense as Mina.

"Well, that was fun." She suddenly pushes herself up on her feet. "I better head off to my room."

Something glints in his gaze, staring at Mina's beautiful face, appearing surprised she's leaving.

She strolls quickly to the door, looking eager to leave us. I scratch my head, puzzled. Was she just placating us?

I honestly believed we were having a genuine conversation.

"See you upstairs," she calls out over her shoulder, then she's gone.

"Wait," I say, but she's gone with the quiet thud of the door, leaving us alone. The desperation I feel for her roars in my chest. I shove myself to my feet, fashioning the blanket around my waist into a kilt. I turn to Tallis, my shoulders bunching up, harsh breaths consuming me. "You scared her."

He bursts out into a chuckle. "Right, me. Not fucking Echo, who captured her and held her prisoner in this room." His eyes grow wide, making his point.

"My gryffin wouldn't have hurt her," I protest.

"She doesn't know that," Tallis counters, a frown capturing his mouth. "Did you see how she couldn't wait to get out of here?"

"All I know is that she was fine before you joined us."

"That's what you think." He stands as well, then we head out of the room. "You're being delusional. We just discovered one of her secrets, and on the inside, she's freaking out. That's what happened."

I scowl. She had been rattled, and I sensed her hesitation. Of course, she was uneasy.

"Don't fret." Tallis slaps my back as we head up the stairs. "She'll reveal her truth soon enough once we complete the Reflective Ritual."

"Tell me, do you actually like her?" I ask.

Tallis frowns. "More than I want to admit to myself."

"Well, for an incubus, you must have been using your allure for too long because you've forgotten how to show it. The girl almost died, and you already want to put her through the ritual? How about you give her a few days to get her head together?"

He pauses halfway up the steps, and I halt alongside him.

"Since when are you dishing out fucking advice?"

"I'm not going to tell you how to run your love life, but fuck, Tallis. The girl was gushing over you in there, and you're questioning her like she's your enemy."

His mouth opens, then hangs there.

"Yeah, exactly," I point out. "You're so afraid to open up and trust her, so you're going to push her away." I turn away from him, heading up. "But, hey, you do you."

Upstairs, we push out into the hallway, crossing paths with Khaos, who pauses mid-march and shoots us a confused glare.

"Where is she?" he demands, then scowls at me. I can see the bubbling blame in his gaze about Echo taking Mina.

Fuck him!

"In her room, I'm guessing," Tallis answers, his voice distant. "The guards at the door will ensure she doesn't leave the mansion."

My focus turns to Khaos, a simmering anger building within me from last night. I had a bone to pick with him.

"Don't think I didn't know what you were playing at during the gala."

The corner of his mouth twitches, a look of faux surprise on his face, the opposite of his smirk.

"You took me away from Mina with that bullshit negotiation story," I continue, my words sharp. "I know you wanted me to babysit your boring friends so you could sneak away from them."

"And you did an incredible job." Khaos grins, an evil glint in his gaze, like he always does when he gets his way.

"Yeah, such a great job that you distracted me from Mina, and she ended up hurt," I sneer. "So, really, everything that happened last night to her is on your shoulders, brother. And just so we're clear, if it wasn't for Echo tracking her down and saving her, I might not have gotten to her in time. So, stop glaring at me like Echo is a loose cannon!"

Tallis grunts a chuckle, nudging Khaos' shoulder. "He's got you there."

"Fine," Khaos growls, his eyebrows pulling together in a frown. "Just remember we're all on the same team here, and I'm looking out for her because she's all of our fated mate, not only yours." He takes off down the hallway, knowing I was about to blast him for his bullshit speech.

"That went well," Tallis remarks dryly.

I shake my head, frustration seeping into my bones.

"I'm going to help Mina. Whatever's lurking in her past, I'm going to find it and set it free."

Taking off toward the kitchen, I don't hear Tallis's response. Not when I had witnessed first-hand the dark fear on Mina's face. Whatever she's hiding, it terrifies her, and I'm going to be the one to fix it for her.

## CHAPTER EIGHTEEN
### BILLIE

A ripple of fear and lust tightens my stomach.

The walls of my room are closing in on me as I pace from the window to the door, clutching my middle. My body's on fire from the heat that's flaring inside me again. The moment Tallis joined us in the basement, my heart tripped over itself at being in tight confinement with two sexy-as-hell Dukes. Evidently, it was too much for me to take.

What I'm experiencing—the attraction to the brothers and discovering my fated mates—is the exact opposite of my plans on arriving in Finland. To make matters worse, they now know about my magic, but I tell myself it might be a good thing.

They already suspect I'm hiding something, so let them think it's my magic, which may distract them from me trying to research my past. If I'm lucky, they'll forget about the whole stupid Reflection Ritual.

Yet nothing changes the gnawing pain rising through me, taking me completely by surprise at how fast and hard it hits. Hours have passed, and the pain grows sharper. Even Helmi bringing me food for lunch didn't distract me. The plate of my untouched meal remains on the table.

Pausing by the window, I stare out at the woods, clenching my fists at the thumping pulse of my heart. I can feel the heat creeping through me, inhaling me. It's billowing with each passing hour, and it's freaking me out.

My breaths come in ragged gasps. What if this is the day I go into full heat, when I'm so desperate for my fated mates, I let them claim me? Then we're bound forever, and what would I do if I discovered they had a hand in my parents' death? Could I live with that? I doubt it... And I don't want to be bound to someone who I'll grow to hate. That would destroy us. But the worst part is that the idea of being with them intrigues me even more than it had a few days ago.

Which is fucking wrong.

A scream bubbles in my throat as I pace again.

Nothing's going to plan. Nothing makes sense.

Collapsing on the bed, tears prick the corners of my eyes at how out of control my life has become. I curl in on myself at the arousal that's going to ruin me. Closing my eyes, I feel broken and tense as another wave of excruciating pressure swells across my lower stomach.

Desire pulses through me as my mind floods with images of Tallis and Eryx down in the basement. Me between them. They're tearing off my clothes, and they lick me, suck me.

A savage moan scrapes the back of my throat as heat flushes my skin.

The force of pleasure dominates me. It crashes into me so hard, when I squeeze my thighs together, my whole body buzzes.

Why's my heat coming so fast?

I need to calm the hell down. Even the three showers I've already taken haven't helped. They eased the pain somewhat, but it wasn't enough. And it's not like I can call the Dukes for help, or I'll end up jumping them. Gods, I blush at the thought.

That's when an idea pops into my head that might help me, without any of the Dukes being any wiser about my predicament. I'm on my feet in seconds, frantically darting for the door and practically running through the empty corridors. I pass a few maids, but they barely pay me attention. Down on the ground floor, I thank my lucky stars that I haven't bumped into any of the Dukes.

And when I hurry into the bathhouse, a sense of relief washes over me.

I'm completely alone.

"Thank you for small miracles," I murmur under my breath, taken aback by the breathtaking view.

The bath area resembles a fairy tale carved out of stone, built to replicate a cave in the room, complete with a waterfall. The built-in half-pool, half-hot tub stretches the length of the long room. Walls glisten with natural luminescence, reflecting off the steaming blue water. Rich scents of minerals waft through the air while tall ferns and water flowers grow in the nooks and crannies of the rock walls. So beautiful.

I hurry over to the stone platforms against one wall, filled with towels, jars of salt, and oils. They've thought of everything, but I can't dawdle when I'm desperate for the ease the water promises.

With a towel in hand, I rush to the side of the pool and quickly discard my clothes in a small pile. With a quick glance at the door with no lock, I murmur, "Please don't let anyone find me in here." Then I dip my toes in, testing the water that's not clear enough to see the bottom.

I gasp at the high temperature. It's almost scalding, but in a way that promises relief. Exactly what I need. Slowly, I lower myself in, the water embracing me until it laps around my shoulders. It surprises me that the pool is so deep. Along the inside walls sits a stone ledge made for relaxing.

I submerge myself completely. It's hard to explain, but already the pain in my stomach eases. Floating there a moment longer, I enjoy the sensation of weightlessness that envelops me. For a fleeting moment, all the complications and dangers I've faced since arriving in Finland dissolve away.

As I drift under the water, I can't help but wish I could breathe underwater and stay submerged, hidden from the world above. It's a ridiculous thought, yet it's appealing and makes me think of my friend, Sasha. What is she doing now? How is her relationship with her Kraken boyfriend going?

With the growing need for air becomes too much, I push myself up, breaking the surface with a gasping breath.

"Certainly a pleasant surprise." The rich timbre of a male voice resonates behind me, causing me to whip around, my heart shuddering in my chest.

I come face to face with Tallis. He's already waist-deep in the water, not wearing a stitch of clothing. My nipples tighten at his sculptured torso. How are there so many muscles on one man, anyway? I don't even know where to look, but he makes the decision easy for me. He sinks into the water, taking a seat on the underwater ledge near the wall.

Finding my voice while my arousal flares between my thighs, I demand, "What are you doing here?"

"What I do most days at this time in the afternoon. I take a hot bath. It helps with my beauty regime as a demon," he says sarcastically.

I glare at him. "I call bullshit. You followed me."

"It's refreshing to be with someone who says it as it is and doesn't bother with all the formalities."

I raise an eyebrow. "Would you prefer if I called you, Your Grace? Would that do it for you?"

"I love your spitfire personality." The corners of his lips curl into a devious grin. "But if you're not comfortable sharing a bath, see yourself out." He glances at the steps in the pool, then the door across the room.

I glare in his direction. "You'd really like that, wouldn't you?"

"You have no idea," he murmurs.

I don't move because here I am naked near a Duke—an incubus, for that matter—and all I can do is drink in his incredibly handsome features. By the wicked grin and the tensing cords in his throat as he swallows, he knows the effect he has on me. I clench my teeth, my chest sticking out of its own accord because my body does that... it betrays me around the Dukes.

Tallis is the opposite of Eryx, darker, unpredictable, and the kind of man who'd most likely enjoy seeing me suffer.

"Well, the pool's big enough that we can enjoy it from different ends," I say, feigning nonchalance. I glide casually through the hot water away from him, as if I'm not bothered by his presence or that we're both naked.

The heaviness of pain building inside me rears its head more viciously and so intensely. I'm nearly brought to tears, but I'll go to hell before I show him. Being mostly underwater, I pray he can't detect my scent. I'll stay in the water until I turn into a prune before I get out first.

I've barely taken a few strokes when something like a super-thick rope snaps around my ankle, making my heart leap into my throat. Panicking, a yelp leaps from my lips, and I'm suddenly wrenched backward, submerged underwater, and dragged all the way back to Tallis.

Fury billows inside me as I splash around to catch my balance. Water fills my mouth, and I finally come back up, spluttering. The cord is still tightly on my leg, refusing to release me. Finally, blinking water out of my eyes, I sneer.

"You asshole."

When I see his face and his body, instinct tells me something's terribly wrong. That's not the Tallis I know reclining in the pool. I let out a small scream, flinching backward at the sight of him in what I can only guess is his demon form.

Horns jut from his head, a hybrid between demon and stag, twisted and protruding in layers like layered branches. They are captivating. Shadows linger under his dark eyes, accentuating the intensity of his stare, that rugged jawline, the dimple in his chin, the thick brows—everything about him screams primal allure. With a horrifying shock, I realize he's more darkly beautiful in his demon form, which I never thought could be possible.

The last thing I need is to be turned on even more above my relentless heat.

I'm breathing harder, my pulse in my ears.

My gaze lowers over the sharp silver-black scales on his broad shoulders that funnel down his arms like armor. They reflect the water's glow, emphasizing his muscles. Somehow, they seem bigger, more pronounced than in his human form.

Clearly enjoying seeing me shocked, he parts his lips, and a wickedly long tongue pushes out and licks them. A shiver slides right between my thighs as if it were his tongue.

*Get a hold of yourself.*

I shift, but I'm tied in place by what I now realize is his tail, still coiled around my leg.

The dark gleam in his eyes taunts me.

"Nice look," I say, filling my voice with sarcasm. "Did you get dressed up just for me, or is this your usual bathtime attire?"

Those devious lips pull into a smirk as he leans back,

clearly making it clear he owns the place. "I can tell you like me in this form better, which surprises me."

I cough, almost choking on my breath. "Goes to show you don't really know me."

"I learn something new every day about you. The quickening of your breath, the dilation of your eyes, the parting of your lips lets me know everything you're trying to deny."

A laugh spills from my mouth at his audacity. "Don't mistake my fear for arousal. I know exactly what you are... dangerous."

"Good, then you know what you're getting into. But I'm guessing you like that, don't you?" His eyes glint with a hint of amber, as though deep down there's a fire from the pits of hell burning.

"You wish," I huff. When I reach under the water, feeling for his tail around me, it feels almost leathery to the touch. I push it off me with determined force.

"Come, take a seat and rest," he finally suggests, his voice unusually gentle, his demon gaze still on me. "This place is where I can be in my demon form and be relaxed. The staff tend to run screaming when they see me this way, especially at night."

I decide to push through the water away from him and settle on the ledge across the pool from him, at least ten feet away, giving us ample distance to chat safely. Besides, I need to focus on calming my breath and quieting the intense pulse that threatens to betray me. Especially with my thoughts channeling on how extraordinary and powerful the rest of his body must look.

He throws his head back, laughing, the sound echoing in the cavernous bathroom. I really hate him for getting under my skin and enjoying every moment of it.

"You know, I saw the marks on your arms the first day you arrived," he admitted casually. "I saw them peeking out from under your sleeves, but had no idea they were magical."

I study him still reclining, the steam around him rippling off the pool's surface. "And now you still think it's a curse?"

"It's possible," he replies. "I've seen marks on people who've been cursed."

I stiffen in my seat. "Marks like mine?"

"Nothing like what you have." He shakes his head, and I slouch once more, watching his tail emerge from the water, splashing as it dips in and out like a sea serpent. "Just saying it's not to be dismissed. Or that your parents didn't tell you the truth about your magic."

My shoulders shoot back. "My parents would never lie to me!"

He lifts his hands in defense. "I get it... parents think they mean the best, but they can also hurt us, thinking they're doing the best. Hell, look at my parents. My father went missing, and my mother relocated to a private location where she could deal with the loss of her soulmate or succumb to death. We were abandoned, just like that. That shit almost destroyed my brothers and me, if it hadn't been for our grandfather, who took us in."

His words hit me hard. Especially the part about being bonded to a fated mate was so intense that their loss could spell my own. Another reason I wasn't ready for such a commitment.

Tallis slides off his ledge, his attention on me, a predatory shine in his gaze taking over as his muscles flex.

I barely have a moment to react when he dives and disappears under the water. His movement is so fluid, so seamless, that panic slams into me that he's coming for me. A cry in my throat, I start to scramble away just as the water churns and bubbles rise. Backed against the wall, the edge of terror swallows me, and I catch a flash of movement of something dark in the water right at my feet.

Suddenly, powerful hands are on my knees, pushing them apart, his head bursting from the water, still in his demon form. Droplets cascade down his face, those dark eyes like opals and aflame with desire.

I gasp with him in front of me, my heart close to giving out. We're inches apart, our bodies almost touching.

"I don't enjoy being so far away from you," he purrs. "I could barely hear you from all the way over there." His devious smile is devastatingly hot as he licks his sharp canines.

I'm on the brink of losing myself to him... to the heat diving between my thighs.

Opening my mouth results in no words rushing out, then I push out a response while fighting his hands off my knees.

"I... I think it was fine."

But he's not moving. His breathing speeds up, and up

this close, I'm completely powerless against the fire leaping off his body to my brain, which cannot think of anything beyond where he's touching me. Or where his tail is sliding up a leg.

My skin tightens, and fear I'm going to lose control twists inside me.

"I'm starving," he whispers in a thick voice filled with hunger, and a vein throbs in his neck. "I haven't eaten for days, saving myself for you."

His words and their intentions hang heavily in the air between us. They terrify me, yet I arch my back, thrusting my breasts against his chest. Because that's who I've become—weak to my heat.

For so long, I've fought to remain focused and find my parents' killers, denying myself enjoying life. Now, every emotion drives me to let go. I'm shaking and have no idea how I'm supposed to get out of this.

The thing is, I'm not sure I even want to.

## CHAPTER NINETEEN
### TALLIS

Her heady scent invades my senses with a savage force.

I stare into her cerulean eyes, enjoying her full breasts against my chest as her body quivers, her gold necklace and pendant with her family crest cradled between them. Desperation to claim her overwhelms me, especially when I inhale her fear. There's something delicious about feeding on someone scared—the flavor is sweeter.

She looks at me with her frightful gaze, yet her body calls to me, responds to me.

"I-I'm not food," she says with a shaky voice. "I'm not fucking you to feed you, either."

A growl purrs in my throat, and I'm completely smitten with her fiery attitude. I've wanted nothing more than to have her fight me while I fuck her and show her how desperate I can make her for me.

Trailing the tips of my clawed fingers up her arm to

her chin, I tilt it back so she studies me. Her lips tremble, and I lean in, brushing mine against the tender skin beneath her ear.

"Who said anything about fucking? I can feed other ways, my little firecracker."

Her body pushes against me once more, even if she pulls her chin from my hold.

"Do you always come on this strong to anyone sharing a bath with you?" she snarls.

I sense her wolf just below the surface, begging to come out and play with me with her sharp teeth. Nothing I'd love more...

"Only when it's you, love." My tail slips up onto her lap, where she sits on the edge of the hot bath, her thighs clenching together. My cock throbs for her, my hunger close to turning me into a madman, and no one wants to see me lose my shit. Yet that primal instinct to pluck my fated mate out of the water and drive into her is unbearable.

"I can help you with your problem, and you'd be doing me a favor, too. Sounds like a win-win situation to me." Yeah, I'm a manipulative asshole, and she'll have to get used to that.

Her features pale, but her hands are on my chest, eager for a feel, no doubt. And who can blame her?

"When you're so close to me, I can't think straight," she murmurs.

"It's incredible, isn't it?"

She's shaking her head while I chuckle. "So, what do you say? Shall I give you a taste of Nirvana?"

Her breath catches, and my muscles flex under her touch. She pushes against me, standing up from the ledge. My tail curls over that curvy ass that's calling my name. He wants in on the action. Waves of heat roll off her and crash into me. She tilts her head to the side, letting her gaze roam over me.

"You know," she begins. "I've never met a demon like you before, especially not an incubus." She lets her voice drip with sweetness, maybe too much, giving her away. But I accept her feigned admiration, playing her game.

"I'm glad you think so," I answer, giving her what she seeks.

"Oh, you do." She grazes her fingers across my chest, the touch heightening my need to feed, my balls pulling up tightly.

She's so close, her head barely reaches my chin, so lifting her in my arms and spreading her legs would be so easy. The temptation is brutal to ignore.

In a flash of movement, she brings her knee up between my legs, but I shift my hips just in time for her to knock it into my thigh. She strikes me hard enough to know it would have hurt like a roaring bitch if she got my balls. I growl at the sharpness of her knee. For someone so small, she's got the bravery of a warrior.

That's all the distraction she needs. Shoving away from me, she dives into the water. Her body slices through the hot surface, swimming frantically to the other side.

I laugh out loud at her brazenness. Of course, I let her think she's getting away. Otherwise, she'd be wrapped around my cock already, but it's hard not to admire her tenacity. The excitement she stirs in me spreads all the way down to my groin.

I need to have her now.

A taste to get her out of my head, enough to sate my hunger.

Muscles flexing, I spring into action and dive under the water after her, shooting across the pool at a speed she won't expect. I'm on her in seconds, hands on her hips, and my sight on that perfect round ass is my undoing. Before she can slip from me again, I wrap an arm around the front of her shoulders as I burst out of the water behind her, bringing her with me.

She cries out, shoving her elbows against me.

"Nice try, but you've used up your one life. You've got a fiery spirit I'm enjoying."

Her ass pushes back against me, and my erection cradles against her cushiony rear. She gasps in response, thrusting her hips forward and away from me.

"What the hell are you packing down there?"

I spin her around to face me and walk her back until she hits the ledge against the wall of the pool.

"Are you asking to see it?"

She bares her teeth at me in an aggressive response, which only gets me harder. Shackling a wrist in my hand, I bring it to the middle of my chest.

"Look how fast you have my heart thumping. You're driving me to a breaking point. You have no idea how turned on I am right now."

"Funny, as I just assumed you had no heart." Her stare darkens.

Desire grips me, my dick hardening until it hurts, and

I can't tear myself from her side. I lower her hand in my grip down my body, letting her touch the muscles she's drooling over, her fingernails digging into my skin.

"I love when you hurt me. Now, let me guide you down to meet *them*."

"Them!" she gasps, ripping her hand from my grasp. Her shock is tantalizing, huge blue irises. Those lush breasts peeking out of the water grab my attention, and her dusty pink nipples are small and tight. She's caught between fear and arousal—just how I love my food.

My mouth waters, but I won't push her too much. She's mine to do with as I please, but I won't break her—not yet, anyway.

She's heaving for breath, her body swaying toward me, even if her lips are poised in a standoff expression.

I trail a finger along her cheek, and she doesn't pull away.

"Tell me what you want," I ask, holding back my growl billowing in my chest.

Her eyelids flutter, her chest rising and falling. My gaze takes in the full curve of her breasts, the glow of her wet skin, and her pouting lips make my mouth salivate. My fingers twitch with the urgency to touch her everywhere.

She shakes against me, a small moan in her throat. Her eyes are suddenly closed tight, and she's breathing heavier.

I lower my hands to her waist and lift her out of the water with ease, placing her to sit on the edge of the pool. Her sky-blue gaze flips open, flashing up at mine, and she draws in a sharp breath at being exposed in front of me. I take in the beauty of her body at a glance—lush breasts bouncing, the thin narrow landing strip of super light hair between the apex of her thighs.

Her hands snap forward to cover herself.

"You're the most beautiful thing I've seen. Never hide from me, understand?" I push her arms down by her side.

"I'm not your doll." She scowls at me, but with her eyes glazed over, she's not exactly herself, with arousal controlling her.

My muscles tense, my cock choking at her goddess body, at the slick trickling between her legs from arousal.

She winces, holding too still, not hitting me with one of her smartass comebacks. That says a lot. She's in the starting stages of her heat and in pain, yet she's stubbornly trying to hide it.

"You need to let me help you," I say, kneeling on the ledge to be at face level with her, her legs spreading for me, inviting me. I catch a glimpse of the slit of her pink flesh, and my balls draw up in anticipation.

Her sugary scent engulfs me, thick and delicious. I hold on to her gaze as she holds mine, but on the inside, I'm teetering on the brink of losing control.

"Why are you concealing the pain?" My words are thin as I barely hold myself together.

She shrugs, then her body breaks into shudders, her nails digging into the stone floor she's sitting on. I run my hand down her arm, feeling the curve of her breast, then skate my fingertips to the dip of her waist and the curve of her hips. My touch slides to her thighs, and she cries out, and she's got her hands on top of mine.

"Please," she pleads, pushing my hand between her legs. She's burning up, her skin slick with arousal. "If you're going to tease me, then stop, and please make the hurt stop."

I'm holding on by a thread. What I want, I take, but Mina is different. She brings something out of me I don't recognize.

Water droplets rush down her body from her hair, weaving down the valley of her breasts to the tips of her tight nipples, rolling down to where I want to be. Her wet hair sticks to the sides of her face, her breaths hitching. She's so petite next to me, almost innocent looking. A devil in disguise…

My other hand reaches for her breast, which fits perfectly in my huge palm, and my fingers pinch her nipple.

She gasps, and suddenly, she's gripping my hair and bending forward. Our mouths clash.

*Fuck.*

I kiss her back, my tongue sweeping into her mouth. She pauses at first—it takes practice to kiss a demon in my form and my long, forked tongue—but then she's sucking on it, seeming to master it quickly. That gives me hope for what else she can suck!

I take her lips, savoring them, ever so gently running my fangs over her flesh. She's shaking, moaning.

Breaking from her, I demand, "Lay back for me." I need to taste her, to have her come all over my mouth, to lick her cream.

Without hesitation, she reclines back, resting on her elbow, her body trembling. She spreads her legs as she nips on her lower lip. Her cunt isn't just drenched; it quivers for me. Those pink, swollen, and glistening pussy lips pull apart for me, and I grunt brutally. Her clit's engorged, and she's wonderfully bared for me.

Fuck me, but she's going to ruin me. I just know it.

"You smell so exquisite when you're soaking wet for me. You're going to come all over my face, aren't you?"

She gasps, and I love her shyness when she stares at me.

Then I'm between her thighs, inhaling her and pushing my tongue along her folds. Unable to hold back, I eat her ravenously, licking, needing more. Her scent, her taste. They fill me, wash over me, pouring into the emptiness inside me. Fucking has always been a quick way to get full fast, but foreplay is like eating the most decadent chocolate cake and taking my time, savoring every crumb.

She writhes, her hips bucking against me. I hold them down, loving to fight her for control. I press my mouth firmer against her and drive my tongue into her entrance, the length spearing all the way in, stroking her, letting her know she's mine.

She cries out, her hand on the top of my head, pressing me tighter between her legs. Fuck, yes, that sets me off. Hands on her ass, I lift her hips for better access and drag her closer to really dive in, needing every inch of her. Her slick coats the inside of her thighs, and her grip on my hair strengthens, telling me she's close.

"Grab my horns," I tell her, my voice muffled with pussy in my mouth.

The moment her fingers coil around my antlers, a

shiver rushes through my body and dives straight to my cock. They're sensitive like that, and I love having them tugged when I fuck.

I go back to enjoying her.

Her inner walls draw down on my thick tongue each time I plunge into her tight, greedy pussy. I curl my tail around one leg, and with my hand on the other, I push them wider, spreading her. Taking long licks, my hungry tongue slips back into her cunt.

Loving the sound of her moans, of her body writhing, I push two thick fingers into her core. She screams, her body arching. She squeezes my fingers, and I almost come. I realize feeding on her one time, tasting her, won't be enough.

I flatten my tongue against her and stroke her clit as I drive into her, dying for it to be more of me inside her. The louder she groans, the faster I eat. Grinding against me, her sounds become raspy, her hold on my horns powerful, and I'm ready.

I breathe her in, unable to imagine myself anywhere but having my face between her legs. Her scent, her candy-sweetness, and her pleasure pour into me, and I'm not sure I can stop.

"That's it, fuck my face like you need it to breathe," I growl, watching the way her cunt pulls down on my fingers, loving how wide I stretch her.

Mina shudders and cries out as she comes, and the sounds she makes are absolutely beautiful. I quickly replace my fingers with my tongue and lap up her slick as she thrashes, floating high on the orgasm rocking her body. I can't get enough of seeing her come completely undone all over my face.

Perspiration coats her forehead, her breaths race, but I'm not even close to being done. I'm hyped up, my hips rocking, and I lose control.

Shoving myself up on my feet on the ledge, I kneel between her legs, my large hand holding onto my two cocks that hurt like hell. I palm them faster.

Mina gasps, her eyes wide at finally discovering what I'm packing. I smell the fear on her.

"Holy fuck, you have two!"

Her fright only pushes me harder.

I howl with arousal as white ropes of cum spew out of both heads, and I lower them to paint her skin with my seed.

She licks her lips and studies me as if she's about to take them both into her mouth. I'll hold her to the promise in her gaze.

I keep coming and grunt at seeing her wearing my cum on her breasts, some drops reaching her neck. Growling, this is euphoria as stars dance in my eyes. With every drop out, I lower my gaze to my gorgeous firecracker, flat on her back, her legs spread and covered in my cum.

The perfect picture of how I want her.

Mina's gaze is on me, the corner of her mouth curling into a quirky grin.

"That's all you've got? I'm pretty sure there's a smidgen of bare skin on my elbow you missed."

I crack out laughing, which I don't expect, but she has a way of always saying the most unexpected things.

"That's just a practice run, my little firecracker. Next time, you're swallowing it."

Her mouth gapes open as I reach over for her towel and start wiping her clean. In truth, I can't remember the last time I built up to coming so fucking hard without anyone even touching my cocks.

# CHAPTER TWENTY
## BILLIE

*Great job, Billie!*

*Let the demon have his way with you. Ask him to touch you. Hold on to his horns as you ride his face.*

And god, he has two cocks! It is bad that it's also slightly arousing to think how he uses them?

My muscles clench as I stalk down the hallway, my frustration and embarrassment turning into a storm inside me.

I'm meant to focus on the job. Well, that's gone out the window when it comes to a sexy Duke wearing no clothes. Groaning under my breath, I shake my head, trying to dislodge the images of a naked Tallis in his demon form, jerking off his two cocks all over me. And I did nothing because I wanted him to do that. It was sexy as fuck, even if my mind was screaming to get out of there.

Yep, I've already gone too far. The heat's ruined me.

and for all I know, next time one of the Dukes makes a move, I'll demand he fuck me.

Sighing, I move faster down the steps of the mansion. My still-wet hair clings to my shoulders. My fresh clothes are comforting against me, but it doesn't remove the memory of his touch.

It's why I can't stay in my room a second longer, and besides, with it being late at night, I'm starving, and Helmi is exactly the person I need to speak with.

I move quickly, my feet practically flying over the plush rugs as I head down the myriad of hallways. The grandeur of the mansion still amazes me. The paintings on the wall, the carved high ceilings, the exceptional ornate chandeliers—the Dukes have wealth to spare.

As I'm about to reach the corridor that leads into the kitchen, something catches my attention through the cracked door of one of the mansion's entertaining rooms.

It's Khaos. He's impeccably dressed in a tailored suit, his deep brown hair swept off his face. He looks like a delicious candy. I grit my teeth at how easily I succumb to his rugged looks.

He's in a deep conversation with four other men, a growl hanging on his words, his shoulders stiff. Standing close behind him is Eryx, shoulders broad, a glare that would slice a person in half. He's ready to fight if he's ordered. I feel the tension pouring out of that room in waves, and I hurry past, even if I'm curious about what's going on.

I'm not going to spy because, knowing my luck, I'll get caught. So, I dart right for the kitchen, the image of

Khaos appearing in control and authority floating in my mind. He runs this place and the business, doesn't he?

There aren't many people in the kitchen. The place is spotless, with only one chef busy frying something on the stove. It smells heavenly of garlic and butter, and I'm suddenly craving garlic bread. I spot Helmi, her curls bouncing on her shoulders, busy storing clean plates on a metal shelf.

"Helmi," I call out from the doorway, my voice crackling with nerves.

She glances my way, her eyes growing in size with surprise at seeing me before rushing over. "Miss, is everything okay?"

"Yes, yes, can I talk to you privately?" I whisper.

"Of course, miss." She nods, wiping her hands on the white apron she's wearing. "Anything I can do. I can have anything you want cooked if you're hungry."

"Well, yes, I would like some food, but first, there's something else."

She takes my hand and rushes me out into the corridor, away from anyone hearing us. My heart's pounding in my chest, my palms slick with sweat.

"Is everything okay, miss?"

I nod, attempting to calm my racing thoughts. I don't even know why I'm nervous, but my hands are trembling, and my stomach is knotting up.

Taking a deep inhale, I say, "Are you still offering those..." I lower my voice, glancing over my shoulder and back. "Pills?"

Her eyes light up, her gaze beaming with an understanding of what I'm asking for. "Oh yes, I do. It's so easy, and you only need to take one a day. Let me grab them."

Before I can say another word, she's shot back into the kitchen.

Suddenly, I feel like I'm about to get caught, even though I'm not doing anything wrong. I'm simply going to suppress the heat for a little while to keep from acting like a desperate fool all the time. Then I can finally focus on finding my parents' killers.

The sound of Helmi's footsteps brings me back to reality, and I brace myself, finally taking control of a situation that's gotten completely out of hand.

## Khaos

I MARCH out of the meeting room, my jaw clenching, my blood boiling.

The conversation is fucking pointless and frustrating because there's little I can do. I can't bring back Darcon and his sons, and from the information I gathered from Eryx, who witnessed most of the event play out at the party, they initiated the attack on Mina. She's my fated mate, so their attack is a direct declaration of war against my family.

Yet his family's demanding justice and compensation. It always comes down to payment and saving face.

Fuck them…

They won't get anything out of me. Pulling my punches has been brutally difficult, so I left for some fresh air. I need space before I lose my shit.

Three of their family members are dead, and if they keep pushing it, their extended family will be joining them soon enough.

Making my way through the quiet corridor, I catch a familiar figure slipping into the atrium in the distance. A strange sensation stirs within me as I study the sway of her hips in her tight pants, and her shoulders are curled forward as though she's staring at something in her hands.

Curiosity has me trailing after her into the atrium, a peaceful haven my mother loved to visit. Vibrant plants spread over the stone pillars, the benches, and even alongside the lofty windows. Small trees with round tops surround the koi pond in the middle of the room, along with a couple of stone benches, and lily flowers float on top of the water. The place is brimming with blooming plants.

I rarely come in here as it reminds me too much of my mother, where she'd spend hours caring for the plants.

But now, Mina's at the pond, peering inside at the water, and being in her presence reminds me I've been so fucking busy with the missing information in our records, with the death at the party, with running the business, I seem to have forgotten to spend time where it most counts—with my fated mate.

"You seem lost in thought," I murmur, breaking the silence.

She spins abruptly, a startled look on her face. At that moment, she swallows quickly, as if she's just eaten something, her hand rapidly shoving into the pocket of her pants. Her cheeks flush, as if she's been caught. What is she up to?

"Khaos," she states with an edge of surprise in her voice. "You look ready to kill someone. Did the meeting go that bad?"

I can't help but chuckle at her blunt observation. Leaning against one of the stone pillars, I note that she's wearing nothing under a t-shirt. The fabric follows the curves of her breasts, her nipples pushing against her shirt. I can't unsee or think about anything else now.

Call it primitive, but our fated mate connection demands I dominate her, to bring her into our family. Images flash of our first kiss, her body flush against mine, her moans in my ears, that inherently feminine sound she makes, and the intoxicating scent that invades me.

She's unlike any female I've encountered. She's wild, anything but submissive, and has me coiled up so fucking hard to claim her, I don't know how much longer I can wait to fuck her and mark her as mine.

She's staring at me, waiting for a response. Right...

"Needed fresh air before I ripped off someone's head, so I walked out of the meeting."

"Ouch!" She raises an arched eyebrow, her hand still in her pocket. "Go on."

I motion with my chin for us to move to a stone bench. In such close proximity, it takes all my willpower not to draw her against me as she sits on the far end. Her sugary scent floats in the air, and it's enough to fog my brain and confuse my thoughts.

"What's going on?" she presses.

Squaring my shoulders, I murmur, "The meeting's with Darcon's family. The ones you were... involved with at the party before they died."

Her face pales. "*Involved* is a very mild way of putting it. So, what do they want? Make me pay for that asshole trying to rape me?" Her voice darkens.

Anger brews in my chest that those bastards dared to hurt her. If they weren't dead already, I'd fucking rip them from limb to limb. My hands curl into fists, fury banging inside me to kick their family out. I've heard enough of their crap. They've wasted more of my time than I should have given them.

"Mina, you should never have experienced that." I place my hand on the bench between us, but she doesn't reach over. "It's my responsibility to shield you from the dangerous monsters who come for you. For that, I'm sorry."

"You don't owe me anything." She glances away from me.

"Is that right, my true mate?"

She makes a small sound in her throat that almost sounds like a moan, which I take as her approval, even if sparks of fire flare behind her eyes when she looks at me again.

"So, seriously, what do they want? Is this something I should be worried about?" She's gnawing on the corner of her lower lip, her cheeks paling.

"The burden falls on me," I state. "I'll fuck them up before I let anything happen to you."

Silence spreads between us.

"You'll do that, no matter what?" she asks meekly.

I nod, yet something unsettles within me. "Is there something you want to tell me?"

She blinks, and her lips part as if she's finally going to open up. Instead, she abruptly gets to her feet as if I touched a sensitive topic.

"Well, I better head to my room... I'm tired."

I study her retreating, my mind spinning with questions.

"Mina," I call after her.

She glances back over her shoulder with a furrowed brow.

"You and I need to sit and have a *genuine* conversation very soon."

Her grin's tight. "Yeah, sounds awesome." Then she's gone.

I scratch the side of my head, turning my attention to the golden koi in the pond, and a thump of frustration burrows through my chest. We have to find out who exactly she is because the very thought of not knowing leaves a bitter taste in my mouth. I'll fight to the death for my fated mate, but I expect the same respect back.

That means no fucking secrets.

I've barely driven the thought away when heavy steps approach me from the direction of the doorway. My heart quickens at the thought that Mina's returning. Except, upon twisting around, I find it's Eryx.

And he's storming toward me, arms swinging wildly by his side, a glare on his face.

What the fuck now?

His nostrils flare as he charges closer.

"You asshole. You left me there with those losers, just

like you did at the party. I'm not your damn babysitter." He's fuming, his voice climbing.

I fight the urge to chuckle at his overreaction, especially when my own anger lurks beneath the surface at having to deal with the entitled dicks in the meeting room.

"Otherwise," Eryx continues, his gaze narrowing to dangerous slits. "I'm never attending these meetings with you again. Get Tallis to be your lackey."

I lean back, crossing my arms, my mind heavy. Mina's face flashes before me, her startled expression, the way she ran from me. Her scent still lingers in my head, and being away from her is starting to get on my nerves.

"Are you even listening to me, or are you thinking about Mina?"

"You know me too well, brother. We have to uncover her past."

The fact that his first guess was her tells me that's where his mind has leaped.

He begins his rant again about me dumping him with guests, but I'm not paying attention... until he says words that seize me by the balls.

"We gotta be careful around Mina. I don't think we can trust her."

## CHAPTER
# TWENTY-ONE

ERYX

Watching Mina sleep has become a ritual. She thrashes, winces, and fights whatever nightmares darken her mind. It's the same every night, but I'm unable to pull myself away. I'm caught in this cycle of heart-wrenching torture, not knowing what she's going through, but not wanting to scare her by abruptly waking her.

Her dreams must be getting worse because so is her writhing and crying. She shoves a pillow onto the floor, her face twisted in distress, sweat on her forehead. She makes sounds that are almost words, except her voice is filled with desperation and fear that she never annunciates them. Yet the agony says it all.

My chest clenches.

Every night, I've come with the purpose of being here for her, even if she doesn't know it. Tonight, though, my purpose has shifted.

When she makes a sudden strangled sound, I jolt out of the chair.

I'm completely smitten by her, captivated by every little detail. From the way her eyes sparkle with intelligence, always looking at you as if she's working out how to play you, to the delicious curve of her lips and the sound of her laughter. Yes, we're fated mates, but to feel the obsession I do for her should come after we've secured our bond. Yet, here I am, teetering on the edge of going insane for her.

She's everything to me, to Echo.

Our world. Our life. Our essence.

Taking a seat at the side of her bed, I trace the contours of her angular face, admiring her beauty.

Beneath the moonlight streaming in from her bedroom window, her skin's pale, almost translucent, her mouth parted as she gasps in her sleep. Dark hair sits messily around her, sticking to her forehead. I reach over and tenderly brush a few strands away. Her skin is feverishly hot, and I'm drawn to her warmth.

She breaks into a sudden explosive scream, then snaps to sit upright in bed, her eyes slipping open. Fear's painted on her face from whatever horror she's still clinging to from her dreams.

Twisting to see me sitting there has her flinching, and she yelps.

My heart leaps into my throat at the sound, and without thinking, I reach out and grab her. She's trembling, her breaths coming in ragged rasps. I pull her even closer, taking her into my arms where she feels fragile.

"You've had a terrible dream, Mina. You're okay now," I whisper, stroking her hair.

I expect her to fight me, to shove against me, but she

sinks into my embrace, curling in on herself. She's breathing heavily, and I can feel her heart pounding against my chest.

Listening to the small whimpers in her throat as she tries to wake up and distance herself from her sleep, I hold her tighter. The desperate sounds she makes are like knives to my throat, each cutting deeper into me.

I inhale her beautiful scent—candy and sex—as it curls around my cock.

It takes a long moment for her to finally calm down and her breaths to slow.

"Are you okay?"

She wriggles out of my arms and grabs a pillow to hug to her chest, her eyes slightly red, her hair wild around her face.

"What are you doing in my room, Eryx?" Her voice is barely above a whisper and croaky.

Meeting her gaze, I have no intention of lying to her.

"Watching over you. Your nightmares must be terrifying. You looked like you were fighting an army of monsters."

She half-laughs. "That's so close to the truth, it's not even funny." Her weak smile escapes her lips as quickly as it came, and I want it back. I hate the pain in her eyes, the way she still trembles.

She slides under the blankets and pulls them to her chest as she rolls onto her side, glancing up at me.

"You can head off to your bed now. I'm safe."

A smirk spreads across my lips. I'm not ready to leave her alone, not when I've seen how much worse her nightmares are becoming. Kicking off my shoes, I feel the cold floorboards against my feet, then I climb onto the bed and under the blankets beside her, facing her.

"I'm going to stay a bit longer, in case you have another nightmare."

Her gaze widens, yet she's not screaming for me to leave. She wants me here.

"Alright, then. Well, if you're going to stay, can you tell me if you're the one who broke the lock on my door the other day? I'm also guessing you've been watching me sleep most nights?"

"Correct on both accounts," I admit, unable to suppress a smile. She's more observant than I gave her credit for, noticing even the subtlest details.

Her lips pinch to the side. "You know, that's kind of creepy, right?"

"Only if you make it creepy. I prefer to call it being protective." I lean back on a bent elbow on the pillow, studying her to gauge her reaction.

She half-laughs at my response, tugging the blanket up to her chin and settling more comfortably into the bed.

"Of course you do. You're just lucky I'm still half-asleep, or I'd have the energy to argue with you and force you out of the room. But you want to know the truth?"

I lean in closer, entranced by her. "Always."

"I like having you here." Her gaze, warm and sincere, holds mine.

My heart flutters in my chest, completely enchanted by her words.

"That's what I want to hear. Now, about your dream…"

Her lips tighten, and pain flashes behind her eyes. With a heavy exhale, she confesses, "I've had this stupid dream ever since I lost my parents. You'd think I'd make sense of it by now, but no. What's worse is that it still terrifies me."

I nod, captivated by the movement of her lips and marveling that I'm lying next to her without having given in to the hungry urge to ravage her already. The temptation lingers, pounding in my head, but that's not why I'm here tonight.

"I've heard it said that dreams are your brain's way of merging memories from the day. In your case, it seems to be stuck in a loop. I've lived a long time with nightmares, too. It's a fucking cruel burden."

"Oh!" Her eyebrows arch. "What were your dreams about?"

My heartbeat thunders in my ears, and I find it increasingly difficult to concentrate around her. Her hand rests on the mattress between us, and I fight the urge to reach out and pull her closer.

"I can't relive those nightmares," I finally say. "They're savage and devastating, gorgeous. I haven't had one in a couple of years now, and I won't subject you—or myself—to them. But don't change the topic. What did you dream about? I want to help."

"I couldn't possibly relive those," she mimics my tone, even lowering her voice a few octaves teasingly.

She always makes me laugh, but I know better than to push her for an answer. I understand too well how nightmares can hover and cling to you long after you've awakened.

As the moments slip by, silence settles comfortably between us. There's only the soft rustle of her breath. Her eyelids grow heavy and eventually close. Her breaths deepen as she falls asleep.

I watch her again, entranced by her peaceful face, my mind replaying our conversation over and over. Her presence, even while sleeping, captures me in a way I've never felt before. I remain by her side, not stirring, not disturbing her until I'm certain she's immersed in a deep sleep. I carefully retrieve an injection from my pocket, flipping off the cap. My heart races, and a surge of protectiveness swells inside me, staring at her calm face.

"Mina, my sweet Mina," I whisper, words that have been on my mind pouring free. "I think I'm falling in love with you. In fact, I believe I fell the first time we met." Relief ripples through me at finally admitting my true feelings. It's a truth I can't keep locked away. "This injection is to ensure what happened in the woods never happens again. I'll find you quicker next time."

With deliberate gentleness, I tenderly brush the hair from her neck and grab the tissue in my pocket with numbing cream. I rub it gently on her arm just below her shoulder. My hands are steady, even if my gut churns with conflicted emotions. Her trust in me is absolute. I wait a long pause for the numbing to take effect, then push the needle into her arm, my movement fast and precise.

She scrunches up her face and twitches slightly before scratching her arm.

I settle back, a smile playing on my lips, completely lost in the moment that I'd do anything for her.

"We are the perfect pair, aren't we?" I murmur to her sleeping form. "Broken pasts that haunt us, though I wish you'd open up more so I can help you with yours."

I shift to make myself comfortable, contentment washing over me. In my heart, I feel confident. Now, nothing will keep me from her. Her safety, her happiness, and finally making sure she stays ours has become my ultimate purpose.

## Billie

WALKING with purpose through the kitchen, just as I had the other night at the party, no one even notices me. They're too busy whipping up breakfast. The smells of baking bread and sizzling bacon have my stomach groaning for food, but there's no time for that. I weave across the room, my target the back door to head to Vanguard Manor.

Gripping the handle, I push it down, my mind whirling with plans for the day. Murmuring under my breath, I plead, "Please be unlocked."

"Fuck, no!"

A sudden booming male voice from behind me stops me dead. My heart leaps, almost snapping a rib in its attempt to break free. Shuddering, I twist my head around, prepared to lie my way out of this.

It's the chef, his face red, curses pouring from his mouth. He's just spilled a large pot of what looks like scrambled eggs all over his front. The other staff all scramble over to him, causing a commotion.

No one notices my presence, and that's my cue. I press down on the handle, and it opens easily. My breaths calm. If this is a sign of my day to come, bring it on.

Shutting the door, I don't waste a second and break into a run toward the front of the mansion, the building looming over me like a giant.

After Eryx's appearance in my room last night and his admittance that it's a regular occurrence, I know two things.

One, there's nothing I can do to stop him. I see the possessive glint in his gaze, and I'm not even going to try to understand why I don't find it repulsive. Or that he and his brothers are on my mind way too much.

Second, he's not going to leave me alone, which means before things become more chaotic with my truth coming out—because it always does—I need answers about my parents' killers… and if the Dukes are involved.

I move quickly while scratching the side of my arm, which feels bruised for some reason this morning. The explosion of trees flanking the winding driveway leading up to the front gates is my target.

But first… I pause at the corner of the mansion, taking in sharp breaths, driving away all other thoughts. Peering out from my position, I spot a guard at the front door, up on the front steps. He's standing with his back to me.

Dashing into the dense woods in the extensive front yard, I step onto a dead branch. The sharp crack rings through the air.

My body trembles uncontrollably, the shock of being

busted and dragged back inside plunging through me like ice. I dive behind a tree, gritting my teeth.

*Please don't see me, please.*

When I don't hear any voices or footsteps, I stick my head out. The guard's not even looking my way, still in his own little world.

*Keep up the good work, universe. You owe me one from the other night from having Tallis join me in the bath as my heat flared.*

I run again toward the front gate, concealed by shadows and trees. Glancing over my shoulder, no one's following me. I only catch glimpses of the imposing mansion, with the numerous lofty windows, knowing that three of the most dangerous mercenaries in Finland live there—my fated mates.

Pausing in the shadows, concealed from the guard at the front gate, I take a moment to collect my thoughts and slow my breaths. He's alone, staring out beyond the wrought-iron gate toward the Vanguard Manor. The tops of the lofty metal gate are fashioned into pointed blades, stone wolves sitting upon the pillars flanking the entrance in attack poses. Ivy has crawled half up the stone, ready to swallow it all, which is extravagant.

Running my sweaty palms down my leather pants, I push aside my fears. With a swing of my hips, I saunter toward the gate, chin high and exuding confidence.

I learned from the best—the Dukes.

The guard with sandy blond hair swings around abruptly at my approach, his gaze narrowing on me.

"Morning." I flash him a casual smile.

But he's not grinning. His expression turns sour and all serious.

"What business do you have here? You're not permitted to leave."

Keeping my tone light, I tamp down the nerves bubbling underneath.

"Don't tell me you forgot Khaos telling you I'm headed into the Vanguard Manor this morning. I'm helping Clark with a bunch of interviews for a critical project."

"I've heard no such thing." The man's brows pinch together. "You better return. No one leaves without instructions from the Dukes, especially their fated mate." His shoulders bunch up to make himself appear bigger.

I huff dramatically, partially irritated that he had to add the fated mate part. Does he think that's an insult?

"Fine, so you want me to wake up Khaos and bring him back here to tell you himself? How do you think he'll react that you can't do your job and forgot his instructions?"

His eyes are spinning like wheels... Good, let him doubt himself.

"Personally, I don't want to wake him up. Have you seen how grumpy he gets in the morning? He's worse than a grizzly bear, and he might even decide to eliminate you for wasting his time. I've seen it done. And it's not going to look good for you when I inform him you caused me to be late for reaching Clark. You know how crazy Clark can get."

He sneers and pulls out a walkie-talk, asking someone for Clark.

*Oh, shit, shit, shit.* A chill drops right through me.

"Clark's occupied and not to be disturbed." The male voice on the other side comes across as crackly. "He's in a pissy mood as nothing's going to plan."

"See, told you." I jump in, seeing my opportunity. "And me being late is making it worse."

Sneering under his breath, he hangs up, and with a clenched jaw, he opens the gate and lets me through.

"I'm watching that you go there and nowhere else."

"Of course." Quickly rushing toward the Vanguard building, I'm keenly aware of his eyes on me.

At the first door, I slip inside, my heart racing with panic that he'll finally speak with Khaos or Clark and find out I lied. Well, that's a problem for another day. My senses are on high alert as I rush down the dark corridor, not knowing where to start my search.

A few people in business attire are bustling around, too occupied to even notice me. Whatever the guy on the walkie-talkie was talking about was real. There's a chaotic buzz in the air, and I take advantage of the moment. That also means avoiding anyone working here.

Speaking of people, two come around the corner at the end of the hall. I dart into the first room, which happens to be a storage room. Cramming myself in there, I hold my breath and wait for them to pass, listening to their footsteps and voices fade.

Then I'm out and on the move again.

I swear I'm going in circles. The layout of this building is confusing as hell. I check room after room, after listening that no one's inside. Frustration tangles through me when I discover nothing but empty offices and a small kitchen with a guy at the sink with his back to me. I was out of there.

Close to approaching someone to ask for a map of the place, I slip open the next door. The room is piled high with messy files, metal drawers, and an old-looking computer. My heart leaps, and I scurry inside, shutting and locking the door behind me.

Then I breathe easily. This has to be it, though whoever had been here last left it in a mess. I dive in to make sense of what I'm looking at.

It's musty smelling in the room, and I hold back from coughing at the dust. With time limited, I slide into the chair in front of the screen, which is flickering on a login page. Sighing, my fingers fly over the keyboard, and I type in the names of the Dukes, one after another. I even try, Echo, but each attempt gives me 'Access Denied.'

Shit.

I keep trying passwords, anything about the Dukes I can think of, but each time I failed, the more I grew ready to throw the keyboard through the monitor.

I'm suddenly on my feet, taking a deep breath. "You're dead to me." I sneer at the computer, then I turn to the cabinets.

In no time, I'm pulling the drawers wider, seeing most of them are already open, and rifle through the contents. I scan documents from what I gather is a recording system with names, dates, locations, and a code allocated to them.

I'm pretty sure I'm looking at printed lists of mercenary hits they've arranged, and those codes are for certain mercenaries. I don't have the main list for those codes, but even just finding my parents' names here would be a ginormous step forward.

So, I settle and dive in.

Hours pass, maybe days for all I know, since the room has no windows. The room becomes a whirlwind of paper and ink, my mind swirling.

My back aches, and my eyes are on the verge of tears at discovering nothing. I'm on my knees on the floor, surrounded by the chaotic evidence of my relentless search, and I can't believe what I'm seeing. The two sheets of paper in front of me, with dates on either side of my parents, have a glaring gap. There are no dates for any hits during that two-month period.

How can that be when I haven't seen that kind of gap across any of the other papers? It's like those papers were removed. Maybe whoever scoured this room before me was after the same thing, and they took the evidence—my evidence.

Up on my feet, I rush back to the computer, convinced I'll find the missing information on there. Right, password. I lean back in the seat, thinking about a password, when I spy a drawer under the table, far from the edge. Unless you're leaning back, you wouldn't see it. Pushing myself forward, I grab the handle and yank, but the wooden table gives a groaning protest.

"Fine, play hard to get."

Rapidly, I retrieve the bobby pin from my pocket I took from my bathroom for such occasions. I jam it into the lock and have it open in seconds. Inside, I find a small notebook. After flicking through it, I land on a password scribbled down.

*ClarkTheGenius47*

Puke. What an arrogant ass.

In seconds, I have access to the files, and I'm speeding through them, sorting by dates. Just like the papers, there's a gap during my parents' killing of missing information.

What the hell? I shift in the seat, frustrated. It makes no sense.

So, I search for Bryant Ursaring, but the search comes up empty. No results. Nothing.

"Fuck!" I mutter.

Checking on my parents' names, and even myself, it comes up blank.

Slouching in the chair, my stomach's starting to hurt because something doesn't add up. How can Bryant not come up at all? It's as if he's been wiped from the system. But my dad was a mercenary, and when I check their database, narrowing it down to South Africa, he doesn't come up. However, I notice the names of their friends.

Irritation and confusion rage in my head, twisting inside me until I can't think straight.

How can there be no information? It's just not possible... it can't be.

I delete the history of my searches, then drag myself out of the room, pulling the door closed, my mind consumed by the lack of findings.

"Can I help you?" a raspy male voice comes from behind me. Clark appears to have just turned the corner, and he stares at me quizzically.

All the blood rushes to my head, and I nearly pass out from the shock of him busting me.

"I'm allowed to be here," I blurt, squaring my shoulders, berating myself internally for sounding guilty.

Clark scowls, stepping into my personal space, his narrowing eyes scalding me. Talk about being hostile.

"Why should the Dukes trust you? You're sneaking around, not revealing your real name or who exactly you are." His voice drips with disdain.

He hates me, so I refuse to give him my fear. I'm not a fearful little girl, quaking in my boots.

"Oh, come on, Clark. Since when did you become the Dukes' watchdog? I prefer you when you're just the grumpy interview guy." My words are laced with sarcasm.

His face turns a shade redder. Not a fan of my humor.

"Don't play games with me. You have no influence over me. My concern is the Dukes and protecting them from fraudsters."

I choke out laughing. "Are you calling me a fraudster?"

With his shoulders rising, him not backing down, a sliver of panic spreads through me that he won't be so easy to con.

"If the shoe fits." He huffs and straightens as if he's said something below his standards. Running a hand through his hair, he glares at me. "What are you really hiding from the Dukes?"

"You tell me, genius boy! Anyway, enough of our lovely chat, but I have other things to do back at the mansion."

His expression changes, and suddenly, he's barking orders to the guards to join us.

Shit, what now?

"I have ways to make you talk, and by the time the Dukes find out, they won't care, because you'll reveal everything. Or you can be honest and speak up now about why you're in this building."

I swallow hard, really loathing him now. The pressure pushes down on my chest, and the moment I catch sight of the guards coming up the corridor, dread engulfs me because I have no doubt Clark will be true to his word. And I'm not exactly a fan of torture.

"I... I was just looking for where the Reflective Test is. I heard someone mention it's in the Vanguard Manor. I wanted to see what it entails before I did it because I've never heard of it before." I shrug. "So, are you happy now?"

His expression twists, his sour frown stretching into a disturbing smirk.

"Good, good," he says, lowering his tone. "I'll take you to it right now. It's all set up and ready for you." He glances at his guard. "Go notify Khaos that we're holding the Reflective Ritual now at the request of our guest, Mina."

"Wait, no, I didn't say that."

He snatches my elbow and hauls me down the hall, his grip firm and relentless.

My heart's in my throat, and I'm shaking. Why the fuck did I have to open my fat mouth? Now look at me... I've walked right into the wolf's den, and he's got his teeth bared.

"Behave, and maybe we can sort out this mess." He looks me up and down. "And move on."

Bastard.

I try to rip my arm from him, but his fingers are like iron, digging into me. Two more guards join us. Suddenly, it feels like I've just reached a dead end.

*Oh, crap.*

## CHAPTER
# TWENTY-TWO
### BILLIE

I'm wrenched from the Vanguard Manor, taken to the mansion, and forced into a room I've never seen before. My heart thumps frantically, but I rip my arm out of Clark's grip and end up stumbling forward to catch my balance.

"Take a seat, Mina. We'll wait for Khaos," he grunts, gesturing to the two leather couches facing each other in front of a massive stone fireplace.

Its empty grate is like a gaping mouth ready to swallow me whole. I shiver at the thought. Nearby is a mahogany cabinet, and behind its glass doors are decanters filled with amber and ruby liquids. Crystal glasses and tumblers are on the same shelf, while a collection of alcohol bottles fills the rest.

I turn to take in the room—the lofty windows, the cinematic paintings of landscapes that hang on the walls, so lifelike they are like openings into another world. Normally, I'd be in awe, but right now, it feels like they're closing in around me.

As elaborate as the room is, what holds my attention is the full-body mirror in the middle of the room. It's unlike anything I've seen before—a thick frame made from what looks like raw wood, untouched by any tools. It's uneven, with knotted protrusions and rough edges. The mirror stands upright, seemingly with no support.

My arms are trembling at my sides, well aware that whatever power it holds, it's going to be used on me in the Reflective Ritual.

Spaced out around the mirror is a circle of thick, white candles waiting to be lit.

Turning to Clark, he's by the doorway, speaking with a guard outside, and aside from windows, there's nowhere else to go.

That caged feeling sweeps over me as I pace the room, thinking I could definitely make the jump from the third floor through the window safely, especially in my wolf form. I'm folding my fingers over one another as I stare out into the woods, falling short on how I'll get out of this without digging myself deeper.

Maybe this is meant to be... if the information in the Vanguard Manor is anything to go by, there have been no hits put out on my parents. Except, I don't trust it. I don't believe Bryant wasn't from Finland.

So, perhaps this is the time to come clean and get the Dukes to help me with the missing data. Coldness runs through me at the thought, convinced they won't share anything with me. Mercenaries aren't exactly known for divulging their secrets or kills.

Pacing across the room again, I flop down on the lounge, eyeing the mirror. Already I dislike the thing.

My fingers drum nervously on the armrest just as Khaos marches into the room with a regal air about him, with power and danger. He scans the room until his attention lands on me.

My breath catches at his presence, my muscles stiff at how incredibly mesmerizing he is. Of course, they are the wrong thoughts, but the guy is my fated mate, and primal instincts are unbearably hard to resist. I just thank my lucky stars that Helmi's pill has tamped my heat.

I'm on my feet, standing tall in the face of danger, and I swallow. Nothing has prepared me for the feelings surging through me. I'm drawn to this man whose biceps flex against his sleeves and whose strong jaw clenches when he looks at me. The scent of him invades me in moments—woodsy and primal, fresh and akin to sex. It's like having my face against the curve of his neck and inhaling him. It leaves me shaking.

Clark's at his side, his lips twitching into a smirk that I loathe.

"Mina," Khaos begins. "I appreciate you agreeing to do this amicably."

Clark's still grinning.

I'd love to shove him into the mirror. I plant a smile on my lips.

"That's me. I'm not here to cause waves." I mentally brace myself for the worst when the truth comes out. I picture Khaos either calling for my death or throwing me into his dungeon, declaring me an enemy of their family. I've heard tales of the brothers killing people for far less than lying to them. The thought has goosebumps skating down my arms.

He strides across the room, a tight expression on his face.

"You want a drink to calm your nerves? You look frightened."

"Your Grace, isn't it best we just commence the test?"

Khaos doesn't respond to Clark, only holds my stare. My heart flutters while the cords of his strong throat flex, the angles of his broad chest pressing against his shirt. It's impossible to concentrate on anything but him.

"That'd be nice," I answer, sparks of anticipation rushing through me.

There's no ignoring my attraction to Khaos, and under any other circumstance, I'd consider myself blessed to be his fated mate. I sigh internally, knowing full well how contradictory I sound, but I live in the House of Gold and Garnet, where so many mercenaries reside. Killings have become almost commonplace, but that doesn't mean I want to be with someone who took part in my parents' demise.

He moves to the mahogany cabinet, where he selects a decanter with an amber liquid and pours some into two tumblers. The drinks glimmer under the soft light. Sauntering over, he extends one glass to me, the other cradled in his grasp. As our fingers brush in the exchange, a jolt of sparks rushes up my arms. My thoughts are swallowed by the time he kissed me at the party and how I couldn't get enough. Even now, I'm staring at these lips, wanting to taste them again.

I'm not sure what's going on with me, especially with

the pills dampening my heat. Dropping my attention to my drink, in the corner of my vision, I note Clark just standing there, watching us.

There's a sliver of pride that Khaos is including me in this intimate moment while Clark is noticeably left on the sidelines. A part of me silently revels in that fact.

"Here's to settling your nerves," Khaos announces, then lifts his glass to his lips. The soothing timbre of his voice is the opposite of the anxiety coiling in my stomach. He takes a sip, his pale blue eyes never straying from mine.

At that moment, it hits me how the calmness radiating off him lends itself to the almost supportive tilt of his head, as if he's secretly telling me everything will be alright. With it comes an unexpected strike of guilt when he finds out the truth. Will he still look at me with the same assurance? The same admiration I've grown accustomed to?

I push those thoughts aside, reminding myself that every decision that's brought me to this point has been a necessary step to my ultimate goal—discovering who killed my parents and getting payback, so that never happens to me.

Releasing a deep exhale, I sip the whiskey, letting its warmth slide down my throat.

As the scent of the candles Clark lights up fills the room, the heavy atmosphere of the room suffocates me, and I cough.

"So, how exactly does this work?" I ask meekly. "It's not every day you encounter a magical mirror." The grin on my face feels forced and heavy.

Khaos collects our glasses and places them on the small coffee table in the corner.

"This mirror is not an ordinary reflection," he begins. "It's been crafted from ancient magic, a gift to our family from a powerful sorceress centuries ago."

My gaze swings from the opulent artifact to the flickering candles while the word *sorceress* echoes in my mind. That kind of magic is powerful and, more often than not, deadly accurate.

Suddenly, I sway on my feet, knowing there's no way I can trick my way out of this.

"It's straightforward," Khaos continues. "If you're truthful, your reflection remains unchanged."

"And if not?" The question slips out before I can stop it.

He pauses, his eyes narrowing on me. "It reveals the lie."

My breaths come faster, and my fingers twist anxiously against my stomach where I hold them.

"You know," I murmur, panicking on the inside and my head starts to hurt. "Sometimes, there are reasons to conceal the truth. Reasons that are… justified. So, perhaps not all reflections in the mirror are truly accurate."

Clark makes a snorting sound from across the room, but I only care about Khaos' reaction. He studies me, holding his expression perfectly stoic.

For a long, breathless moment, I half-expect him to press me for more information on my comment. Instead, he reaches out and takes my hand in his reassuring grasp. His hand swallows mine, and being that close to him reminds me of how incredibly tiny I am at his side.

"We will find out," he says in a firm voice.

As we walk across the room, every cell in my body screams at me to flee, to escape the test, but wouldn't running confirm their suspicions? And worse, they'd have every reason to pursue me and treat me as a traitor. Either way, I'm screwed.

Before I take another step, I pause and glance up at Khaos, my throat tight, feeling the blood leaving my face.

"Maybe we shouldn't do this," I whisper as I pull my hand free from his. "I'm not feeling too well."

Just as I turn toward the door, it swings open to Eryx and Tallis pouring in, their faces eager. They pause there like a barrier to my escape.

"Hope we're not too late." Eryx meets my gaze, giving me one of his devious grins, my insides lighting up in response. Tallis doesn't say a word. He just stares at me, like he already sees right through all the lies I've created and told.

Something in my eyes prick, my heart constricting.

I can't do this...

"It won't take long." Khaos slips his hand into mine once more, drawing me gently into the circle of candles.

If I thought I had any chance of getting out of this, I've now lost that opportunity. All I can think is that I actually care about not disappointing them, about what the Dukes will say and do, aside from punishing me.

I shouldn't care... yet I do.

Facing the mirror, I stare at myself, and right now, I hate who I see. The red rim of my eyes, my chin doing that thing where it quivers. A girl who's been hiding most of her life. Who's been strong because she didn't know any other way to be. A girl who's barely survived or… lived.

My parents' faces flash in my mind's eye.

I didn't lose everything not to go through with my plan.

I have to do this for them.

Eryx and Tallis position themselves on either side of me for a better view because, of course, none of them truly trust me. And I'm about to prove them right.

With the person looking back at me looking no different, I say, "Seems to be all good from my end. I think we're done here."

And with all the candles, it's becoming unbearably hot in the circle. I take a step back when Clark's voice rings out, "That's where you're—"

But his sentence never quite makes it out, silenced by a mere hand gesture from Khaos.

Khaos leans in close to me, the warmth of his breath against my face comforting while I feel like I'm burning up in the pits of hell.

"For the magic to work, you need to spill blood," he murmurs, placing a small, sharp blade into my hand.

I turn to him, our gazes clashing. I can't find my response because I'm falling apart.

"Like most magic, it demands a sacrifice… a payment," he explains, then retreats.

The weight of the four sets of eyes on me is destroying me. But I remind myself of the horrors I've already encountered—my parents' death, my world crumbling. I've lost it all.

So, how much worse can this be?

Wearing my faux bravery, I straighten my spine, holding onto the blade with determination. Without a second thought, I slice the flesh on my palm. I hiss at the sting while blood wells up, and a line of red instantly rolls over the edge of my hand. The cut is deeper than I anticipated.

With a shaky hand, I press my bleeding hand against the icy surface. My other hand clings to the blade, the metal hilt digging into my skin. Drawing my hand away, I press my wound against the side of my shirt, applying pressure so the bleeding stops.

Blood drips down the mirror like a true horror show.

My vision blurs, the edges of the room wobbling with my fear.

I concentrate on the mirror's reflection, where the candle's smoke is behaving strangely. Where seconds ago, they were wisps, they now appear thin, elongated shadows that are stretching outward.

No one around me reacts to the change. Is this normal?

Gripping the blade harder, I keep staring at my oval face, at the ocean-blue irises standing out against my dark hair. Shadows are under my eyes from exhaustion, and despite my best efforts, I'm shaking on the spot.

"So, let's begin," Clark drawls. "Just answer my questions. First, what's your name?"

"Mina Steward," I answer with feigned confidence.

The artifact in front of me reacts almost immediately,

growing cloudy and fogging over until I can hardly make out my face.

My arms are shaking by my sides because I suspect this is the evidence showing that I'm lying. I can't bring myself to even look at the Dukes, not when my insides are shattering like someone's set a bomb off.

Those wisps of smoke from the candles in the mirror also darken, creating distorted forms.

"Liar! I told you not to trust her. She hasn't even told us her real name." Clark snorts, which snatches my attention.

But the Dukes concentrate only on me.

For a heartbeat, the room stills.

Clark's abruptness has me burning up with fury. I hold my ground, forced to look at him, at his nostrils flaring from his simmering anger.

"Who doesn't use a fake name in this line of work?" I snap, trying to sound casual, but I fail with my shaky voice.

He takes a menacing step forward, his expression painted with rage.

"Then you should have no problems telling us your real name and who your parents are. And why are you in Finland?"

Before he can move closer, Tallis lashes out with his arm, landing a brutal punch to the side of Clark's face. The force sends him sprawling onto the floor. Blood oozes from the gash on his cheek, and he's cradling it, whining.

"That's better. His voice was grating on my nerves," Tallis groans, the darkness deepening on his face, but I could have kissed him for doing that. Then he glances down at Clark. "Don't you dare speak in such a tone to our fated mate," he warns coldly. "Next time, I'll rip out your tongue."

Eryx exhales loudly. "Fuck, about damn time someone shut him up."

I want to cheer, except with their attention back on me, they aren't exactly in a cheerful mood.

Khaos looms closer, shadows playing on his face. His expression is so intense and unwavering, I fight the urge to retreat from him.

Of course, the Dukes are waiting for my response, and I've reached the point of no return. With a powerful voice, I let it out.

"My name's Billie Tempest. I have no siblings, and six years ago, my parents were murdered in cold blood in front of me. What else can I tell you? That I work at a boring data entry job and live with my best friend? That I've barely kept my life from spiraling out of control, terrified I'll be killed next?" I hadn't meant to sound bitter, but there's only so much a girl can take.

Instantly, the mirror pulses with life, emanating a glow. Strands of iridescent energy jolt at me, wrapping around me.

A startled cry spills past my lips as the energy digs into my flesh. I flinch to get it off me, but it comes and goes in less than a second, and I'm left stumbling, rubbing my itchy arms.

"Min... Billie," Khaos states questionably, with a dark voice.

Lifting my gaze, I catch my reflection. A cascade of

blonde hair falls over my shoulders, shimmering in stark contrast to the dark hue that was there just moments earlier. This... this is the color I was born with. How on earth did this happen?

A shocked gasp escapes my lips.

"It suits you better this way," Eryx remarks.

"We have more questions," Tallis states, but the rest of his words become background noise, drowned out by my pounding pulse.

Because it's not just my hair that seizes my attention to the mirror, but something that makes my blood run cold. My stare fixes on the billowing wisps from the candles that have now twisted into the shadowy monsters from my nightmares.

Shadowy creatures are lurking ominously in the room's reflection, closing in on me.

I can't move, can't speak.

Khaos is calling my name, and I think he's touching my shoulder, but I can't look away.

Then in my horrifying-induced nightmare comes-to-life terror, the tallest of the monsters, just like in my dreams, the one with the glowing white eyes, thrust toward me. His bony, clawed hands break the barrier between the reflection and the room.

That itch deepens over my arms as panic collides with me.

I flinch back, a scream ripping from my throat. My feet stumble, tripping over myself. My heart hammers so loudly that it drowns out the Dukes shouting at me.

Panic has me tightening my grip on the blade, still in

my grip, and I'm slashing it out blindly, trying to fend the attacker off as they pull themselves out of the mirror.

"You can't be here... you can't be real." But he doesn't stop and is coming for me.

I can't breathe quick enough, and my chest's heaving.

"Seal it!" Khaos roars somewhere in the room. Tallis and Eryx rush to blow out all the candles, but they're not pulling away or reacting to what I'm seeing.

Then he lunges at me.

A raw, primal scream tears through me, replicating the dread consuming every inch of me as I retreat, tripping over the candles. Before I can even make sense of what I'm seeing, my magical swords are floating in front of me.

I drop the small knife and clutch them instead. Then I'm slashing at the escaped monster.

"Billie, stop," Eryx's bellowing, but I won't.

My sword rushes right through the attacker across his middle, slicing into him as though I'm cutting air. Breathing comes in shallow, panicked gasps. But just as I swing my arm for another attack, he disintegrates, dissolving into harmless tendrils of smoke, retreating into the mirror.

Suddenly, I feel hands on me, warm and solid, drawing me back. I wrench myself free for a second, believing it's another monster sneaking up on me. I whip around, my glowing swords raised, and my muscles tense. My pulse is on fire, thundering in my ears.

But they aren't attackers.

It's only the three Dukes standing there, their mouths and eyes open.

My skin's prickling, their terror, their accusatory glares studying me like I'm crazy. It's too much to handle. The room spins just as my swords fade away, sliding from my grips and slipping back onto the skin of my arms. My knees are already buckling, and I sink down on them.

Everything spins. Everything's too much.

Suddenly, I'm in Khaos' arms. He rushes me over to the couch, barking orders for his brothers to bring me water.

"Billie, are you alright?" he asks, kneeling before me. "What happened? What did you see?"

Tallis and Eryx are at his side, not leaving.

I wrap my arms around myself and draw my knees up to my chest.

"Th-They're c-coming for me."

"Who?" he asks, his brow furrowed with worry, his hand on my knee. "Who's coming for you?"

Swallowing hard, I struggle to tell the difference of what's reality. Hugging myself and rocking on the spot, the words pour from my quivering lips.

"The monster from my nightmares. He's found me."

Darkness swells over me, and the next thing I know, I'm falling to my side and blacking out.

## CHAPTER
# TWENTY-THREE
### KHAOS

"She manifested swords," Tallis splutters, leaning forward on the couch across from me. "I know you told us, Eryx, but seeing them is just unbelievable."

"Something she insists she was born with." Eryx is grinning and looking proud of himself, as if he's responsible for her abilities.

I'm still coming to terms with it all myself, unpacking so much that happened during the Reflective Ritual, which we never completed. Hell, this whole time, she had us calling her a different name. I groan when I think about it, furious about being lied to, yet when I recall the fear on her face, the impossible battle she faced, my heart cracks.

She reminds me so much of the tormented soul Eryx had become when we saved him as a young child from his kidnapper, the psychopath who tortured him.

My ribcage constricts my lungs from the blame I've

lived with my whole life, the blame squarely on my shoulders.

He had been under my responsibility, and I fucked up.

*Sunlight filters through the trees on a warm summer's day, where the sounds of laughter and chatter fill the surrounding park. Families dot the area, kids running and playing. I stand there, just twelve years old, acting like an adult, which I hate. I'm on the verge of exploding with the rage curling in my fists.*

Stop being a child. Your parents would want you to care for your brothers.

*My grandfather's words stream through my mind. I had no intention of heading to the park, but he forced me. So here I am, watching my brothers and ignoring my friends.*

*Tallis is climbing a tree, joining other kids, always so social and making friends without effort. Eryx is four years younger than me and is content by the pond alone, crouching at the edge, tossing pebbles into the water.*

"Khaos," *someone calls out, and I turn to find Pedro and my other friends waving for me to join them across the park.*

*Glancing back at my brothers, they seem occupied enough.*

*Shit. This is so unfair. Without another thought, I choose my next actions based on what I want for a change. My brothers will be fine.*

*I run over to join my friends.*

*Minutes pass. I glance back for a quick check. Tallis is still in the tree, and Eryx is... nowhere in sight. My breaths rush out.*

*"Eryx?" I murmur under my breath, a sharp fear burrowing through me. Where did he go? When I don't spot him in the park, I frantically dart back to the pond.*

*"Eryx," I call out, panic in my voice that he's wandered off. My grandfather is going to murder me. Running around madly, I try to track his scent, but there are so many smells at the park, I can't pinpoint his. I'm back by the pond's edge, fear draining the blood from my face.*

*I rip my shirt off, my wolf growling in my chest, and dive into the clear water, searching desperately for him in case he hit his head or something. I don't know, but I'm freaking out.*

*He was last by the pond... He wouldn't go in, would he? He hasn't used his gryffin wings yet, so he wouldn't fly anywhere.*

*Beating my legs furiously, I scan the bottom of the pond, not seeing a sign of him. I keep searching. My lungs scream for air as I push deeper, the water stinging my eyes.*

*He's not down here.*

*Emerging with a gasp, I frantically glance around as onlookers gather around the bank.*

*"My brother, Eryx," I cry out. "I can't find him."*

*Before I know it, everyone in the park is looking for him, calling his name. My wolf pushes forward, and I transform, joining the hunt like a manic creature. Trying to catch his scent, I end up in the parking area. A black van speeding away from the parking area, its tires screeching.*

*Wait! Could someone have taken him?*

*My world spins, my stomach drops through me, and I fall apart.*

I fucking hate that memory, hate myself, hate that

it took us two months to finally locate the warlock who abducted my brother for his own personal experiments.

Fury sizzles down my spine at the past, at how much joy I took in watching my grandfather rip the warlock apart, one limb at a time.

That's the day I learned that in my position as Duke, I'd lost my privilege of being a child. I had my brothers relying on me. My grandfather couldn't always be around, and the bodyguards he'd appointed to watch over us were outmaneuvered by anyone who was truly motivated to get to us. That is why I had to step up and protect us.

Now, that same empty, hopeless feeling engulfs me when I think of Billie—about her suffering and us sitting on the sidelines, doing nothing to help her as she drowns.

Since she arrived, I had no idea how far I'd already gone in accepting her as one of us, how much I vowed to protect her. Part of my brain reminds me I don't deserve to feel happiness, not after what Eryx went through, and that now I'm repeating history—sitting back while my fated mate suffers.

Right now, Billie's passed out in her room, a guard at her door. The longing haunts me to go to her, to check that she's okay, to find out every goddamn detail of what happened earlier.

I lift my head to my brothers, who both watch me.

"You're doing that thing again," Eryx says.

"Yeah, where you murmur under your breath to yourself but don't actually say anything," Tallis adds.

I arch an eyebrow. "Well, at least you're both observant."

"So, what's our plan, then?" Tallis asks.

"We have her real name. I'll start researching her past and discover exactly who her parents were and how her ability is possible as a pure wolf shifter," I explain, my head still whirring with the events—her screams, her fear, her magic.

"You think she saw something in the mirror?" Tallis asks. "She was swinging those swords, staring into thin air, and I was seriously worried for her sanity."

"I just don't fucking know." I run a hand through my hair. "She seems to be under the illusion that whatever monster was in her dreams is coming for her. Notice how she called it a *he*? She might know who it is."

"Thing is, she hasn't gotten over the trauma of watching her family being killed in front of her, so isn't it normal to assume that whoever took them out would come for her?" Eryx is up on his feet, moving over to the fireplace, running his finger across the marble mantle. "She must know more about it because her reaction wasn't to run and whimper but to fight like she's been preparing for the confrontation."

"Wait," Tallis murmurs, reclining on the couch. "You sound way too logical to be my brother, Eryx."

"Fuck you."

"No thanks," Tallis grunts with a smirk.

The door to the room opens up to Clark marching inside with two guards behind him, not paying us any attention. He's a loyal worker, but doesn't know when he's crossing the line. Right now, he's pissed and barking orders at the guards on how to carry the mirror while he's meticulously wiping the blood from its surface.

"She has nightmares every single night, thrashing about on the bed like she's fighting to the death."

Tallis raises an eyebrow. "Did she tell you that, or have you been spying on her?"

Eryx grins his answer.

I exhale loudly, but there's nothing I can do to change my brother. His passion is you don't exist to him or he's in your face, buzzing like a gnat, making everything his business. There is no in-between. The fact Echo also adores Billie tells me she's not a horrible person.

I watch the guards and Clark take the mirror out of the room, and once they leave, I turn to my brothers.

"Listen, what we just witnessed was fucked. We know she's been lying to us, but just hiding her name is not a big deal. The real question is why? I have a horrible feeling she's in real trouble. I'll put feelers out with my contacts to investigate further." Standing, I'm too irritated, too worried for Billie to fully make sense of my emotions, so I'll focus on figuring out her mystery. "You two keep a close eye on her to ensure she doesn't leave the estate. If it's all in her head, then we'll work with that. If there's danger coming for her, then we can unearth the world to protect her."

"So, you're okay now with her not telling us the truth?" Tallis murmurs sarcastically.

"You tell me." I grizzle, keeping my voice casual. "Is your fated mate not worth a second chance?"

"Absolutely." He folds one leg over the other. "But have you asked yourself the question of why she's in

Finland? Why has the person she was visiting still evaded us when he was asked to come in for questioning about the missing information in our records we're investigating?"

Waves of annoyance roll over me.

Tallis shrugs. "Hey, look, I'm not trying to be the prick here, just the devil's advocate."

"Sounds to me like you want her to be guilty," Eryx butts in. "Just so you don't have to deal with trusting someone again, right?"

Tallis' chest rises and falls rapidly, the corners of his mouth pinched. "Is that your go-to every time I oppose anything you agree with?"

Eryx smacks his lips, leaning a shoulder into the fireplace mantle. "Only when it's so obvious you're letting your fear make your decisions."

"Right, says you, who's so scared she's going to leave you, you stalk after her."

"Well, I'll let you two battle it out. I have more important things to do." I turn away from my brothers, rolling my eyes, when Eryx's words hit me.

"Trust me, she's not going anywhere. Not after I injected her with a tracker."

"You what?" I roar, swinging around, the fury lingering in my veins coming alive.

"What's the problem?" he quips, his shoulders stiff, standing several feet from me. "I did what was needed. To ensure next time she vanishes in the woods or anywhere else, we find her before she gets killed."

I grind my back teeth because I can't even argue that point, seeing that I'd wrap her in cotton wool to keep her safe and close to me if possible. A thought that suddenly takes me off guard...

"She's gonna be fucking furious at you," Tallis says, mirth behind his words.

"She won't find out. Besides, her safety is paramount to me."

The room goes silent as the weight of worry and anxiety floods me.

My gaze drifts to Eryx as he keeps bantering with Tallis. He believes that happily-ever-afters aren't just stories but normal realities. Normally, I'd scoff at such notions.

I pause, glancing out the window, and my hand clenches in my pocket as I exhale softly. With everything that's happened—seeing Billie struggling and the reality of how much something scares her—I'm beginning to think she's crawled under my skin faster than I anticipated. But there's something more... Maybe a happy ending wouldn't be such a bad thing to believe in, especially when death and deceit shroud our world.

~

I CAN'T STAND it a second longer—the restlessness that strangles me and the fury seeping into my bones. The confusion billowing in my head is akin to the promising storm lurking over the mountains.

The afternoon sun stretches shadows over the landscape as I burst out from the back door of the mansion, landing on all four paws. The desperation to escape the walls closing in on me from inside is becoming too much.

Shaking myself, the wind ruffles my fur. The world around me is striking colors, every moment catching my attention, the smells sharp. Crisp pines call to me in the woods at the rear of our mansion, and my powerful back legs send me hurtling into the dense underbrush. A few leaps and I burst into the forest.

I crave the hunt, the chase, asserting dominance over my territory.

Trees blur past as my claws dig into the earth, propelling me forward faster. The woods embrace me— the decaying leaves, the heavy fragrance of flowers, whispers from the ancient trees. They are part of me, bound through my bloodline to my grandfather, the God of Forests. Each exhale of their leaves is a breath I sense in my veins, the pulse of the forest thumping in my chest. I've always been able to tune into the woodland, down to being able to sense when a tree is injured.

But I'm distracted as the tantalizing scent of prey calls to me.

Ears twitching at every little sound, my inhales catch it all, and I scan the grounds for my first target. When I can't think straight, I can't think of anything better than hunting and feeling the spill of warm blood on my tongue from a fresh kill.

All I care about is the present and escaping real life, how fast I can run... Except, it seems no matter how quickly I speed through the woods, I can't escape the thoughts of... Billie.

Since her arrival, I've been careful... so fucking careful

to keep my distance, not to let myself fall so hard that it shakes my resolve. Like Eryx and Tallis have done. They're completely captivated by Billie, and I can't blame them.

Until today, I like to think I've held on strong to my belief of needing to understand who I'm going to spend my life with as my fated mate. But after seeing her so vulnerable—tears in her eyes, fear draining her face of all color—something inside me shifted, broke.

My heart aches, a sharp throb that refuses to leave me, and I realize I've been fighting a losing battle.

Problem is, this is precisely where I didn't want to end up—drowning in my obsession with her. For the first time in what feels like forever, I'm terrified of losing control and letting my guard down. And right now, every inch of me yearns for her, blurring all my other thoughts.

A rustle at my left grabs my attention. I snap my head in that direction, eyes locked on a deer in a small clearing, feasting on grass. A perfect target for my first kill, its muscles rippling beneath the reddish brown pelt.

With a surge of energy, I lunge. The deer flinches and bolts in the opposite direction, but I'm on its tail. The chase is fast and fierce, my heart thundering, and I'm exactly where I feel the most comfortable.

Hunting.

Then why can't I get Billie out of my head?

# CHAPTER TWENTY-FOUR
## BILLIE

The semi-darkness of my room is suffocating.

After waking, the memory of the Reflection Ritual has been a storm in my thoughts. That bastard from my dreams showed up in the mirror. How the fuck did that happen? No one else saw it, so did I imagine it?

In truth, it scares me half to death—more than what the Dukes will do with their newfound information that I lied to them. But the image of the figure in the mirror had to be in my head, right? Though for a moment, I swore he'd found me in the real world and was coming to get me.

After taking a hot shower and slipping into my nightdress, I feel restless and anxious in my room. I desperately want to talk it out with the Dukes, yet I don't want to see them. Talk about being conflicted.

Unable to stand the silence a second longer, I grab the robe and put it on as I leave my room. There's a guard outside my door, blocking my path with his imposing size. So, it seems they've put me under surveillance.

"Going somewhere?" he asks, mocking me.

"I need fresh air. Surely that's allowed?"

His gaze roams over me, and I pull the robe tighter across my chest.

"I've been instructed to watch you," he states, standing stiff as a statue.

Frustration mounting, I huff. "You can watch me from a distance. How does that sound? I can't stay cooped up in here right now."

Despite his hesitation, I push out of my room, and he's forced to step back.

"Fine," he grumbles. "Just don't try anything, understand?"

"You have my word." Grateful for even the smallest opportunity to get out of the room, I nod and push past him, making my way down the corridor. His heavy footsteps remain close behind me.

My thoughts keep circling back to the Reflection Ritual. I passed out before I could find out exactly what the Dukes thought of my ability and me going into fight mode with an invisible opponent.

Gods, they must think I've gone insane.

I shouldn't care, yet every breath feels constricted.

I walk past double French doors that lead onto a balcony and change direction. Stepping outside, I inhale Finland's fresh, cool air as the guard's shadow looms over my shoulders.

"Please, I need some space," I plead, lifting my chin toward the wide balcony that spans half the length of the mansion wall. I twist my head to glance at him. "You can keep an eye on me from the doorway."

With a grunt, he nods and stands there, hands folded over his chest in that classic, clichéd bodyguard pose.

Stepping across the balcony, I'm immediately taken by the elegant arrangement of furniture—tables with polished marble surfaces, lush seating, and intricately wrought iron lanterns that sway on the breeze from poles.

Beyond the railing are the sprawling woods. I'm drawn closer, staring out farther to the rolling hills, reminding myself that not everything in this world is dangerous and trying to kill. There's beauty amid the darkness.

Glancing down, my attention catches on a massive black wolf tearing through the underbrush along the perimeter of the mansion's yard. Its muscles flex as it tears free, then struts toward the building, huge paws hitting the ground like he's the king of the world.

I've never seen a wolf so big, so wild, so terrifying. Its power dances up my arms, and a low growl rumbles in my chest in response, my instincts sensing the danger.

Then the impossible happens.

The colossal animal, in one mind-blowing leap, springs up from the ground and reaches the balcony's height. I scramble backward as it soars onto the balcony, its teeth bared and heading straight for me.

Suddenly, all the anxiety, the nightmares, that ghastly test, and my lies don't matter.

Not when I'm about to be eaten alive.

I flatten myself against the wall, my instincts screaming, *don't run, don't you dare run.*

My skin ripples with the promise of my wolf pushing free to meet this beast head-on.

The black creature steadily approaches me with his gargantuan paws, capable of tearing off my head. Shoulder blades rise and fall across his back with each step. But it's those cold, lethal, pale blue, almost white eyes that scare me, promising a swift end.

The guard finally arrives on the balcony in a casual stride, examining my situation, but his aloof expression irritates me.

"Took you long enough," I say with a strained voice. "Why is this monstrous wolf up here? Can you get rid of it before it kills me?"

Rather than responding, the guard chuckles, even as the wolf snaps its jaws at him.

Pausing abruptly, he lowers his head, saying, "Your Grace, I'll leave you to it."

I freeze in shock. "Wait, what?" Did he just say, Your Grace?

The reality check crashes over me. The wolf in front of me is Khaos in his animal form. It has to be. I should be relieved I'm not facing down a wild animal, but I'm not exactly loving the idea of answering to Khaos right now. I've barely had time to process what happened during the ritual.

By the snarl in his throat and his intense stare, he doesn't look happy to see me.

"Look, I understand if you're upset with me," I say, attempting to defuse the situation. "I get it. But don't you think dismembering me over a few lies is a bit... excessive?"

The rumble of his growl vibrates in the air between us. Closing the gap between us, his head is at the same level as my shoulders. He sniffs me, suddenly shoving his nose between my breasts.

"Hey! Personal space?" I protest, pushing my hand against his huge head, his fur lush beneath my touch. Except instead of backing off, he does the unthinkable.

He pushes himself up onto his hind legs, bones in his spine clicking as if adjusting to his new posture. A sound that normally makes me cringe doesn't bother me so much when I have bigger things to worry about. So big that I'm tilting my head back to stare at a standing wolf, who glares down at me. He presses one paw to the wall behind me, effectively boxing me in. I swallow hard, feeling like I'm back at the party, trapped under him at the side of the mansion.

"Déjà vu, right? This must be your favorite pose in human and wolf form."

His gaze, more human now than wolf, even as he remains in his animal form, studies me. Is he deciding how he'll punish me?

With his razor-sharp claws, he delicately slides the robe off my shoulder. The light, silken material follows gravity's call and pools at my feet, and I'm left just in a flimsy pajama dress, the chill of the evening causing my skin to ripple.

"Really?" I question, trying to infuse my voice with bravado. "We're doing this now? How about you show me your human form?"

Instead of responding, he tilts his head slightly, observing me. Then, as if to prove his point that he won't take any commands from me, his clawed paw moves to the thin strap of my nightdress, lowering it gently over my shoulder and down my arm.

My mind races, and every instinct is screaming to push away, yet there's part of me, deep down, that doesn't want to move. Perhaps it's that for all the intimidation, there's an intimacy between us that I haven't often experienced.

His gaze follows the path of my fallen strap, of my exposed breast.

"Khaos." My voice is but a whisper as the cool wind swishes against us.

My nipples harden, and I cover myself. The back of his paw slides under my chin, lifting my attention to him.

A sudden crack of thunder erupts, so loud and unexpected that I jolt on the spot. The sheer force of it causes me to flinch, and it feels like the whole mansion quakes under its power. The winds pick up, bringing the first trickle of rain. Leaves in the woods nearby rustle frantically.

Khaos blocks most of the rain from reaching me.

"We should head inside," I suggest, just as lightning streaks the heavens, so bright and sudden, it catches me off guard, and my heart jumps into my throat. Instantly, it's followed by a clap of thunder.

I flinch, my back flat against the wall, and I can't breathe. I start to wriggle out, that frantic desperation of feeling trapped and needing to escape enveloping me.

Khaos groans, studying me like he's trying to decide whether to stop me.

"I need to go inside, please, Khaos." Words barely leave my mouth when another crash of thunder comes, louder and closer this time. I jump as echoes of the past rush over my thoughts.

My parents' dead bodies flash in my mind every time the lightning bolts strike. A reminder of the storm that raged the night of the attack. My chilling scream, their lifeless eyes staring at the ceiling on my bedroom floor.

When I whimper, my legs soften beneath me.

Raw pain strikes my chest, twisting and twisting.

"Please, I can't be out here." I'm shoving against Khaos when he finally steps back, his long nose creasing.

Panic coils tightly in my chest, squeezing my lungs. Heart racing, I try to move, but each gust of wind feels like a slap. I'm spiraling, my breathing growing erratic, and I have to get indoors.

Khaos falls to all fours, and I sense my skin tingling from his oncoming transformation, except I'm already turning toward the door. My skin buzzes, every hair standing on end.

Another thunderclap, louder than before, snaps the last of my nerves. Tears blur my vision, and a cold sweat drenches my skin. A scream escapes my lips. Without a second thought, I make a mad dash indoors, darting past the guard. I feel nauseous and dizzy, as if I'm about to pass out with my parents' dead faces on my mind.

I run faster than I've ever done before, unable to stop seeing my parents being killed over and over.

My throat tightens.

Behind me, the sky roars, but no matter how fast I escape the storm that always reminds me of that devastating night, I'll never outrun the memories of their last breaths.

## Khaos

THE WEIGHT on my chest deepens with each fast step I take to Billie's room. Dressing quickly to avoid barging into her room naked, I pause outside and raise my hand to knock.

But the door swings open, revealing her dark room bathed in a stream of golden bathroom light. The lock on her bedroom door, I notice, is damaged. Unease ripples through me, even more so when I find her bed neatly made with no sign of a struggle.

Where is she?

A thunderous boom echoes outside when a soft whining sound comes from the side of the bed, out of my line of sight. I sidestep and move toward the noise, my pulse racing in my veins.

The moment I lay eyes on her, fear grips my heart and crumples until I can't breathe. She's crouched in the corner, her back against the wall, knees hugged tightly against her chest. Tucking her chin low, all I see is the wall of blonde hair covering her face.

She's shaking.

"Billie?" I step closer, but she doesn't respond, and that terrifies me. "What happened? Did someone hurt you?" She had sprinted off the balcony and back inside, yet I kept thinking I scared her with my wolf prank. Fuck, I'm an idiot.

Tension hangs thick in the room. Her soft sniffles echo in the silent space. I slowly move closer, taking a moment to kneel beside her.

"Billie? I'm sorry if I scared you." I keep my voice low, placing a hand on her knees. She doesn't brush me off, so maybe she's not furious at me.

Thunder cracks so deafening, the entire room trembles.

She gives a sharp flinch and a cry rips free from her lips as if the storm itself has wounded her. Holding on to her legs tighter, she rocks back and forth, eyes screwed shut.

My heart splinters as the realization that this fiercely strong woman is petrified of storms sinks in.

"Billie," I murmur. "Let me take care of you. I'm going to lift you and take you somewhere peaceful, okay?"

She raises her head just a fraction, and the sight of her tear-stained cheeks, her ghostly pale complexion, and her quivering lips punch the air from my lungs.

Tenderly, I collect her in my arms. She curls into me, every inch of her tense body still wincing with each roar of thunder. Her head cradles under my chin, finding her safe place.

Rain pelts violently against the window. I march her out of the room, memories flooding me with searing pain. The painful similarities of Eryx's trauma when we finally got him back from that fucking warlock undoes me.

Not a word is exchanged, but we don't need to when I feel her trembling. I need to know what's scaring her. If it's related to what she saw in the mirror earlier today, then I need to find a way to heal her.

One thing I notice about her tonight is her scent as I inhale it deeply into my lungs. There's something different about her, as if she's no longer releasing that sugary smell from her heat that grabs hold of my cock and doesn't let go.

A savage growl rolls through my chest at the protectiveness I feel, desperate to find out every damn thing about her, down to why her smell changed.

The intensity of Billie's fear, the shaking of her body, makes me want to take her somewhere safe, away from the storm's fury, and I know just the location.

"It's going to be okay," I reassure her, holding her a bit tighter, absolutely adoring the feel of her in my arms. She clings to me, her breaths still racing.

We reach the end of the corridor, and I swing right into the empty library. I don't pause until I'm in the far corner, as far from the entrance as possible to a dead end, but I know better. Gripping her in one arm, I stretch my hand to a concealed button camouflaged into the decorative wallpaper.

It gives off a muted click, and instantly, a section of the wall slides back, revealing a narrow stone passageway. I step inside, and the wall closes. A faint light flicks on overhead.

The floor descends slightly, and the farther I walk, the more the muffled boom of the storm fades, soon replaced by a comforting silence. Reaching a room at the end, I enter with Billie, and the lights flick on automatically, controlled by magic.

There's a low table in the center with a pile of books on astronomy from the library, telling me Eryx visited the nook last. A couple of plush lounge chairs, longer couch crowded around a cozy fireplace and a bookshelf fill the space. The ceiling has a mural with intricate details depicting a serene night sky.

My grandfather showed me the location when I was a child. A place he'd told me I'd need when the world felt like it was ganging up on me. When things became so much, that I was at a breaking point. I used the location all the time, mostly to get away from my brothers. Except it's impossible to keep anything from them. They were onto my hideout in no time. Now, it's a shared sanctuary if any of us need it.

Billie hasn't stirred in my arms, so I settle down on the couch with her resting in my lap.

"You know what I like about this place," I whisper. "It's that here, time seems to stand still."

Her breathing gradually slows, and she pulls her head up, her eyes wide. Then she glances around the room, wiping the tears on her cheeks.

"It's beautiful," she murmurs, her gaze landing on the starry ceiling. "So, is this your secret serial killer den where you drag your victims?"

I laugh, knowing that if she's making jokes, she's feeling better.

"You're my first victim. I've never brought anyone else here, well, aside from my brothers, who use the room. It's perfectly insulated, meaning no outside sounds. Sometimes, we all need an escape from this fucking world... even from storms."

Her gaze lowers to me, and she gives me a cute, lopsided grin. Then she slips off my lap and flops onto the couch next to me, folding her bent legs under her, facing me.

It's the first time since entering her room that I notice she's still only wearing her flimsy nightdress. I get up to collect the blanket from the shelf. Returning, I wrap it over her shoulders, and she tugs it around herself.

Settling down next to her, I twist to face her, my arm draped across the back of the couch.

"You must think I'm so weak that storms freak me out," she says, her breaths quickening.

"Thing is, dealing with a traumatic past in any way our body deems fit isn't a sign of weakness." I search her face for her reaction, but she just watches me with huge blue eyes that call me to her.

"How so?"

"Well, it's a testament to your strength. It means you've found a way to confront your demons and not let them consume you."

She blinks up at me, giving a small nod. "You know, I like that." Her fingers tap to an unknown rhythm on her thigh as she gnaws on her lower lip.

"The trauma in your past," I venture, studying her closely. "It was during a storm, wasn't it?"

She reclines against the sofa's armrest. "Is that your way of getting me to open up about my past?"

"I'm assuming it has something to do with your parents' murder," I answer, deciding to be direct.

Her face loses its color, and her hint of a smile vanishes. She averts her attention from me, followed by silence.

And more silence.

But I'm nothing if not a tenacious bastard until I get what I want.

Gently, she presses a shoulder into the back of the sofa, resting against it, and sighs.

"It was a fierce, stormy night six years ago, much like now," she murmurs. "I remember the footsteps in my bedroom while I lay in my bed. Two men attacked me that night, and I swore I'd die because those assholes had every intention of killing me." Her fingers tighten around the fabric of the blanket, her knuckles white.

I'm seething on the inside at hearing what she went through. I'm going to murder those two fuckers.

"But my parents burst into my room to rescue me," she continues. "They fought the two men, but it wasn't enough. Nothing was enough." Her face changes, squeezing and blinking away fresh tears.

My fury spikes, every inch of me tense at the thought of a younger Billie experiencing such brutality. I place my hand over hers on her thigh, squeezing lightly, vowing to find out who did this to her and make them pay.

"How did you escape?"

Sighing, she says, "That night was the first time I discovered these." She stuck out her arms, showing me the lines of magic on her skin. "By some miracle, I killed one man, but the other ran when my neighbors came to my rescue. But you know what?"

"What's that?" My head's spinning with the idea that

these men came intending to kill a young girl. What the fuck had she done to them? Raw, primal anger builds up in me, demanding retribution for her.

"There was something odd about the hooded attacker who survived. Not only did he take his dead friend with him, but when I cut his arm, he hissed and quickly covered his wound as if afraid he'd leave some blood behind."

"He didn't want the murder traced back to him," I state, anger licking my spine at the men who dared break into her room to kill her.

"Yeah, I get that, but there's something more, as though he knew me. And it was a personal attack, not just getting back at my parents, you know." She shrugs. "I don't know. It's just how it felt at the time."

"Was there anything else you remember about him? Anything unusual? His voice, his walk, something..." I'm tense all over, leaning closer. She has to know that the smallest clue will help us find him.

"I wish I knew more."

The room feels smaller and more oppressive as Eryx's earlier words come to mind that her parents' killers would very well be making plans to come back for her. I'm more convinced than ever that he will. It explains her nightmares, and perhaps the magic in the mirror manifested her worst fear. The killer who came for her.

Which begs the fucking questions... why her. "I'm curious. How have you managed to avert the hooded man after all this time?"

She sighs, glancing down to the gold pendant hanging from a chain around her neck. "This is the only reason I'm still alive. My mother arranged for my pendant to be charmed to conceal me from him." She's quiet for a long pause. "I think my mother knew the killer well, but I never got the chance to ask her who he was."

She suddenly drops her gaze before she starts getting up off the couch. "I've been wracking my brains for years and haven't found a damn clue, except the one..." She suddenly falls silent.

"One what?" I press, snatching her wrist. No response, so I don't release her, needing to know. "Billie!"

She wrenches her arm free from my grip.

"I found the name of the man who either put the hit on me or was involved in the attack."

"Who?" I'm on my feet in seconds, savage fire ripping through me. "I need the name," I growl, darkness looming over my thoughts.

She hesitates, and it's killing me on the inside.

"Billie, I can't help you unless you share everything you know." Closing the distance between us, she turns her back to me.

"Bryant Ursaring. That's his name, and he's from Finland."

Everything she's said rolls over in my head.

"That's why you're here, to find him and get revenge?"

She spins to face me, her features firm. "To find both men and why they came for me. Then to cut out their fucking hearts."

Her brutality is music to my ears.

"And it's why you broke into one of our rooms in the Vanguard Manor, then? Did you find him in the records?"

She shakes her head. "There's a chunk of information missing exactly during the date of my parents' death."

I go still at her words, blood rushing to my head, my pulse pounding in my ears. Wait... so the missing information in our records is somehow connected to Billie's attacker?

*Fuck.* My stomach clenches, my head spinning to make sense of what the hell's going on. Someone's trying to hide their tracks. I have dominion over Finland, and all hits in the country must come through my brothers and me for the final sign-off.

Does that mean we agreed to the death of Billie's parents?

An icy terror sinks through me. Our team reviews every job for us because we won't take hits on innocents out of pure vendetta and no children, either. We have ethics we live by, so for the job to go through our estate, it means at least one of the mercenaries works for us.

"Why is your data missing? Are you hiding something?" she asks, striding across the room.

"We're currently investigating that ourselves as we recently discovered the breach, and some of our records were removed."

She absentmindedly fiddles with the astronomy books on the table as I approach her.

"Why didn't you just come clean with me?" I ask. "It would have been easier. Time will heal the pain. I know this firsthand and would have shown you how."

She exhaled a heavy sigh. "Because you weren't

supposed to be my fated mate. For all I knew, you could have signed off on my killing. And I had to find out the truth." Lifting her gaze, she meets mine, darkness behind them but also fear.

My heartbeat spikes as every word she speaks ignites fury that churns deep in my gut. A cold, sharp stab pierces through my chest with anger.

"Tell me, Billie, what would you have done if you found records that showed we signed off the hit?" There's a rawness in my voice, hurt in my heart. It shouldn't be there, but Billie's grown on me, and I understand her intention. But even after spending time with us, she never came clean and still intended to spy on us to what... end us?

The ache blurs in my head.

"If you think I'm not the villain here, you're dead wrong," she finally answers. "You have no idea the things I'll do to make those pay who ripped my life apart. And don't you dare lie to me about time solving the pain because it fucking doesn't..." She's gasping for breath, her eyes glistening with tears.

My insides rattle like I'm barely holding myself together. Anyone else, and I'd have them fucking bleeding and on death's door. Except she's my fated mate!

"I'll avenge their deaths and destroy the fucker responsible," she says firmly. "I'll make sure that he'll never come for me again. It's all I've wanted for the past six years. All I've thought about. So, maybe you shouldn't trust me because I wouldn't." Quivering, she turns to the doorway. "I want to return to my room now."

Her words are like knives to my throat.

Do I hate her for it?

*Fuck no!* I would have done the same thing in her position. It stings like a bitch to be on the receiving end of knowing the woman I'm completely captivated by arrived at my home with dark intentions.

At that moment, I begin to understand the depth of what she's done to me, the crazy way she's made me, the savagery she's brought out of me. I assumed the fated connection that called us together was responsible because I'm falling so hysterically hard for her.

But now I see the real Billie behind the mask and the reason we're meant to be together, why she'll accept it, too. She's just as broken and dark on the inside as my brothers and me. She knows that no one reaches rock bottom without truly understanding what it feels like to stand at death's door, banging to be let in.

I hunt with a deep-seated need to tear things apart, to kill. Eryx gives himself to his gryffin, and Tallis hides behind his intrusive research into anyone he meets, using that to hide the real pain of his past lover betraying him.

While my wild girl wears her raw fury like armor.

I adore every fucking inch of her, even if she might have thought about killing us. I can live with that. And she will come around to being ours forever, fighting and screaming. She will learn to finally accept her fate.

Raw tension ripples through the room. Her demand to leave hanging in the air, except I'm not done with her. I stride toward her.

"Billie, it may not mean much without proof, but my

brothers and I would never authorize a hit against a child."

Her gaze widens, but she doesn't back away from me. Good, I don't want her to cower.

"Khaos, don't."

Before she can move, I scoop her into my arms. She gasps at my abruptness, but she's light, and I push her legs around my hips as I press her back firmly against the door, trapping her in place. Her eyes lock onto me, stormy and defiant, while mine are on fire with a hunger to remind her who I am to her—her fated mate.

"Khaos, please... we shouldn't." Her quivering voice fades, her palms firm against my chest.

"I'm right here and always will be in the darkness with you, Billie. I'm not letting you get away from me that easily."

Then I capture her lips with mine. Our mouths clash —teeth, tongues, and a tornado of emotions behind our searing kiss.

# CHAPTER TWENTY-FIVE

## BILLIE

I'm breathless as Khaos kisses me.

Chest tight, my legs grip his hips, and I grind into the hard erection in his pants as he plunges his thick tongue into my mouth.

His exhales and inhales are racing as his powerful hands grip my ass. Excitement coils around me, and where he touches me is all I can concentrate on. He licks my lips, and I tingle all over.

That earlier anger has shifted into untamed arousal through every inch of my body. I'm buzzing, completely drenched from rubbing myself against his cock. He kisses me like I'm his whole world. My toes curl with the passion and addiction he lavishes on me, tasting me, inhaling me.

He's rough, but I crave his pain as he sets the fires alight inside me.

When our mouths pull apart, I gasp for air. Dipping his hand lower across my ass, he reaches my pussy and pushes two fingers into me unceremoniously. I cry out from his thickness, with how badly I need him inside me.

"P-Please, don't tease me," I moan.

"You're so horny, I could happily drown in your body, but do you deserve it?"

I stiffen just as he draws his fingers halfway out, then pushes them all the way in, stretching me.

Quivering, I try to keep my thoughts together because my body's already lost to Khaos. Of course, I'm telling myself we shouldn't do this because it's going to end with him fucking my brains out.

Am I ready for that?

My body screams yes, my pussy purring around his fingers, which he keeps deep in me as if he belongs there, only moving now and then to remind me he's in control. The smidgen of rational thinking that remains in my head reminds me that once I go there with him, I'm his forever.

Call me sadistic, but I want that. Yet a nagging feeling at the back of my head tells me I've only just shared my secrets with him and don't have all the answers I need or how involved they were in my parents' killing. I'm rushing, making decisions based on emotions, and those kinds of things never end well.

"Hey," he says, pulling me out of my head. "Focus on me. Don't overthink it, my horny firecracker."

I grin at him, melting, my response coming out as a moan.

"Is this what you want? For me to be inside you? To spread you open and be used by me?"

"G-Gods," I groan, evidently unable to string a

sentence together. I blink up at him as he pumps into me a few more times. Our gazes lock, his tongue on my lips. My hands tighten around his shirt, my legs quivering because I can't get enough. My thoughts are consumed with having him thrust into me, fucking me.

Then his fingers move to my clit, sliding over my silky folds.

"I love the way you grind against me, so desperate for my cock."

"Yes, I am." He gives me huge Daddy vibes, and the word just slips from my mouth. "Yes, Daddy."

What in the world is wrong with me?

He chuckles, the sounds intoxicating while I shudder, on the verge of coming undone.

His mouth is on my ear, that devious tongue looping around my earlobe before scooping it between his teeth.

"Good girl. Tell Daddy what you've done to soften the scent of your heat?"

I didn't see that twist coming, and he must have seen the shock on my face. Teetering on the edge of an orgasm while being asked sneaky questions is completely unfair.

My mouth opens, and a moan spills out as he rubs my clit in tight circles, my pussy dripping wet, nipples so hard, I'm thrusting my breasts against him. The last thing I need to talk about is me blocking my heat.

"I-I don't know what you mean."

Shaking from being so close to bursting, he suddenly releases me from his teasing, removing his hand from between my legs. My chest tightens as he lowers my legs. Embarrassment swims over my cheeks, along with rising anger.

I barely touch the floor, already pulling from him, and he grabs hold of my waist, holding me next to him.

"Did I say you could go?"

"But you—"

Pinning me in place, his savage lips on mine once more, his hand rises to my throat. He only applies pressure that holds me under his control, but not that I can't breathe. I've always been strong, but being under his control this way fills me with unbearable excitement. I squeeze my thighs together, desperate for release, but he rips the nightdress off my body.

I gasp against him, and he stares deeply into my eyes.

"I need you naked."

That intoxicating spark in his pale blue eyes that screams wolf pierces into me. My own wolf purrs through me, drawing to him, demanding I claim him as ours.

He clears his throat as he releases me, pulling back just enough to lower his gaze down my body to take in everything. The curl at the corners of his mouth might as well be an aphrodisiac.

My body's rocking on the spot, his manly, earthy scent pouring over me. I inhale it as it weaves through me, making it harder for me to think beyond needing him.

He studies me. "Absolutely beautiful. I just knew you'd ruin me from the moment I first saw you."

The game he's playing is by his rules. I see that now, especially as he unbuckles his belt and rips open the button on his pants, pulling them open.

A massive cock pops out, thick and heavy. He tugs his

shirt up and over his head, revealing his Adonis body, carved out of stone with layers of muscles. My attention dips back to his ready hardness, my body struggling to resist him.

His cockiness is on full display, taunting me to the point of falling apart in the arms of a powerful Duke.

"If you're still going to hide secrets from me, we can rectify that, can't we?"

I swallow as he moves closer and slides a hand between my thighs. Apparently, I'm too weak to protest. Who am I kidding? I'm starving for him.

"Are you going to finish what you started?" I whisper.

He slides his fingers between my folds, and sparks dance across my nerve endings, catching on fire from that single touch.

I shudder.

"Will you tell me what you did to cover your heat?"

"Don't know what you're talking about." I gnaw on my lower lips, shaking as I ride his fingers, then he pulls them away again.

"Be a good girl and get on your knees for Daddy."

With an evil grin on my face, I kneel in front of him, holding his gaze.

"Never thought you'd ask, Daddy." I know something's wrong with me in how easily I give in to the Dukes, but at that moment, eye level with a monstrous-sized cock, I don't care.

When he kicks off his boots and drops his pants, tossing them aside, I'm in awe. The man is huge, has powerful legs, a solid body, and he's mine.

Then he steps closer, his erection right there, close to slapping me in the face. Fuck, he's big. And I'm soaking.

"Hands in the air," he instructs.

I follow his instructions, and he clutches both my wrists in his large hand and presses them in a locked position on the wall above me. I'm kneeling before him, my legs spread.

"Are you afraid?" he asks.

I shake my head. "Are you?"

He barks a laugh, throwing his head back.

"Open up for Daddy," he purrs, that tempting smile never leaving his mouth.

My body clenches, the sensation of his fingers on me still lingering. I part my lips for him, keeping his stare as he slides his cock into my mouth.

Khaos tastes salty, with a hint of honey, as he slips over my tongue.

"Fuck, Billie," he hisses, tightening his grip.

His free hand snatches my hair at the back of my head and holds me in place as he pushes deeper. I lean into him because this isn't my first time giving head, but never with someone so huge. My lips are stretched to the limit, with only so much space in my mouth.

"Just knowing that your delicious pink pussy is dripping wet for me, hungry and waiting, is driving me crazy." He goes harder, the tip of his dick hitting my throat. Tears spring to my eyes while lusting over the idea of taking him deeper.

I groan my approval, then work my throat to take more of him. My mouth is tightly wrapped around him as I sense him gliding down my throat. With my tongue,

I run it under the length of his shaft, giving him the ultimate sensation.

He groans, his body shaking, staring down at me with a wide grin.

"You're ruining me. The view from here, your mouth stuffed with my cock, is sexy as fuck."

I'm barely breathing when hearing his words. My muscles tense, but he never releases me and starts fucking my mouth. Every inch of me seizes, a moan vibrating in my chest while my pussy is dripping with how much I love being taken by him this way.

"Billie..." My name rumbles from him as he draws his cock out of my mouth and pushes it past my moist lips, deeper, teasingly. "Your mouth feels fucking incredible."

He hits the curve of my throat, testing me, going deeper still, and in all honesty, I am slightly stunned that I haven't gagged yet. It has everything to do with how turned-on I am and how much I love sucking his dick.

"That's it, take it all for Daddy. Open your throat for me." He tilts his hips just enough to gain better access, then he growls, "I need more, Billie. I need to fuck your throat."

A thrill runs through me, and I moan in response, my nipples hardening at the idea.

His hand tangles more in my hair, holding me in a position as he tilts his hips a bit more.

"Would you like that?" he asks, drawing out of me.

I lick my lips, tasting him as I bat my eyelids at him. I'm shaking with arousal, that heavy sensation of how close I am to exploding teasing me to no end.

"Yes, Daddy. Fuck my throat."

"Sweet hell!"

With his grip on my hair, he slips into my mouth again and thrusts. I take it, loving being under his command and letting go of how in control I am every second of my life. This is different. This is ecstasy and escape. To know what it feels like to have someone else in charge of me makes me want more.

Each time he shoves into me, my eyes roll back, and he exhales and groans louder. On the last push, he's in me to his hilt and pauses. He has me at his mercy, staring down at me with a smirk. I tremble, then his orgasm slams into him.

A growl rips from his mouth as he comes. I work my throat to take it all down and not choke, surprised by how much there is. But I'm never one not to accept a challenge, and I take it.

Once he pulls out, I lick the last drops of his seed from my lips, greedily swallowing it.

He releases my hands, which hurt slightly from being held up, but as if he senses my discomfort, he swoops me up into his arms. Then his lips are on mine, tasting himself on me, and we kiss fiercely, as if there's no way we could ever be apart again.

He sits on the couch with me in his lap, my legs straddling him, and I know exactly what he wants.

Gasping for breath, I position myself comfortably over his erection, ensuring he's horizontal as I sit down on him, straddling him.

"My little firecracker, you have no idea what you do to me."

"I have an idea," I tease. His cock's already hard,

nestled between my legs. I rub myself against the shaft. "But I'm not going to fuck you."

He growls, a wildness in his eyes. "It's difficult for you to completely give up your control, isn't it?"

"Would you have me any other way?"

His hands are on my hips, trying to guide me higher so he can slip into me, but I nudge them off me.

"This is my turn, Daddy." I wink at him as he grinds against me, his jaw clenched tight.

His eyes gleam dangerously sexy when he studies me, and I barely recognize myself. The slick length of his cock against me is pure bliss, the perfect thing to scratch that itch.

Those busy hands move to my breasts, kneading them and pinching my nipples hard.

I shake as my hips rock over him, back and forth, always staring at him. When he takes my nipple into his mouth, biting down a bit too hard, I completely lose the savage desire I've been drowning in.

Quivering with desire, I scream out, the orgasm ripping through me, tearing me apart. Stars dance in my eyes as I pant for air as jolts of pleasure swirl through me. Gripping Khaos' round shoulders, I press myself against his chest. I come all over his cock, cradled against my pussy. Every cell in my body tingles, and when I finally float down to reality, I'm slumped over his chest.

He pulls me close, his broad hands rubbing my back, grounding me after the storm, after our argument, after orgasming so hard, although I still see stars.

Time seems to blur and stretch as he sits there, catching our breaths in each other's arms. I've never understood the pure euphoria of being held by someone who'd shield me from the world's cruelty.

For so long, I trusted only myself and told myself that to survive, I could only rely on myself. While that same voice in my head tells me I'm soft for giving in to Khaos, for enjoying his company, maybe I haven't been exactly accurate in my views.

His hold tightens, and it hits me that maybe there's also strength in finding someone who won't make you face the darkness alone.

## CHAPTER
# TWENTY-SIX
KHAOS

The coldness of the day cuts through my clothes as I stand at the front door of my new mercenary's home on the outskirts of Rovaniemi. It stands solitary by a river, away from the busy city. The place is mine, as is the property. So, when Ayla agreed to work on my team and locate Lapland, I offered her and her friend, Issy, the place to find their feet.

I press the doorbell, and it chimes. Moments later, the door swings open, and Ayla greets me with a tight grin. She's in tight jeans and a loose, long-sleeve T-shirt. Raven dark hair, swept off her face, cascades over her shoulders. She's radiant, with a captivating beauty, and has that kind of smile that easily takes you off guard. In that spark of a moment, Billie comes to mind, her wicked grins and sarcasm that has me wrapped up and obsessed with her.

I hate leaving her. Hate that when I close my eyes, I relive her fear during the storm, hearing her words about her attack. The burning ache in the pit of my stomach to keep her safe intensifies.

Ayla lifts her chin toward me, drawing my attention.

"Khaos, you got here fast. Don't you live across the city?" Her brows pull together as she wears a lopsided grin.

"I don't mess around," I answer, chuckling as she waves me into the house. Stepping inside, I toe off my boots and shut the door. I'm hoping to get her started on researching Billie's parents as soon as possible, then I get back to Billie.

"Is Issy home, too?"

Ayla shakes her head. "She's out for a stroll in the woods. Might be gone for a while."

"That's alright," I reply. "I won't keep you long."

I haven't been in the house since it was redecorated before Ayla and Issy moved in. Lots of white walls with blue and green cushions, a vase of flowers, and lush chocolate rugs.

"Hopefully, I haven't caught you at a bad time," I say, knowing I gave close to no notice of my arrival. Thing is, Alya comes with highly specialized mercenary and tracker skills, something my team is sorely lacking. Her abilities were exactly what I needed, so I snatched her up when the opportunity arose.

She manipulates dark magic, her power revolving around souls, and she's powerful—the perfect ally.

I follow her into the main living room, where two walls are almost entirely made of glass, creating an illusion of the outside as an extension of the inside. The view is a serene, enclosed lawn dotted with trees and a patio.

Near the kitchen, she pauses by a large wooden table and pulls out a chair for herself. She's quiet, more than when we last met weeks ago, but beneath her serene appearance, I feel a storm brewing. She's patiently waiting to hear what I need from her.

As a leader, it's my responsibility to ensure every member is ready and feels comfortable to take my lead. Ayla's no exception because with her skills, she's invaluable.

Sensing the shift in the mood, she smiles as if physically shaking her nerves. "Get comfortable. I'll grab our coffees." Once settled, she sits across from me, a steaming cup of coffee in front of each of us.

"So, what can I do for you? It sounds urgent."

"I have a personal situation I could use your assistance with," I explain, choosing my words carefully. "Given your specific skill set and your hobby of researching missing people, you might be interested in this."

Her eyes light up, and she leans forward, waiting. "I'm listening. You've said the magical words." She half-grins, but I can already see the seriousness settling on her features.

"Your reputation as an information tracker is unparalleled. There are two persons of interest I want you to dig into. Their records seem to be *non-existent*." I emphasize the last word.

Ayla's on her feet, fetching a pad and pen from the

kitchen counter. "Give me everything. Names, addresses, descriptions, favorite color... the lot."

I nod. "Lorelei Tempest and Draven Tempest." Last night, Billie gave me her parents' names and a few details.

Ayla stiffens, staring at me with her brows pinched together.

"You've heard of them?" I ask.

She takes a moment to respond. "The surname is familiar, but before I say anything, I won't jump to conclusions. Go on."

I delve into the information I have from Billie—her family address, what they did, and that they were both pure wolves. Then I move on to Bryant Ursaring, not holding back that he might be involved in Billie's parents' killings.

My own research has brought up minimal findings, especially with our records on them wiped. This is Ayla's specialty–finding the lost–and she's fast.

She doesn't say a word as she scribbles notes on her pad. The weight of the conversation grows, and my eagerness to get to the bottom of who's targeting Billie is my priority. She slowly lifts her gaze to mine with an intensity that takes me aback.

"You know, Khaos," she begins. "This might not be as difficult as we think. I may have come across some... interesting leads in my personal research on someone I've been investigating with the surname Tempest. If it turns out to be the same person, you'll be shocked by what I have to share with you."

I raise a brow, intrigued, my heart thundering in my chest.

"Give me less than twenty-four hours," she says confidently, tapping her notes. "If it's not who I'm thinking of, I'll let you know."

A deep breath escapes me. "I'm counting on you. We need answers, and we need them fast."

**Billie**

WHY DO cravings for cake always happen at night?

My stomach rumbles as I lay in bed, unable to sleep. The rest of the mansion is silent, yet I've been stirring. I can't think of anything but eating something sweet. Chocolate cake. Freshly baked cookies. Fudge. Drooling, I crawl out of bed.

Dragging on the robe, I quietly open my door to find the guard Khaos insists on keeping outside my door snoozing away. After the mirror incident, Khaos said I'm not to leave the mansion alone.

The man's sitting on the floor, his back to the wall, and his chin tucked into his chest. Seems Khaos underestimated his top-notch security.

I tiptoe past the guard, and once I'm no longer in earshot of him, I rush down the stairs. The mansion's unsettling so late. A few lights are on, as though the place never completely goes to sleep. Otherwise, it's eerily silent.

Hurrying across the cold floor, I make a beeline for the kitchen. My stomach is starved while Khaos still lingers on my mind. More specifically, our time together two nights ago.

I haven't seen him since. Helmi told me the three brothers were called to an urgent meeting with other families and explained this happens all the time. The matter of *urgency* is questionable when it comes to these gatherings. She giggled. I really like her, especially when she pops into my room to check on me, but we end up chatting for an hour. The rest of the time, I've been investigating the mansion, keeping occupied. By some miracle, Clark is not treating me like a piece of dirt on his shoe.

He even went as far as to tell me Khaos was getting external help to find out about the breach in their data. I have my fingers crossed it turns up information about the monsters who killed my parents.

When I reach the vast kitchen, I find myself alone with the high ceilings, gleaming countertops, and pots and pans hanging off a metal hook over the stoves. I'm in the fridge in no time, poring over what's on offer. Finding nothing sweet, I grab the bottle of milk. Placing it on the counter, I open the door to the pantry and gasp aloud.

The powerful smell of dried herbs invades my senses, then...

"Holy crap. How big is this place?"

The pantry's larger than the entire apartment Sasha and I shared back in South Africa. There are lines of shelves and so much in here, I have no idea where to begin or where to even find the lights. So, I delve into the first couple of rows lit up by the kitchen lights.

Moments later, I emerge with an armful of treats and lay them out on the far counter—a jar of chocolate chip cookies, a wrapped loaf of what looks like an orange poppyseed cake with white frosting, cinnamon rolls with a syrupy sheen, a small container of pink and blue macaroons, and lastly, freshly made fluffy marshmallows with a bar of chocolate. My mouth's drooling. Yep, I went overboard, so I decide to create a small platter with a sampler from each goodie.

As I bend over to collect a plate from the shelves under the counter, footsteps echo from the hallway. I jolt back up, my heart rate picking up. Did the guard find me missing? Or is it one of the Dukes? I don't move, hoping whoever it is will pass by and not bust me about to devour all this food.

A powerful arm coils around my waist, and a hand slaps against my mouth. A sudden pull and I'm dragged across the kitchen into the pantry. The doors shut, turning everything dark. The smell of herbs is crazy potent, almost watering my eyes.

Panic grips me, and I thrash against the attacker, cursing myself for not grabbing one of the kitchen knives to take back to my room for such occasions. My breaths come in short, sharp bursts against the hand clapped over my mouth. Confused, disorientated, and scared, I throw my elbow back, but it makes no difference.

Then the chilling sensation of something leathery snakes its way up my legs, wrapping tighter the higher it climbs, and a scream bubbles in my throat.

"Hush," the deep, male voice whispers in my ear,

with it the familiar scent of charred wood after an old camping fire, tinged with the sweet smell of cherries.

I know this scent, his touch, his tail. I groan.

"Asshole," I mumble against his hand. "Let me go, Tallis!"

His hold doesn't relent, and I can just picture the smirk on his face—the same one he'd worn in the steamy bath. And like then, he's in his demon form, clear by his frisky tail sliding around my legs.

His warm breath remains on my ear. "Do you want him to find us?"

"Him?" I exhale, confused and trying to see past the firm hand that muffles my words and half covers my face.

Through the thin gap of the pantry door that isn't completely shut, there's only the empty kitchen with a perfect view of my treats across the room.

"He's been following you, you know that? Except you're out of your room, and that means you're mine. I got to you first."

"What are you talking about?" My voice is close to being inaudible behind his hand. Gripping it, I try to push it down, but it's a losing battle. As is the tail that's now snaking up my inner thigh, covering me in excited shivers. How fair is it that my body has no control around the Dukes?

So, I bite down on his finger, and he hisses, but there's no letting up in his grip.

"Really, you're biting now?"

"Whatever it takes. Now back off!"

He laughs softly behind me. "Not happening. You'll

run away." His lips are on my neck, those dangerous sharp fangs grazing my tender skin like a threat that I better do as he asks, or he'll be the one doing the biting.

"Do you have any idea what it feels like?" His tongue licks me from my earlobe down the curve of my neck. "To crave your touch, to long for your taste, to have a constant hard-on?"

I'm at a loss for words at first. Not just because he's speaking of such raw emotions that squeeze my chest, or that his tail is getting dangerously high between legs, but because, honestly, he's coming between me and the chocolate cake I had my heart set on.

Except now that the tip of his tail slips in under my pajama shorts, I gasp.

"Hey, that's not fair," I murmur, trying to squirm and push his tail out, but with Tallis' arm around my middle, forcing my back against his chest, it makes it impossible to reach down.

"Did you know my tail is covered in sensitive receptors? So, wherever I move it, I feel the touch as if it's my fingers, even my mouth. Well, except for taste."

I can't help but laugh at him, my voice still muffled by his damn hand.

As if to prove his point, the tip of his tail slides over the seam of my pussy. Shivers cover me, electricity tingling across my body at how easily he arouses me. A moan purrs in my throat when he grabs my breast, squeezing a nipple.

Desire ripples down my spine, and I groan, licking the inside of his palm this time instead of trying to draw blood.

He nudges my legs wider with his foot, and I moan as his tail slides up close to my entrance, teasing me. I feel the smoothness of his demon skin and the round tip that pushes in just an inch.

"Tallis, please..." My breaths are coming so quickly, I heat up. My pussy squeezes him, trying to take him deeper. My body rejects me and embraces the Dukes.

"I'm addicted to you after just one taste," he growls in my ear, squeezing my breast again.

I tremble, unable to focus on anything but his tail between my thighs. Already, I feel myself grow wetter. Is it bad that I just want him to do it instead of taunting me?

"I think I have a problem," he confesses in my ear.

"Just one problem?" I say breathlessly. "Oh, how humble of you."

He does that thing where he laughs in his heavy tone, then pushes his tail into me.

I grip his arm because, let's just say, his tail isn't on the thin side.

"You like that?"

I can't find my words, so I nod, my insides fluttering. There's something erotic about being held by him while he has his way with me. It's a fantasy I have, and somehow these Dukes know exactly how to deliver.

A low purr rubs across my throat as he inches deeper. I feel the circular ribs on his tail as he slips in. He grips me, breathing heavily in my ear. I can barely feel my feet, and he's mostly holding me up at this stage as stars burst behind my eyelids.

My stomach cramps up, desire swallowing me. I shudder, moaning.

That's the moment someone strolls into the kitchen.

"Shhh." Tallis is in my ear, his breath hot and heavy, but his tail moves deeper, then out and back in, ensuring he's rubbing those ribbed circles against my entrance because he's evil. And he knows I can't resist.

Through the tiny gap of the pantry door, I stare out and find it's Eryx. He's dressed only in loose pants, his sculpted upper body on full display, and I can see the cut of his muscles, the play of shadows and light over his abs.

I'm completely mesmerized.

"You like him a lot, don't you?" Tallis whispers so softly, I barely hear him. He's holding me possessively, tugging on my nipple over my pajama top.

Not trusting my voice, I nod as I rock my hips. I study Eryx, who doesn't seem to notice our whereabouts, which I put down to the overpowering scent of the herbs in this damn pantry.

My thighs flex then wobble at Tallis' relentless teasing, the intensity he brings out in me. It takes all my control not to cry out at how good it feels to be fucked by a demon's tail. And I'm thinking about the two cocks he's packing, currently grinding against my ass, and how incredible they would feel.

I'm so far gone down this path of arousal, I don't want to stop. Tallis owns my body, and he knows exactly how to play, so it sings to his tune.

Eryx moves over to the collection of sweets I'd gathered at the table and pokes at them. Then he flips open the jar and starts chomping into the chocolate chips. Three down, he grabs two more and devours them on the way to the fridge.

I eye him, willing him to leave my cookies alone while floating on wave after wave of torturing arousal from Tallis. He finally removes his hand from my mouth and slips it down my front and to where I'm rocking with his tail. With two fingers, he pulls my lips apart, and one finger taps on my clit.

"Want me to change things up a notch?" he murmurs in my ear, all while I'm watching Eryx retreat from the fridge with an enormous ham and a jar of pickles under one arm. He snatches a blade and a full loaf of bread.

I make a small sound in response to Tallis to say no way in hell.

"What about a small touch of my incubus power right here…" He presses down on my engorged clit, his tail deciding to move faster. My legs almost give out, and all I can think is I need more.

Slick's dripping down the insides of my thighs. I recall his last use of incubus power, which made me a completely sex-starved maniac. More than I already am, which says a lot.

I stiffen, shaking my head at him, my insides tightening as I twist my head around to look at him. "Don't you dare!" I mouth what is barely a whisper.

His lips peel back into a smirk. Shit, he's not going to listen to me, is he?

Glancing back, Eryx is staring at my pile of yummies again, and I'm mentally willing him to hurry up and leave the kitchen. I adore him, and the last thing I want is to fall out of the pantry, crying from an orgasm, with a tail up my hoo-hah in front of him.

I have no doubt he'd get a kick out of it, then want to join—I see it already playing out in my mind—but I'm not ready for how fast things are escalating. The more I fool around, the more likely one thing will eventually lead to full-on sex. I barely have control over my heat...

Tallis suddenly pushes deeper into me, and I gasp, then shut my mouth.

Eryx pauses and glances around the room.

My heart thunders as I can feel Tallis smirking as he teases my clit. *Asshole.*

Fire flushes my skin, and sweat breaks out over my brow.

Just as Eryx scoops up my chocolate cake into his grasp and marches out of the kitchen, Tallis' next touch on my clit is like electricity.

It zaps through me, sizzling across my pussy, and I completely lose it. Euphoria devours me as I cry out, and my knees give out.

He holds me up while I shake. The pleasure is so intense, I can't stop from coming again and again. My body convulses, my pussy squeezing his tail, and he's hissing behind me, but I can't think of anything but how I'm coming harder than I ever thought possible.

Hot slick drips out as he cocoons me, saying, "I've got you. Look how beautiful you are, coming all over my hand and tail."

When I finally return down to earth, my body goes limp, and I'm in Tallis' arms, cradled close to his chest. My gaze falls to his tail, slipping out of me and sitting in a small puddle of my cum that has the end tip glistening wet.

"That was stunning," he purrs. "I can't wait until you're ready for me to fuck you, to give you both my cocks."

Stunned, I'm still shaking from a mind-blowing orgasm, but I'm spent. It took every bit of strength I had and zapped me.

"I said not to use your power," I say with a crackling voice, barely able to talk clearly.

He grins at me, then leans his head forward and kisses me. "Was that not the most incredible sensation in the world?" He walks me out of the kitchen, empty-handed from my goodies.

"Well, yes, it was insanely good, but—"

"Then that tells you everything. I knew exactly what you needed, and I'm always here to please. Like now, I'm going to take you to the bathhouse to wash up."

I blink at him, narrowing my gaze at him, unsure what he's up to now.

"And what are you going to do?"

The corner of his mouth curls upward. "I, my sweet girl with the most delicious pussy, am going to make it up to you. I promise."

"Wait... make what up to me? That you held me hostage in the pantry, then turned me on so much that I enjoyed having sex with your tail, or was it when you touched me with your incubus magic?"

The full glow of his smile is breathtaking. "You'll see."

"To be honest, your surprises kind of scare me. I'm happy without them."

He studies me as if he's memorizing me, and I'm trying really hard not to swoon at this demon who drives me crazy.

"Prepare to be surprised." Then he kisses me again, and I can't help but be swept away by his charm, with that intoxicating scent and how deliriously handsome he is, even in his demon form. Despite how angry he makes me, I'm still fanning myself, even when he pulled that stunt in the kitchen.

"Oh, and by the way, I hate you," I snarl. "You lost me my chocolate cake."

"I love you, too, gorgeous."

The bath's water laps gently against my shoulders as I float in its embrace. I feel completely relaxed, but there's an edge of anticipation I can't shake off. Tallis brought me to the huge bathroom that resembles a cave, promising to make it up to me. That terrifies but also excites me.

I can't explain it, but the feelings inside me for these Dukes are changing. They're a lot more different than I expected, but I'm getting ahead of myself and need to pull the reins on my emotions.

Harder said than done.

Just as I contemplate the meaning of my life, the door to the bath creaks open.

Tallis steps into the light, and he's in his human form, dressed in jeans only. But my attention hooks on the decadent, frosted chocolate cake, complete with two forks sticking out of the top, in his hand, presented on a golden plate.

My mouth waters, eyes wide. I'm utterly speechless because that isn't the cake I pulled out of the pantry. It smells like freshly baked chocolate.

A sexy smile teases his lips.

"What's this?" I finally moan aloud, nodding toward the dessert, trying to keep calm and not get over-excited. Just in case this is some test, and he's going to taunt me with it. Then I'm officially going to kill him.

His grin spreads into a full-blown smile.

"Consider it my peace offering. Eryx stole your cake because of me, so I've made you my famous Demon's Chocolate Cake. Fresh out of the oven, so much so that the frosting is melting, so it needs to be eaten quickly."

"Wait." I stop floating in the water and lower my feet to the bottom of the bath. "You bake?"

His eyes gleam, and I enjoy seeing the excitement in them, how proud he looks at his creation. "You'd be surprised how many things I can do."

For a moment, we both gawk at the cake before he sets it down on the edge of the pool. He looks ready to dive into the bath.

"Planning on taking a dip with your clothes on?" I ask. "Are you channeling your Victorian Lady side?" I poke my tongue out at him as he chuckles.

He strips in a second flat, and my gaze lowers to his groin because that's the kind of girl I've become. And he's got only one huge, heavy cock hanging between his legs that has me tightening my thighs. But what's interesting is that in demon form, he has two dragons down there.

He hops into the pool, causing a small tidal wave in the process. Swifty, he grabs the cake and moves over to sit on the ledge in the bath.

"So, are you joining me?" His eyebrows raise suggestively.

I smile. "Absolutely. Who could resist a cake and bubble bath date?"

Hell, did I just say *date*?

I grab my fork and dig into the dessert. The moist and still-warm sponge is velvet and heaven on my tongue. The chocolate cream has partially melted, but it doesn't ruin the taste. It's sweet and rich, and suddenly, I'm moaning.

"Oh my God," I murmur, putting another forkful into my mouth.

"I'll take that as a compliment because, yes, I am half a god and your god." He grins at me. "Also, if you keep making those sounds when you eat, you're going to be wearing the frosting all over your body, and I'll be licking it off."

I almost choke on my food, then burst out laughing.

"But seriously, you made this cake? For real? Or did you conjure it up with some magic spell from someone in the mansion?"

His brows draw together. "Should I be insulted that you don't believe I can make such an amazing cake?"

"No, it's just that." I take a huge bite, needing to shut up now before I dig myself deeper. "Wait." I swallow the mouthful. "Is there some kind of spice in the cake? There's a tiny zing on my tongue."

"Ah, yes." He's beaming again. "There's a dash of chili in it. My own twist."

"It's ridiculously good." I dig in for more, already making a nice big hole in my side of the cake.

He leans in closer, so much so that our faces are almost touching. My breath catches when he kisses the side of my mouth, then licks it. Pulling back, he says, "You had some frosting there."

My heart's galloping, and the longer I stare at him, the more I'm letting strange thoughts into my head—like, what would it be like to be with a man like him? Then the words roll past my lips as if they have a mind of their own.

"How come someone like you, who could have anyone, is alone? I picture you inundated with women begging to be with you."

He snorts a laugh. "Because I've been waiting for someone like you."

Rolling my eyes, I say, "Stop lying. I'm serious."

A sigh spills from his lips, and he glances out across the water's steamy surface, but when he doesn't answer, I decide to open up.

"For me, I kept telling myself that I didn't have time for anything serious. That first, I had to find who killed my parents." I shrug.

He tilts his head to the side, studying me. "Has that changed now?"

"When I first arrived, I was adamant I knew the

answer. But now, I'm feeling so many emotions, and it's more complicated with us being fated mates."

"Feels straightforward to me."

I give him my best deadpan look. "Okay, now you go."

After another long pause, he says, "I thought I found someone once. Someone I actually believed was the one. And she played the part flawlessly, telling me everything I wanted to hear, doing everything I desired. She spoiled me and stood by my side. Hell, I was convinced that the universe messed up by not designating us as fated mates." He glances across the room, lost in thought.

I hadn't meant to bring out his painful memories. My heart aches seeing this side of him. I curl up against his side, resting my chin on his arm, wanting him to know he's not alone.

Tallis leans back, the water up to his chest, flowing around us as if the jets had been switched on.

"Turns out," he begins. "She played me. I should have seen it and known that no one is perfect. Everyone has flaws that make them unique. She was no different, but I was an idiot and blind to it. She wasn't with me for love, not even infatuation. She had been infiltrating our family, spying on behalf of a rival mercenary family."

"That bitch!" Anger flares within me, something fierce and protective. "Please tell me she's out of your life now, or I might just have to unsheathe my swords on her," I say, half-joking, half-serious.

"She's far gone. Put it this way, once we found out, my brothers and I paid their family a visit that no one in that family will ever forget." He studies me carefully, those dark eyes of his revealing golden flecks like tiny starbursts. Then a smirk plays on his lips. "I didn't know you had a touch of the green-eyed monster in you."

I laugh louder, the sound echoing in the cave-like room.

"Neither did I, honestly. Who would have thought?"

"You know, I haven't trusted anyone since I was in a relationship," he explains. "Until I met you."

My heart pounds in my ears at his words, at the depth with which he stares at me.

"Well, that must mean I'm doing something right." I chuckle at my sarcasm, seeing I managed to do everything you're not supposed to do when hunting down a killer.

He strokes my cheek and curls his fingers under my jawline. "Or perhaps it means you're starting to fall for a demon."

## CHAPTER TWENTY-SEVEN
### TALLIS

I stretch my legs out in the heavy wooden chair, uncomfortable as hell in these damn meeting room seats. So, I get up and leave the table where Eryx is dwindling his thumbs while Khaos is getting himself a coffee. My brother can't operate without his caffeine fix in the morning. He's called us urgently, so here we are. I'm standing on the top floor of Vanguard Manor, staring out at the guards at the front of our property. The lofty electric fence around our property provides security because, in our business, there's always someone trying to kill us. Beyond the gate lies a quiet road that leads into the city.

Billie's on my mind, like every other second of the day. She consumes my thoughts, and I'm desperate to see her again. I can't stop picturing her last night, naked in the bath, her mouth covered in my chocolate cake. Her laugh still rings in my ears.

Khaos' voice breaks my concentration, and I swing back around, then flop into my seat.

"Okay, hit us. What's going on?" I ask.

Eryx perks up across the table from me while Khaos grabs the spot next to him.

"I received some preliminary findings from Ayla on Billie's parents early this morning."

I lean forward, suddenly interested. Here I thought it would be another snore-fest meeting about mercenary hit stats and which mercenary family has started a feud with another. Sometimes, I swear we're dealing with children rather than professional killers.

"Don't make us wait," Eryx presses, watching Khaos lower the coffee cup from his lips and set it on the table.

"Ayla only told me a couple of top-line findings as she has to keep investigating, but what she uncovered is a great start."

Eryx and I aren't saying a word but watching our brother intently.

"First, it seems Billie's mother was involved in an enormous human trafficking ring that's been going on for over twenty years."

I stiffen in my seat at the news, which came out of left field, but considering we knew nothing about her, I guess it was possible.

"So, what?" Eryx asks, beating me to the punch. "She's one of the victims or... what?"

Khaos swallows hard. "From what Ayla's been able to discover, she was kidnapped over twenty-one years ago and dragged into the Arcadia portal up in Portland. And you know that what used to go in there rarely comes back out."

I shuffle forward in my seat, muscles tense at hearing

the word Arcadia. A world of shifters ruled by Pan, the King of Arcadia. And yeah, the portal is now fixed, but when it was broken, the vast majority who went in vanished. They weren't heard from again... just like our father.

My heart slams against my ribcage.

He'd been thrown in, and to this day, we haven't been able to find our father in Arcadia.

"So?" Eryx barks, drawing me from my thoughts. "What's this got to do with Billie? Okay, her mother probably got out of Arcadia with the handful of lucky people who actually made it out. What does it mean?"

"Well, for one, she had no memories of how they ended up in Arcadia or what happened there," Khaos adds.

"And?" Eryx prompts, in a pushy mood today. "Maybe whoever took her mother to Arcadia returned to kill her and the husband, fearing she'd regain her memories and expose the traffickers."

"Doubt it," I pipe in. "They broke into Billie's bedroom and attacked her first. They would have gone for the mother if they wanted to shut her up."

Khaos is quiet, which tells me there's more he hasn't revealed yet. It's in the tightness at the edges of his mouth.

"What else?" I ask abruptly.

Khaos lifts his hard gaze to me. "I don't think Billie's parents told her the truth of what her mother endured. Billie explained to me that her mother arranged for the pendant she wears to be charmed to conceal her from *him*... the man who attacked her and killed her parents. So, I'm certain the mother had to know the killer."

The sensation of icy fingers grips my heart. Exactly how much does Billie know about her parents?

Khaos heaves a raspy breath, raking a hand through his hair.

"According to Ayla, her parents were pure wolf shifters with no magic in their bloodline. The father was a mercenary, the mother a nurse. So, how do you explain the magic Billie wields? And it's strange how the timelines match suspiciously well. Her mother vanished into Arcadia roughly twenty-one years ago. How old is Billie?"

"Twenty-one," Eryx responds instantly.

I swallow hard as we exchange glances. "So?" I ask. "You're saying something happened to her mother in Arcadia that affected Billie?"

"Perhaps her mom was pregnant when she went into the portal?" Eryx asks.

Khaos' expression turns grim. "Or she got pregnant while in Arcadia by someone else."

"Fuck!" I grunt.

"Of course, it's all speculation right now," Khaos murmurs.

I recline in my chair, my thoughts already going wild. If Billie discovers her dad may not be her biological father, it could devastate her.

"We don't tell Billie any of this until we're 110% certain, understand?" I state.

"Fuck yes. No blurting it out," Khaos mutters, glancing at Eryx.

He's got his hands up in the air to declare his innocence. "I won't say a word. You think I want to break her heart?"

Khaos is on his feet, tugging down on his business jacket.

"For now, let Ayla keep working on the case. We jack up our security to ensure Billie's protected. We assume the worst-case scenario, and no one comes in or out of the mansion without us knowing."

As he turns to leave, I call out, "Hey, Khaos, any news on the mercenary, Bryant something, who Billie said was involved in her parents' killings?"

My brother nods, rubbing the bridge of his nose.

"It seems that Bryant Ursaring was indeed a mercenary from Finland, so he must have been on our records, yet there are no details of him in our files. But he died six years ago, found in a ditch, and his death was not reported to us. With no living family or friends, we have no one to ask more about him."

"Hell," I groan under my breath, a darkening sensation coming over me that we're about to uncover something horrific. And it'll revolve around our Billie.

My brothers leave, and the room settles into a heavy silence. The weight of the news, of the ominous feeling crawling under my skin that something so horrible could have happened to Billie's mother, suffocates me.

But Billie's safe. And she's going to stay that way. That's all that matters.

Dragging myself out of the boardroom, the situation bears down on me, but with every step, I fear we don't know enough to understand exactly what enemy we're fighting.

## Eryx

MARCHING TOWARD THE MANSION, each thump of my heart reminds me of Billie. After what Khaos had discovered about her mother, I'm under no illusion that she's going to face the darkness from her past. And it fucking destroys me to know she'll be devastated. I want to steal the pain from her so I can face it for her. I'm already partly ruined, so what's a bit more?

The grunt of my protesting gryffin resonates deep within me.

"Don't tell me you wouldn't do that for her?"

He goes silent, and I laugh. "I thought so."

Stepping into the mansion, my gaze immediately finds her. She's halfway up the grand staircase, balancing an armful of thick books, and clearly, she's struggling from the way she wobbles on the next step, her arms grappling not to drop them.

I dart up after her to help, taking a few long strides up behind her. Suddenly twisting and seeing me, a surprised yelp spills out, and the books tumble out of her grasp.

"Eryx!"

But I'm fast. Reflexes that are unmatched. In one swoop, catching my gorgeous girl with one arm around her waist, with the other, I snatch a falling book, then another.

"I've got you," I quip.

Yet the third book slips past my fingers and smashes onto my foot.

I roar and hiss out loud, the pain sharp and my big

toe already pulsing. Fuck! The sudden pain causes me to lose my footing, and for a heartbeat, my world tilts.

Billie's crying out as she's falling with me, her arms flinging into the air, and the books in my grasp falling.

"Don't worry, sweetheart," I murmur in the same split second she clutches onto me, her face twisted with panic. My legs are rapidly catching me as I stumble backward, but I'm barely hitting the steps.

Only one thing darts over my mind—I won't let her get hurt.

That's when I feel the buzz over my body...

"Hell no, you don't!"

Echo bursts out of me in a flash, like the big hero coming to the rescue. *Damn him.*

Clothes shredded, my body stretches. Echo shoves me aside and takes over the reins. I still feel like I'm in my body, except the controls don't listen to me. I'm surprised he hasn't completely taken over and blocked me like he usually does.

Wings explode outward from his back, spreading wide, catching the air to stop us. But there's no stopping the falling impulse, even with claws digging into the steps, carving their scratching mark in an effort to grip onto something.

Billie's screaming, and instead of bracing for impact, I feel Echo's intentions, his movements. Back legs kick out, and we're suddenly launching upward, sending us airborne.

My girl's grip on me tightens, her fists clutching onto the feathers around Echo's neck, her voice booming with my name on it.

Then we're swooping back down with unstoppable momentum before we hit the ceiling, and Echo has his sights on the oversized arched windows.

Billie's shuddering, crying out, "Stop. Don't you dare."

The wings pull tight against our body, one of them cradled over Billie, covering her completely.

We smash right through the window with a shattering crash. Shards of glass shoot in every direction, and we're shooting upward instantly. Powerful wings beat the air, each thrust propelling us farther toward the sky.

The whirlwind of motion causes the cool air to crash into us.

Now and then, I glance down at Billie, who's holding on with dear life, her face pale, her eyes wide. And when she looks at me, it's with a death glare. Someone is angry.

Echo swings his front leg awkwardly upward to press up against her back and give her support to ensure she doesn't fall.

"Put me down," she yells, her voice barely audible over the rush of air.

But Echo's speeding over the land, leaving behind the estate, and heading to the mountain we often escape to. A place we use for his solace, away from the rest of the world.

The great expanse of the forest spreads out beneath us, but we're approaching the mountain looming ahead of us, its rugged surface of rocks and trees making it too steep for most animals to climb. My sights are on the oversized outcrop, a ledge made of solid stone nestled on its side. Behind it lies the shadowy mouth of a cave, a place I've slept in many times. Rushing upon it quickly, we're suddenly touching the ground, coming to a complete stop.

Billie tears away from Echo's side, stumbling and trying to catch her balance just feet from the sheer drop down the mountain.

"What the hell, Echo? You need to take us back... now." She gasps as Echo stretches out a long wing and scoops it across her back, forcing her forward a few steps and away from the edge.

I smell her perspiration, her fear, and I turn internally on Echo. *Listen up. You've got to give me control because you're freaking her out. Look at what you've done. She's close to tears!*

Echo comes back with a loud chirp, shaking himself and abruptly pacing across the stone overhang.

*She's ours, and this is our realm together. You don't need to steal her when she's in danger. We'll do it together.*

Echo grumbles, rubbing his back against the stone wall while making whining sounds directed at me.

*You can be a stubborn ass all you want, but you know I'm right. You're making her scared. Is that what you want?*

He doesn't answer, just stares at Billie, still scratching his back on the cave wall.

Sighing from his stubbornness, I know the only way I'm going to win this battle is to be straight with him.

*Billie wants us as one. Not a man by day and a raving beast by night. And I don't know about you, but I'm utterly in love with her. Don't you want her love in return? You won't get that if you keep acting like a rogue gryffin, stealing her out of the blue and flying her to a mountain.*

Echo pauses. Maybe I'm finally getting through to him.

Then he shoves me aside and takes off the ledge... Fuck!

# CHAPTER
# TWENTY-EIGHT
## BILLIE

"What the fuck!" I call out.

One second, Echo's scratching himself on the wall, staring at me intensely. Next, he bursts into the air. Now, he's doing some weird-ass stuff, like chasing his own tail or fighting himself. God knows!

I blink up at him, unsure what's going on, but considering how quickly Echo pushed out of Eryx and zipped me up the mountain, I'm going to hazard a guess that the pair are battling to gain control.

So, with a sigh, I decide I should get used to this. Having a gryffin as a fated mate is bound to lead to batshit crazy stuff happening.

I turn to the cave behind me, figuring I might as well check out the place, considering the way out is to either climb a sheer wall straight up or plummet to my death. With tentative steps, I enter the cave, rubbing the chill out of my arms. To my surprise, there are piles of blankets and a simple fire pit, including a bunch of kitchen containers that are empty of food. I venture deeper and find animal bones scattered in the farthest corners. A shiver races down my spine.

I leave the cave quickly and am drawn to the ledge, where I take a seat, my legs dangling over the dizzying distance below. The ground is barely visible in a blur of rock and greenery. I'm not normally afraid of heights, but this leaves me slightly nauseous, so I lean back on my arms.

The powerful beat of wings draws my attention higher in the sky.

Suddenly, Echo is descending at neck-breaking speed, coming right in my direction.

I cry out, panic squeezing me, but I barely have time to get out of the way, so I duck, covering my head with my arms.

He soars right over me, the curl of his talons grazing my arms, knocking me over before he crashes behind me with a thundering thump and exhaled breath.

Barely able to catch my breath as I cough from the dust and debris, I whip around. The gryffin is gone, replaced by Eryx.

His chest heaves, and he's grumbling, getting to his feet, completely naked.

"Eryx," I mutter, getting up and approaching him. "Are you okay? What the hell happened?"

"Fuck, Echo's a stubborn bastard, but I wasn't letting him shove me aside that time." He dusts himself, saying, "Give me a sec."

I fight the urge to hold his gaze and not lower it to

what hangs down there, but I get a glimpse and I gasp aloud.

When he marches into the cave, my gaze drops to that firm, gorgeous ass that has me biting my lower lip harder. Moments later, he's back, wearing only loose pants. It makes sense that he'd have clothes up here if he's arriving in gryffin form. He also has a blanket draped over one shoulder.

He's breathtaking. That body and the confident air about him do something to my brain where I lose the ability to focus on anything but him. Brushing his messy hair out of his face, his grin is captivating, and the sun glinting against his amber eyes makes them look like gold.

"I know Echo scared you today, but he gets carried away, especially around things he's passionate about. Mainly you... and food."

I can't help but laugh. "Hopefully, not in that order."

He quirks a grin, and it's almost impossible to think beyond how spectacular he looks, towering over me, broad shoulders and muscles everywhere. My fingers tingle with the craving to reach over and trace every inch of him. His pants are hanging so dangerously low on his hips, he's clearly trying to kill me with those sharp V-edges on his hips. Then there's the obvious outline of his cock in the thin fabric of the pants. Is he wearing them on purpose, knowing they show every ridge and line of how massive he is?

"Up here," he says.

I lift my gaze. "Huh?"

"My eyes are up here, sweetheart." That sly smile stretches his lips, loving the attention.

I blush, but never one to miss a beat, I say, "I know. I'm admiring your black toenail."

"What?" He's staring at the toe the book landed on is already black, the skin red around it. "Were you carrying the heaviest book in the library on purpose?"

I laugh as he's wiggling his toes.

"It seems to be still working." I glance around at the beautiful landscape, breathing in the crisp, fresh air, hearing no sounds but bird calls in the distance. "What do you do when you come up here?"

He goes to lay the folded blanket near the edge, then sits down, leaving one side ready for me.

"I use the place to calm my thoughts when things get to be too much. Sometimes, I can't cope with people or heavy noises. I need silence."

"So, it's your hideout, then." I move closer and join him, taking a seat. "I get it. Some days, I would love to escape the world. You're lucky you found your little haven."

His attention slides over to me, and I shake from the need in his eyes. He rests a strong hand on my thigh, studying me.

"When I look at you, all I can think about is how much I want you. How I can't hide any part of myself from you, and how I tell myself to fuck it all and claim you."

"Oh." It's not like me to be lost for words, but I didn't expect him to say that or how easily it caught me off-guard.

"I'm not going to hide what I feel," he continues. "You're mine, and as my fated mate, get used to how much I'm going to fucking love you. How I'll protect you and give you everything you need."

With my heart fluttering, I lean in closer. "Just so you know, you're making me swoon right now."

When had I fallen so hard for these Dukes that I wanted everything they promised? Here I've been holding onto my emotions, or at least thinking I was, except I've been kidding myself. I've only known them for a couple of weeks, yet I long for them desperately. I blame the damned fated mate connection.

He lets out the deep, guttural laugh that always melts my insides.

"Good," is all he says. "Then kiss me."

I cradle closer to him because my body now answers to him. An arm loops around my back, and he twists his body to face me. His other hand spears through my hair, pushing it off my face.

Then he's kissing me, and it's commanding and forceful. For some reason, I expected him to be more tender, except he's showing me the true hunger inside him. He claims my mouth, sucking on my lower lip, stroking my tongue with his... taking ownership of me.

Gasping for air, I place my hands against his chest, his muscles firm beneath my touch, his skin on fire.

He traces his fingers along my jawline before gripping my chin in place to kiss me to his desires.

I shuffle closer, moaning and inhaling his masculine scent, tasting him. Listening to every exhale, my heart beats faster. Goosebumps cover my arms, the sensation of him and me together billowing in my chest.

There are hundreds of things I want to say to him about the things he awakens in me—how just seeing him has my stomach erupting with fluttering butterflies, how I can't wait to see him every day.

Our closeness isn't enough, but at the same time, it leaves me dizzy with euphoria. He's intoxicating.

I know what's happening to me, and it scares me.

I'm losing my heart to Eryx. To his brothers.

Breaking our kiss, I'm breathless, but he's grinning like he won first prize in a marathon.

"You feel that, too?" he asks, placing his large palm over my heart. "It's like our souls are calling to one another. It's been like this with me since first meeting you. And once my brothers and I mate you, we will be bound forever."

"The feeling is beautiful." My words come out in a whisper, choked with a flood of emotions. I never truly grasped the concept of fated mates or the extraordinary pull they have toward one another.

It's mind-blowing.

Even the word, *forever* doesn't scare me. But I'm not ready to go there yet... not until I have the truth of what happened to my parents.

"Yes, you are," he says.

Laughing at him, I cup his cheek and kiss him again because, you know, how can I resist this irresistible man?

"I have no idea what you've done to me," I say. "But don't stop."

"I've been longing for you to say that." In an instant,

his hand slides farther up my back, anchoring me to him. He nudges me gently, urging me to recline as his body presses against me. He shifts his body, and before I know it, he's nestled between my legs, his body lying on top of mine.

My heart's thumping louder because when I stare into his eyes, I knew this was meant to be. I can't recognize myself anymore, but the emotions curling around my heart are persistent. I know I'm playing with fire, considering there is still so much I don't know, but I can't stop myself.

When he leans down, his lips brushing against mine, I soften beneath him and curl my legs around his hips. He's taking his time, kissing me slowly, as if he's savoring every inch of me.

A moan dances in the back of my throat, and I kiss him back.

There's only the thin fabric of his pants and my panties between us, but with the way he pushes his cock against my entrance, it feels as if it's not enough to stop him from getting through.

Exhaling loudly, he's got his arms bent on either side of my head, his face inches from mine, our bodies burning up. He covers me in kisses, sliding down to my neck.

"This is how I want us," he murmurs. "But preferably naked and me buried balls-deep in you, sweetheart. To have you scream out my name and to feel your pussy squeezing around my cock."

I gasp for air, his words triggering my hips to rock

against him. Somehow, the darkness I've lived with for so long seems brighter with him.

Bunching up my shirt, he pushes it up to my neck and tenderly peels back the lace of my bra. He licks his lips, staring at my exposed breasts.

"I love how hard your nipples are for me, so pink. You know, I'm going to have to find out if they are the same color as your pussy."

I laugh out loud. "Is that your way of getting me naked?" I push myself up on my elbows, staring down at this beautiful man who's wrapping his lips around my nipple. Those sweet lips are wicked, and he sucks down on it to the point of undoing me.

A groan spills past my throat as my body writhes. I can't look away, loving the way he takes my breast with savage hunger. I tingle all over at the promise of what his mouth can do to me.

Releasing me, he moves to the other breast, enjoying himself. His gaze clashes with mine as his wicked tongue flicks over my nipple. Tingles swarm to the pit of my stomach, and I'm drenched in seconds. At the same time, his hand slides down my body, tugging my skirt up to my waist.

I shiver as his body keeps my legs forced open. He traces the pads of his fingertips lightly down the middle of my panties. His touch is so tender it sends me into a shuddering moan.

"Eryx, more," I beg.

Without releasing my breast from his mouth, he tugs on the elastic at my hip, ripping my underwear right off me.

"Hey."

But he's already tucking them into his pocket and moving down my body, his lips tracing down my stomach.

"You don't need them."

My body clenches, and the moment he kneels between my legs, he wastes no time. He leans in, and his tongue slips between my folds.

My pulse booms.

"Is this the *more* you're asking for?" he asks.

His hot breath against my sensitive skin leaves me panting.

"Yes, please, yes." Here I thought taking the heat suppressant pill would keep me grounded. But if this is me on the brakes, then without that pill, I'd probably be expecting by now. Thoughts that scare me and I push them aside, not ready to think about them.

"Look at how pretty your pussy is," Eryx purrs, spreading my lips, smiling, studying me like it's the most beautiful thing he's ever seen. Then he glances back up at my exposed breasts. "Yep, same gorgeous dusty pink color. I love how perfect you are."

I'm swooning hard right now, my world spinning around Eryx.

Before I can respond, the flat of his tongue is on me, and he's lapping me up. I cry out, shivering at how incredible he feels, how my body hums. His head is buried between my legs, and those licking sounds he makes are sinful.

He pushes his tongue inside me, and I cry out, soaring to the heavens.

Licking.

Sucking.

I'm too far gone to think that this gorgeous man is going to destroy me.

Two thick fingers slide into my pussy, and I arch my back, feeling the stretch. I lift my hips, needing that ache badly.

He pumps into me so hard, my whole body shudders. I notice him staring up at me, watching my breasts bounce, and I love that he enjoys my body so much. It means the world to me.

His mouth releases me, but his two fingers never relent.

"Think you can take three?"

My mouth drops open. "No, it's too much."

He chuckles. "I think you can take it, sweetheart. You're so wet and ready."

"Eryx." I push myself forward to stop him, but his hand is on my breast, squeezing, holding me back. All while he wriggles in another finger. I cry out because the stretch is real. Shaking, I lift my hips, wanting it. "It's not going to fit," I moan.

"Oh, sweetheart, I promise it will fit. I need to get you ready for when you're finally ready for me."

I feel him working his third finger in there slowly. The sensation is ridiculously arousing to be so spread, so wet. And yet his words play on my mind about when we'll have sex. I'm dying on the inside, desperate for him to fuck me... and every time I think about just giving in, a spike of fear comes through me. That I'm going to be bound to men who participated in destroying my life, and even if unknowingly, I have to know the truth first. I've lived with so much heartache already, that I can't bear to be torn apart again.

"You're so tight," Eryx says, distracting me, dragging me from those dark thoughts to the present. "I can't wait to fuck you. If you tell me now to sink into you, I'll make you mine forever. Just say the words..." His words are so sincere, I have no doubt he'd do it in a heartbeat.

I collapse onto my back, riding his fingers, knowing I won't stop him. Sweat runs down my neck, the pressure pushing me so close to exploding, I'm not seeing straight.

"That's it, gorgeous. You should see how beautiful you look from my view." He's got a thumb on my clit, and I lose all control.

The climax slams through me.

I scream, fisting the blanket beneath me, my body convulsing.

"Scream, let the world hear your song."

He doesn't stop as he watches me thrash on the blanket. The sensation is utter bliss as I fly, soaring through the clouds.

When I collapse, gasping for air, he's crawling up my body, caging me with his.

"I've never seen anything more beautiful," he purrs, then gathers me into his arms, holding me close, as if the world beyond the mountain ridge we're on doesn't exist.

Staring into his deep, amber eyes, I tease, "Well, you owe me a new pair of panties, and damn, Eryx, that was incredible. I'm still buzzing."

"I know, and I absolutely adore your body." He kisses the corners of my mouth.

"But what about you?" I wiggle my hand down between us, but he catches it.

"Don't shatter this moment. It's only us, the vastness of nature, and your undeniable growing love for me."

I burst out laughing but then catch the intensity in his gaze. Oh, he's serious.

"Wh-What gives you that idea?"

He traces a finger down my cheek, sending a shiver down my body.

"It's in the way your eyes light up when they meet mine, how your body gravitates toward me whenever I'm near, and... they sparkle when you look at me. How your body leans closer whenever we're close, and our chemistry is electric. You may not realize it yet, but you already love me."

"Mr. Confident, huh?" I'm breathing rapidly suddenly because what if he's right? All I know is that with each day, I'm more drawn to the Dukes. Their presence drives me crazy, yet I can't get enough. Is that love?

He chuckles softly, his kisses on my face again. "Just observant. And hopeful."

The sincerity and vulnerability in his voice touch something deep inside me. As much as I want to brush off my feelings, I can't stop thinking he might be right.

"You don't have to say anything," he explains. "I already know you will feel the same way I do about you, and I am here for you for anything."

My chest tightens. "Eryx, I have to find out who killed my parents, who came for me, or I'll be on the run for the rest of my life." A gnawing fear sweeps over me that I'll be hiding for the rest of my life. "I'll be honest. I'm scared of what I'll find out about my parents and the killer."

"Whatever you find out, remember you have us." Eryx's lips pinch as he draws me into his arms, lying on the blanket as a cool breeze swishes past us. "You're not going through this alone."

Closing my eyes, I rest my head on his chest, wanting to embrace his words of comfort. But that knot of dread in my chest remains, especially when every nightmare reminds me that I'll never be free.

"It's brutal," he whispers. "But none of us can change the past. Whatever you find out about your parents, remember they made their choices for a reason. It might not always make sense, but you can't let yourself drown in anger or regret."

His words resonate with me, yet they keep repeating in my mind over and over, sounding... heartfelt and painful.

Lifting my head, I ask, "Do you... do you know something about my parents?" Fear spikes through me.

He hesitates, and for a fleeting moment, a shadow ripples over his features. Then he shakes his head, but I'm already narrowing my gaze on him.

He exhales heavily, glancing away. "Billie, it's not that simple."

My heart's pounding loudly in my ears. "Not simple? You say you love me, but you hold back the one thing I've been searching for all these years."

He rakes a hand through his hair. "I do love you, and that's exactly why I'm trying to protect you."

I'm on my feet, stepping away from him. A sense of dread ripples over me. "How are you protecting me by keeping me in the dark?" I gasp. "What do you know about my parents? Please, tell me."

The fact he won't reveal anything, tears me up inside. Whatever the Dukes discovered must be really bad.

"Billie," he pleads, his shoulders curling forward. "There are things I don't understand yet, so there's nothing I can tell you because I'm not going to speculate when you only need the absolute truth."

I stare at him, my whole body shaking, my chest feeling like it's going to shatter open like broken glass.

He reaches out for me, but I pull back.

"No, don't."

The wind whistles between us, and I breathe quickly, my pulse drumming. I feel like I'm drowning. Those old wounds where it's me against the world surge through me, and I hate it.

"Billie, I understand—"

"No, you don't." Tears prick the backs of my eyes. "You're a Duke! You've never been terrified or alone or..." My voice breaks.

Neither of us say a word for a long moment.

"I was a child when it happened," Eryx finally murmurs, and I'm not sure where he's going with this. "I was snatched away from my family, put in a cold, dark place. I spent two months in a small cage like an animal." He's staring at his hands, shadows darkening his gaze, his posture defeated.

I'm frozen in place, my brain trying to catch up to what I'm hearing. I remember him mentioning something briefly before, but he refused to speak about it at the time.

"That bastard warlock experimented on me, wanting to see where my magic of transformation came from. Gryffin are rare, so the fucker cut into my flesh, ripped my wings apart. Get this, that psycho wanted to see how I worked, mumbling about replicating what I was for himself."

My heart splinters, my stomach turning with revulsion. "Eryx." His name falls from my lips like my crushed insides. I'm not sure if he's trying to distract me, but it's working.

"He used bolts of electric shocks on me, tortured me every damn day." His voice is trembling.

"Eryx, it's okay." I step closer to him.

He raises his head, eyes glistening, his expression belonging to a man defeated like nothing in the world could take the ache from his soul.

"No, you have to know the real me. Because you know what kept me going through all that darkness? The unwavering belief that my brothers and grandfather would come for me, that they'd never stop searching for me. You see, if I let my fear consume me, I wouldn't have made it."

Stunned, I rock on my feet as fresh tears in my eyes stream down my face at the depth of his pain.

"Eryx," I choke out, reaching for him, our fingers touching and interlacing. "I had no idea."

He wraps me in a tight embrace, and for a moment, I

can't stop crying for him. Every gasp I draw in is like a sharp edge of glass that's become part of my soul. The weight of his suffering as a child, the image of him alone, caged, and tortured, carves out a hole inside me that will never leave me.

He strokes my hair, kissing my brow, but I feel his shaking hands against me.

"I'm not telling you this to gain your pity, Billie. You need to understand that just as Echo emerged from within me, split from me to become his own personality and entity to shield me from the warlock's torture..." He takes in a sharp inhale.

"It's okay." I reach up and stroke his cheek, feeling the cold on his skin.

His hand clasps over mine, and he stares deep into my eyes.

"Let me absorb the terror of the truth of your past. Let me face them and be your strength. Just like Echo was for me."

I clutch him tighter, my emotions whipping through me, tearing me apart, the tears never stopping.

"I don't want you to face any more pain," I whisper. "Not for me, not for anyone."

Without his response, I know he won't listen to me. I want to be strong for him, for me, but I'm quivering to hear how much he suffered.

And I'm scared to death that whatever he's hiding from me will devastate me completely.

# CHAPTER
# TWENTY-NINE
## KHAOS

My jaw clenches as the fiery burn of anger rushes through me.

The staff are telling me Echo had Billie in his clutches and burst through a window, then flew away with her. What the fuck?

I'm fuming, balling my hands into fists, and I can't even be furious at Eryx when he can't always control that fucking gryffin. Standing by the window in my office, I glare out at the mountain right behind our property, knowing they're up there now. It's where Echo always goes to escape, which I have no issues with, but fuck!

We're going to have a major problem if he thinks taking my fated mate up there will be a regular thing.

A knock comes at the door. I turn around to find Clark sticking his head inside.

"You got a moment?" he asks.

I flick a hand for him to enter. "What's going on?" I ask as my thoughts funnel on Eryx, hoping he has this situation under control and that Billie isn't terrified up there, or I'll skin him alive.

Clark stands in front of my desk, fingers threading through each other like he does every time he's nervous.

"I've tried every route I know, but I can't find the missing data from our breach. What I have discovered is that magic was used to remove it. There's a faint trace of it in our data."

I frown. "What kind of magic?" There are different forms in this world, and there are ways to trace elements of what might be left behind. What I have issues with is when it's used against me.

"It's not that simple," he heaves. "I hired a professional team to work on it. They said they weren't able to pick up the source, but that magic was used."

"That's fucking useless information, then." I glare at him, frustration bubbling inside me. "Whoever you used, scratch them off our books from ever using again." Exhaling, I turn my back to him once more, my gaze up on the mountain. Maybe Echo's got the right idea. Get the hell as far from the estate and everyone.

They've been gone for half a day already, and if they don't return soon, I'll be going up there to fetch her.

Swinging back around, I find Clark still standing there, and my tension flares.

"You're still here?"

He bows and gives me his apologetic expression, then leaves. Lately, Clark has been getting on my nerves, and I can't even pinpoint it. He's always there, in my face, getting in the way, yet not providing any benefit.

And why the fuck come tell me he failed at a task I

demanded a solution for instead of finding another answer?

Shaking my head, I march out of my office. Downstairs in the main entrance, the gryffin team is already working on fixing the smashed window. We had to hire them as permanent staff, considering how often Echo breaks into the mansion. I make my way upstairs in case I missed Eryx and Billie returning. She's been on my mind endlessly.

I'm the Duke, a harsh asshole who rules this land and the mercenaries who reside here, yet I'm constantly thinking about Billie's needs. That's not who I am, but it's who I've become.

Since getting a taste of her, feeling her soft body against me, listening to her moans, her banter, her laughter, all rational thoughts fly from my mind. By now, I should have gotten to the bottom of our data breach, but instead, I'm distracted by her. And each time I do, blood rushes to my cock.

She's my fated mate. I'm her Duke.

That's all that matters to me right now. I have to rethink my priorities, and that means addressing the mess coming to light from her past.

A surge of tension flares over me. I take the steps two at a time, making my way upstairs, needing to see if Billie's returned. At her doorway, I hear faint footsteps from inside. Anticipation tightens around my ribcage. I knock lightly as I gently push open the door.

I catch her bent over something by her bed, popping something into her mouth. She straightens swiftly, swallowing what's in her mouth while nudging the bedside drawer shut with her hip.

"Khaos, great to see you," she remarks, her voice a bit too sugary sweet to be real.

"When did you get back?" I ask, stepping inside and leaning against the wall near the door.

"Not long ago." Clearing her throat, she pushes loose, wet strands of hair out of her face from the shower she must have recently taken. "I was just...tidying up. I wasn't exactly expecting a direct flight into the mountains while clinging to a gryffin." She laughs, but it's forced.

"You seem different today," I remark, my gaze never leaving her.

She steps around the bed, closer to me, as she tugs down the long-sleeve shirt she's wearing over black leather pants that trace her toned, stunning legs.

"Yep, that happens when you think you're about to die," she teases, approaching the door and opening it wider. "Feel like going for a walk? We should probably talk."

My nostrils flare, and I inhale her perspiration, her fear.

She wants me out of her room, doesn't she?

"Sure." As she steps out of the room, I head to the side of the bed where she'd been moments earlier. I can't shake the feeling she's hiding something. What did she just swallow?

She's fast and already on my heels. "Hey, the way out is this way," she says nervously.

Ignoring her, I tug open the drawer.

"Khaos, please don't..."

I'm absorbed by the small transparent bag with several white pills sitting there. Snatching them up, I turn toward her, holding back my anger. I know what these fucking pills are... Hell! This is why her scent has smelled differently. She's been suppressing her heat, and I'm fucking furious. I want her to come clean now that she's been busted.

"What are these, Billie?" I growl.

The color drains from her face, and guilt flashes behind those radiant blue eyes.

"They're mine," she states, trying to grab them from my hand.

I pull them out of her reach, studying the little pills, confirming they are exactly as I suspected—heat suppressants. They're bought illegally and for the purpose of deceiving a fated mate, by a female not ready to mate with him. I've heard others using it for pain control, except they're dangerous.

"Did you at least find out the consequences of taking these?" I demand, holding the pills in my fist between us.

She narrows her attention on me defiantly. "They're safe."

"Who gave them to you? Did they tell you about the aftermath? That once you stop, the pain will be so severe, you'll find it unbearable? The heat you're trying to suppress doesn't just vanish. The heat lingers, builds up inside you, and can overpower you."

She blinks faster, swallowing more frequently.

"I won't tell you who gave them to me," she murmurs. "But I chose to take them. My heat was getting worse, and well..." She takes a sharp intake of breath. "The things I was starting to feel for you and your brothers were too much, too quickly. I came here to find answers about my parent's death, not to... just jump into bed with you three." She exhales, her shoulders drooping. "But you don't need to worry. Even with these, it's like they're not even working. My feelings are just as intense."

There's a vulnerability in her voice. She's struggling, and I can't fault her when the connection between us is so powerful. I struggle to sleep most nights thinking of her, jerking off or anything to calm myself. Nothing works.

"Then why are you still taking them?" Walking into her bathroom, I tip the pills down the toilet before flushing them away.

"Because I'm scared of how much worse it can get," she says from the bedroom, then sighs heavily. "So, what now? I'm going to become a complete slave to my desires? And what about the answers I seek? They aren't important anymore?"

When I return to the bedroom, she's pacing, her brow furrowed.

"Now we wait and hope the effects on your body don't slam you so hard that they send you spiraling into full-blown heat. The rest... it can wait. It's not going anywhere, Billie."

Her pacing halts abruptly, and she stares at me with a challenging look.

"No more hiding from us, either, okay?" I say, taking a step toward her, desperate to bridge the gap between us. I'm eager to take her into my arms to eliminate the tension in the air. There's so much about her I want to discover, so much I want to show her in my world.

It feels like I'm in a sprint to get her to open up her eyes and see how ready we are for her to accept us as her fated mate.

She raises an eyebrow. "What about you?"

I shrug. "Yeah?"

"When are you going to stop hiding things from me?" Her voice trembles, her arms stiff by her side.

I don't need to work out what she's going on about. Fucking Eryx opened his fat mouth. I should have known he would. My brother couldn't keep a secret if his life depended on it.

I inhale deeply, choking on the emotions twisting me inside. I never wanted her to endure the agony of her past. But the distrust, the burn in her eyes, is eating away at me and at the bond we're meant to be cultivating.

"Look," I start, stepping closer to her, but she recoils, and that simple act is a dagger to my heart. "I'm not playing games with you. Sometimes, knowledge can be a double-edged sword. Misinformation can be as harmful as no information."

"Guess what?" she huffs. "Keeping me in the dark doesn't feel like you're being protective. It feels like imprisonment." Especially since she still doesn't know if they're involved in her attack or in her parents' death.

My gut hurts in response. Her feeling caged is the complete opposite of what I want for her.

"Alright," I concede. "I should have told you about it earlier, and you shouldn't have had to hear from Eryx up on a mountaintop that your father may not be your real dad and what your mother endured."

She's staring at me, her cheeks pale, her eyes glistening. I expect her to pepper me with more questions for all the details, but she hasn't moved, and it scares me. I extend my hand toward her, but she draws away, her breath catching.

"I just... need a moment, okay? Alone." She's visibly shaking, and my chest tightens.

How the fuck do I fix this, return the light to her eyes, the curve to her lips?

"Okay, if that's what you wish. I'll let you know once my friend arrives, and you can join our meeting."

She nods and turns away from me.

My heart shatters, and it's killing me not to grab her into my arms and kill the pain away. I've never felt this strongly about anyone before, so to leave her in the room upset destroys me. I know she needs time... we all do sometimes, but I'll be back.

First... I need to track down Eryx and fucking strangle him.

## Billie

ON THE INSIDE, I feel like fragments of a life I once had.

Tears stream down my cheeks, and my body is shaking uncontrollably. Weak-kneed, I crumble on the wooden floor of my bedroom, curling up and engulfed by the weight of Khaos' words.

He hadn't realized that Eryx kept details about my

parents from me, but now, with the truth, I'm not ready to deal with the past.

My father, not bound to me by blood, is still my father in every way. But he lied. They both did. Panic burns through me, crashing into me like a tornado. My heart races so hard, so fast, the room sways with me.

More tears flow, the hurt in my stomach thick. Each shuddering breath grows heavier, and I hug my sides, trembling from the sobs wracking through me. My hands are wet with tears.

The painful torture of losing my parents has been a constant ache, a reminder of the hollow of my heart. I desperately wish I could look them in the eyes to ask them about these truths, to understand what really happened and their reasons.

And the looming question... who's my real father?

All these questions, the agony, swirl inside me when powerful arms suddenly encircle me, lifting me effortlessly. Startled, I release a gasp.

"I've got you," Khaos murmurs soothingly into my ear. "I couldn't bear to leave you in this state. I just can't see you this shattered."

He lifts me onto my feet, and I twist around, burying myself against his hard chest. My hands grab hold of his shirt like I forgot how to stand. His arms around me are life-belts.

"You're shaking so hard, my little firecracker." Suddenly, he's got me off my feet and lays me on the bed, where he crawls in alongside me. Then he drags me to him and wraps around me. He holds me close, stroking me.

I can't stop crying.

The tears.

The heartache.

"I'm going to take good care of you," he whispers.

I try to answer, but only a hiccuped cry comes out, so I nod. I'm not sure how to take the news, but as I start to quiet, my mind's spinning. The clues were there... the magic on my arms, the vagueness of my parents' explanation of why I was always so different.

I press closer to Khaos, and he kisses my brow.

"Please," I manage with a croaky voice.

"Anything," he answers.

"Please don't break my trust. I'm destroyed, and I'm blindly believing you won't."

Slipping a finger under my chin, he tilts my head back so I can look up at him and wipes the tears from my cheeks.

"Never. I will die before I ever betray you. You're my everything. My fated mate. My love."

I blink at him, adoring his words, the warm glint in his gaze. Even if, on the inside, I'm beaten down and unsure how I'm supposed to go on.

Stopping the tears is a losing battle, so I close my eyes, pressing my cheek to his chest, listening to his heartbeat. I hate how weak I feel, how everything seems too hard, how I always thought, even if the world is against me, I held onto the thought of my parents' support and love. Now, I can't even say that I can trust everything they told me.

Khaos' large palm caresses my back, the soothing

motion lulling me into a sleepy trance... then I'm floating away. Finally, sleep takes me.

Awakening in a dim room, my eyes sting and feel puffy. With it comes the heaviness of my parents' lies, squeezing my heart.

I roll over in bed and find I'm alone. With that comes the knowledge that Khaos is receiving information on my parents today. Scrambling out of bed, I push down the sorrow, needing answers. Swiftly, I pull my boots on, determined not to miss out on anything. I know Khaos well enough to know he wouldn't have woken me after I cried so much.

The usually guarded hallway is surprisingly empty. Odd, but I don't have time. My urgency propels me down the corridor, weaving my way downstairs, then through more corridors to reach Khaos' office.

Rounding a corner, I almost crash into a beautiful woman with raven-black hair framing a face of undeniable beauty. Her gaze pierces into me, not appearing flustered that I almost ran into her. Her calmness is both unnerving and curious.

"I'm Ayla." She introduces herself with a hint of amusement in her eyes, studying me as if she can look into my soul.

Still catching my breath, I blink up at her. "Do I know you?"

She shakes her head. "Not yet, but I know you're Khaos' fated mate."

Frozen on the spot, her admittance takes me off guard.

"I better be off. I'm running late for a meeting." Then

she hurries right past me, and I glance back, having zero idea who Ayla is.

I make a mental note to ask Khaos, but right now, I have to track him down. I rush past Helmi, who waves at me, and finally, I turn the corner toward Khaos' office.

That's when a fleeting shadow from the edge of my vision catches my attention. Before I can fully process the movement, a hand clamps over my mouth harshly, and an intoxicating smell of something bitter and sickly sweet fills my nostrils.

Panic hits me at how brutally they grab hold of my throat, and I can barely breathe.

I thrash against the person behind me and stomp down on their foot.

But the corners of my vision are already blurring, my head dancing.

My thoughts rush to the Dukes...

But darkness sweeps over me, and I'm collapsing before I can respond. Then I pass out.

## CHAPTER THIRTY
### BILLIE

Waking up with a gasp, I gulp for air, feeling like I've just resurfaced from deep water, my lungs burning for oxygen. I'm sitting in a chair, blinking rapidly, trying to take in my surroundings.

I'm at one end of a grand ballroom that's intimidating by its sheer size, dimly lit by chandeliers. The thick curtains are drawn, blocking out any indication of time or place.

Where the hell am I?

Pushing myself up, I take two steps forward when a rush of dizziness hits me, and I slump down to the floor on all fours, waiting for everything to stop spinning.

Heart raging with fear, I wrack my brain for what I remember last—someone ambushing me in the corridor, then knocking me out with the cloth doused in sedative shoved against my face. Shivers race up my arms.

I've been kidnapped, and no one will know where I am. I don't even know where I am.

Heavy footsteps echo in the cavernous room, and I shove myself to my unsteady feet as a familiar face emerges from the shadows. I blink hard, my heart thundering at the man strolling toward me.

"Awstin?" What's my uncle doing here? Was he responsible for kidnapping me?

He rushes over to me, helping me back to the seat.

"Billie, you need to stay still."

"Did you drug me?" I groan, pushing him off me. Panic seeps into my bones, that ominous feeling billowing in my chest that something is really off. I'm in a world of trouble, yet when I look at his face, he reminds me so much of my father. They look so alike that it hurts staring at him.

Awstin hasn't answered my question as I settle in the seat, trying to calm the fear of why I'm so lethargic.

"Please tell me you're not trying to save me from the Dukes? And where are we?"

He grips my shoulders, his firm fingers digging in. With an enormous sigh, he studies me, his lips pulled into thin lines as if, somehow, I've disappointed him. I'm so confused.

"I told my brother, fuck, I told him a dozen times that you're going to bring him bad luck and it would kill him."

His words are razor blades to my throat, and part of me is unsure if I'm hearing him correctly.

"Wh-What are you talking about? Are you okay?"

He's huffing, a conflicted expression playing over his facial features, and the longer I watch his struggle and replay his words about him telling my father that I'm bad luck, the more I choke on a growing panic.

He pulls back, grabs another chair, and sits in front of me, so close our knees are touching.

"I have so much to tell you, and we don't have much time." His expression is tight, and he keeps glancing over my shoulder expectedly. "But I guess you should know the truth. It's the least I can do for my brother. For some reason, he loved you as his own child."

"Wait... you know he wasn't my dad?"

"Good, then you know, so we can do this fast."

Shuddering, I lean sideways, trying to shuffle my legs in that direction, needing to get the hell out of here. By the looks of the opulent ballroom, the wallpaper and the curtains, it looks like something in the Dukes' mansion. So, if I can just get out of here, I might find some help.

I shove my seat back and twist to get up, but I fall forward just as fast. Rapidly, I climb to my knees, breathing heavily, exhausted, my muscles aching.

"What the hell did you give me?" I groan.

"Something to slow you down," Awstin snaps and grabs me by my shirt, as if I'm nothing more than a scrawny alley cat, and shoves me back into the chair. "I've given you sufficient sedatives to keep you tame until *he* comes."

"He? Who the fuck's coming?" My mind's scrambling, and my heart's hitting my ribcage. I feel like I might pass out. "Please, just take me back to the Dukes, and we can sort this out."

"Fuck those bastards. They got in the way when I had you in my house, when I could have finished this," he snarls, the wolf in him flaring behind his eyes. "Listen very carefully, Billie. I'm not going to sugarcoat this."

I'm trembling while my body feels heavy and exhausted. I hate hearing him talk to me so callously or the fact he knows things about my family I wasn't privy to.

Sitting tightly, clenching my jaw, I hiss, "I'm listening." My plan is that if he talks long enough, my lethargy will wear off, then I can draw on my magic. Right now, every time I concentrate on calling to my swords, a sharp pain stings in the back of my head. "What do you need to tell me to clear your conscience?" I snap.

Darkness spreads over his expression as though he is taking pleasure in what he's about to reveal.

"Twenty-one years ago, your mother was captured, thrust into a trafficking ring operation. Something that's not too uncommon," he says casually while I'm trying not to burst into tears from the shock rattling me. "But one particular handler became… fascinated with her."

Each word is like another boulder being added to the weight on my chest, and I struggle to breathe at hearing the truth. All the memories of my mother are of her kindness, her smiles, her love. She never once shared her history with me, but made out as if her life was mundane. And yet… my insides are breaking.

"He shoved her into the Arcadia portal, where he joined her. I have no idea what happened, but when she finally escaped the portal, she was pregnant."

I suck in a sharp breath, pressing against the chair as though I can't pull far away from my uncle. Yet, Khaos' words come to me, telling me the story about my father not being my flesh and blood…

The reality crushes me.

"She... she was pregnant with me," I gasp, voicing the obvious, but the news still stuns me. "Who's my father?"

A grin curls on his lips. "Your real father is a fucking bastard with dark powers, and before your parents went into hiding from everyone, I warned him that Vayr would come back for the child... for you. And that he'd kill my brother to do that."

Vayr... is that my father's name? I'm shaking so hard, I have to tuck my arms against my body to control myself.

The past comes barrelling forward from the night of the attack. The dark figure who tried to kill me.

Sickness twists in my stomach, and I'm going to vomit. Bile hits the back of my throat to hear the truth of my real father killing my parents to get to me. It explains why my mother had the pendant around my neck charmed to protect me, why she also wore one identical to mine, to not be tracked down with magic, why she told me with her dying breath... *"Leave this house, change your name, don't go to anyone else in the family, or he'll find you."*

A sob rips from my throat, raw and painful. The truth is too much, too intense. I adored my parents. Now, the life I thought I had is crumbling down. It's not me I pity, but the agony and all those secrets my parents lived with, hiding, their lives completely upturned to protect me.

"It's too late for crying, buttercup," my uncle sneers.

Glancing up at him standing over me through blurry eyes, I want to rip his fucking face off. I push the tears away, attempting to form words, trying to piece it all together.

"So, what then?" I snap, fighting the lethargy, battling the fog in my head. "What role do you play in this? Receiving a big fat payment for letting my real father know where I am? Is that why I'm here?"

He barks a laugh and grabs my chin to force me to face him, but I use what strength I have to kick him in the knee. It's not enough to shove him away, but he stumbles back, nudging his chair out of the way.

"Listen up." He's towering over me. "Because of you, my brother died, and this payment is long overdue. I'm just doing the right thing and fixing the order of things. I tried so long to take you away from them, but your mother never left your side. She suspected me, never liking me."

"Fuck you. And yeah, my mother saw what a gutless pig you are." I push forward, but the back of his hand comes out of nowhere, slamming into the side of my head and knocking me right out of the chair. I cry out from the sharpness that cracks over my skull.

With the room buzzing around me, I refuse to be weak in front of my uncle... except I won't call him that anymore because he's nothing to me.

He straightens his shirt and physically shakes himself like hitting me was hard work.

I'm furious with myself that I didn't heed my mother's warning to stay away from family members.

Shoving myself up on my feet, I fight the exhaustion in my muscles. I'm trembling with anger, but I won't let him shove me down.

"If you want revenge, then do it yourself. Make me suffer."

"Sit the hell down. The kind of suffering I can cause you won't come close to what Vayr has in store for you."

"You fucking bastard. Vayr killed your brother, not me, when he came for me."

The nerve in his temple pulses. "And that wouldn't have happened if my brother had just damn listened to me and got rid of you. I told him to dump that bitch and leave you both."

My wolf is in my chest, but when I call her, nothing happens. I sense her, but the exhaustion has affected her even more. Hell.

An oppressive feeling settles in my chest as I hold his stare, watching him for what he really is... a fucking asshole. I've known a lot of cunning people, but the glint in his eyes is something else entirely. There's anger and darkness there, a fierce rage he's barely holding on to. He's not the man I once thought he was, and the realization hits me like a punch to the gut.

He shoves a hand into my chest, sending me reeling back.

I miss the seat and hit the floor. He laughs at me.

Fury blinds me. This weakness is irritating me.

"You've held on to this resentment for six years," I spit out. "Stewing on your bitterness, just waiting for the perfect moment to strike. How pathetic! Do you really think this vengeance will replace all you've lost?"

I push myself up from the floor, my muscles trembling. Each movement is like a colossal task, and I sense my adrenaline is working overtime to keep me up.

"Resentment?" Awstin's voice cuts sharply. "I've lived with this torment for twenty-fucking-one-years, ever since my brother fell in love with your mother... and you." His face contorts with a fierce anger. "Year after year, as they faced attacks from your real father, I watched in terror, knowing it was only a matter of time before my brother would pay the ultimate price... all because of you. But once I lost contact with them, guess who came knocking on my door searching for you?"

I swallow hard, not needing him to answer... "Vayr." His name feels gritty in my mouth.

He pauses, and my heart's breaking to hear how much my parents endured for me, how much they loved me.

"I had a conversation with a local mercenary, the one you were searching for. *Bryant*. Six years ago, he was discreetly hired for a job, something off the books because the target was a minor. The Dukes never authorize hits on kids, but Bryant was known for doing special hits. Being registered with the Dukes, he had to submit all work through them. That's when I learned he had an insider at the Dukes' estate to fudge the records, to conceal hits. So, imagine my surprise when I discovered that Bryant was hired by Vayr... to help him eliminate you—in case things went pear-shaped."

"It sure as hell went belly up for Bryant because I killed him when they attacked." Rage bubbles inside me. The room is closing in around me, every breath shorter, sharper, every word he says slicing into my soul.

"No real loss." He grins.

"And you," I begin, barely able to speak. "You told

Vayr I was at the Dukes' estate, didn't you? That's how he found me." I'm heaving for each inhale, my hands curling into fists.

"I tried, trust me, but I couldn't track him down." He chuckles to himself, and I want so badly to shove him through the wall. "You did that all on your own with the use of that magical mirror. You let him know exactly where you were. But don't worry, he found me soon after with a plan."

"Fuck you and fuck him." The cold metal of the chair bites into me.

The distant creak of the door across the ballroom breaks through Awstin's laugh.

My head whips around, every nerve on edge, the heaviness in my body not relenting.

Then someone walks into the room dressed in a black cloak, head covered.

A figure enters the room after him instantly. I recognize the black hair slicked off his face, shining beneath the lights.

Fucking Clark.

My blood turns to ice at the newcomer. Clark is dragging that damn reflective mirror inside with him, grunting in the process.

"Hurry up," Awstin yells out. "You sure took your time."

Clark grumbles in the distance.

My mind races at what they're going to do. Of course, he's involved. He's a worm, and I knew he couldn't be trusted from the moment I met him. He's to blame for so much, and the Dukes have no idea that he's been undermining them.

My heart's beating furiously, already terrified of the dark stranger.

Awstin marches over to help Clark, who's looking like he might drop the mirror... which I can only pray for.

I push myself up on unsteady legs and frantically search this end of the ballroom, which has no exit but stacks of chairs and folded-up tables. Hurrying toward the curtains, I rip them back to get someone's attention. Even doing that much has me gasping for air, my body shaking.

Beyond the window reveals the woods in the distance. That's when I realize we are at least two floors up in the Dukes' mansion, and down below is the backyard. Except, there's nobody out there. I bang on the glass, which barely makes a thumping sound.

"Don't waste your time, no one ever checks this room," Awstin asserts from behind me, his hand suddenly snatching my hair and tugging me backward.

My legs give out, the room starts spinning, and I can't stop it. Awstin drags me to my feet by my hair, and I cry out, grabbing hold of his hand to stop him. Stumbling on my feet, he halts, and Clark's staring at me with that stupid grin. God, I loathe him.

"I like her like this. Weak. Once we get rid of her, things will be back to normal in the estate."

"Why?" I spit out, pushing myself toward him. My limbs still feel like they're made of lead. Every movement, every attempt to fight back, is slowed by the sedative still in my system. It's as though my energy has been siphoned away, leaving me fragile. And I hate it!

"Because I don't like you taking Khaos's attention from me." Clark's voice slithers past his lips. "And besides, my payment for this will ensure I live a life of luxury once it's done." That righteous smirk spreads on his mouth, and that earlier repulsion sweeps through me.

Driven by instinct, I lash out, my fist connecting with his face. It's not a devastating hit, but forceful enough to make him recoil and whimper. One point for me.

With a snarl in his throat, he seizes my arm and wrenches it behind me, pulling me tight against him, his chest against my back. Pain shoots up my arm, intensifying by the sharp bite of his fingernails breaking my skin.

His breath is in my ears, grunting. "I think it's about time you met your real father."

He shoves me forward, and the force sends me directly into the towering figure in a black cloak.

I recoil instantly, my heart about to give out at how fast it beats. I glance up, gasping loudly. I'm face to face with my nightmare. The man from my dreams with glowing eyes stands before me. The very same figure who broke into my bedroom years ago to kill me.

"Hello, my child." His voice is gravelly. He reaches out for me, and I'm not fast. His fingers, cold and clawed, tighten in my hair. The moment he touches my head, a pulse of energy races over me, giving me what I've been lacking... strength. It's as if I'm drawing it from him.

"Even now, you keep taking the power from me," he growls so loudly, the walls of the room seem to rattle.

Clark and Awstin both cower away.

He yanks my head back to make me look at him. With his other hand, he throws off his hood, and the dim light reveals his face—a face I've seen before.

Memories flash back to a day outside our home when he had been arguing with my father loudly enough that authorities arrived. That very night, we packed up and moved away, cutting all ties with everyone we once knew. My mom said to forget I ever saw that man...

His icy blue eyes fix on me with a look of triumph. With high cheekbones and a sharp jawline, he appears regal, especially in his black robe, which pulls apart, revealing his black fitted jacket and pants underneath, thick boots. It's only when he shifts closer that his long, white hair falls off his pointed ears.

The chilling truth dawns on me—he's fae. If I share those traits, the magic on my arms... I'm part fae. I don't know how to feel because I've never paid much attention to the fae I've met back in South Africa. What I do know is that their magic is formidable and dangerous. There's a reason they say never to make a deal with fae—you can't trust them.

My father has visited my dreams, always with shadows, with death.

A dreadful ache creeps through me that the same darkness powers my magic.

"Finally," he murmurs, sending shivers down my spine. "Do you know how long I've hunted you?"

"Some things are better left alone," I state with more bravery than I feel.

He tugs my hair harder, and I scratch at his arm, but he doesn't so much as flinch.

"You're just like your mother, unable to keep her thoughts to herself, always back-talking, showing no respect."

"You're nothing to me. Let me go!" I demand.

"Yes, you are right. I am nothing to you. You're just a mistake. But you took something from me. And even now, you keep on taking my energy." He yanks my arm up and drives down my sleeve with his claws. "This magic is mine." He points to the ancient script on my skin. "The moment you were born, you took it from me. And I want it back," he snarls.

Suddenly, he hauls me across the room.

Terror surges through me as my feet trip over one another, then he throws me down in front of the mirror.

"We cannot coexist," he states. I move to recoil, but he pushes me down, then steps on my back, shoving me flat to the floor. The cold boards press against my chest, his boot adding weight onto my back.

Dread grips me, a primal fear that screams I'm going to die.

He chants in a language foreign to me. The room's atmosphere grows thick and heavy. The mirror begins to radiate an eerie luminescence.

Frantic, I struggle beneath his boot, scraping the wooden floor as I desperately try to distance myself from him, from the mirror.

"Please," I plead. "Don't do this."

His chant is unrelenting, and the hairs on my arms stand on end. I shoot a quick glance to Awstin. He's watching me, a chilling smile on his mouth. Clark stares with the same disturbing grin.

They're fucking enjoying themselves. These assholes want me to hurt, to die.

A sharp, searing pain bites into my arm, and I wince. Whipping back around, dark tendrils are rushing out from the mirror and ensnared my arm like a tether.

Terror swallows me.

Desperately, I'm fighting against them, pulling away desperately.

Vayr's foot lifts off my back, but the energy from the mirror draws me closer to its gleaming surface.

A scream tears from my throat. I scramble, clumsily attempting to roll over and stand, fighting against the force pulling me into the mirror's embrace.

"Awstin, your brother wouldn't want you to do this. Please help me."

"Well, my brother didn't exactly listen to me when I asked him to get rid of you. Call this fate."

"Enjoy the show," Clark taunts behind me. "I've heard it's quite a spectacle when magic is torn from someone. Painful, too."

I push my heels into the floor, trying to anchor myself against the relentless pull.

My father...no, I will never think of him that way. Vayr is still chanting, his eyes completely white at this stage.

Fuck!

The scorching pain on my arm deepens, and I scream, tears streaming down my cheeks.

This isn't my time to die... not when I have so much to live for and three fated mates I truly love.

## CHAPTER
# THIRTY-ONE
### KHAOS

"Fuck, she's going to be devastated. A dark fae impregnated her mother. Her father is a goddamn asshole who works in the trafficking ring." Tallis spears a hand through his hair, his lips thin and tight.

"We tell her today. She needs to know the truth," I suggest, as much as I know it will destroy her. But holding her in my arms while she cried, it completely ruined me. Her past is just as broken as ours, and it makes me realize how perfectly she fits in with us. And that means we'll tell her together, be there for her. She'll never be alone again.

"You sure Ayla is right about the information on Billie's past?" Eryx glances at the door she left minutes ago. He clenches his jaw, a storm of emotions burning in his eyes as he stands behind a chair across the desk from me, his knuckles white from how hard he grips the back of it.

"I stake my life on it," I state.

"Then I'm going to destroy that asshole," Eryx declares. "For what he did to Billie and her mother. We track him down and take him out. We now have a name...Vayr Giedene."

"Agreed," I snap, my nerves at the breaking point. "He's a rogue, gathering his power in the trafficking ring for years."

"Who gives a shit about his past," Eryx snaps. "I want to rip his head off his shoulders."

"I'm in on this. Let's fuck him up. I'll burn him alive. But I don't want him to die easily." Tallis bursts into a maniacal laughter.

Up on my feet, I nod and grin. "We track him down today."

A knock comes from the door, which suddenly swings open. Ayla, usually composed, storms in, looking like she's run a marathon. Her cheeks are flushed, and her chest heaves, but her eyes are sharp, the kind that doesn't miss a beat.

I swiftly move around my desk to approach her, my gut twisting with concern at her return.

"Everything alright?"

My brothers are there, by my side.

"I just saw Vayr, Billie's father." Her words slam into me.

"What? Where?" Tallis demands.

My shoulders curve forward. I'm going to murder that son of a bitch if he's thinking he can come into my home.

Ayla straightens her posture. "I was on my way out of the mansion when I walked past him. He wasn't alone. A smaller man with dark slick hair and a beak-like nose accompanied him as they hurried into the mansion."

"Clark," Tallis snarls. "I told you all he's a fucking bastard."

"How can you be sure it's Vayr?" Eryx asks.

She practically all but rolls her eyes at him. "Their Auras. Everyone's unique, but family auras resonate with me. I can sense relations. Earlier today, when I arrived at the mansion about an hour ago, I bumped into Billie, and just like I saw her fated mate bond to you three, I can sense her family ties."

As a powerful witch, Ayla uses death magic, her specialty having something to do with souls. Another reason I jumped at the chance to work with her.

"Which direction?" I snarl, already charging toward the door, urgency hammering into me.

"Front entrance is where I saw them last."

I turn to the door to leave, my brothers rushing to do the same.

"Khaos," Ayla calls out, and I glance over my shoulder at her. "Be careful. I sensed a significant surge of dark energy on him."

"Will do. Thank you for everything."

She shrugs nonchalantly. "Now, I'll focus on other searches I've started. But you owe me for this job, so expect to return the favor soon."

"You got it." I bolt from the office, Tallis and Eryx already several paces ahead. Eryx leaps from the balcony to the floor below, Tallis doing the same. Without a second thought, I mirror the move, urgency pounding in my head.

We reach the front entrance in mere seconds, but he's nowhere in sight.

"He's gone for Billie. That bastard must have taken him right to her room," I grit out, already darting upstairs.

Eryx blurts out, "Wait a sec. I'll find her quicker."

I spin around, heaving for breath to find him with shut eyes, his brow scrunched up.

Tallis nudges me. "What's he doing?"

I shrug. "No clue, but we don't have time for this. Eryx!"

Then his eyes snap open. "I've got her. She's still in the mansion. This way!" Without waiting, he dashes up the stairs like a madman. He calls out over his shoulder, "Remember you doubting me about the tracker I put in her? Who's laughing now?"

With the tension of needing to find her, I can't even give Eryx a comeback. We have to find her first. Then not only am I killing this fucking Vayr fae, but I'll personally rip out Clark's spine for betraying us.

"She's in the ballroom," Eryx growls, charging up the corridor.

Throwing myself forward, I reach the door first, and without hesitation, I kick my heel into it with all my strength. The door splinters, swinging open to reveal my nightmare.

Clark and an unfamiliar man with striking white hair and a beard are watching with predatory glee as Billie fights for her life against our reflective mirror. She's being dragged closer, her feet digging into the floor while dark tendrils spilling from the mirror are coiled tight around an arm, wrenching her closer to its surface. My first thought is that it's trying to swallow her, to take her from us. Next to her stands a tall figure in a dark cape, chanting a spell, watching over my firecracker.

My bones chill, and madness consumes me at that bastard for hurting my fated mate.

All three of them, except Billie, turn our way.

Fury lashes inside me, unlike anything I've felt before, blazing alight. It's primal, the wolf within me pushing for release, for battle.

"Billie, hold on, we're here," I yell.

She twists her head, fear painted on her face. Our gazes clash, and a spark of hope glints in those gorgeous blue eyes.

"About damn time," she cries out.

Clark cowers near the older man with the beard.

The lofty man in a black cloak and pointy ears gives me a toothy grin.

Finally, I meet Vayr.

And he's about to die.

I lunge, ready to tear the fae apart.

My brothers have the same idea.

With a flick of his hand, Vayr sends a shock wave that crashes into us, a wall of air that blows us backward as if we're mere ants. We crash to the floor.

"Is that all he's got?" Eryx's already shuddering, and Echo bursts out of him in seconds, wide wings stretching out as he ruffles his feathers. He unleashes a thunderous roar that sounds more like a lion than his eagle.

Tallis' clothes shred off his body, and he's in his demon form. Then, we're all charging to destroy these fuckers, Echo with his wings expanded, unleashing a fierce battle cry.

My adrenaline's in full force, but I'm barely a few steps forward when a brutal grip of something solid, icy cold to the touch, clasps around my arm. Caught off guard, I'm tugged backward. My feet lose balance, and I stumble as I snap back around to face my enemy with a snarl.

Standing in front of me, clawed fingers digging into my arm, is a lofty shadowy figure with no defining features, just hollowed-out holes for eyes and elongated fingers. Smoke waves off its body, a hiss rolling from the throat.

Instinct takes over. I attack, throwing my fists, aiming for the bastard's head, but my fist sweeps through it, as if I'm striking a mist. The fuck! They're forged from darkness, yet its hold on my arm feels solid as hell.

Attempting to shake him off, I glance back to find four of the shadows on top of Echo, mostly on his wings, holding him down, and I can't even see Tallis.

Billie's shouting for help.

Vayr's chanting louder, his voice echoing in the ballroom.

"Clark, you fucking piece of shit. If you were ever going to redeem yourself so I don't murder you later, this is your chance," I shout, just as two more shadows emerge from the dark edges of the room. They come at me with the full force of the storm, and I'm off my feet in seconds, winded.

That's when the lights overhead go out, and we're plunged into darkness.

Fear beats into me, and Clark's somewhere in the room, chuckling.

Something tackles me, stealing my response. I hit the floor on my back hard, the weight on me like a mountain.

Darkness threatens to swallow us whole, to destroy us before we can even reach Billie.

"Light," I bellow desperately. "Tallis, we need fucking light now."

Suddenly, a fabric-like shadow wraps itself around my face, a cold force stifling my breathing. A harrowing panic surges, and I struggle against it, kicking and thrashing against an enemy I can't touch.

In a flash, a fiery brilliance sparks alight.

The shadow suffocating me leaps off me.

Gasping for air, I blink against the searing light from the hellish flames soaring from Tallis' hands.

The air around us crackles with energy as the writhing shadow shrieks and slinks back into the shadows. There are dozens of them, and it terrifies me that we barely stand a chance.

Swinging around, my brothers are there, and we rush to Billie.

"We need to form a circle with the fire to keep the shadows out," I command.

My sights are on Billie, who's screaming, standing in front of the mirror, her hand inches from nearly slipping into its surface.

"I'm here," I call out, noticing Vayr has moved to the opposite side of the mirror, chanting, with Clark and his buddy, both looking petrified. Oh, they haven't even seen what real horror looks like until they've faced me.

In that same split second, I rush to rescue Billie, calling out, "Echo, take out that fucking fae."

Behind me, Tallis's sudden movement catches my eye. He thrusts his hands outward, and a burst of flames erupts from them. The flames spiral outward, swirling and spitting embers as they rapidly enclose everyone in the room in a ring of blazing light. The fiery barrier closes, taking up most of the ballroom, leaving us all locked in with Vayr and the other two.

He can't leave his post. If he steps out or loses focus, the flames will surge out of control, spreading with a savage hunger that will consume the entire mansion.

We're down a man, but Echo and I have this.

Vayr recoils, a sneer on his face, revealing his apprehension.

Beyond the circle, the shadows hiss back, keeping their distance.

I lunge for Billie and I'm at her side in seconds. "I'm here." My arms loop around her waist securely, my voice in her ears. "I've got you." She's trembling against me when a sudden force tugs her forward, pulling us both with astonishing strength.

A scream bursts past her lips as her hand begins to meld into the surface of the mirror. Terror seizes me as the force drags her deeper yet. More black tendrils lash out of the mirror and seize her free hand. Billie's breath comes in short gasps, perspiration on her brow, and she's shaking uncontrollably.

"Khaos, please help me. Please." Her pleas kill me because I feel helpless.

Echo and Vayr are locked in a battle of the gryffin attacking and the fae shoving him against the floor again and again. The chilling scene intensifies as Clark joins in and, with a chair raised over his head, he slams it into Echo each time he's down.

But Billie's screams are destroying me, and she's my priority. I know Echo can look after himself.

"Silence the fae, Echo," I bark, needing the chanting to end to save Billie.

With the crushing weight of her cries, of Echo making no progress, a frantic idea flashes through my mind.

I hurl myself at the mirror, striking its frame and backing with everything I have. If I destroy it, this nightmare ends. But with each blow, it feels as though I'm smashing my fists against a boulder. Pain radiates up my arms, my knuckles bleeding, so I draw on my wolf's power.

Billie's crying louder, and I rush to her side, cradling her, fighting to pull her out of the mirror. I'm shaking from my strained muscles.

"Listen, Billie. I won't let you go," I vow. "Fight this. Focus on your magic."

She nods, but her fear rips me apart.

"Khaos, find its weak spot," Tallis yells over the commotion. "Every piece of wood has one, and you can tune into it with your power."

Desperation makes Tallis' words fuel a spark inside me. I have always been able to connect with and tune into trees and nature. Normally, I can connect to the heart of a tree, but the wooden frame of the mirror is dead wood. I concentrate regardless, not feeling the breath of a forest, but beneath that, I sense a faint hum, a tiny tremor in the bottom left-hand corner of the frame.

"Hold on," I whisper to Billie. "I'm right here."

Throwing myself to that section of the mirror, I crouch low and trace the frame until I locate an almost undetectable split in the grain. It's a fracture, a weak point. Adrenaline courses through me, and with a deep growl, I pull back.

"Billie, pull... pull as hard as you can, now!"

I throw my foot forward, my heel landing with force. The wood groans, and determination grabs hold of me. I slam my heel into the spot, over and over. Each thud echoes louder in my ear, my breath in ragged pants.

With another forceful strike, there's a tremendous crack. The fracture widens rapidly, snaking up the frame. Instantly, the wood crumbles away, chunks falling on the floor with loud thuds. The mirror, teetering for a split second, falls backward.

Billie is violently thrown backward from the force of being released, her scream piercing the chaos. I spring into action, lunging after her, arms outstretched. Just in time, I catch and draw her against my chest.

"You're safe."

The room fills with the deafening crash as the mirror shatters, fragments splintering into hundreds of pieces, reflecting light from Tallis' flames everywhere.

Vayr roars, darting toward the mirror.

It all blurs into a whirlwind of motion.

I leave Billie's side, leaping toward the Fae, my wolf splitting out of me in that same heartbeat.

My paws pound the floor with force as I attack.

I barrel into him, sending him reeling back, and knock him off his feet. He groans, arms flinging out. I sink my teeth into his shoulder fast, tearing flesh. Blood spills down my chin as he howls in pain.

Just as quickly, a burning sensation erupts on my side and I'm suddenly flying across the room. Crashing into a pile of chairs, I snarl, furious. The sting sears across my ribs, but I won't back down. I shake off the impact and lunge at him once more.

Magic surges from his hands once more. Dark bolts fire at me, and before I can launch out of the way, they hit me brutally.

I wince as the attacks smack into the chest, feeling like punches.

I'm teetering backward, breathless. But I'm not even close to finishing this.

A dark figure rushes right past me and collides into the fae. A vicious battle explodes, until moments later, Tallis is flung aside.

"You're leaving this room in a bodybag today," Tallis booms toward the fae.

Vayr stumbles, which makes me happy, before he faces Tallis and I.

But from the corner of my eyes, Billie shoots toward her father, coming up at his back. Her determination, her strength warms my heart. She's holding onto one sword that gleams menacingly from her hand.

Tallis and I lunge toward her and Vayr. But the

moment the fucker spins around to face her, Billie launches herself at him. There's no hesitation in her movements, only pure fierceness. With a powerful thrust, she drives her sword deep into his chest.

His eyes widen in shock, a crackling cry on his throat. Disbelief etches on his face. He drops to his knees, gurgling out a groan.

Billie steps back, and I collect her into my embrace.

"For my parents, you psychopath," she spits out.

A sudden piercing shriek fills the room, almost deafening, coming from the shadows in the room. They thrash, recoiling from the fiery light, but just as suddenly, they're silent. And in front of us, the fae has dropped face-first to the floor. Dead.

Killing fae is close to impossible, but I've heard using their magic against them can work.

Tallis groans, "About fucking time he's dead. I don't know if any of you noticed, but I was losing control of the fire but held the fuck on."

I couldn't help but laugh at him, considering what we were all facing.

The lights come on with a flicker, and a curdled scream has us all turning toward Echo.

He snaps his gaping mouth toward Clark and bites down on him, engulfing his head, taking it right off with a savage shake of his head. Blood sprays across the wall and the older man, who's suddenly shouting with fright.

"Echo did promise to rip someone's head off," I murmur, mostly to myself. Then I groan, especially when all I can hear is him crunching down on the skull.

I glance down at Billie, and she's scrunching up her nose. "You kiss that mouth."

"It's not that bad." She then wanders over to the older man, her sword still in her hand. "Tell me, uncle, is there a reason I shouldn't finish you off?"

Trembling, he falls to his knees, his face splattered in Clark's blood.

So that's her damn uncle! Fuckhead. He deserves to die.

"Take pity, please, Billie. I loved and lost my family, just like you did. I promise to show you I'm a changed man."

She stares at him, and my brothers and I do the same, curious what she'll do.

Tallis staggers to our side, back in his human form, his arms charred black up to his elbows from the fire.

"I vote for not giving him another chance." His voice streams across the room.

Billie shrugs. "You heard my fated mate, and I'm inclined to listen to him." She turns away from him, smiling at us, her sword dissolving and sliding back into her arm.

Echo pivots toward the man, who starts screaming in terror. Billie positions herself between Tallis and me, her gaze fixed on the unfolding scene as Echo takes charge.

The gryffin's talons close around the man, the sudden force causing him to let out a horrifying scream. With a powerful beat of his wings, Echo launches them both into the air and smashes through the windows, sending shards of glass everywhere. He rips the curtain, taking half of it with him in the process. The rest flutter in the breeze.

"Well, the room needed to be renovated anyway," Tallis says.

I turn Billie by her shoulders to face me. "How are you? Are you hurt anywhere?"

"I'm still in shock, I think, because of almost dying and all that. Plus..." She lifts her hands, pushing the sleeves up to her elbows. "I lost one of my swords. I fucking hate my real father. He tried to take everything from me. But in the end, I still have one and my three fated mates."

"I didn't even notice," I say. "The magic from the mirror must have stripped it from you." Ink remains only on one arm. Tallis reaches out to touch her, and she gasps at his burned arms, pointing at them.

"Tallis, you're hurt!" She gasps.

He laughs. "It's alright. Fire burns don't hurt demons like me, and this will heal in no time."

She breathes easier and glances up at me. "I have no idea how I survived that, and it still feels surreal. But I need one thing." She pushes herself against me, and I scoop her into my arms because I can't be close enough to her.

On my next inhale, I take in that sugary slick scent she's hidden from us for too long with the pills. And she's eyeing me intensely.

"Oh, why do you smell so good?" Tallis is there, pressing his nose to her neck, inhaling deeply.

I meet Billie's eyes.

"It's time."

"Yeah, I feel it coming really fast. Before I lose my mind and can't think straight, take me to your room. The answer is yes."

Tallis howls with excitement, and I rush out of the ballroom. The chaotic mess will be cleaned up later. The dead aren't going anywhere.

Right now, my fated mate needs us.

## CHAPTER
# THIRTY-TWO
### BILLIE

"Grab hold of the headboard, little firecracker. You're going to need it," Khaos demands, laying me on his king-sized bed.

I'm still holding onto him, not ready to let go. Every cell in my body calls to him, needs his touch, his kiss, his cock. My core is wet and swollen, and I groan each time I clench my thighs together.

With black sheets, the mattress is firm beneath me, and there's something sexy about his room. Maybe it's the darker walls and the black-framed photos of the woodland peppering the wall. It's not what I expected, but I love the feeling, as though I'm out in the wilderness. I can picture myself sleeping here at night, naked under the sheets, being ravaged by him.

Khaos kneels on the bed next to me as his fingers sweep across my cheek.

"You have no idea how beautiful you were out there when you fought. You're everything I want in a fated mate. And now I'm ready to claim you as mine."

Lifting my gaze to this powerful man with his handsome face cut in sharp angles and pale blue eyes hungry for me, I tremble at his words. No one's ever been this passionate toward me, so adamant I'm the right person for them. It's incredible.

I lean against his hand, and the familiar heat I've suppressed floods my insides. Where before, it rose intensely, at this moment, it's like a tornado, ripping through me with ferocity.

A moan spills from my lips as my nipples harden. Fire erupts within me, and my thoughts begin to fog over.

He inhales, his nostrils flaring, and a groan rolls through his chest.

"I love the way you smell." He's looming over me, blocking out the rest of the room. "Are you ready for this…. after everything you just went through?"

I stretch a hand to the back of his neck, dragging him down to me. Our mouths clash, and I kiss him to show him how desperately I crave him. Breathless, I sweep my tongue in his mouth, and I'm already drenched.

His hand is on my breast, squeezing, his breath racing. His searing heat engulfs me, and I raise my pelvis, so needy.

Breaking from my lips, breathing heavily, he reaches down to adjust the bulging cock inside his pants.

"Let him out," I purr, knowing I don't sound like myself, but then being so horny I can barely breathe isn't like me, either. Well… evidently, I might be when I'm around the three Dukes.

"I'm ready," I gasp. "I've had a long time to think

about this, to learn the truth of my past, about who the Dukes really are. And you know what?"

"What's that?" he growls, as if he's barely holding himself together. He licks his lips, his gaze dipping down my body and back to my mouth.

I wriggle on the bed, reaching over, tugging at his belt, wanting it off.

"That I spent too long being careful when I should have listened to my instincts that I'd be safe with you and your brothers."

The corner of his mouth pulls up into a grin as he rubs his chin. "What I'm hearing you say is that you regret not having sex with us earlier?"

"Maybe." I giggle. "God, who am I kidding? Yes." I roll toward him, ready to jump him at this stage.

Tallis struts into the room, shuts the door, and stands at the end of the bed, hands on his hips. He does what he always does—distracts me. The man's hypnotizing—brooding face, chiseled cheeks and jaw, framed by longer, dark hair. How in the world did I resist him this long?

He's watching me writhing on the bed, curling my finger to call him to me. Just as he'd done to me back in the bath.

"She looks ready," Tallis murmurs, starting to unbutton his shirt. I notice his arms are still charred black, but it doesn't seem to bother him, and I don't care as long as he's not in pain.

"You make me sound like a roast chicken in the oven," I tease.

"Oh, my horny little one, I am going to stuff you so well."

I burst out laughing. I walked into that one.

Khaos rips off his shirt and shows off his spectacular body. My thighs are quivering, my pussy fluttering like it knows what's coming, and it can't wait.

"She's wearing too many clothes," Tallis says, already grabbing my ankles and hauling me across the bed.

I cry out, mostly out of happiness, the rest out of sheer arousal.

His hands skip up my legs, then pop open my buttons and zipper. He moves fast and tears my jeans and underwear off in one go.

My heart's pounding loudly as I pull my legs together, but when Khaos unleashes a growl, something inside me shifts, and my body responds to the sound instantly. Leaning toward him, I thrust my breasts at him.

"I love when she does that," Tallis teases.

Khaos' smile is contagious. "It's one of those moves that gets my dick so fucking hard."

"Is Eryx joining us? I want all my fated mates with me."

With my shirt flung across the room and Khaos's lips on my shoulder as he slides my bra strap down my arm, I hold Tallis' gaze.

"He'll be back soon," Tallis says, yanking his shirt off. "Trust me, he won't want to miss out on bonding with you."

Just hearing those words leaves me quivering with excitement. I'm actually doing this—accepting my fated mates, partners who will share my life. Going forward, I'll never be alone. So many thoughts cross my mind, from telling Sasha to moving my stuff up to Finland, but when Tallis drops his pants, I go blank.

In the blink of an eye, he transforms into his demon form.

I gasp, my toes already curling at how much larger he is, those horns, sharp teeth, the tail already coiling around my leg. But what has me interested are the two large cocks sticking upright. Thick and coated in precum, they are stacked on top of each other, as though they're made for the front and rear entrances.

They both scare and exhilarate me.

"I think she wants them both inside her." Tallis is taunting and relaxed, but when he claps both in his huge palm, I remember him coming all over my stomach and chest in the heated bath room, and just how much he came.

"You might be right," Khaos says, taking off his pants in record time.

Glancing over, I do a double-take, remembering how huge and delicious Mr. Big Cock was deep-throating me.

"I'm being spoiled for choice." I reach over to Khaos, my fingers curling around his shaft. He hisses, and I love watching a powerful man like him come undone.

"There's no *choice*," Tallis reminds me. "Today, we're all fucking you. Deep and fast, and filling you with our seed."

"Seed, hey?" I'm no fool and know there's a big chance this could lead to pregnancy... It's what going into heat is primarily about. The idea doesn't terrify me, not when I know I won't be alone, and I have three men who love me.

"We're going to fill you, breed you, put a baby in your belly," Tallis states. His tail sneaks up between my clenched legs. He's grinning, and I know him well enough to understand he wants a reaction out of me.

An excited shiver rushes over at the way he said that he's going to breed with me. There's something about being dominated by these three Dukes that makes me wild.

"Oh, is that so?" I say as I slowly part my knees, my hand starting to stroke Khaos in my fist. "And what if I said I want lots of babies?"

"Fuck yes, I'll scream from the rooftops." Tallis holds my stare, those dark demon eyes sincere, then his gaze lowers to between my legs. "You're already so wet for us."

Okay, that didn't exactly go to plan. Tallis is the last person I'd expect to be desperate for a family.

"I want a big family, too," Khaos adds, unfurling my fingers from around his erection, so he can go stand next to Tallis and stare at me. "I'm ready to start one."

"Okay, you're both surprising me."

That's when I feel the soft tease of Tallis' tail across my inner thigh.

"Spread them wider," Khaos demands with that dominating tone that slams into me and curls around my insides, forcing me to obey him.

Khaos is purring, and Tallis is breathing heavily.

I feel myself heating up as I widen my legs, feeling

my muscles relaxing. Then the tail slithers between my slick folds and pushes into me.

Moaning, my chest arches upward as my walls close around his tail. Shivers coat me, and I rock my hips, wanting more... so much more.

"Fuck, I could watch you all day," Khaos groans, palming his cock, Tallis doing the same, and they're having a grand old time watching the tail teasing me.

My breath catches, and with it comes an unbearable arousal. Muscles flexing, I cry out from the ache growing inside me. The air thickens in a split second, and every part of me screams for my mates.

"It's getting intense and fast," I manage to say. "I love your tail, but I need more, please."

The men climb on the bed, crawling toward me.

"You heard her. She needs us now," Tallis growls like a starved predator, his tail drawing out of me before sliding up to my clit and rubbing it.

A sound more like a scream and moans roll over my throat when suddenly, Tallis pushes his body between my legs.

"I want her first," he almost pleads, glancing up at Khaos.

"Is that what you want?" Khaos asks me.

Nodding, I thrash, ready to grab them both and pull them over me.

"Please, just fuck me. The pain's hurting me. I've been dying for this for so long. I want to mate with you as my fated mates."

My skin prickles with anticipation, their scents pouring over me. Khaos flops his huge cock on my breast as he straddles my arm, his hand on my nipple, pinching, squeezing. His other hand loops under my knee while Tallis pushes the other, both of them keeping me open.

Their earthy, masculine scents crash over me while moisture trickles out of me. My stomach aches, and my breasts feel swollen and so sensitive all over.

Those dark eyes hold on to me as the tip of his cock pushes into me. But when he pauses and the second tip nudges to squeeze in, I freeze.

"W-Wait, not both in the same hole," I stammer.

Tallis is grinning. "Of course, it's two at once. You're made for them, for us."

"My mouth waters, just watching," Khaos says, leaning down my body. With his finger replacing Tallis' tail, he plays with my clit, pinching it.

A primal lust tightens my skin, and with it comes a fear that it's going to hurt so much, I can't cope. When Tallis pushes both his tips into me, I cry out, writhing. The stretching ache finds the vulnerable part of me that's so sensitive and responsive, I feel like I'm about to explode with a thousand orgasms.

But that fear returns, and I'm suddenly shuffling backward, drawing away from his cocks. The moment I pull from him, a terrifying pain jolts through me—sharp and deep—as though I'm being sliced in half.

"Billie," Khaos coos, his hand on my shoulder. "There's nothing to be afraid of, but if you don't do anything, your pain will become unbearable."

My head spins, confusion mingling with the ache, and the arousal simmering beneath it is a strange sensation I've never experienced.

I roll over, thinking if I get up, I'll feel better.

Except large hands grasp hold of my hips and tug me back across the bed, me on my stomach.

"You're not going anywhere. What you need is cock, and lots of it." Tallis has his hand between my thighs, sliding up to where more slick slips out. Then he lifts my hips so my ass is high up in the air. When his fingers graze the length of my pussy, I shudder.

It's alarming but also makes me want to just give in.

Khaos maneuvers himself to kneel in front of me, his heavy cock in his hand, lifting it to my mouth. "There's no running away, firecracker. This is how we're going to stop your pain and create our bond."

I don't have time to say I'll think about it because Khaos pushes his cock into my mouth. Tallis has his two cocks at my entrance, sliding into me.

The shimmering need surges through me, eliminating the pain, but I can't work out what's best. Crying from debilitating pain or doing the same with arousal that strangles me, demanding I get fucked until I pass out.

Tallis takes his time, but the stretch of pushing two cocks into me has me breaking out into a sweat.

I scream from the pleasure, the urgency to take more. His fingers dig into my hips as he slides deeper into me, doggy style.

Khaos slips deeper into my mouth, and that savage need sweeps through me. Nipples hard, pussy seeping, I wrap my lips around his bulging erection tighter, sucking him off.

Every inch of me hums. Heat wraps around me, and

the deeper they both go, the harder I shudder. My body bucks, hips rocking, my breaths coming fast.

Tallis moves my hips for easier access, and he suddenly plunges into me. I don't know how I'm taking two cocks at once. But I feel it, and the pleasure-pain sensation has me moaning loudly.

I thrash, but neither lets me go. They hold on, Tallis thrusting into me to the hilt. My spine curves as intense pleasure rolls through me.

Then something shifts inside of me. It starts as a tremor in the pit of my stomach, moving through me, and quickly blossoms into an explosion of tingles. Everywhere the sparks touch is like I'm being branded, and my heart is alight.

Tallis is in my mind, in my heart, and the intensity of what I'm feeling makes it feel like my soul's being fused with his.

I'm floating suddenly, no longer tethered to reality, and for the first time, I'm not frightened. I'm drowning, but I don't want to be saved because Tallis is by my side.

I sense his heartbeat as it's linked to mine. Tears prick at my eyes from the overwhelming sensation of belonging and happiness I haven't experienced for so long. As I lose myself to Tallis, I know that our forever bond has locked us together, and I'll never be alone again because he'll forever be in my heart.

I gasp around Khaos' cock as if ripped out of a dream. Tallis exhales loudly, a startled sound in his throat. Both my men fuck me until I can't think straight, until I'm shuddering and moaning from an exhilarating orgasm. I come hard, my walls clasping Tallis' cocks.

Khaos pulls out of my mouth, and the scream in my chest springs free.

I collapse onto the bed, drawing myself off Tallis. I turn, knowing I'm not even close to being done, but I need a reprieve.

"I felt the bond," I whisper, my throat feeling hoarse. "It's beautiful."

The love in Tallis' eyes is new. I get up, then throw myself into his arms. He embraces me, kissing my face.

"I never knew it could feel like this."

I adore the feel of his body against mine. In his demon form, he's warmer, and I love it.

Khaos is at my back, his hands on my waist, his breath on my ear.

"Are you ready to keep going?"

"Yes, please," I say, twisting myself to be taken into his arms. His mouth is on mine, and I kiss him with sparks. Tallis is behind me still, his mouth on my shoulder and down my arm. There's something exhilarating to feel them both, but I feel the emptiness of Eryx's absence.

As if he read my mind, the door bursts open, and he bursts inside, butt naked.

"Fuck, tell me I'm not too late." He's gasping for air, and we all glance at him, me laughing at knowing he'd probably created another gaping hole somewhere in the mansion, then proceeded to run naked through the mansion. "Echo was a bastard to tame today, but I'm here, sweetheart."

He joins us, his hand on my cheek, and he pushes

forward, our mouths meeting, tongues tangling, that powerful way he kisses me, burning me up.

"Never too late," I whisper. "I would have waited until the end of days for you."

Suddenly, Khaos steals me away from them, chuckling. "You'll both have to wait. She's mine next." Those tropical ocean blue eyes are on me, and I melt against him, wrapping my legs against him.

"I've been waiting for you to claim me," I tease.

"Is that so?"

I lean in and lick his lips, shivering all over.

"I want you to always look at me the way you are now. Like I'm your everything." He shudders against me, and we don't even make it to the bed. He's got me up against the wall, his mouth against mine. Curling my legs around his hips, his massive cock pushes into me.

"My beautiful firecracker, I never thought I'd find love, then you came into my life and brought it all down."

Suddenly, Eryx and Tallis are there, on either side of us, eyes on me, as if they can't bear to be away.

"I'm loving all this attention, and—" My words morph into a groan as Khaos drives into me. There's no pause, just him taking what's his—me. I need him inside me, my pussy tightening him as he fucks me.

My other two men only have eyes for me. Leaning against the wall, they study me as I moan and grasp onto Khaos. There's no resentment, just pure bliss.

Khaos kisses me, and I lose myself to him while Tallis and Eryx move in closer, their lips on my neck and arms.

"You're so beautiful when your pussy's being

fucked," Tallis purrs in my ear while Eryx, my breast in his hand, squeezing, breathes heavily as if he's barely holding it together.

I slip my tongue into Khaos' mouth. His hips thrust overtime, then an intoxicating sensation envelops us. We're floating through the woods, slipping away. The strong perfume of pines, of nature and woodlands, fills my senses. My lover is one with nature, and it surrounds me. The love I feel for him deepens as if molten gold threads our hearts together.

The sheer intensity billowing between us is breathtaking, every inch of me screaming that I can't get enough of being this close to him. In that moment, we are one while everything else fades away.

I want to cry at the heaviness of emotions that pour through me, and when my eyes do flip open, we're so close that we're breathing in each other's air.

"Hello, my fated mate."

I hiccup a cry of happiness. All the while, he never relents pumping into me. I'm dripping wet, but that seems to be a turn-on to my men.

The word 'forever' feels too inadequate to describe the eternity I crave with my men. Suddenly, Eryx is there, his arm across my chest. With a playful growl, Khaos smiles and slips out of me, then hands me over to Eryx, as if I weigh nothing.

Wave after wave of emotions inhale me, tears brimming in my eyes. I never understood fated mate bonds or how powerful they can be. Sure, I've heard they vary, especially when hybrid forms connect, but what I'm feeling is beyond my expectations.

The emotions are overwhelming.

Eryx whispers, "Are you ready to have your mind blown and become mine?"

"I need this." He has me on the bed on my back, and he's on top of me, between my legs, just like up on the mountain ledge.

"I want to watch you when I fuck you for the first time, to memorize every reaction, to see how absolutely beautiful you are when I fill you."

Tilting my pelvis, I curve upward to better accept him, and his thick cock pushes into me. Like with my other fated mates, my walls clench in around Eryx. With his arms on either side of me, caging me in to keep me all to himself, he moves into me, spreading me.

I mewl when he slams into me, the tension on his brow telling me how much he's holding back. He pushes in and out, those fevered golden eyes never leaving mine. Khaos and Tallis are beside the bed, watching everything, their hands on their cocks. I want them all, but Eryx draws me into his world.

The harder he fucks me, the more I shudder. His lips are on my neck, his teeth grazing over my skin.

Intensity builds inside me. There's only so much a girl can take when being claimed by three men in a row. Yet I'm quivering beneath Eryx, moaning for more.

"Yes, like that, harder." The bed creaks beneath us as my heart flutters.

The room fades away, and electric tingles race through me, setting my skin ablaze. It's just Eryx and me, and we're in the heavens, stars blinking around us, and the small distance between us is like a chasm. It's too far, too much. I ache to close the space. Our hearts beat in rhythm, his thoughts intermingled with mine, our souls merging.

The air around us crackles, and the threads of love between us echo through time. That magnetic pull that makes me his, and him mine, is simmering, boiling over into an explosive surge of emotions.

And it's so much more... with Eryx, I'm home. I've finally found myself.

His kisses have me floating back to reality, tears in my eyes, and they're in his as well. The thread between our souls is unbreakable, enchanting.

Suddenly, I'm crying. I've never felt such intensity before today. Never had such love poured into me, let alone from the three men I first considered my enemies.

Eryx pauses but remains buried deep within me. Then he kisses away my tears. Khaos and Tallis are lying on either side of me.

"I don't even have words for what I just experienced, but it was something I'll never forget," I murmur.

Their gazes hold on to me, and no one speaks at first, but I know they're feeling it, too. Then they kiss me, and Khaos' whisper tickles my ears.

"We're yours now and forever. Nothing changes that. No one takes you from us."

"I've never felt such love in my heart, and all I can think of is that I need to get back inside you before I blow," Tallis adds.

I giggle as Eryx thrusts in and out of me again.

"I'm envisaging that we stay locked in, fucking our fated mate for at least the next week."

"A week?" I gasp.

"Not long enough," Khaos adds.

"Agreed. A month is a good length," Tallis says.

"Right, you're all dreaming," I burst out.

"Do you see any of us laughing?" Eryx murmurs as he picks up speed.

I shudder as slick gathers between my legs. The bed's moving again with all of us in it from Eryx's thrusting.

"I won't be able to walk straight," I manage.

"We'll carry you around," Khaos says.

But I can't respond in words, only in screams, because the friction from Eryx's cock is like fire. He suddenly pulls up off me, pausing just long enough to lift my legs and grab hold of my ankles. He holds them up, my ass off the bed for better access, and hammers into me.

Khaos and Tallis are kneeling on either side of me, their cocks sticking out. My body craves them, and I reach out, grabbing their shafts and working them fast.

It's a miracle the bed hasn't broken.

What does break is me when the climax crashes over me. I come so hard, I scream loud enough for everyone in the mansion to hear me.

Eryx keeps plunging as my hands work my men, then they lose it.

Tallis comes first, ribbons of cum bursting out all over my chest. I direct his cock lower to avoid spraying us, all while shaking from the most incredible climax.

Khaos howls, his cock pulsing in my fist, white cum all over me.

Eryx growls, unleashing a strange bird-like sound

when he thrusts one last time, where he stops, almost balls deep. He's coming inside me, and I feel the heat of his seed, how much keeps ejecting into me.

I'm gasping for air, collapsing onto the bed, covered in semen inside and out.

"Beautiful," Khaos murmurs, kissing my cheek. "And you're ours now."

The world suddenly seems to fall into place, as though every inch of me feels connected with a purpose. Before, I spent too much time hiding, telling myself I needed no one.

But I was wrong.

Being here with my fated mates is where I've been yearning to be. This is my home, my family.

"Well, it took you guys long enough to finally make your move. Good thing I'm worth the wait!" I say.

Suddenly, Tallis is tickling me. "We made *you* wait?"

Khaos bursts out laughing.

Eryx is still buried inside me like he never plans to leave.

I have never found such happiness until now... but Tallis refuses to cease his tickling. I howl with laughter, trying to wriggle away. So, I snatch a pillow.

"You wanted a war. Let's go!" I declare, giggling as my men pounce on me.

# EPILOGUE
## BILLIE

The winter cold is fierce, but inside our fancy glass igloo, it's all toasty vibes and snuggles. I'm nestled comfortably between my fated mates, Khaos on my left, his broad arm a cushion under my head, and to my right, Tallis, his muscular forearm serving as a second pillow. Eryx is sprawled out next to Tallis, pointing out at the bright flares of the sky above us.

We're on our backs, staring up through the translucent dome where, thankfully, it's not snowing at the moment, so the vivid reds and purples of the aurora borealis dance across the inky blackness of the night sky.

It's been several months since my real father found me, and then... well, I killed him. What did he expect when he came with the same intentions toward me?

"Did you know the Northern Lights are created when there are charged particles from the sun that collide with the Earth's atmosphere?"

Eryx groans. "Really, Mr. Encyclopedia. Thanks for ruining the mood with science."

Tallis chuckles, Khaos howling with laughter before he says, "Well, someone's got to light up the dim world every now and then."

"I'd rather talk about Billie." Tallis rolls over and lays his large palm on my tiny baby bump stomach. "We know she's having twins, but the question is, who will they take after?"

"Me," I answer truthfully. We've had this conversation, and it always ends in debates, which inevitably lead to baby names, which we still haven't decided on.

"I told you, she's a girl, and she'll be a gryffin. I felt my seed connect with her egg during our mating bond."

Tallis is laughing louder. "Sure you did."

"I want two girls," Khaos says, leaning in and kissing me on my head. "And for them to be as gorgeous and dangerous as their beautiful mother."

"Thanks, babe. You're making me swoon again." I cradle against Khaos when Eryx suddenly jumps up off the layers of fur blankets beneath us.

"Alright, Echo is being insistent that he wants to come out, saying it's his turn to snuggle Billie."

"No!" we almost shout in unison. The last thing we need is a gryffin inside the glass igloo.

But our protests are ignored. A tingle of energy fills the enclosed space, and in seconds, an enormous gryffin replaces Eryx, his vast wings fanning out against the glass walls. Every movement sends us into panic as we scramble to get up.

In moments, I find myself swept off my feet, a cry in

my throat as I'm drawn toward Echo, as are Khaos and Tallis, despite their flailing arms.

Seconds of squished movement, feathers, a whipping lion's tail, and we're all lying back down, nestled inside Echo's wings, the tip curled up to keep us cocooned in place.

I'm sandwiched between my two men. Echo has his huge wing over us like a warning if we think we're going anywhere.

Gasping for air, I have no idea what just happened.

"Well, this is... intimate," I remark, pressed up against my men in an awkward snuggle with a gryffin.

"When I'm free, I swear Eryx isn't going to see me coming."

Khaos is chuckling as if he can't stop. "I've heard of group hugs, but this?" He's howling, then winks at me, brushing a feather from my face.

I press in against his chest, all of us staring up at the sky.

"This is perfect if you ask me," I say. "Echo *is* one of us and deserves snuggles, too."

Lying there with my fated mates, the men who are about to become fathers and me a mother, I think back to everything I've experienced. And despite the crazy journey, something feels right inside of me.

Like this is exactly where I'm meant to be.

# DEMON'S CHOCOLATE CAKE

## COCOLATE SPONGE:

**Ingredients:**

1¼ cups all-purpose flour

1 cup granulated sugar

½ cup unsweetened cocoa powder

1 tsp baking powder

1 tsp baking soda

¾ tsp salt

1 large egg

¾ cup milk

⅓ cup vegetable oil

1½ tsp vanilla extract

¾ cup boiling water

½-1 tsp chili powder (adjust to your heat preference)

### Instructions:

- Preheat Oven: Preheat your oven to 350°F (175°C). Grease and flour a 9-inch round cake tin.
- Dry Ingredients: In a large mixing bowl, sift together the flour, sugar, cocoa, baking powder, baking soda, salt, and chili powder.
- Wet Ingredients: Add the egg, milk, vegetable oil, and vanilla. Beat for 2 minutes on medium speed.
- Add Boiling Water: Add the boiling water to the mix. The batter will be thin, but that's okay.
- Bake: Pour the batter into the prepared round tin. Bake for 30-40 minutes, or until a toothpick or cake tester inserted in the center comes out clean.
- Cool: Allow the cake to cool in the tin for about 10-15 minutes, then transfer it to a wire rack to cool completely.

### Chocolate Frosting:

### Ingredients:

½ cup unsalted butter, softened

2⅔ cups powdered sugar

¾ cup unsweetened cocoa powder

1/3 cup milk

2 tsp vanilla extract

A pinch of salt

**Instructions:**

- Mix Butter & Cocoa: In a large mixing bowl, beat the butter until creamy and light. Slowly add in the cocoa and mix until well combined.
- Add Remaining Ingredients: Gradually add powdered sugar, milk, vanilla, chili powder, and salt. Beat until smooth. If the frosting is too thick, add a bit more milk. If it's too thin, add more powdered sugar.
- Frost the Cake: Once the cake is completely cool, spread a generous amount of frosting on top and sides of the entire cake.

***Enjoy***

# About Mila Young

**Find all Mila young books at
www.milayoungbooks.com**

Best-selling author, Mila Young tackles everything with the zeal and bravado of the fairytale heroes she grew up reading about. She slays monsters, real and imaginary, like there's no tomorrow. By day she rocks a keyboard as a marketing extraordinaire. At night she battles with her mighty pen-sword, creating fairytale retellings, and sexy ever after tales.

Ready to read more and more from Mila Young?
**www.subscribepage.com/milayoung**

Join Mila's **Wicked Readers group** for exclusive content, latest news, and giveaway.
**www.facebook.com/groups/
milayoungwickedreaders**

*For more information…*
mila@milayoungbooks.com

Made in the USA
Columbia, SC
09 May 2024